KU-020-392

Betty McInnes was born in Aberdeen and trained as an architect in Dundee. She lives in Dundee with her husband, and her hobbies include delving into local history, gardening and travelling around Scotland and England. Betty McInnes's previous Scottish saga, *The River Calls Us Home*, is also available from Headline.

'Written with integrity and with a tender feeling for its characters and settings that is appealing' *The Sunday Times*

BOOK NEUK
£3
STONEHAVEN

Also by Betty McInnes

The River Calls Us Home

The Alexander Inheritance

Betty McInnes

HEADLINE

Copyright © 1994 Betty McInnes

The right of Betty McInnes to be identified as the Author of
the Work has been asserted by her in accordance with the
Copyright, Designs and Patents Act 1988.

First published in 1994
by HEADLINE BOOK PUBLISHING

First published in paperback in 1994
by HEADLINE BOOK PUBLISHING

10 9 8 7 6 5 4 3 2 1

All rights reserved. No part of this publication may be
reproduced, stored in a retrieval system, or transmitted,
in any form or by any means without the prior written
permission of the publisher, nor be otherwise circulated
in any form of binding or cover other than that in which
it is published and without a similar condition being
imposed on the subsequent purchaser.

All characters in this publication are fictitious
and any resemblance to real persons, living or dead,
is purely coincidental.

ISBN 0 7472 4493 6

Typeset by Keyboard Services, Luton

Printed and bound in Great Britain by
Cox & Wyman Ltd, Reading, Berks

HEADLINE BOOK PUBLISHING
A division of Hodder Headline PLC
338 Euston Road
London NW1 3BH

For my husband David

Chapter 1

'No, Pa! Oh, Pa, please don't!' Ishbel Mackie studied the empty evening sky anxiously. It was clear and bright, an ideal night for a Zeppelin raid over the Forth, though she couldn't see any of the German airships, thank goodness.

Donald Mackie lowered the shotgun regretfully. 'Och, dinna fash yoursel', lassie. They'd be out o' range anyway, more's the pity.'

Ishbel was not convinced. After recent Zeppelin raids on Edinburgh, her father had appointed himself unofficial anti-aircraft observer for Dalkeith district, and she had a healthy respect for his aim. Her pa was gamekeeper on Craighill estate on the outskirts of Edinburgh, and a crack shot on the grouse moors. Ishbel wasn't sure what damage a scatter of shotgun pellets might inflict upon the fabric of an enemy airship, but she wasn't taking any chances.

'You might just annoy the Jerries, Pa, then they'd attack the Big House for spite. They'll likely know it's a convalescent hospital for wounded officers,' she warned cunningly.

Craighill House, known locally as the Big House, was Sir Dudley Hawkerton's ancestral abode. It stood serenely behind them in the shelter of the wooded hill which

1

shielded the mansion from the rude stares of Dalkeith folk. It was a focal point in the rural landscape, as its architect Robert Adam had intended it should be, and presented a tempting target for vengeful German aviators in the spring of 1917.

Donald sighed. 'Aye. You're right. The safety of those poor lads is more important. They've suffered enough, God knows.' He stared north-east to where a grey pall of sooty smoke rose from city lums beyond the Pentland Hills and the distinctive pinnacle of Arthur's Seat.

I wouldna care to be living in the Cannongate these chancy nights, he thought with a shiver. He remembered one overcrowded tenement in particular; the high land, where he'd spent an urchin childhood. He shook his head. 'Och, there's nae honour in war, Ishbel. When I fought against the Boers I tried to spare innocent women and bairns, but other fighting men aren't so fussy.'

He slipped the safety catch on the shotgun, broke it, and eased the stock into its customary place in the crook of one arm. Ishbel took the other, fitting her own light tread to her father's uneven gait. She rejoiced silently in that legacy from Donald Mackie's soldiering days. They'd introduced conscription for single men in January 1916 and spread the net wider last May. If it hadn't been for his game leg, Donald would have gone. He was only forty-nine, and if he'd been called wild horses wouldn't have stopped him from going. But there was the leg, and the army would not have him, and thanks be to God!

He glanced down at her. 'Shouldn't you be putting on your glad rags, now you've milked the kye?'

'Och, there's time yet, Pa.'

His eyes twinkled. 'Weel, weel! Eighteen years auld this

very day, and invited to a swanky concert in the Big Hoose like a gentry lady! It doesn't seem a minute since you were just a wee wildie, falling in the midden an' comin' out smelling of sweet violets,' teased her father.

She gave him a little shove, laughing. 'Och, Pa!'

Ah, but she was bonny! She was dark-haired, clear-skinned, and tall and lissom like her mother. There was a graceful dignity about the women from the Western Isles. It had struck Donald forcibly the very first time he'd set eyes on Ishbel's mother, Catriona Sinclair, and their only child had inherited that natural grace.

'And that was Sandy's card you had through the post this morning,' he said aloud, following a certain train of thought.

She smiled delightedly, cheeks pink, hazel eyes bright. 'Oh yes, a lovely card, Pa! Violets woven in silk, with "Remembrance" stitched beneath. So pretty. I'll keep it forever.'

'Aye. Sandy's a canny lad. You could do worse.'

Donald was careful to say no more on that score, wise in the ways of unbroken colts and young lasses. The more you urge the young ones to scttle to harness, the harder they kick. He couldn't resist a gentle prod, though. 'The MacArthurs are hard-working, God-fearing folk, Ishbel. Don't you forget I owe my job to Sandy's father. Auld MacArthur soldiered wi' me in Natal, and put in a good word for me wi' the laird when I was in sore need o' work.'

'Aye, I know.' Ishbel frowned. She thought, Why must he remind me I must make up my mind to marry Sandy one day?

This war unsettled everything, made the simple path of life complicated. Her childhood sweetheart Sandy

3

MacArthur, once the laird's fourth ploughman, was a Tommy now, stationed in Glasgow's Maryhill Barracks. She worried day and night that he would be sent to France, after recent dreadful losses on the Somme and long columns in the papers listing the dead.

There was plenty of work on the land with all the young men gone to fight the Germans, and that meant a new freedom for the women who'd stepped into their shoes. Ishbel worked on Wotherspoon's farm, which bordered the laird's estate. Hugh Wotherspoon was a dour, middle-aged bachelor who glowered when you passed him by, but the few shillings she earned in his dairy were welcomed by her parents, and the sense of independence the money gave her was worth even more. Ishbel was loath to give up that precious independence even for Sandy MacArthur. There was time enough yet.

They had reached the river bank and her father glanced up and down, looking out for poachers. 'The salmon are running early this spring. I saw two or three louping the falls yesterday, and that'll bring the poachers out, sure as fate. I'll sit here awhile wi' my gun handy. That'll mak' them think twice.'

'It's daft to stop folk catching salmon when food's in short supply,' declared Ishbel stoutly. 'What right has the laird to own fish that come freely up the river from the sea?'

Her father smiled tolerantly and gave her a gentle spank on the bottom. 'Ach, run away and put on your bonny frock, young miss, and dinna bother your pretty heid wi' politics!'

Ishbel laughed and ran. She soon forgot her indignation in contemplation of the treat ahead. A concert in the Big House! A lovely concert organised by Lady Hawkerton to entertain the convalescent officers, to which Ishbel had received an invitation on the strength of a long-lasting friendship with Hannah, Lady Hawkerton's daughter.

Ishbel gave a skip of delight. Oh, she'd always loved concerts! Not that she'd been to many, mind. A soiree or two in Dalkeith kirk hall, one magical pantomime in the Gaiety Theatre, Leith, with her father's sister, Auntie Nellie, and a wonderful, never-to-be-forgotten evening watching Harry Lauder perform at the Empire, Nicolson Street, before it burned down in 1911. Harry Lauder was born in a tiny house in Portobello, which was Edinburgh's fashionable seaside resort, and he'd made such an impression upon Ishbel she'd learned all his songs by heart. Heading home through the twilight, she began to sing one of her favourites: 'Roamin' in the gloamin'. . .'

Catriona Mackie lifted her head from her sewing to listen to her daughter. Ishbel's voice was sweet and true, yet had a lilting, husky note that made you want to grin. Smiling, she returned to a last-minute adjustment of her daughter's new dress. New to Ishbel, that is. It was one of Lady Hawkerton's cast-offs, of silk faille in a creamy-yellow shade.

'Pa was looking for Zeppelins to shoot but I stopped him, Mama,' said Ishbel blithely, coming in.

Catriona tut-tutted. 'I keep telling the man those things are best treated like wasps and ignored, then they'll get wearied and go away.'

Ishbel turned her attention to more important matters. 'Is my dress ready?'

'I shortened it a bit more, like the gown I showed you in the catalogue. You have good ankles, fortunately.' Catriona held up the dress and there was a short silence while mother and daughter studied their handiwork critically. They'd both had a say in transforming my lady's unbecoming gown into a garment of unusual style and beauty.

'Those pin-tucks on the bodice just made all the difference,' decided Catriona. She was pleased to find she'd lost none of the flair she'd shown as lady's maid and dressmaker to the Big House, before the war put a stop to it.

'And the lace collar makes a lovely finish to the neckline,' enthused Ishbel. She hugged her mother. 'Mam, you are a dear, taking the collar off your Sunday blouse just for me.'

'Aye, well, I want it back before next communion, mind!' warned her mother with a twinkle in her eye. She hugged her daughter close for a moment. This one ewe lamb had almost cost Catriona her life at the birth, and so was doubly dear. 'Away you go now. The tub's waiting ben the hoose, buckets of hot water, and mair in the washboiler if needed. There's the pink soap and attar of roses your Auntie Nellie gave me last Christmas. You may as well use them. I've no call for such fal-de-rols at my age.'

Ishbel choked back emotional tears. She knew how highly her mother prized such rare luxuries. 'Oh, Mam, I wish you were going to the concert instead of me.'

Her mother laughed. 'It's the young, pretty ones the officers want to see, lovie, not auld wifies.'

Ishbel tossed her head. 'Och, the officers! I'll be struck dumb faced wi' those toffs. I wish there were Tommies going, they're much more fun. I'll no' open my mouth. I don't know what to say to officers.'

* * *

6

She was greatly excited all the same. Her heart raced as she washed her hair in one bucket and rinsed out the soap in another. It was sheer luxury, lying soaking in the wooden tub in front of the fire with the clothes horse drawn discreetly around it, draped with towels and clean undies. When I'm rich, thought Ishbel dreamily, the water lapping her chin, I'll have hot, scented baths every single day. She laughed at her day-dream. Fat chance, Ishbel Mackie, and you the wife o' a fourth ploughman!

Vigorously, she towelled her long tresses dry in front of the fire, then hurried ben the house. Her mother was waiting with hairpins, comb and curling tongs.

'A chignon, I think,' decided Catriona. 'That's what a' the swanks in Morningside are wearing, Nellie says, so you'll be upsides wi' them.' She set to work pinning up her daughter's dark hair.

'Now the dress. Careful, Ishbel. Don't spoil the hair-do.'

She slipped the dress over her head, and with trembling fingers Catriona fastened the long row of buttons down the back and stood aside to study the finished effect.

Ishbel twirled to face her. 'Mam, how do I look?'

Catriona was silent. How to answer, when her heart was aching with pride and a queer, wistful sadness? Sadness for my ain lost youth and beauty maybe, she thought, but more likely because life is hard for the likes o' us, and to think of cruel hardship withering this lovely young flower is like a knife in my breast.

Ishbel sensed mixed emotions. 'What is it? Is the colour wrong for me?' she demanded anxiously.

'No, no, dear, it's just wonderful, like the sun coming out in this house. I was struck dumb for a moment, that's all.'

Ishbel giggled. 'Then I hope the officers will be struck

dumb as well, Mam. I'll no' feel out o' place if everyone's a dummy.'

She turned away to study her reflection – what she could see of it, that is. Oh, I wish we had a mirror that went all the way down to the floor! she thought wistfully, as she peered into a looking glass that showed little more than her mother's lace collar set on a patch of creamy-yellow silk.

'Save us! Who's the leddy?' Her father had come in, joking as usual. She turned to him, laughing.

'Pa, it's only me.'

He peered short-sightedly, then made a great show of astonishment. 'Och, so it is. And here's me bowing and scraping to the bonniest young leddy in the land.'

His wife snorted. 'Donald, will you stop your nonsense and escort the girl. It's time she was on her way.'

Father and daughter halted uncertainly when they reached the mansion. The question was whether to go boldly up the front steps or take the servants' entrance. In the end custom prevailed, and Donald left Ishbel to steal past the kitchen premises and up the servants' staircase.

She clutched her mother's Paisley shawl nervously closer when she reached the green baize door which separated downstairs from upstairs. She'd been upstairs many times over the years, of course, assisting her mother with pincushion and measuring tape when Lady Hawkerton and Hannah required fitting for gowns. She was in awe of her ladyship, but loved the Honourable Miss Hannah, the laird's only child, just a little older than Ishbel herself. She loved Hannah and pitied her too for Hannah had triumphed over a tubercular hip in childhood, at some cost to her looks and mobility. Nevertheless, although the laird's daughter would always limp on one shortened leg, she was good-natured and friendly, with a lively sense of humour which appealed greatly to Ishbel. So the two girls had become friendly, and Ishbel hoped she would be present at the concert tonight.

Taking a deep breath, she pushed open the door and stepped into the concealed space behind the great staircase. She could hear talk and laughter coming from the ballroom. Evidently the concert hadn't started yet. She felt awkwardly shy. Oh, the dress, she thought anxiously. Is a reach-me-down really suitable for this grand do? If only I could see how I look!

She suddenly remembered there was a long gilt mirror in the library. Hannah had fostered Ishbel's love of reading and the two of them had spent many happy hours browsing through the library shelves together. She folded the shawl and laid it on a chair, then set out quietly along the passageway.

For the first time, Ishbel noticed how shabby the house had become. There had been rumours recently about the laird's financial difficulties, but she hadn't believed them. Now she began to wonder if they might be true.

The library was just as she remembered, and there before her was the beautiful gilded mirror which stretched from floor to ceiling. Her mouth fell open as she gazed at her reflection. Was she really as pretty as this? Could this be the same lass who milked the kye and churned the butter in Wotherspoon's dairy? Surely no'! This was a stylish stranger. Delighted, Ishbel spun round holding out her skirt and someone clapped energetically, frightening her out of her wits. She stared up at the gallery above the bookshelves, and laughed with relief.

'Och, Hannah, I didn't notice you perched up there.'

Hannah Hawkerton slid down the banister of a spiral wooden staircase and limped towards her friend. 'My word, Ishbel, you look lovely! Mind out for those officers. They'll be buzzing like bees round a honeypot.' There was no hint of envy in the remark for Hannah had long since come to terms with her own shortcomings. She paused a moment before going on in a different tone. 'I was hoping to see you tonight, Ishbel. I wanted you to be the first to know I'm getting married.'

There had been no word of Hannah's courtship in the cluster of cottages, known locally as farm toun, which housed the workers on the Hawkertons' estate, and Ishbel was surprised and delighted. She hugged her friend. 'Oh, I'm so happy for you, Hannah. Who's the lucky man, do I know him?'

Hannah looked at her strangely. 'Yes, you do. It's Hugh Wotherspoon.'

'Wotherspoon!'

Ishbel recoiled with shock. She couldn't hide her dismay. Wotherspoon, that hard, dour man, to marry Hannah, who was so pleasant and full of fun! She didn't know what to say. She felt like weeping.

Hannah gave a brittle laugh. 'Yes, Wotherspoon. Hugh asked Father for my hand in marriage last week, and he consented with alacrity as a Heaven-sent way out of our difficulties. Of course, the poor man must take the rest of me as well, but the fact that I'm heiress of the estate and he will have the working of all Father's land has no doubt sugared the pill.'

'Oh, Hannah! I'm so sorry,' whispered Ishbel tearfully.

'Don't be sorry for me!' Hannah cried passionately. 'I

10

want to be married – I don't care to whom – so long as the estate can be saved. I love this place with all my heart, but I haven't the strength to save it from the ruin my father's brought on us with his mismanagement. I'm a weak woman with a crippled body, but Hugh Wotherspoon, whatever else he may be, is a shrewd farmer. Oh, Ishbel, don't look at me like that! Can't you see why I'm doing this?'

She nodded slowly. 'Yes, I see. It's just that I couldna marry without love.'

Hannah's mood changed. She laughed and gave Ishbel a little push. 'Well, go ahead, you little beauty. Laugh, love and be merry tonight. Break a few hearts. You have my permission to wreak havoc amongst His Majesty's forces.'

'Aren't you coming to the concert?'

'No. My intended doesn't care for music, and Mama, bless her heart, doesn't dare let me loose with all those penniless young officers around in case I lose my heart to some unsuitable man and confound dear Daddy's plans. I shall retire obediently to my room with a good book.'

Ishbel had made herself late. She could hear violins tuning up as she hurried towards the ballroom. It had never been her intention to make a dramatic entrance, but the doors were closing and she rushed at them desperately. She burst into the room and stopped dead in the open doorway. There was a sudden hush as every eye fixed upon her.

Paralysed with shyness, she saw the room was packed with people: convalescent soldiers, staff doctors and nurses, local members of the Voluntary Aid Detachment, or VADs as they were known. The big room wasn't lined with rows of seats like other concert halls; the seating was arranged informally, many of the men being in bath chairs, knees covered with rugs, some disguising amputated legs. Some had an arm missing or awkwardly pinioned in splints. Others, in the uniform of the Royal Flying Corps, had young faces so burned and disfigured the sight almost brought shocked tears to Ishbel's eyes. But these poor men have had enough of tears, she thought. She looked unflinchingly at these tragic statistics of a war to end all wars, and smiled. Had she but known it, her youthful presence suddenly lit the austere room with the warm radiance of a lovely spring day.

Lady Hawkerton hissed, 'Get to your seat, Ishbel. I've a good mind to turn you out for putting the string quartet off.'

She stared around anxiously but every seat was taken. A young man sitting nearby moved a heavy walking stick aside and patted the empty space beside him invitingly. Ishbel squeezed on to the seat with a grateful smile, and a voice from somewhere in the gathering muttered loudly, 'Well, I'll be damned! Trust old Freddie!' A ripple of amusement ran through the male audience, drowned by opening chords from the earnest quartet.

Ishbel settled down to listen, but it soon became apparent to her it wasn't the sort of concert she'd been expecting. She'd hoped for cheery music hall songs and dancing, and jokes from a comedian in between, but the Salvation Army band outside Dalkeith's pubs on Saturday nights dished out cheerier fare than this dreary scraping. The quartet was followed by a soulful baritone mourning his lost loves, a great many of them. And no wonder they'd ditched him wi' a girning voice like that! she thought. Ishbel turned her attention to her companion, curious to find out what an officer looked like.

12

Untidy, for a start. Officers didn't wear the regulation blue of convalescing Tommies, and this one had carelessly thrown on a jersey over a crumpled silk shirt and wore a pair of shapeless trousers. There was a patterned cravat knotted round his throat, giving him a debonair look. The clothing was all superior quality though. Ishbel had gleaned enough knowledge from her mother's occupation to know good stuff when she saw it.

'If I'd known you were coming, I'd have worn a tie,' the officer remarked dryly.

Ishbel blushed scarlet. 'Och, there's no call to dress up for the likes o' me, Mr – er – sir.'

'Captain Alexander. Or Freddie, which sounds friendlier, don't you think?' he said with a grin. 'Captain in the Royal Flying Corps, presently withdrawn from active service.' He tapped a leg gingerly.

'Oh, dear. Is it bad?'

'Bad enough, but could be worse. The Red Baron tends to pursue two-seater scout planes, you see. They're slower than single-seat escorts, and everyone knows they're up there to spy on Jerry lines. Anyway, Von Richthoven got my observer straight off and was back on my tail in no time. I was dashed lucky. He shattered the leg, but I dropped the Sopwith's nose and dived. The aircraft didn't fall to pieces for once so I hedge-hopped home – and here I am.'

They noticed Lady Hawkerton glaring daggers in their direction. The baritone had ended his melancholy repertoire and departed, his place taken by the ample lady seated at the piano. She sang a couple of preparatory scales then launched at full volume into a quavering Italian aria.

'Oh, my gosh!' groaned Freddie, sinking lower in his chair. One of his more mobile companions leaned across and handed him a half-full bottle and two glasses. 'Fancy a splash for yourself and the lovely lady, Fred?'

'What is it?'

'Bubbly of sorts, but it has a mighty kick. It'll buck you up no end.'

He dispensed full glasses for Ishbel and himself. She stared at the sparkling drink warily. 'I don't think I ought to.'

'Of course you ought to, with this caterwauling going on! Drink up, Miss – d'you know, I don't even know your name!'

'I'm not Miss anybody, I'm just plain Ishbel Mackie.'

He studied her, serious for once. 'You could never be plain.'

She sipped gingerly, her heart racing. She'd never met anyone like him. He wore clothes her pa wouldn't be seen dead in, yet you could tell he was a gentleman, just as you could tell that Pa was only a—

What am I thinking? she thought aghast, pulling herself up with a jerk. It was the champagne, of course. She'd only taken a few sips, but already her head was spinning, and she felt – well, to be quite honest, rather jolly.

The opera singer finished her third selection and retired to thankful applause. There was a lull in the entertainment, and someone called out, 'Hey, Freddie old man, give us a tune!'

Other voices added weight to the request, and the officer smiled at Ishbel. 'Give me a hand, will you?'

She jumped up obligingly and grasped his hand. Hard work had made her strong, and she pulled him easily to his feet. He swayed and flung out his arms, ostensibly to steady himself, and Ishbel found herself enclosed in a warm embrace. The audience whistled appreciatively.

Freddie let her go with an apology. He wasn't quite so unsteady as he'd made out, and had received rather more from that wickedly casual embrace than he'd bargained for. In fact his senses were reeling, and he shook his head in an effort to clear it. What a kick that cheap plonk has! he thought dizzily.

The mood in the room changed when Freddie started to play. He launched into a medley of popular songs, but these proved too poignant to be borne by men who'd viewed the carnage on the Somme. He ended the sing-song quickly and glanced up at Ishbel. 'Do you sing?'

'Yes, but not in front of all these folk.'

'Why not? Go on, be a sport. Sing something for me.'

Like all his sort, he could charm larks out of the sky if he put his mind to it, she thought as she hesitated nervously. Well, she decided, if I do sing, it'll be for poor Harry Lauder, who lost his only son just before Hogmanay in the cold mud of the battlefield. Ah, poor Harry, with such high hopes pinned on his one clever laddie!

The champagne gave her reckless courage. 'Och well, Freddie, Harry Lauder says a Scot can aye sing if there's a free supper at the end o' it,' she laughed. Stepping in front of the piano, she began to sing one of Harry's favourites, the funny one about a daft wee boy that never failed to make Mam and Pa laugh.

'I'm the saftest o' the family . . .'

Freddie picked up the melody, and bursts of laughter echoed through the crowded room. Ishbel's confidence grew. She enjoyed performing to an appreciative audience, and boldly improvised a few dancing steps which showed off slim legs and ankles to advantage. The audience went wild. When the song ended they howled for more, and growing bolder by the minute, she launched into the naughty one that had sent Auntie Nellie into gales of loud laughter in the Empire.

'Will you stop your tickling, Jock?'

That nearly brought the house down. The audience applauded thunderously and yelled for more, but Ishbel shook her head firmly, blushing and laughing. Freddie reached for her hand and pressed it, his eyes shining softly. 'That was wonderful. Just what these poor boys needed, my dear. Thank you indeed.'

Holding his hand, staring fascinated into his grey eyes, she wondered dazedly what was happening to her, for she'd never experienced such strong feelings at the mere touch of a man's hand. The uplifting influence of the drink subsided and she felt oddly weak at the knees.

A soldier had slipped unobtrusively into the room during Ishbel's performance, but Lady Hawkerton's eagle eyes had spotted the intruder. Her ladyship was annoyed because Ishbel had lowered the edifying tone of the evening. Now she sought to redress the balance. She called out loudly, 'I'm sorry, soldier, other ranks are not permitted.'

He came forward. 'Dinna fash yoursel', I'm no' staying to affront onybody, my lady. I came to escort my lass home.' He removed his bonnet politely and Ishbel cried out: 'Sandy!'

She didn't know whether to be shamed or delighted. He must have seen her carrying-on, and the MacArthurs would be black affronted when they heard. Well, it was done now, even if Sandy didn't look too pleased. He marched over, kilt swinging, very smart and military.

16

'Ishbel, are you ready to leave?'

Freddie smiled disarmingly and said sotto voce: 'I say, old chap, don't heed the old battleaxe. We don't pull rank with this bunch of crocks. You're very welcome to stay.'

He smiled awkwardly. 'Thanks, sir, that's kind, but it's near ten o'clock and Ishbel's folks are anxious for her wi' Zeppelins about. I'd best see her safely home.'

'Oh, very well,' Freddie sighed. He began to play and sing softly, watching Ishbel as he did so.

'Goodby-ee, don't cry-ee,

Wipe the tear, baby dear, from your eye-ee . . .'

It was a cheery song usually, but the way he sang it sounded sad. Of course, others picked up the popular melody and began singing merrily. Sandy put an arm round Ishbel's waist and led her away. She went obediently, turning just once to smile at the man seated at the piano. He waved a hand.

'Bon soir, old thing, cheerio, chin chin,

Nah-poo, toodle-oo, goodby-ee!'

Walking in the dark, hand tucked under Sandy's arm, Ishbel didn't know what to say, and that was odd because she'd chattered away to the strange officer. Her childhood sweetheart had come back so changed she hardly knew him. The coarse khaki jacket he wore with the kilt had a strange and different smell, not unpleasant, rather like the Lysol she used to scrub the dairy. She stole a cautious glance at Sandy in the light of the moon. He was handsome and well-built. A good, steady lad any girl would be proud to take.

'Your card was lovely. Thanks, Sandy. And fancy you getting off on my birthday!' she remarked.

'The training and square-bashing's finished so they're

mair generous wi' days off.' He looked down at her. She looked so beautiful he'd hardly known her when he'd barged into the Big Hoose and found her making an exhibition of herself, showing off her legs. That was an eye-opener! He didn't know what to think. 'You fairly enjoyed yoursel' larking wi' the officers,' he said grimly.

She was glad it was dark under the trees so she could hide her blushes. Yet why should I feel guilty? she thought with a burst of defiance. 'Och, it's another way o' life when you're in the Big House, Sandy. It's free an' easy, though the officers are perfect gentlemen. I even had a wee drappie o' champagne,' she admitted boldly.

'Aye, so I noticed.' He itched to shake some sense into her, but he loved the lass dearly and would never lift his hand to her. He stopped in a patch of moonlight, forcing her to face him. 'Listen, Ishbel, since I've been in the army I've learned something about mysel'. I've learned my roots are deep in the earth. In the past I've walked behind the horses wi' plough stilts in my hands and clarty boots in the furrows, and if I have a future it'll be in farming, a way of life we both love and understand. Mind that when fine gentlemen give you the glad eye.'

She'd never dreamed he had such passion in him, the steady lad. For some reason she was reminded of Hannah Hawkerton and felt afraid. Sandy bent his head and kissed her fiercely. 'I'm sorry to preach, love, but they're sending us to France. It concentrates the mind.'

'Oh, Sandy!' She clung to him in tears. He would die, of course. He'd die on the battlefield like thousands of fine young men. 'This awful war, I can't bear it!' she sobbed.

'Aye. The future's hazy,' he agreed sadly. 'A man canna mak' plans, but—' He fished in his pocket and brought out a small leather box. 'This is for you, Ishbel. Your birthday present.'

She opened the box with dread because she guessed what was in it and didn't know how to deal with the complication. Her fears confirmed, she gazed at the ring, at chips of diamond winking coldly in the moonlight, a dark little ruby in the centre like a drop of congealed blood. She didn't know what to say.

He took her hand and slipped the ring on to the betrothal finger. 'Will you wear my ring, Ishbel? Will you wear it with no promise given an' none taken, until I come home safe and can see the future clear?'

She looked at him with tears in her eyes. He was going to France. It was a death sentence. She reached up and kissed him. 'Aye, Sandy, I'll wear it 'til you come back home, safe an' sound,' she promised.

Captain Freddie Alexander had been unusually quiet all morning. He'd been racking his brains for a plausible excuse to visit Ishbel Mackie. There had been several beautiful women in Freddie's past, and he didn't claim to be a saint, but Ishbel's beauty and innocence had touched the remnants of chivalry within him. His last love, Marietta, had been French; very chic and charming, but her charms paled into insignificance beside this country lass's. He was glad the brief, passionate affair had ended by mutual consent.

Anyway, thought Freddie happily, who needs an excuse to visit a pretty girl? He set off slowly down the drive, stick swinging as he stepped out, following directions supplied by a giggling ward maid.

He arrived at Catriona Mackie's door and knocked,

taking care to lean pathetically upon the stick. His leg was actually quite painful after the walk, though not quite so painful as he made out. A tall woman with calm eyes and a strong resemblance to Ishbel answered his knock and he smiled disarmingly. 'Please excuse me, ma'am, but my name is Frederick Alexander, and I had the pleasure of meeting Miss Ishbel at the concert last night. I could not pass her door without calling to pay my respects.'

Catriona's glance took in the merry grey eyes, the heavy stick, the good clothes worn casually. Even without the educated accent, she would have guessed he was a gentleman. 'Ishbel is at the dairy, and will be there till lowsing-time. There's churns to be scalded and kye to be milked before she gets off.' Catriona deliberately stressed her daughter's lowly tasks. It seemed necessary somehow.

He looked regretful. 'Ah, well. Another time, perhaps.' He turned away, then staggered and groaned, leaning against the wall. Catriona hurried to his aid.

'It's this dashed leg, ma'am. It packs up sometimes, but please don't worry about me. I'll make my way back to the hospital,' he gasped.

'You'll do nothing of the kind, you poor lad. You'll come into my house and rest for a bit,' Catriona insisted.

Freddie allowed himself to be assisted into the cottage. His hostess seated him in a comfortable chair beside a gleaming, black-leaded grate, and bustled around bringing out the best china, while a kettle hanging on the swee over the fire was brought to the boil. Freddie looked around curiously. It was a simple enough dwelling, but everything was spotless. Indeed, there was evidence of good taste in the furnishing of the pleasant room, he noted with surprise.

He was further impressed when Catriona served tea in

willow pattern cups, accompanied by warm scones which melted in the mouth. He found himself feeling more at home than he'd done for years. Catriona sat opposite, chatting away and sipping tea in genteel fashion in honour of her guest. Conversation was just beginning to flag when Freddie heard the sound he'd been hoping for. The door opened and Ishbel came in laughing, followed by a burly, older man whom Freddie guessed correctly to be her father. Donald had been smiling, but his expression changed when his eyes lit on the visitor.

Ishbel could hardly believe her eyes when she saw Freddie sitting there. Her heart gave a wild lurch which left her slightly breathless. 'What are you doing here?' she cried in a joyful tone which made her mother look up sharply.

'I called to pay my respects to you and your family, Ishbel, then this leg played up. Your charming mother came to my rescue and has been spoiling me with her wonderful hospitality.' He smiled at Catriona who was flattered despite herself.

Donald's hackles rose. Buttering up Catriona, was he? Well, sweet talk might fool women, but it cut nae ice wi' him! 'Och, man, my wife takes in any rag-tag tinker who spins a hard luck yarn, and Ishbel's no' much better,' he said loudly.

Freddie recognised hostility. 'Then you're most fortunate in your wife and daughter, sir,' he said smoothly.

Donald was ashamed of his own churlishness. The poor lad was badly wounded, after all. 'Aye – well – you're welcome in my hoose anyroad,' he muttered gruffly.

'I mustn't outstay my welcome though, Mr Mackie!'

Freddie stood up to take his leave and made for the door,

limping so pathetically Ishbel gave a cry of concern. 'I'll see you home,' she offered, and he did not demur.

When the two young people had gone, Donald turned on his wife. 'What's that fine gentleman after?'

The visit had flustered Catriona, which was unusual for her. She could understand why he was suspicious for he doted on their daughter. If any harm befell his lass, her husband would likely shoot the man. She hugged Donald, as much to reassure herself as her husband. 'My dear, dinna fash yoursel'. Ishbel wears Sandy's ring, and our lass would never break her young man's heart for the sake o' a gentry officer.'

'Your leg must be awful sore, Freddie,' Ishbel said sympathetically, as he leaned more heavily upon her.

'Oh, it is! Maybe if I put an arm round you like this . . . ? There, that's much better.'

It was indeed. Very much better, he thought. It took all his willpower not to kiss her, she was such an adorable little innocent.

But not quite so innocent, it seemed! She shoved his hand away indignantly from her breast and turned on him hotly, eyeing the walking stick which he'd absentmindedly tucked under his arm in the heat of the moment. 'Here, what are you playing at, Freddie Alexander? You're not lame at all!'

'Oh, blast! I forgot to limp.'

Ishbel stared, then her lips twitched and she burst out laughing. She laughed until she was weak, and he daringly took her in his arms to support her. She wiped her eyes on the back of her hand.

'Och, Freddie, you are a wicked rascal!'

He didn't say anything. He was noting the cheap little ring on the betrothal finger of her left hand, and wondering what could be done about that complication.

Next day, Freddie turned up in the byre while Ishbel and the other women were milking the kye. She leaned her head against a cow's warm brown flank and smiled up at him. 'Well, you've seen it all now, Captain Alexander, this is what I do for my living.'

He studied her, so bonny and natural, her cheek resting against the big brown and white beast, and an oddly painful emotion twisted his heart. 'It's the prettiest sight I've ever seen, Ishbel,' he told her truthfully.

She'd been on his mind ever since he'd met her. He'd sauntered casually to the dairy that day because he'd little else to do, but that chance visit was proving to be a momentous event in his life. He recognised the feeling: he was falling in love. He would never forget this scene, the women milking the cows in the big byre, the hiss of warm milk into the burnished pails, the pleasant smell of hay and oat straw. And at the heart of it, Ishbel.

'I must see you tonight,' he said urgently.

She stood up, milk-pail brimming. 'Then you'll come to supper with my mam an' pa for I'm a respectable girl. I don't go walking in the gloaming with flying officers who kid on they're lame when they're not!'

He smiled. 'I accept with pleasure, and promise to behave impeccably.'

'Oh, Pa will see to that, dinna you worry!' She turned away and strained the milk into a nearby churn, carefully reserving some which she poured into a stone trough.

23

There was a flurry and cats came streaking from all directions to lap at the trough. She saw Freddie watching.

'Please don't tell Wotherspoon or he'll have my lugs for breakfast. But who would care for the poor wee starved beasties if I didn't?'

'Ah, yes, who indeed?' said Freddie gently.

The pace of life in the farm toun went on quietly over the following weeks. The ploughed parks were harrowed, there was a fresh sowing of oats, turnips and potatoes. Wotherspoon stalked the laird's idle parks, planning a new rotation of crops – a more profitable way of doing altogether. He was not yet wedded to Hannah Hawkerton, but everyone knew he was already master of the place. The laird was no more than a spent tattie-bogle: a sad ineffectual scarecrow in his own parks.

Ishbel wore Sandy's ring and prayed for him nightly for he was fighting in France. She wore it to keep her feet on the ground, too, since Captain Alexander visited the cottage every day. He was due to be discharged from hospital soon to continue convalescence at home, a privilege afforded to officers. He didn't relish the prospect of returning to his Edinburgh home, he told Ishbel.

'What do you work at anyway when you're not flying aeroplanes?' she asked curiously.

'I'm a shopkeeper,' he admitted.

This was news to Ishbel who laughed heartily. 'Och, Freddie, imagine you behind the counter!'

He looked at her, unsmiling. 'Yes. Imagine me. Would you care to come and see?' Catriona was sitting nearby, sewing, and he turned to her. 'May I take Ishbel to Edinburgh for the day, Mrs Mackie?'

Catriona hesitated. She felt a chill of apprehension strike her. She liked him, had grown fond of the charming lad, but didn't want him for her lass. What am I afraid of, though? she rebuked herself. It's only an outing to Edinburgh, and Ishbel wears Sandy's ring. Slowly, she nodded her consent.

'Aye. It'll be a nice day out for Ishbel, on the holiday.'

Freddie turned up on Saturday morning in a Rolls-Royce Silver Ghost, and Ishbel's jaw dropped. 'Is this a taxi, Freddie?'

He grinned. 'Could be. Hop in.'

She climbed in gingerly and waved goodbye to her parents. The limousine purred down the driveway and into Dalkeith, and soon they turned off the main street on to the ancient Edinburgh road, picking up speed heading down-hill past Bridgend. Ishbel clung to the seat in terror.

'Oh, do stop it, Freddie. It's going too fast!'

He laughed. 'We're only doing thirty, you goose! I've had her up to sixty, when the police weren't about.'

But he did slow down to the regulation twenty miles per hour. The metalled road surface wasn't too good, and besides, Freddie wanted this journey to last forever. He dreaded what she'd say and do when they reached the shop.

Ishbel enjoyed herself once Freddie reduced speed. The beautiful countryside of the Lothians unfolded around them as they drove along, and in no time it seemed they'd reached the outskirts of the city. She could see the high tenements ranged on the spine of the castle hill, where her father had been born. On this fine summer's day there were few lums smoking, and church spires rose high into clear air like castles in a fairytale. She was very happy.

She was still in a happy dream when Freddie pulled up at a kerbside in the West End. 'We're here,' he announced.

Ishbel looked up. She saw a uniformed commissionaire standing at the foot of marble steps leading to a polished expanse of glass doors; huge windows draped with red silk, displaying fabulous clothing and priceless objects. As she gazed, her heart grew cold as a chuckie stone. Her dazed eyes scanned the sign in huge gold letters above the doorway: ALEXANDER.

Everyone in Edinburgh had heard of Alexander's. It was a posh shop for wealthy folk, and a legend in the city. She turned on Freddie furiously. 'Why didn't you tell me you were *that* Alexander?'

'Would it have made any difference?'

She wouldn't look at him, for she didn't know the answer. The commissionaire hurried to open the car door. 'Welcome, Mr Freddie! My, but it's grand to have you back safe an' sound!' His glance flickered discreetly over Ishbel as Freddie helped her out.

Freddie tucked her hand firmly under his arm and led her into the shop. She looked around, stunned by the luxury goods on sale. This was all his – or at least, his family's. The carpets on the floor, the mahogany counters with superior assistants in charge, the silks, satins and perfumes, the jewels. A fabulous display of wealth even in wartime. And I milk the kye! Ishbel thought, sickened.

Freddie was popular, greeted left, right and centre. It was 'Mr Freddie this' and 'Mr Freddie that', and 'How very sad about your brother, Mr George'. Aware how cheap her Sunday best must appear to these fine folk, Ishbel endured curious stares proudly, looking neither right nor left until they had been whisked upstairs to Freddie's office in a lift operated by a diminutive lift boy. Freddie closed the office door and they stood facing one another.

'Oh, Freddie, why didn't you tell me?' she asked miserably.

'I *did* tell you. I'm a shopkeeper, and not a very good one at that.'

She was bitterly angry. 'You know what I mean, Freddie Alexander! You're a cheat. You sat in Pa's cottage and patronised us, eating bannocks and supping broth. How you must've laughed up your sleeve at us poor folk and our country ways, with all this at your back!'

He grabbed her by the shoulders, giving her a furious little shake. 'Listen to me, Ishbel! Those hours spent in your home were the happiest I ever knew, your mother's hospitality the kindest. The last few months have been a dream of happiness for me, all because of you, my dearest girl.'

He hadn't meant to kiss her. He'd made up his mind to be a model of propriety so he could meet her mother's keen gaze with a clear conscience. But that was before they'd faced one another with passions roused. He seized her and kissed her with all the pent-up longing of the past months. For a moment she was taken by surprise and was warm and yielding in his arms, then she tore herself away. Her arm swung back, and she slapped his cheek.

'How dare you kiss me like – like that!'

Ishbel ran to the door and flung it open. He called out but she wouldn't stop. She flew along the passageway to the lift where the boy stood gawping. 'G-going down, miss?'

'Aye. Right down to the ground,' she cried bitterly.

Freddie leaned against the desk. He was so badly shaken the injured limb refused to do his bidding, and that was how his father found him when he hurried in to discover what all the fuss was about.

William Alexander was delighted to find his son in the office. Freddie had shown very little interest in the family business, but now war had claimed William's elder son George, he hoped Freddie would step into his brother's shoes. It was over a year since his beloved son had died at Ypres, but William's grief was still fresh and raw. It had helped a bit, putting off his retirement, but the strain of running a business in wartime was telling on him. He looked at Freddie with renewed hope.

'Getting the feel o' the business, son?'

Freddie had the grace to feel ashamed. 'Er – yes.'

His father nodded. 'Adam McPherson's worth his weight in gold as manager, but he's near as old as I am. We look to the younger generation now, Freddie.'

And that reminded William. His wife Eleanor had arranged one of her dinner parties for that evening, and it was vitally important Freddie should be there. Sir Stewart Allsop's pretty daughter had been invited, and Eleanor had high hopes of an excellent match for their son.

'Don't forget your mother's dinner party tonight. Sarah Allsop is dying to meet you.'

Freddie knew perfectly well what his mother was up to, and it turned his stomach. His thoughts cleared. He could see the way ahead with a clarity that had been lacking until now. He moved the leg cautiously and it was right as rain. 'Sorry, Father, but I can't attend tonight. Tell Mother I have an important engagement, will you? Now I must dash.'

Heads turned as Freddie erupted from the lift downstairs. He raced through the shop and ran outside, pausing to stare up and down Princes Street. He knew Ishbel's Auntie Nellie lived in Leith, so it was a safe bet she would head for there. He set off at a run towards the top of Leith Walk.

To his relief, Freddie soon saw Ishbel ahead, hurrying along with head held high. With a desperate burst of speed he caught up with her and whirled her round. People jostling past on the crowded pavement stopped and stared indignantly but Freddie was oblivious. 'Ishbel, my dearest girl, I love you so much. Will you marry me?' he asked.

Chapter 2

Ishbel stared, doubting if she'd heard correctly. 'You want to marry me?'

He laughed. 'Of course I do! You keep reminding me in no uncertain terms you're a respectable girl, so there's nothing else for it. Besides, I'm head over heels in love with you, my darling.'

Her heart was racing. To be Freddie's wife! She felt quite breathless at the prospect. To love him faithfully all her days. She looked into his grey eyes, shining with love for her, and knew she wanted him too, aye, every bit as much as he wanted her. But he was a gentleman, far above her station in life. And besides, she wore Sandy's ring. Her fickle emotions shocked her. *How can I forget Sandy so easily and love Freddie so much?* she wondered.

They were hindering impatient Saturday shoppers, and Freddie seized the opportunity to hold her closer. 'Darling, please say yes!'

His attractiveness, and her own overwhelming response, only served to heighten Ishbel's dilemma. She'd woven many ambitious daydreams whilst milking the kye, but never in her wildest dreams had she expected to escape the harsh drudgery of the land. Yet this dear man was asking

31

her humbly to share his gilded life. Folk would call her gold-digger if she took him, yet rich or poor, she loved Freddie Alexander and wanted with all her heart to marry him.

She suddenly remembered Mam and Pa, and what they would say. Her parents would be dead set against it. They liked Freddie, but they had their sights fixed on Sandy for their daughter. She almost wept.

'Oh, Freddie darling, I do love you so, but – but – there are so many "buts"!'

'Sweetheart, I'll settle for your love!' he cried exultantly. 'I promise the "buts" will be overcome.'

He grabbed her arm and joined the throng of shoppers until they reached the junction with Hanover Street where he daringly launched himself into a stream of horse-drawn cabs, carts, honking motor cars and charabancs navigating Princes Street. He wove merrily through the mêlée, dragging a terrified Ishbel behind him.

'Freddie, where are we going?'

'To a haven of peace, my dear. I want to kiss you.'

She hung back, laughing. 'Don't be daft, man. Everyone in Princes Street will see us canoodling, I'll be so ashamed.'

'Och, I keep for-rgetting you're a r-respectable gir-r-rl,' he mimicked, in a creditable impersonation of Harry Lauder.

Hand in hand, they left the street and ran down flights of steps leading to Princes Street Gardens. The green warmth enfolded them, and the sound of traffic faded. Now they could walk in lazy sunshine with the scent of summer flowers in the air. Other refugees from the hustle and bustle strolled here: elderly folk, young couples with children, lovers like themselves, most of the men in uniform like Freddie, snatching a few moments' peace in the midst of war.

A shadow still clouded Ishbel's happiness. 'Freddie, I wish you'd told me from the start your family owned that swanky shop.'

He slipped an arm round her waist. 'Would it have changed anything?'

'It might,' she answered honestly. She might have been frightened off. She wouldn't have dared to invite Freddie to her parents' but and ben if she'd known who he was. Maybe she wouldn't have let herself fall in love.

Freddie guessed the drift of her thoughts. He paused and gripped her shoulders, making her face him. 'Ishbel, listen to me. The Alexanders come from humble stock. The founder of the firm way back in 1830 was a poor widow in the Trongate, at her wits' end to feed a young family. Elspeth Alexander rented a small booth near the Tron Kirk for a few pennies and set up as mantle-maker, designing ladies' gowns and hats. She worked night and day and her fashionable designs and careful attention to detail became well-known in the city. When she died at a ripe old age, Elspeth had laid the foundations of the firm which eventually became Alexander's.'

The story appealed to Ishbel who was reminded of her own mother. She could imagine Mam buckling to like that. 'Elspeth must have been a remarkable woman,' she said.

'Oh, she was, but she also had an element of luck. She was blessed with a clever son.'

Something in his tone made Ishbel look up. He sighed and tucked her hand under his arm before walking on.

'Four generations of clever Alexander sons kept Elspeth's business flourishing up to the present day, but since my brother George was killed at Ypres it all depends on me. It's a grave responsibility, Ishbel. I'm not sure I'm up to it, to be honest.'

Frowning moodily, he paused to watch as a train puffed past at the base of the castle rock. It gathered speed coming out of Waverley Station and rumbled in a cloud of smoke and steam into the tunnel. Ishbel hugged him tenderly. 'Oh, Freddie dear, you never told me about your brother. You must've been so sad, and you never let on.'

He sighed and drew her close. 'Yes, it was a bad show, my dear. George had bright ideas and was destined to carry on the family tradition. I was never interested in running the shop, you see. It was a crushing blow to my parents when George was killed, and though Father struggles to keep the firm going, he should be retired at his age. I know he's counting the days until I can take over.'

Ishbel's imagination was fired by Freddie's dilemma. She could help! Her mind was bursting with ideas, and from an early age she'd learned useful skills from Mam, who was a wizard with the needle and had a sure eye for fashion. If need be, she'd work her fingers to the bone for Freddie, and between them they'd win through. She traced the forlorn droop of his mouth with a fingertip. She hated to see her laughing Freddie downcast. 'It's a sair responsibility, dearest, but you can do it.'

'Only if you marry me, dear girl. Otherwise I'm sunk.'

She made up her mind there and then. 'Yes, I'll marry you, love. To tell the truth, my life would be bleak without you.'

With a joyful whoop, Freddie whirled her round and kissed her. It was a long, searching kiss they shared beneath the trees, and when it ended, Ishbel rested her head breathlessly on her man's shoulder. She caught sight of Sandy's ring winking on the betrothal finger and came down to earth with a thud. For the first time she faced the consequences of her love for Freddie Alexander and realised she would hurt other trusting and innocent folk.

'Your family will not be well pleased when they find out you've been courting a farm worker, Freddie,' she warned. 'And my parents had set their hearts on Sandy MacArthur for their son-in-law. I'm afraid there are battles ahead for us.'

'San fairy Ann, my love!' Freddie laughed. He felt euphoric, welcoming a fight, though his arms tightened protectively round his newly won lass as he recalled his mother's dinner party scheduled for that evening, and the well-born Sarah Allsop lined up as a suitable mate for him. A vision of his mother's wrath, coupled with Donald and Catriona Mackie's tight-lipped displeasure, was enough to quench his ardour momentarily. He took Ishbel's arm and urged her towards the steps. 'Come on, dear. I've had enough of Edinburgh's smoke and grime for one day. I'll take you home.'

Freddie drove decorously along Lothian Road and by way of the Meadows to join Dalkeith Road, Ishbel nodding dreamily by his side. The populace on the city's outskirts was indulging in the great Scottish institution of High Tea, and the road in front was temptingly deserted. Recovering his ebullient spirits, he rose to the challenge stretching ahead.

I'm expected to trundle along at twenty in this powerful machine as if it were a bloomin' milk-cart! he thought. He had a quick look all round. There wasn't a bobby to be seen. Joyfully, he opened the throttle and let the car rip.

Ishbel sat up with a jolt. 'Freddie, what are you doing?'

'Speeding. Hang on to your hat, my darling!'

Exhilaration coursed through Freddie's veins. What a memorable day! He'd asked his girl to marry him and been accepted. This was the only fitting way to end such an outing. Every nerve in his body tingled as the car sped faster. He felt vibrantly alive, senses sharpened, hands sure and steady on the wheel. He scanned the empty road for hazards, confident his reactions were speedier than any danger confronting him. He'd never felt so completely in control. He let out a joyful roar that must surely echo to the high Pentlands. 'Hurrahhh – I love you, Ishbel Mackie! I'll love you 'til I die!'

Trees, hedges, houses flashed giddily past Ishbel's frightened gaze. She clung to the seat in terror as the car sped even faster. Finally she screamed in panic. 'Freddie, stop it! Oh, please stop!'

It took several seconds for Ishbel's genuine terror to get through to him, but he slowed down at last and reached for her hand reassuringly. 'Sweetheart, don't be scared. I know what I'm doing.' He gave her an exultant grin. 'Darling, do you realise we touched seventy miles an hour on that straight stretch?'

'No! Did we? Oh, michty me!' She shuddered and buried her face against his shoulder.

Freddie hovered dutifully round the speed limit for the rest of the journey, but the incident left doubt at the back of Ishbel's mind, a shadow on her happiness. Nearing the laird's estate, they encountered Wotherspoon's farm baillie on the road, blocking progress with a herd of slow-moving cattle. Stockmen were lonesome lads and rarely had a holiday, for beasts must aye be fed and tended. Ishbel guessed these were bound for fresh pastures on Wotherspoon's orders. The farmer was creating a great uproar on the laird's estate on the strength of his impending marriage to Hannah. Everyone in the farm toun was talking about the changes made. Freddie slowed the car behind the herdsman and the ambling beasts, and Ishbel found she could laugh again at her fears.

'Freddie, this is my pace. It's safer!'

Catriona Mackie couldn't settle that Saturday. Her mind kept turning towards Edinburgh and her lass. Donald, bless him, had set off for the inn with a carefully saved shilling or two in his pouch to stand his friend auld MacArthur a dram and a game of dominoes. Catriona had looked forward to an idle afternoon's reading, but that wasn't to be, she was so nervous. She'd ended up restlessly scrubbing the spotless stone floor, and had just made a fresh batch of bannocks on the girdle when she heard Freddie's car. They were back early. She hurried to the window.

What braw manners the man has! she thought admiringly. He was handing Ishbel down as if she were fine bone china, but for a moment his hand lingered, high and familiar, on the swell of her young breast, and the two of them stood motionless, gazing deep into one another's eyes. Catriona turned icy cold. They are deep in love! she thought in panic. How far has this gone?

She was outside before she knew she'd moved, breaking

the intimacy, driving them apart, stepping between the tall young man and her vulnerable lass.

'Well, how was Edinburgh this fine day?'

Freddie glanced at her sharply, detecting challenge in the tone. She hoped her glance was keen as a knife because she wanted him to see how she felt about his philandering, and no mistake! She wanted to drive a warning sharp as a kitchen blade into him. If you dishonour my lass, Freddie Alexander, so help me, I'll . . .

He smiled, a charming, ingratiating smile to get himself off the hook. No' so easy, my fine lad! thought Catriona grimly. It was a silent battle they fought while the innocent lass stood by with stars in her eyes, staring at her lover with devotion in every line of her.

Freddie, more worldly-wise, guessed what was in Catriona's mind. He answered warily. 'Auld Reekie was hot and crowded, Mrs Mackie, so we came home early.'

'But we walked in Princes Street Gardens for a spell, Mam. That was ever so nice,' Ishbel added.

Catriona nodded, her thoughts running cynically. Aye, I'm sure it was nice, my dear, and I can guess the spell that was woven. I've loitered there mysel' wi' your ardent father when we were young and courting, and been kissed and fondled beneath the shady trees. I ken fine how nice it can be!

Recalling her duties as hostess, Catriona turned to Freddie. Even with misgivings, hospitality came first. 'Will you stay for your tea, Freddie? You're very welcome.'

'We–ell . . .' he hesitated. Those clear eyes were looking right into him, searching his soul. Well, so what? He'd behaved honourably and done nothing to harm her beloved daughter. It was no sin to love Ishbel truly and wish to marry her. All the same, Freddie deemed it wiser to refuse the invitation. Better to give Ishbel time to prepare her parents before he came wooing in earnest. 'Thank you, Mrs Mackie, but not tonight.' He lifted his cap politely and climbed into the car. His exuberant spirits returned as he drove off, and he sounded the horn while the two women waved goodbye with very different emotions.

'Are you hungry, love?' asked Catriona when they were back in the cottage.

'Aye, Mam. I haven't had a bite since breakfast, we were so busy – er – seeing the sights.'

'I can imagine,' said her mother dryly, setting the supper table.

Ishbel pulled hatpins out of the crown of her hat. 'Mam, you'll never guess! Freddie's shop is that posh store in Princes Street, Alexander's. It's ever so grand, with marble steps and mahogany counters and lovely things for sale. He showed me all over, then up in the lift to his office.'

Her mother swung the kettle over the flames. 'So he's better off than we thought. What's he playin' at, befriending us poor folk?' She faced her daughter squarely. 'What's he wanting from you, Ishbel?'

She found her mother's tone insulting and answered hotly, 'It's no' what you're thinking! Freddie's an honourable man. He asked me to marry him the day, and I said I'd take him.'

Catriona collapsed in a chair, flabbergasted. In her experience, his sort never married the innocent lasses who took their fancy, if they could have their way without it. 'I'll tell you now, my love, it'll no' work,' she declared flatly.

'Aye, it will! We love one another.'

39

'Och, love! That's no' near enough,' her mother laughed
scornfully. 'Love won't heal your hurt when those fine
Edinburgh ladies cut you deid.'

'Why should they? I'm as good as them!'

'You try telling them that!' Catriona's tone changed then
and she wrung her hands. 'Oh, Ishbel! What about Sandy?'

She was near to tears. 'Mam, I don't love him.'

'But you wear his ring!'

'I promised I would 'til he comes home safe, and so I
will,' she said wretchedly, holding out her hand to stare at
the little jewel.

Catriona studied the blood red ruby set around with icy
chips of diamond, and suddenly knew she was looking at
heartbreak and tragedy. She shivered. Often she had a fey
Hebridean premonition about such things, but on this
occasion she prayed with heart and soul she was wrong.

She sighed heavily. 'If you're set on this path, Ishbel,
you'd best leave me to break the news of it to your father.'

Catriona had sympathy for the lass, for she wasn't too old
to remember how it felt to be young, and head over heels in
love. She wouldn't distress her daughter at this difficult
time, but secretly she feared this union would break
Donald's heart.

Because of the unexpected disruption of his plans for that
evening, Freddie returned to the Alexanders' Morningside
mansion earlier than intended. His mother's select little
dinner party was just ending. The ladies had withdrawn to
the drawing room to partake of coffee, whilst the gentlemen settled down to brandy and cigars in the dining room.
Freddie stole silently towards the kitchen premises.

He found his sister Dorothy supervising the washing up

of the Spode dinner service. Maggie, the latest skivvy, was a notorious butterfingers. You couldn't get reliable domestic staff these wartime days, Freddie knew, domestics had gleefully deserted in droves to work in munitions or to act as conductresses on Edinburgh's trams. Still, the large mansion functioned smoothly with Dorothy in charge, ably assisted by Florrie the cook-general who'd been with them for years.

Freddie grinned beguilingly. 'Any scraps for a hungry dog, Dorothy?'

'Not if Mother has her way, my dear. She is not best pleased.'

Dorothy pushed the remains of a large roast sirloin of beef towards her brother. He carved off two thick slices, and she sat down to watch him eat. An established old maid at thirty-six, Dorothy delighted in Freddie's free and easy behaviour. He made her laugh, and there wasn't much to laugh about in her drab existence.

'How's the leg, Freddie?'

He reached for the mustard. 'Oh, it stood up pretty well to the rigours of Princes Street.'

'Will they send you back to the Front?' she asked anxiously. She mourned her brother George sincerely, but thought she'd fade away and die if Freddie was killed.

'Well, the CO writes they're desperate for experienced pilots in the squadron,' he answered seriously. 'The replacements they send from Blighty are wet behind the ears and only last one or two missions, poor young devils.' He didn't want to think about going back. He knew that at twenty-seven, with a game leg, he was past peak performance.

He sandwiched meat and pickle between slices of bread

41

and ate hungrily, studying his sister who kept an anxious eye on Florrie and Maggie, dealing precariously with a large soup tureen. Dorothy was a good sport who'd fished him out of many a scrape in younger days. She was small and dumpy, as plain and wholesome as good fresh bread. He loved her dearly.

'How was Mother's dinner do?' he asked idly.

'Somewhat flat, dear, since the object of the exercise was to introduce you to Sarah Allsop, with a view to matrimony.'

He scowled. 'Mother needn't bother!'

'Don't be too hasty, Freddie dear. Sarah's quite presentable. Drives an ambulance for the Red Cross. I do admire her skill. My one ambition is to master a smooth gear change without excruciating screeches from the engine and a series of kangaroo hops.'

Freddie smiled, but all the same he was irritated by his mother's persistent match-making. He'd always been popular with girls, and had sown his wild oats in France like many other young men, but he considered the final choice of wife and helpmate to be his. Ishbel Mackie was the girl he'd chosen, the only girl in the world for him, and he loved and wanted her madly. The sooner his dear, well-intentioned mother got that into her head, the better!

Dorothy eyed her brother. She recognised that mutinous look. Freddie was digging his heels in. Well, good luck to him! She only wished she'd had the guts to live her own life, but as the unmarried daughter of ageing parents her duty was plain, and her future dully predictable.

Florrie came over, drying red hands. 'We've done the Spode, Miss Dorothy. You said no' to let Maggie touch the Royal Worcester fruit service, so I've set her to scouring the pots. Nothing she can break there, bar the sink.'

Dorothy reached for an apron. 'Thanks, Florrie. I'll do the fruit service myself. Don't let Maggie near the coffee cups and brandy glasses when they come down, will you?' She turned to Freddie, smiling. 'When you've demolished the remains of the roast, love, you can go and make your peace with Mother. The poor darling baited the hook very temptingly for Lady Sarah, and was so disappointed when you failed to show up.'

He gave in with bad grace. 'Oh, blast! Very well.'

While his sister bustled off to attend to the family heirlooms, his thoughts turned moodily to Catriona Mackie's willow pattern, of which she was so proud. He could foresee a sharp conflict between Ishbel's mother and his own dear mama when they met. Freddie had long recognised that Eleanor Alexander's main ambition was to bridge the sizeable gap between rich tradesfolk and titled gentry, hence her tender cultivation of Lady Sarah. It would be prudent to have smelling salts handy when his mother discovered he intended marrying a milkmaid, no matter how beautiful.

A replenished brandy decanter stood in reserve beside the service lift and Freddie poured himself a stiff drink. He had a feeling he might need it.

The dining-room door was firmly closed upon the gentlemen enjoying brandy and cigars in a more free and relaxed atmosphere. Freddie hovered longingly outside before heading resolutely towards the sounds of small-talk coming from the drawing room. May as well get it over with.

His mother's face lit up when he walked in. 'Freddie! I'm so glad your other – er – engagement was over sooner than expected. Have you dined, dear?'

'Yes, thanks, Mother.' He smothered a grin. Engagement! A most appropriate choice of words, if she only knew.

While introductions were made, he cast an expert eye over the ladies. Sarah Allsop sat a little apart from the fashionable matrons his mother had assembled. Freddie eyed her warily as he bent over her hand. He had to admit she wasn't bad – pretty and interesting-looking. She had a resolute look. You could imagine her carrying the banner in a suffragette parade or chaining herself to railings. She met his speculative gaze with a hint of amusement, as if reading his thoughts accurately. He settled down beside the grand piano with a cup of black coffee, the brandy having gone straight to his head.

Eleanor Alexander had no intention of letting her son off the hook, however. 'Won't you play for us, Freddie dear?' she asked sweetly.

He sighed and stood up obediently. His mother turned eagerly to Sarah Allsop. 'My dear, do you sing?'

'Not a note. I'm tone deaf. The music teacher at Queen Street School used to bribe me with sweeties to shut up,' she replied blithely.

There was an uncomfortable hush in which Freddie chortled appreciatively. Feeling somewhat tipsy, he made his way to the piano and daringly struck up the opening bars of one of Ishbel's favourites.

'Will you stop your ticklin', Jock . . . ?'

His mother gave a horrified squeal of protest. 'Darling, isn't that rather vulgar for present company?'

'Not at all, Mother. You should hear Ishbel sing it. You'd die laughing!'

'Who's Ishbel?' asked Lady Sarah curiously.

'The girl I'm going to marry.'

There was a stunned silence. That's torn it! he thought, dashing off a resounding chord. The cat was out of the bag, and he didn't give a damn. The brandy certainly helped.

His mother had turned pale. 'Marry? Freddie, what are you blethering about? Who is this girl?'

'Her name's Ishbel Mackie, and her father's a game-keeper on Craighill estate, Sir Dudley Hawkerton's place. She's beautiful and talented and practical. You should see her milking the cows. That's a picture worth painting!'

The respectable matrons drew breath sharply, quivering with excitement, and poor Eleanor cringed. The news of Freddie Alexander's indiscretion would travel round Edinburgh's drawing rooms with the speed of light. Sarah Allsop burst out laughing. 'Freddie, you're wonderful!'

'I know,' he agreed modestly, and settled down to play in earnest, silencing all further speculation.

'My dear lass, if you marry Freddie it'll be a disaster,' Donald Mackie told his daughter.

'I don't see why,' she said coldly. She was fighting hard for her loved one, and her parents' disapproval only served to strengthen her resolve.

'Aw, Ishbel lass, see sense! It wouldna work,' Donald said. Ever since Catriona had told him of Freddie's intentions, he'd felt as if his world was collapsing round him like a badly built haystack. His wife had warned him to go softly with their daughter, but he couldn't stay silent. Little good his protests had done him! The lass he worshipped was glaring at him like a stranger.

'Pa, Freddie and I love one another!'

'Love!' He shook his head. 'Och, what's love? I love your

mother dearly, but has my love given her anything but hard work and insecurity in her auld age? Na, na. Dinna put your trust in love, my dear.'

'I'd rather marry for love than marry without it, like Hannah,' declared Ishbel stoutly.

'Och, there's no comparison. Hannah's a poor, crippled cratur who must tak' what she can get. If she doesna have love in her marriage, she has the satisfaction of saving the laird's estate. Wotherspoon may be a dour devil, but he kens the way o' the land.'

Donald studied his stubborn daughter and felt like weeping. 'If you marry Freddie you'll live in a grand hoose in Edinburgh and forget your poor auld pa.'

That brought her rushing to his side, hugging him emotionally. 'Never! Oh, Pa, I'd never forget you an' Mam. Even if I lived in the finest mansion in Edinburgh, I swear I wouldna!'

And so Donald was comforted and the future seemed brighter. After all there was no talk of a wedding just yet. There's mony a slip 'twixt the cup and the lip, he thought hopefully. He continued to play dominoes in the pub with auld MacArthur, but never mentioned Ishbel had changed her mind about marrying Sandy. He just hadn't the heart to confess to his old friend, and that was a fact.

The Honourable Hannah Hawkerton married Hugh Wotherspoon, farmer, after the tattie drills had been checked for rogues and the certificate obtained from the official inspector certifying the crop could be sold for seed – a profitable business. It was a quiet wedding in the family chapel on the Craighill estate; quiet, that is, so far as the gentry was concerned, for none was invited. It was doubtful if they would have attended, for word had got round that Dudley Hawkerton was near bankruptcy. To swell the numbers, all the folk from the farm toun crowded in.

Ishbel attended her friend as bridesmaid. Wotherspoon, who had few friends, ordered his stockman baillie to be best man. The two men stood before the altar, awaiting the arrival of the bride, when Wotherspoon happened to glance down. He whispered furiously, 'Bert, for God's sake, tak' aff your nicky tams!'

'Ach, maister, I forgot!'

Bert lowered himself into the front pew beside her ladyship and unwound a length of binder twine securing the wad of jute sacking round the leg of his breeks above the working boots. He grinned amiably at the frosty lady. 'I've just been muckin' oot the byre, your leddyship, and the nicky tams keep the clarts aff my breeks. The beasts come first wi' me, and a' this tomfoolery comes a long way doon the list. Would you mind keeping an ee on my nicky tams for me? I'll leave them here beside ye.'

Ishbel followed Hannah and the laird down the aisle with mixed feelings. If anyone could save the estate it was Wotherspoon, but how could Hannah marry without love? She listened intently to the solemn words that made Hugh Wotherspoon and Hannah Hawkerton husband and wife, and her eyes filled with tears. Her own marriage to Freddie would be sore disappointment to many folk, and that was a sobering thought.

Hannah's feelings were rigidly controlled. When the gold band was placed on her finger she smiled shyly at the stranger who was her husband. He scuffled his feet awkwardly and refused to meet her eye.

Kisses and congratulations, followed by showers of rice

at the chapel door which the hens gobbled up, passed like a strange dream for Hannah. Luxuries were scarce as the war dragged wearily towards its fourth year. There was no sugar to bake a wedding cake, let alone ice it, but everyone had brought something to lay on the table in the barn, and there were the first sweet strawberries of summer heaped in punnets, and cool dishes of whipped cream won from Ishbel's contented kye. Hannah moved through it all in a daze. She was hardly aware of her limp, for her feet seemed poised above the ground. Her thoughts were lonely and afraid, but she refused to dwell upon them.

When Hugh Wotherspoon glanced at his gold watch, then took her by the elbow and guided her from the merry festivities in the barn, she followed without a word. Their departure went unnoticed.

They walked in silence through the empty cornyard. It had been a neglected tangle of nettles and rotting wood when the laird had care of it, but Hannah noticed the founds had been cleared and prepared for corn stacks at harvest and the space between widened to accommodate a threshing mill at the back-end of the year. It was evidence of her new husband's foresight, and the sight cheered her.

Wotherspoon led her through ripening fields of oats and barley towards the grey stone farmhouse that would be her home. He went before her into the house to light the lamp, and Hannah paused for a moment to draw in one last breath of sweet night air, one last breath of freedom. Then she went obediently into the house when her husband called, and resolutely closed the door on her past.

Meanwhile, there were ructions going on in Knoxhall House, the Alexanders' Morningside mansion. Freddie

48

had received a communication from the War Office, warning him his period of recuperation had officially ended and to prepare for a medical examination to assess his fitness, prior to his return to the squadron. The pace of life had suddenly speeded up for the Alexander family.

His father secretly lived in hope that Freddie would fail the examination and be invalided out for good. The strain of running the shop under wartime conditions was telling on William Alexander, and he could do with his son's help. There was also a heated argument raging over Freddie's engagement to a country lass, and William's head was aching as he rustled through the pink pages of the *Evening News* and laid the paper down with a sigh.

'Let's get this straight, Freddie. You intend to marry this girl?'

'The sooner the better,' declared his son staunchly.

Eleanor wrung her hands. 'It's this war, William! It speeds everything up and addles people's brains so it's impossible to live an orderly life. This is indecent haste, Freddie, and I shudder to imagine what decent people will think.'

'They can think what they like,' he declared stoutly. 'My conscience is clear, Mother.'

'I'm glad to hear it,' she retorted frostily. 'I've decided the time has come to visit the girl and her parents. No doubt they're as upset about the whole affair as I am. You will take me to visit them tomorrow afternoon, Freddie,' she ordered.

'Mother, no!' he cried in horror. He had a nightmarish vision of his mother in headlong confrontation with Catriona Mackie, and couldn't think how to avoid it.

* * *

49

Ishbel hurried joyfully to the window when Freddie's car drew up outside the cottage next day. Her pleasure turned to dismay as she watched Freddie assist a determined-looking elderly lady from the vehicle.

'Mam, Freddie's brought his mother to visit! I can't let her see me like this!' she cried in panic.

She'd been in the turnip fields till lowsing-time, and was hot and work-stained after a wearisome stint singling young turnip plants. Nobody relished the monotonous task of clatting neeps, but it had its compensations. Many a funny story was told as the workers stood hoeing in line, and there was laughter and joking and farm gossip exchanged. It was a dusty job in the warmer weather and a muddy one if it rained. Ishbel still wore stout boots and a coarse sackcloth apron.

'Don't worry, I'll see to her. You run ben the hoose and change,' ordered her mother quickly. Catriona took off her apron and rolled down her sleeves. With a quick pat to tidy her hair, she went outside.

Standing beside her son, Eleanor Alexander straightened to her full height to receive the woman approaching them. She was agreeably surprised by what she saw. The woman was taller than Eleanor and carried herself well. Her dress was simple, but expertly cut and sewn. As the daughter of a Leith tailor, Eleanor recognised fine tailoring when she saw it. She smiled pleasantly while Freddie made the introductions.

'You are very welcome indeed to my house, Mrs Alexander,' said Catriona politely. She led the way into the cottage and seated Eleanor with some ceremony in the best chair. Freddie looked round eagerly. 'Where's Ishbel?'

'She will be in presently,' Catriona said blandly.

Meanwhile, Eleanor had been taking in her surroundings with a critical eye, but could not fault the room. Everything was neat and spotlessly clean. 'I must thank you for giving my dear son your kind hospitality in his time of tribulation, Mrs Mackie,' she said with genuine gratitude.

'Och, that was our pleasure indeed, Mrs Alexander. Freddie is a fine young gentleman.'

Freddie cleared his throat and looked apprehensive. He was expecting fireworks sooner or later.

'Quite so.' Eleanor coughed delicately. 'I gather your daughter, though accomplished in – er – many ways, is still quite young?'

'Aye. Ishbel is but newly turned eighteen.'

'An impetuous age, Mrs Mackie.'

'I say, Mother, listen here—' began Freddie. The two women paid no heed to the interruption.

'Eighteen is indeed a chancey age, Mrs Alexander, but Ishbel's a sensible lass. Wisdom can often prevail even wi' impetuous young folk, given time for reflection.'

Eleanor beamed. 'Exactly. How aptly put, dear Mrs Mackie! Time for reflection is never wasted, especially with the young.'

The glance the two women exchanged assured them they were in complete agreement. With the best interests of their beloved children at heart, they were both firmly set against the match.

'Listen!' broke in Freddie desperately. 'Ishbel and I don't have time for a normal courtship. I'll be called for a medical soon, and after that I could be sent back to my squadron on the Western Front. My luck could change. Time for reflection is a luxury in wartime. Time could be running out. Who can tell?'

The meeting was not going the way he had expected. A united maternal front unnerved him, and by speaking out he'd gone and upset his mother.

Tears rose in Eleanor's eyes at this reminder of danger. She'd already lost one son in this terrible war, and had borne up as bravely as she could. If she lost Freddie as well, it would be the end of her. Tears slid down her cheeks, and she was appalled. Such bad manners in someone else's house! The other woman saw but made no remark, only squeezed Eleanor's shoulder comfortingly. The sympathetic touch was enough, and she gained control of herself with a grateful glance at her newfound friend.

'Here's Ishbel now,' said Catriona with relief.

As Freddie leaped to the girl's side, Eleanor studied her with interest. She could understand why he was so smitten. Ishbel Mackie was very striking, dark-haired and lovely, with her mother's natural style and grace and a certain sparkling spirit which was her own. Freddie led Ishbel forward to meet his mother, an arm defiantly round her waist.

'Mother, this is Ishbel, the girl I'm going to marry,' he said, flinging down the gauntlet.

There was an awkward pause while Ishbel and Eleanor Alexander took stock of one another. Ishbel first noted the beautiful black gown embroidered with jet beads and the smart black bonnet trimmed with curling black feathers, then lifted her gaze shyly to meet the shrewd blue eyes studying her keenly. The firmly set lips and stubborn chin were reminiscent of Freddie's. This was a formidable little lady, thought Ishbel with a touch of awe.

'I am very pleased to meet you, Mrs Alexander,' she said demurely.

Catriona bustled around. 'You'll stay for your tea, Mrs Alexander? Wait 'til I warm the pot. There's fresh scones and jam in the press, Ishbel, and see that our guest has a clean napkin for her lap,' she ordered.

She was determined to have no unseemly argument in her house, though she feared a fight could break out any minute. Catriona was not deceived by her daughter's docile manner, and was alarmed by the obstinate jut of Freddie's jaw. Calm before the storm, she thought.

Donald Mackie chose that moment to come home. He stood in the doorway surveying the guests with an oddly smug and satisfied air, then looked towards Ishbel.

'There's someone to see you, lass.'

Donald ushered in a young soldier. The Tommy's chest was heavily bandaged beneath a loosely buttoned khaki jacket, and the blood drained from Ishbel's cheeks as she recognised the injured man.

'Sandy! Oh, Sandy, it's you!' she cried.

Chapter 3

'It's what's left o' me, anyway,' he said wryly.

She crossed the room with a cry, looked into his face, touched the bandages sorrowfully. 'Oh, Sandy dear, what have they done to you?'

He smiled. 'It was a piece of shrapnel from a Jack Johnson. That's no' the prize-fighter, mind, it's a great big brute o' a heavy shell. I was hit in the chest but they patched me up in Le Havre and sent me home after a while. I've been lucky. The army's finished wi' me, Ishbel. I'm discharged from active service to work on the land.'

Sandy glanced curiously at the two strangers. They were well-dressed toffs, and looked out of place in the Mackies' but and ben. No doubt the motor he'd noticed outside in the yard belonged to them. The man's face seemed familiar, but Sandy couldn't place him. Their presence was puzzling, and he wished they'd go away and leave him alone with his lass.

To be sure, there was much that had puzzled Sandy MacArthur since he'd climbed down from the mail-cart a short time ago. He'd expected pity from the cottars, the state he was in, but folk became shifty when he'd asked eagerly after Ishbel, and he'd found it disturbing. During bad times in the nightmarish trenches, a vision of the girl he'd left behind had kept Sandy sane and given him hope for the future. He'd been hurrying anxiously to see her when he'd met her father. It had been a reassuring meeting, for Donald had welcomed him with open arms.

Sandy caught sight of the ring on Ishbel's finger. 'You're wearing my ring!' he cried delightedly.

She bit her lip to keep back tears. 'I promised I would, Sandy.'

Eleanor Alexander stiffened. She leaned towards Catriona, who was standing as if turned to granite. 'Mrs Mackie, who is this man?'

'He's – he's – oh, dearie me!' Catriona put down the teapot with a clatter. She'd tried hard to avoid an unpleasant scene, and now she feared a row was brewing.

Donald wanted the whole affair brought out into the open. 'Sandy's the man Ishbel was all set to marry, until Freddie Alexander came along and upset the applecairt!' he said loudly.

Sandy was stunned. He turned to Ishbel. 'Is this true?'

Freddie had been quiet too long, and Ishbel's stricken expression was more than he could bear. He stepped forward bravely and put an arm round her. 'Of course it's true. I've asked Ishbel to marry me, and she accepted.'

Recognition dawned as Sandy glared at his rival. 'I mind who you are! You're the officer from the Big Hoose who gave Ishbel strong drink and made her mak' a fool o' hersel' at the concert!'

'I did nothing of the kind!' protested Freddie hotly.

'I saw you wi' my ain eyes, man! She was tipsy when I went in, singing a risky song.'

'Oh, nonsense! It was harmless fun.'

Donald had gone pale with indignation. 'My lassie, tipsy?'

'Freddie, this is scandalous!' breathed his mother, outraged.

He wheeled round angrily. 'Mother, you stay out of this!'

Catriona joined the fray. 'I'll thank you no' to speak to your mother in that tone o' voice in my house, Freddie Alexander!'

In a trice they were all shouting at one another furiously. Ishbel struggled to make herself heard. 'Stop it, all of you!' she screamed.

She gained a startled silence. Sandy looked at her with a piteous expression. 'Ishbel, since we were wee bairns we've been happy together. I thought we'd be together for the rest o' our lives. Dinna tell me it's over just because of him?'

She wished she could comfort her childhood sweetheart, kiss him better as she'd done when he was a wee lad with skinned knees and she was his best friend. But that wasn't possible. 'Sandy, I'm sorry. Folk grow up – and – and they change,' she faltered.

'Aye, maybe some do,' he said bitterly. He looked at her sorrowfully, then turned on his heel and blundered out of the cottage.

Catriona clutched her daughter's arm frantically. 'Oh, how could you do this to the poor lad? He's a sick man, Ishbel!'

She wrenched her arm away. 'Leave me be, Mam! I'll go after him. Maybe I can make him see it's for the best.'

She ran to the door, but Freddie caught up with her and held her back. 'Darling, let him go.'

'I can't, Freddie. Not like this!'

'Then I'm coming with you.'

He would have followed, but she pushed him aside. 'No! Can't you see that would only make it worse? Wait here for me, Freddie, please!' She turned and ran after Sandy.

His breath laboured in his damaged chest and Ishbel soon caught up with him. He faced her angrily. 'What do you want? There's no more to be said. Away back to your fine officer!'

She went to him and laid a hand on his arm. 'Sandy dear, don't take it like that. I care for you and always will, but it's a different caring I have for Freddie. It's a love I can't fight, though I tried hard. I've read in books about love at first sight, but I never believed it until it happened the night Freddie and I met. Can't you understand?'

'Oh, I understand perfectly!' he cried caustically. 'That's the same night you promised to wear my ring, and kept me hoping. The night you had the first glitter o' the man's gold in your eye, and saw your way clear to being a lady instead o' a ploughman's wife.' He pushed his face so close she could feel the heat of his anger and contempt. 'You know what you are, Ishbel Mackie? You're a cheap gold-digger!'

He had gone too far. Her head jerked back as if he'd struck her. She was too hurt and insulted to care what she did then. 'I promised to wear your ring 'til you came back safe, and I've kept the promise,' she said coldly. 'It seems you've a low opinion o' me, Sandy MacArthur, so I'll wear it no more. You're welcome to it!' She dragged the ring off her finger and hurled it in his face. It scratched the skin and fell at his feet.

Ishbel stared in horror at the drop of blood forming on the young man's cheek, red as the ruby that lay in the mud.

With a cry of anguish she whirled and ran. Away from him, away from memories of an innocent first love that had ended disastrously, in the dirt.

When the young people had gone, Catriona sank on to the nearest chair, groaning. 'Oh, Donald, what a to-do! Could you no' have stopped Sandy coming here?'

Her husband looked shame-faced. 'It's no' my fault. He was off the mail-cart and on his way afore ye could wink. I'd no time to warn him about Ishbel's change of heart.'

His wife suddenly recalled her duties as hostess. 'Aye, weel, it's just a disaster, but we'll no' waste the good tea. Draw in your chair, Donald. Be good enough to pass your cup over, Mrs Alexander.'

Her cup filled, Eleanor Alexander stirred the refreshing brew thoughtfully. 'One's heart goes out to the poor young soldier, of course, dear Mr and Mrs Mackie, but one wonders if this sad situation might not be turned to our advantage. I gather we're agreed my son and your delightful daughter would be happier in the end if they – er – parted company? Then let's put our heads together, shall we?'

Donald leaned eagerly over the table. 'What do you suggest, ma'am?'

'Perhaps we should remember the old maxim: "A bird in the hand is worth two in the bush",' she answered cannily. 'Freddie could be kept occupied in the shop if his father takes a much-needed rest. Then my dear boy must go before a medical board at Larkhill airfield, to assess his fitness to fly. I pray he won't be sent back to active service, but there is a possibility he will be called on to serve in some capacity, I fear.' Her eyes had filled with anxious tears, and Catriona patted her hand.

'There, there, love. The laddie can hardly walk, let alone fly an airyplane.'

'Aye, God forbid he should have to fight.' Donald spooned some scarce sugar into his cup. 'But, ma'am, I think you're hinting Ishbel could be meeting with Sandy every day while your lad's kept busy elsewhere?'

'Exactly. It would give Sandy an opportunity to continue his interrupted wooing, and he's a fine-looking young man.'

Catriona looked pensive. 'Ishbel's a sympathetic lass wi' a kindly heart, and he's badly wounded. Sandy's a stubborn chiel who'll fight tooth an' nail for his sweetheart. A little time for reflection could be all that's needed to change our lass's mind.' She stared at her friend hopefully. 'Mrs Alexander, I wish nae harm to befall dear Freddie, but his absence for a wee while could work to our advantage.'

'Oh, no, it won't!'

The conspirators sprang apart in disarray. They'd been so engrossed in hatching the scheme they hadn't heard Ishbel come in quietly with Freddie at her back. She crossed swiftly to the table. They saw how angry she was, and couldn't help but cringe. This furious young woman bore little resemblance to the tearful girl who'd left the room only a short time ago.

'Stop your wicked scheming, Mam!' she cried. 'Nothing you can do will change my mind. Sandy won't come courting because he knows now it's hopeless. Look, his ring's gone. I threw it back in his face.'

Catriona put her hands to her cheeks with a cry. 'The poor lad! How could ye?'

'Good for you, my darling!' Freddie cheered.

Catriona still couldn't believe a daughter of hers would be so cruel. 'Oh, Ishbel! What's got into ye?' she wailed.

Ishbel's eyes blazed. 'He dared to call me cheap, and a gold-digger besides, and that's cruel, Mam, and no' true forbye. I love Freddie. It doesn't matter whether he's rich or poor. I would marry him whatever his state, and so I will, in spite of your sly plans!'

Freddie swept her gleefully into his arms. 'Oh, my darling, you're magnificent!' They kissed with an abandon that shocked the older folk. It was not done in their day to parade such wild emotion in public, and they were outraged and highly embarrassed.

Donald stood up, the chair scraping loudly on the stone floor. 'Enough o' this! Ishbel, your conduct's unseemly in a modest lass. Think shame o' yoursel'!'

She broke free from Freddie's embrace and stared at her father incredulously. He was looking at her in disgust, as if she were a bad woman of the streets, a hurtful glare which wounded her deeply. She felt no shame! She had kissed the man she loved with a joyful abandon as natural to her as breathing. 'I'll no' be shamed, Pa, for I've done nothing to be ashamed of,' she told him with icy defiance. She turned her back on her father and clung to her lover.

Donald sat down abruptly, deflated. It took all his willpower not to drop his head on his arms and sob like a bairn.

Eleanor Alexander had seen enough. She rose to her feet and drew on her gloves. 'Freddie, you will drive me home now,' she ordered. She took Catriona's workworn hand in both of hers. 'My dear, my son and I have brought trouble and unhappiness to your house. I'm sorry.'

'It's no' you that brought trouble, ma'am, it's me that gave birth to it,' Catriona said, her glance going sadly to her lovely, rebellious daughter.

Everyone in the farm toun had an eye trained on the sky these warm July days, for they knew it was the weather that made the hay. The grasses were ready for mowing, the flower heads wilting and the stems on the point of 'going over'. A fall of rain would ruin the crop, for wet hay could heat and ferment and spoil in the coles. Next day there were ominous signs of a break in the pattern of sunshine, and Wotherspoon rallied all his workers to help bring in the valuable crop.

Sandy MacArthur moved from his family's cottage into the bothy shared with three other older ploughmen and a young halflin. He'd had dreams of setting up house in the toun with Ishbel as his wife, but those dreams lay in ashes. He moved in with nothing but two wooden chests. One held a poke of oatmeal and a jar of his father's honey, the other his spare clothing, a few precious tools and a melodeon. He sat on one kist, and ate his bowlful of oatmeal brose off the other.

Sandy lacked the strength to walk behind Big Bob and Bertie, his Clydesdale pair, so Wotherspoon, ever watchful, ordered him on to the new mowing machine that had recently replaced an army of scythers. Sandy found he could ride and spare his chest, while the two canny horses harnessed to the contraption did their noble best not to jar his weak arms on stones and boulders. Strange, he thought, how the huge, gentle beasties sensed their young master's shortcomings!

All the women were out helping to turn swathes of drying

grass in the sun and wind. Ishbel was out too, but he never looked her way, nor she his. They passed one another like strangers, he seated on the machine, she with the pitchfork on her shoulder. It hurt to ignore her, but he had his pride and would not let her glimpse his unhappiness and pain.

And gradually new ideas and ambitious plans began forming in Sandy's head, as he played the melodeon for the lads in the bothy to sing ballads after lowsing-time. One day he'd be rich. He had a fair idea how to set about it, and when he'd made a great fortune, he'd seek Ishbel out and taunt her with worldly wealth far above Freddie Alexander's. Then he'd laugh in her face and walk away and leave her.

When the hay was safely ricked in coles, and spread dry and sweet for the Clydes in the hayloft above the stables, the rain came down in torrents. The farm workers looked for employment indoors. Freddie, who'd been impatient with Ishbel's involvement in hay-making, arrived unexpectedly when she was vigorously churning butter in a metal-banded, wooden churn in the cool dairy, a twice-weekly task she enjoyed. He leaned against the wall in the doorway, arms folded. 'Sweetheart, I love watching you work, but how long will this blasted process take? We must talk.'

She could tell by the heavy thumps as she turned the handle that the butter had formed at last within the churn. She smiled at Freddie. 'Won't be long, darling. Wotherspoon says I've to save the skimmings for the pigs, and salt the butter in a barrel. An Edinburgh grocer's collecting it tonight wi' his cart. We're in big business now Wotherspoon's in charge, love. City folk will pay sweetly for fresh butter and bacon to eke out their rations, and that canny man knows it.'

She kept busy as she spoke, her feet clop-clopping in the wooden clogs she wore for dairying. Ishbel tipped the solids into a butter press on the scrubbed slate table, carefully reserving the skimmings. Freddie sniffed appreciatively. The butter smelled creamy and fresh.

'Sweetheart, I've had orders to leave for Larkhill tomorrow for a medical,' he told her.

She ran to him with a cry of distress, and they hugged one another. 'Oh, Freddie dearest, I pray they won't send you to France, and I pray you'll be found fit. I don't know what to pray for!'

He kissed her tenderly. 'My sentiments exactly! Heaven knows I don't want to fight, but on the other hand, four German Gothas bombed London in June, Ishbel. They were after the Silvertown munitions factory, I believe, but civilians were killed in the City and East End. It was a cowardly attack on innocent people. I'd dearly love another go at Jerry's airfields.'

She was terrified when he talked like this. Ah, but she hoped the doctors would say he was unfit. She would rather have him lame and limping for the rest of his life than fighting in the dangerous skies. It was an appalling thought for a loving woman to entertain, but it was heartfelt.

He tilted her chin and made her look at him. 'Don't look so woeful! Remember, we're getting married very soon, no matter what.'

'I'll iron my Sunday best and trim my old bonnet, Freddie,' she said with a smile.

He kissed her. 'Oh, no, you'll be dressed like a duchess on our wedding day, my love! You'll choose an outfit from the shop, a gift from the family. I'll see to it.'

Ishbel was shocked. This smacked of charity and she was sure Mam would object. 'I couldn't do that!' she protested.

'Of course you could. You'd be doing us a favour, advertising Alexander's range of readymade garments. We'll have photographs taken to put in the shop window, and Father's sales will rocket sky high.'

He made her laugh, and after that it was hard to refuse such a tempting offer.

'You'll come to see me off tomorrow afternoon, won't you?' Freddie begged. 'I have some wretched legal affair to attend to in the morning, but my sister Dorothy offered to pick you up and take you to the station. She's not much of a driver, but she's a good sport. You'll like her.'

'I wish you didn't have to go. I wish the war would end,' Ishbel said tearfully. It was difficult to keep up a brave front when she loved him so.

'It won't go on much longer now the Americans have come in, my love. Kaiser Wilhelm must be scared stiff. It'll soon be over and the boys will come marching home, yours truly well to the fore.'

Secretly, he wasn't so sure of his own safety. Dog-fights were a young man's game. You needed nerves of steel and reactions quicker than a cat's. You needed fierce aggression and iron discipline. And above all, you needed not to be in love, with dreams of a peaceful future with wife and children.

True to her promise, Dorothy turned up outside the cottage next morning in pouring rain, driving an odd-looking car with a dickie seat at the back. Ishbel had sought permission to see her man off, and been granted the favour because rain had stopped outdoor work. The weather showed no sign of relenting and there was anxiety for the grain harvest. Everyone knew Wotherspoon needed the co-operation of Heaven if his bid to rescue the laird's land was to succeed.

Dorothy, who was always in a thundering bad temper when driving, honked the bulbous horn loudly, and Ishbel came scurrying out. Catriona followed curiously, shawl over her hair. She'd never seen a woman driver before, and found the sight a great source of wonder.

Dorothy shouted, 'I say, do hop in quickly! I daren't stop this wretched thing or I'll never get it started with the blasted handle.'

Ishbel climbed on to the running board and was hauled into the front seat beside Dorothy. Her passenger safely installed and the engine ticking over healthily, Dorothy relaxed and held out a hand, smiling.

'Pleased to meet you, Ishbel. You don't drive, do you?' she asked hopefully.

'Not yet.'

'Pity.'

Dorothy grabbed a brass-handled brake on the running board, simultaneously let in clutch and gear and advanced the throttle in what seemed to Ishbel a perfect frenzy of movement. The car shot forward through the puddles, while rain pattered noisily on the canvas hood over their heads. 'Dear God, don't let the brute stall!' prayed Dorothy.

Once safely in top gear and birling along the road at a steady twenty, she was more relaxed. 'Sorry about that. Never can get the hang of gears.' She smiled cheerfully at Ishbel. 'Would you mind twiddling that little knob above your head occasionally, dear? It wipes the windscreen, and quite frankly, I can't see a thing.'

Hiding her alarm, Ishbel energetically operated the windscreen wiper arm. Sitting beside Freddie's sister on that hair-raising journey, she began to appreciate how skilful a driver Freddie Alexander was.

The rain had eased to a steady drizzle when Dorothy drew up triumphantly in Princes Street opposite the Waverley Steps. Freddie was waiting, very smart in RFC uniform. He helped Ishbel climb down, then smiled at his sister.

'Thanks for bringing her, old dear. How was the gear change?'

'Oh, coming along. I fancied the engine sounded less tortured today. Must be Ishbel's calming influence.' Dorothy leaned over and laid a hand anxiously on her brother's arm. 'Freddie, don't look too healthy when you face those doctors, will you?'

He grinned. 'Don't worry, I'll look positively ghastly.'

His sister turned her attention to Ishbel. 'I'll see you outside the shop after you've seen Freddie off, shall I? I've instructions to help you choose an outfit before I drive you home. I warn you, my taste runs to sensible tweeds and felt hats, though.' With a wave and some stern grappling with the gears, she drove off.

Freddie took Ishbel's arm and they descended towards the railway platforms down that famous and draughty Edinburgh landmark, the Waverley Steps. A damp breeze blew, and Ishbel clung on to her hat with one hand and Freddie's arm with the other. ' "East-windy, West-endy", my Auntie Nellie says,' she told him, smiling to keep her spirits up.

He laughed. 'I must meet your Auntie Nellie someday.'

'You will. She'll be at the wedding. Wild horses wouldn't keep her away.'

He was travelling First Class, Ishbel noted. The seats had freshly laundered linen headrests to protect the plush upholstery from hair oil. Studying the gleaming LMS coachwork, she recalled a trip to Portobello before the war with her aunt in a dingy excursion train. They'd travelled Third Class in a packed compartment smelling of smoke and vinegary fish and chips. It had been cheery though, with everyone in high spirits at the prospect of a day at the seaside. Auntie Nellie had started singing a popular Leith ditty at the top of her voice:

> *'Isabella, Isabella, bring out yer umberella,*
> *We're goin' away for a holiday,*
> *Down to Portabella . . .'*

The gentlemen sharing Freddie's compartment looked a frozen-faced lot by comparison, Ishbel thought.

Oh, but the minutes ticked by fast! Freddie kissed her then climbed in, letting down the carriage window to its fullest extent and ignoring the frosty-faced gentleman who rustled newspapers and coughed disapprovingly. He leaned out. 'Darling, don't cry. I'll be home very soon!'

The guard was blowing the whistle, waving the green flag. Steam hissed and the train moved ponderously from the platform. Ishbel waved, smiling through a blur of tears. She knew there would be other partings, but this first separation, the shortest and most crucial, seemed hardest to bear.

* * *

Dorothy was waiting patiently outside the shop, much to Ishbel's relief. She doubted she could have plucked up courage to enter the swanky portals by herself. Dorothy conducted her briskly past the curious gaze of shop assistants. The little lift boy was still in attendance, and his face lit up when he saw Ishbel. 'I ken you. You gave Master Freddie the brush-off.'

'That will do, Archie!' Dorothy remonstrated with a twinkle in her eye. The wee lad operated the lift, whistling cheerfully through his teeth, then clanged open the metal doors with a flourish. 'Third floor, ladies' gowns, nighties, an' unmentionables,' he announced modestly.

The lift doors opened upon a wonderland of beautiful clothing. Ishbel wandered after Dorothy, awed and entranced by fine silks and satins – then suddenly came down to earth with a bump. There was Mrs Alexander, sitting bolt upright on a pink-upholstered couch, gloved hands resting on the handle of a black brolly.

'Mother!' sighed Dorothy.

'Yes, indeed,' retorted Eleanor. 'You are a dear girl, Dorothy, but your dress sense leaves much to be desired. I thought it wiser to be on hand to give Ishbel the benefit of my taste and experience.' She thumped the floor imperiously with the brolly, and a middle-aged sales assistant came scurrying like a frightened rabbit.

'Yes, Mrs Alexander?'

'This young lady will choose a hat and gown from our readymade range, Miss Taylor. Kindly bring a selection in her size.'

Miss Taylor ran a tape measure over Ishbel's vital statistics, then opened a nearby glass case.

She produced gown after beautiful gown until Ishbel's head was reeling, but none met with Mrs Alexander's approval. Miss Taylor grew more harassed, but returned presently with a simple, cream-coloured outfit, beautifully embroidered round hem and bodice, the matching straw hat trimmed with veiling and roses. Ishbel touched the fine material thoughtfully with a fingertip, then allowed Miss Taylor to slip it over her head and adjust the hat. She studied the effect in the mirror. It was perfect. She knew Mam would approve. She'd kept silent so far, but now she spoke up.

'This is the one I'll take.'

Mrs Alexander raised her brows. 'Well, I admit it's pretty, but it shows a great deal of ankle.'

'That's fashionable and quite practical. I would prefer it shorter,' said Ishbel firmly.

The others stared, then Mrs Alexander shrugged, with a hint of amusement. 'Very well, my dear. It's your choice.' She turned to the bemused sales assistant. 'Miss Mackie requires the hemline raised. See to it, will you?'

Ishbel's decision produced a flurry of activity. A weary little woman appeared like magic, and went down on her knees, pinning up the hem. When she'd finished, Eleanor Alexander nodded thoughtfully. 'Yes, I believe I agree. That does look elegant.' She stood up, satisfied. 'See that the gown is finished and delivered first thing tomorrow morning,' she ordered casually.

'Very good, madam,' replied the fitter woodenly, but Ishbel noted the little woman's fatigued expression. She looked exhausted. Doubtless the poor soul had alterations to finish for other customers that Friday afternoon. The dress was full-skirted, and taking up the hem would be a long, tedious business. She spoke up boldly in the fitter's defence.

'Excuse me, Mrs Alexander, but there's no hurry for my dress. I wouldn't want this lady working all hours of the night on my account. That wouldn't be right, and I won't agree to it.'

Eleanor drew in a startled breath. Dorothy, who had maintained a low profile throughout, looked intrigued. There was a breathless hush before Eleanor smiled graciously. 'Why, how thoughtless of me, Ishbel! Next week will do perfectly well, of course, Miss Taylor.'

Ishbel turned to her with a radiant smile. 'Thank you, Mrs Alexander. Thank you from the bottom of my heart for everything. It's the most beautiful outfit I've ever had.'

Her genuine pleasure brought a painful lump to Eleanor's throat. She fiddled with her gloves to hide her emotion. 'You're very welcome, my dear,' she replied awkwardly.

When the sales assistant had left the fitting room with Ishbel's dress, she and the fitter stood for a moment in the corridor and gazed at one another speechlessly. 'Well, what do you make o' that, Doris?' whispered Miss Taylor in awed tones.

'I would say madam has met her match – I hope,' answered weary wee Doris, gleefully.

Shortly after Ishbel's expedition to Edinburgh, Freddie arrived at the cottage unexpectedly. She ran into his arms to greet him with a curious mixture of joy and trepidation. Looking at him, she couldn't tell what the medical board's decision had been. 'Well? What did they say?' she asked breathlessly.

'It's either good or bad, love, depends how you look at

it,' he said. 'I've been passed fit. I've to report to the squadron in a fortnight.'

Colour drained from her cheeks. 'A fortnight! Oh, my darling, what are we going to do?' she wailed.

He held her close. 'I'll tell you. We'll get married by special licence before I leave.'

'Oh, Freddie!' The thought took her breath away. Under normal circumstances she would have been thrilled, but now haste seemed ominous, underlining the danger.

He laughed at her. 'Don't look so tragic! This is meant to be the happiest time of our lives. At least, one of the happiest times. There'll be more joy in the future, Ishbel. You can count on it.' He put an arm round her waist. 'Come on, my love. Let's tell your parents what's in the wind,' he urged.

The news took the feet from Catriona. She sat down abruptly. 'Forty-eight hours! Save us! How can I organise a grand do in forty-eight hours?' she grumbled.

'There's no need for a grand do, Mrs Mackie,' Freddie said anxiously.

Catriona looked indignant. 'If you think Kaiser Bill will stop me putting on a good show for my daughter's wedding, you're mistaken. I'll send word round the toun, and hopefully everyone'll contribute a wee something to the wedding breakfast, to help out.'

Donald fondled the ears of his gundog. 'What about the Edinburgh toffs?'

'Och, Donald, you can't expect fine folk to fork out like us,' his wife said.

Donald sighed and stared mistily at his daughter, standing close beside her man. The sight hurt him.

72

Recently he and Ishbel had lost the precious rapport they'd once had. She favoured the other man. 'My lassie to be married by special licence! Sucha thing's never been heard of in Dalkeith,' he remarked mournfully.

The old ways were changing and it scared him. It was rumoured Wotherspoon the farmer had plans to turn the moors into profitable farmland. Donald saw the danger of this policy only too clearly. There was no call for a gamekeeper on a working farm.

'Ishbel Mackie asked me to be maid of honour at her wedding on Saturday, Hugh. You don't object, do you?' Hannah Wotherspoon asked her husband.

'It's a fell hasty marriage, isn't it?' he observed.

'It's not what you think. Freddie has to report to his squadron in a fortnight.'

'Och well, do as you like, lass.' Her husband returned to his ledger. Hannah stared despairingly at the crown of his dark head. She'd been prepared for indifference, but nothing had prepared her for the hurt of it. She wanted to love him if he would only allow it. She wanted to make him smile, but she could not break through to him. He had not been unkind. On the contrary, he had been scrupulously polite and surprisingly gentle, and slowly and surely he was breaking her heart. She turned quietly and limped sadly from the room.

Hugh Wotherspoon laid down the pen and stared after her. Before his marriage all he'd thought about was the land. He'd watched the laird's estate go to rack and ruin, and it was more than he could bear. Unobserved, he'd watched the heiress limp through the parks, and had stood aside dourly while she rode by with a pleasant smile, sitting well on her pony. The thought had come to him slowly that he could wed her with the laird's blessing. She was flawed and destined for spinsterhood, they whispered. He could wed her, and it would be nothing more than a business proposition for both of them. And so the land would be saved.

A business proposition! He was ashamed. Och, he hadn't meant to touch the lass, but he was a man, and she was young and innocent and his lawful wife, and he couldn't stop himself. The sight of her chestnut hair loosened almost to her waist, her graceful arms as she brushed the beautiful tresses around her shoulders, gave him so much nightly pleasure. But he'd learned the hard way to hide his feelings and bury them deep in the soil. He couldn't tell his young wife of his unexpected pleasure in her. He couldn't speak of his growing love for her, because he didn't know how.

Preparations for the wedding went on in the Mackies' cottage. Catriona collected a quantity of currants, raisins and rationed sugar from the kind folk of the toun, and made the largest clootie dumpling ever seen in Dalkeith, in lieu of a wedding cake. Prior to the ceremony, the pudding mixture, well laced with brandy, was enclosed in floured muslin and lowered ceremonially into bubbling water in the boiler in the wash-house, the only receptacle on the laird's estate large enough to take it.

Donald had been brooding over his daughter's coolness, but with the dumpling on the go, he brought out his best boots in preparation for the walk down the aisle, and oiled them in an attempt to get rid of the squeak. At Hannah's suggestion, the happy pair were to be wed in the little chapel on the estate. It was handy, and you could squeeze in a fair wheen o' folk.

Ishbel went around in a daze – one moment deliriously happy, the next plunged into sadness, for news of the war went on unabated in the press. There were rumours a British secret weapon could finish hostilities at a stroke, but the top brass didn't see eye to eye on tactics. Lloyd George and Mr Churchill were impatient to end the stalemate in the trenches, but General Haig still urged caution. It seemed the war would never end, and Freddie would be drawn back into the horror of it. The thought clouded the morning of Ishbel's wedding day, though the sky itself was clear and blue.

When Ishbel had bathed and dressed, Catriona inspected her daughter's wedding outfit with a critical eye. She thought she'd never seen her lass look so lovely, and wanted to cry as if her heart would crack though she wouldn't allow herself. Every eye in the kirk would be trained on her to see how she was taking this union, and she wouldn't shed a single tear to satisfy them. 'It's no' too bad for readymade,' she conceded. 'Mind you, I could've done better mysel', lovie, given time.'

Ishbel hugged her mother. 'Of course you could, Mam.'

Catriona dabbed her eyes, then drew on her gloves. 'Here's your pa wi' the dogcart, Ishbel. It's time to go.'

There were no invitations out, because of the speed of events, but the wee kirk was packed. Eleanor Alexander had recruited a selected few of her Morningside neighbours, but these were outnumbered by the folk from the toun who crowded in. Ishbel was touched by the turnout as she walked down the aisle through the crowded pews,

holding her father's arm, with Hannah limping behind.
Donald's boots squeaked despite the oiling, but she hardly
noticed. She'd just caught sight of Freddie, waiting
patiently before the altar. Ishbel went forward happily and
confidently, to be married to the man she loved.

After the ceremony everyone came pouring out of the
chapel in high spirits. Ishbel and Freddie were swept along
with the crowd to the big barn where Catriona and her
assistants had been busy since early morning, setting up the
trestles and arranging bales of straw for the dancers to rest
on after their exertions in the reels. The food was carried
in, the huge steaming dumpling taking pride of place beside
large jugs of custard. The grieve tuned his fiddle, and the
festivities began.

Ishbel hadn't spared a thought for Sandy as she laughed
and danced her way through the reels with Freddie. It
hadn't occurred to her he might attend, for he never so
much as passed the time of day when they met. It was a
shock therefore when she glanced laughingly across the
barn and found him standing unsmiling in a dark corner, his
eyes fixed upon her. Her heart gave a lurch and she looked
quickly away, hanging tighter on to Freddie's arm. Why did
he come? Surely just to sadden me, she thought.

'Your Auntie Nellie is trying to persuade my mama to
join in the jigging,' Freddie whispered in her ear.

It was true. Nellie Armstrong, on her second glass of
port, was making friendly overtures to Eleanor Alexander.
The pair were surrounded by a curious group of genteel
Morningside ladies seated on the straw bales, tucking into
clootie dumpling and custard.

'You all come frae Morningside?' Nellie was saying. 'Oh,
my, that's an awfy pan-loafy district!' She took another

swig of port and giggled. 'D'you ken what a creche is?'

Eleanor arched her brows. 'A creche?'

'Aye. A creche is a collision between twa cars in Morningside.' She went off into gales of mirth at this old Leith joke, and the ladies, after a few moments of stunned silence, smiled politely.

The fun in the barn was fast and furious, the dumpling demolished to crumbs, when Freddie took Ishbel's hand and whispered, 'Darling, let's slip away. They're dancing Strip the Willow. Nobody'll notice.'

Ishbel nodded. She longed to leave the heat and the din, to be alone at last with her new husband. They waited 'til the reel was at its most strenuous, the red-faced couples birling madly, then sneaked quietly out of the barn door. Outside, the evening was cool and peaceful, and Freddie's car waited in the stackyard.

'Your father put your case aboard earlier, Ishbel. Hop in while I crank the engine,' said Freddie, reaching for the starting handle.

'Where are we going?' she asked, once the engine was ticking over and she was settled snugly by his side, a rug over her knees.

'We're going to visit a friend of mine. He has an inn not far from here, and more importantly, he has a petrol pump. There's not many of those around,' Freddie answered as the car began moving. He frowned, startled. 'What the devil's that?'

Their progress was accompanied by an incredible clattering and banging from the old shoes and tin cans tied beneath. Freddie turned pale. 'What a din. I thought the big end had gone.'

Alerted by the clatter, the whole crowd came pouring

out, screaming and yelling from the barn. 'So you thought you'd sneak awa' withoot so much as a pour-oot for the bairns, did ye!' roared Donald. Catriona was laughing by his side.

'Oh, help, I forgot!' Freddie fumbled in his pockets for a fistful of coppers and scattered the money broadcast with a jingling sound across the stackyard. The bairns pounced with whoops of glee.

Ishbel leaned out and kissed her mother, while Freddie shook Donald's hand. 'Thanks for giving me your daughter, Mr Mackie.'

'Aye, weel, look after her, mind!' urged Donald gruffly.

'God bless you both,' said Catriona softly, shedding the first sentimental tears of the day. Freddie drove off with their rattling accompaniment amidst cheers and laughter, while Ishbel nestled closer. He looked down at her tenderly. 'Happy, Mrs Alexander?'

'I'm the happiest lass in Scotland this night, Freddie,' she declared. They were brave words, but not true. There was a feverish quality to this hasty wedding and the few precious hours they'd spend together, as if time was running short. She'd felt it keenly and was frightened, not daring to look to the future. Will there be a future for us now Freddie must go back? she wondered.

The car rattled on, Freddie singing as he drove to keep her cheery, quite unaware that his young bride shared all his fears, on this, their wedding night.

Chapter 4

'But, Freddie, what about the butter-making?' Ishbel asked anxiously, swinging her legs out of bed on the Monday morning after the wedding.

'My darling, hang the butter! We're on our honeymoon.' A quick glance at his watch showed it was barely six o'clock on a misty morning. Freddie pulled her back into bed.

Ishbel laughed, snuggling up to her husband. 'Farm folk don't have honeymoons, love, they're much too busy.'

'Ah, but you're not farm folk, you're my wife.'

He embraced her and she returned his kisses eagerly, but the words had given Ishbel an unexpected chill. Frederick Alexander's wife. That was an unknown state of affairs, and she wondered anxiously how she was expected to fill the position.

The talk at breakfast in their little honeymoon inn was all about motor cars as usual. Ishbel had become resigned to the conversation going over her head as Freddie and his friend the proprietor talked endlessly of refinements to carburettor and cylinder head, and the alteration of drive ratios to produce more speed.

Speed, speed, always the quest for more speed! The

men's preoccupation disturbed her, but the pleasure of watching Freddie's face as he spoke glowingly of improved engine performance, compensated a little.

'Brooklands paddock, Freddie. That's the place to be if you're really interested in motor racing,' remarked the proprietor.

He thoughtfully speared another slice of bacon. 'You think so?'

'That's where it was all happening before the war. It's a banked circuit, built in 1907, to take speeds of up to one hundred and twenty-five miles an hour.'

Freddie whistled. 'That's fast.'

His friend laughed. 'Snail's pace to a fighter pilot like you, old chum.'

'I admit when I dived the dear old Sopwith I achieved record speeds, but the Red Baron's flying circus was on my tail at the time.' He caught sight of Ishbel's tortured expression and paused. By tacit consent they hadn't mentioned flying or the war which could separate them all too soon. Freddie reached for her hand and pressed it reassuringly. 'But I'm a reformed character, married to the most beautiful lass in the Lothians. No more risk-taking for Freddie Alexander.'

'Pity!' the proprietor sighed regretfully as he polished a beer glass and set it on the bar counter, ready for opening at noon.

Sandy MacArthur had been doing a deal of thinking since Ishbel Mackie's wedding had taken her out of his reach, into a world a man could only enter with money at his back. The outcome of his deliberations was a conversation with Wotherspoon.

'Can I have a word?' Sandy asked one day.

The farmer gave him a canny stare. 'Fire awa'.'

'It's about clearing the moorland. You canna do it wi' just horses, and the best o' men away to the war.'

The farmer nodded. 'Maybe so, but it must be done if this place is to pay. I've no choice but to try wi' the men an' beasts at my disposal.'

'Aye, you do so have a choice. There's machines.'

Wotherspoon made no reply, but there was a speculative glint in his eye which encouraged Sandy. He drew closer. 'There was a woman demonstrating a motor plough in Edinburgh, in Roseburn Park. I went to see just for a laugh. She was a weakly thin lassie, but the contraption ploughed a fair furrow for her. I was impressed. They say there's a tractor working the land at the Mains o' Rannieston, near Ellon. It easily pulls a grubber that needed three beasts or two pair yoked, before. That's the way ahead, Mr Wotherspoon.'

The farmer sank his chin on his chest. 'If I bought a tractor the gear would a' need converting. It'd be a sair cost.'

'I could do that mysel'. Me an' the smith. I've thought it oot,' said Sandy calmly.

Wotherspoon gave him a long, considering look. 'Aye, but will you be off to the feeing market wi' the rest at the Martinmas term?'

The younger man met his eye, thinking of Ishbel Mackie and his need to get away. 'I'd considered it,' he admitted.

'Then don't. I'll get you a tractor if you'll convert the gear to clear the moorland.'

Sandy remained obstinately silent, and there appeared

a glimmer of what might have been amusement on Wotherspoon's dour countenance. 'If it's done weel, you get paid weel,' the farmer added.

'I'd better be, Mr Wotherspoon,' retorted Sandy.

Freddie's orders came through earlier than expected, resulting in an urgent telegram being sent to the inn. When the bad news arrived, Ishbel clung to her husband on the point of tears. He kissed her tenderly. 'Cheer up, sweetheart. I'll be home in no time, once we've stopped Jerry planes bombing Britain. It's high time the blighters were given some of their own medicine.' He studied the telegram, frowning. 'I have to catch the London train tomorrow afternoon. It doesn't give us much time.'

'We must tell Mam and Pa what's happening first, Freddie,' she said worriedly. 'They'll be wondering where we've got to. I told you, farm folk don't have honeymoons.'

He sighed resignedly. 'Oh, very well, love. In that case we'd better leave at once.'

'They're back, Catriona!' Donald had been seated by the window cleaning his shotgun when Freddie's car drew up in the yard. The faithful old gundog at his feet had been trained not to make any noise that might disturb game during a shoot, but at the note of joy in his master's voice he gave a deep 'Woof!'

Catriona had been up to the elbows in soapsuds, but she quickly dried her hands and ran outside to greet her daughter and son-in-law. Donald and the dog stayed behind. It would take time for Donald to adjust to his daughter as a married lady.

'Welcome home, my dears,' cried Catriona, holding out her arms. Ishbel hugged her, while Catriona studied the lass anxiously. She looked well and happy, thanks be! Catriona smiled warmly at Freddie, and laughingly accepted his smacking kiss. 'Come away in. The kettle's on,' she said happily.

Donald was more reserved. He kissed his daughter lovingly, then shook Freddie's hand. 'What kept ye? We were just aboot sending oot a search party.'

'Four days! It wasn't much of a honeymoon, Mr Mackie.'

'Och, me an' the missis never had a honeymoon yet,' said Donald scornfully.

'Well, the honeymoon's over now, with a vengeance. I'm leaving to join my squadron tomorrow,' Freddie told them.

Donald was silenced, but Catriona gave a cry of distress. 'Oh, Freddie, that's bad news!'

'But not unexpected, Mrs Mackie.' He put an arm round his wife. 'At least I know Ishbel will be well looked after while I'm gone.'

Donald's eyes misted. 'Aye, Freddie, have no fear. We'll care for the lass, same as always.'

He looked perplexed. 'Oh, but Ishbel will stay in Edinburgh at the family home, Mr Mackie. It's all arranged.'

The two older folk stared at him in such consternation Freddie was startled. Donald's countenance darkened. 'Listen here, I joined the army years ago to get oot o' thon city, and you'd make my lass live there, in a' that dirt and reek!'

Freddie's temper was up. 'Excuse me, but there's no question of Ishbel's living in dirt and reek. My wife will live in luxury. She's had a hard life, and I want her to enjoy her leisure.'

'A hard life? Will you listen to the man! You'd think we made a skivvy o' the girl!' exploded Donald indignantly. The old dog cast an apprehensive eye over his master and slunk beneath the table.

Ishbel had been standing by, stunned by this unexpected turn of events, but now she came to life and rounded on her husband. 'Do you think I'm a wee bairn that needs looking after and decisions made for me, Freddie?'

'Well, no, my love, but—'

'Then I'll make up my own mind what's to be done while you're away, thanks!'

'Good for you, my lass,' cheered Donald. He subsided hastily as she wheeled round.

'I'll go to Edinburgh with Freddie, Pa, because he's my man and I want to be with him on his leaves. I'll accept his family's invitation to bide, because it's kindly meant and it'd be discourteous to refuse; besides, I need to know my in-laws. But when I decide the time's right, I'll come back to work on the farm.' Donald looked chastened, so she dropped a kiss on his brow to soften her decision. Freddie stared open-mouthed at his young bride as she crossed to her mother and kissed Catriona's cheek. 'We'll no' bide for tea, Mam. I just wanted you to know what's afoot. There's precious little time to spare.'

Catriona looked at her daughter, her eyes bright. 'But you'll be back, love?'

Ishbel lifted her chin. 'Aye, Mam, we'll be back. Both of us,' she said. And hoped to goodness she wasn't tempting fate.

* * *

When Freddie pulled up outside the coach-house of a Morningside mansion later that day, Ishbel began to appreciate how drastically her life was changing. He gave strict orders concerning the garaging of his precious car to a chauffeur on duty, then led Ishbel through a warren of kitchen passages until they reached the quiet opulence of the upper floors. She had been accustomed to the laird's Big House, where she and Hannah had played since she was a little lass, but this was different; on a smaller scale, but much more tastefully and luxuriously furnished, the paintwork fresh and gleaming. She wrinkled her nose. You could almost smell the wealth that had been lavished on the place, and she wasn't sure if she cared for it.

However, Dorothy Alexander was plain and wholesome enough, with a shiny, scrubbed face and no-nonsense air about her as she greeted her brother and his wife. 'Mother's resting, and Father's enjoying a sneaky whisky and cigar in the smoking room. I've put you and Ishbel in the Blue Suite tonight, Freddie. I thought you'd prefer that to bachelor quarters.'

Freddie grinned. 'Thoughtful of you, old girl.'

Dorothy gave him a look. 'Not so much of the old, thank you! We dine at eight prompt, mind, Freddie. Just time for a quick bath before you change for dinner.'

For her first meal in her husband's family home, Ishbel wore the gown given to her for the wedding, because she'd nothing else fine enough. Flustered by an intimidating array of cutlery, she gave Freddie an appealing glance when the soup arrived. With a grin, he delicately indicated the soup spoon. Suppressing a giggle, Ishbel dealt serenely with the soup, and worked her way successfully through

85

fish, meat and pudding under her husband's discreet guidance. She refused the offer of fresh black grapes at the end of the meal, however. Mam had impressed on her that if you swallowed as much as one grape seed you'd be struck down with appendicitis like the late King Edward VII, and Ishbel was taking no chances.

Eleanor Alexander had taken note of Ishbel's conduct during dinner, and been pleasantly surprised. She warmed to the girl. To tell the truth, Eleanor had found Lady Sarah an intimidating young woman, and was secretly relieved Freddie had dug his heels in and chosen this beautiful young lass who would no doubt prove more amenable. She smiled kindly at her daughter-in-law. 'Perhaps we could have a hand of cards after dinner. Do you play whist, my dear?'

Ishbel met the challenge calmly. 'No, Mrs Alexander, but I shall learn.'

Eleanor regarded her thoughtfully. 'Yes. I believe you will.'

Next day another sad parting, on a station platform crowded with anxious relatives and men in uniform. Rain fell, wetting Ishbel's cheeks as she stood on tiptoe to kiss her husband. She was glad the rain hid her tears as she smiled for him. She didn't want him to remember her with eyes red from weeping. Her face felt painful with smiling. 'Mind and keep warm, Freddie,' she said brightly as he leaned out of the carriage window. 'It'll be cold up there high in the clouds, higher than Ben Nevis.'

'I'll think about you and stay warm as toast,' he joked. He didn't want to leave her, her lips so warm and loving against his. His heart was down in his boots. It was true what they said: fighter pilots shouldn't be married. His chances of coming out of this show alive were slim, he knew. The war had already taken its toll of far better pilots than himself. The guard blew the whistle and waved a green flag. With a hiss of steam the train jolted forwards, carrying Freddie away from everything he loved dearly. The scene blurred, and he leaned out, shouting a defiant song, trying to sound merry for Ishbel's sake.

'Goodbyee, don't cry-ee,
'Wipe the tear, baby dear, from your eye-ee . . .'

He was gone so quickly, Ishbel was suddenly lost and alone. She walked blindly from the station on to Princes Street, busy as usual with tramcars and motors, and congested with horse-drawn traffic. Somehow she found herself outside the shop, taking comfort from it because it bore his name: Alexander. Her name, now. Maybe it was the bleak, grey clouds, the rain coming down, but the scales fell from her eyes. The shop was not so imposing as it had once seemed. Paintwork was flaking, and the marble steps were chipped and muddy. Ishbel stared into the nearest window. It contained a display of drab overalls and practical footwear, and a discreet notice.

'We take great pride in our smart overalls, 7/11d in good quality casement cloth, for the well-dressed lady engaged in war work. Also National Service boots at 45 shillings, suitable for ladies employed in the manufacture of munitions.'

Ishbel turned away. War invaded all aspects of life, making everything look coarse and ugly. Depressing lists of casualties filled pages of the newspapers on sale on the streets, and still there was no end to it.

'Well, fancy meeting you!' cried a familiar voice. Ishbel wheeled round.

'Auntie Nellie!'

Nellie Armstrong gave her niece a keen look. 'Your face is longer than my airm, lass. What's up?'

'I just said goodbye to Freddie. He's away to the war and I've to go and bide wi' his mother in Morningside,' she explained.

'Ah, you poor wee soul!' said Nellie. She was humping a big bundle tied in a blanket on one arm, but took Ishbel's arm comfortingly with the other. 'I'll get ye doon the street. I do the washing for a wifie in Morningside, but dinna tell my neighbours I'm poor as a mouse in a manse, will ye? They think I'm weel aff because I keep brass rods polished outside my window like a sea captain's widow. My poor Wullie was skipper o' a barge on the Forth–Clyde canal when he drooned, but whaur's the difference?'

Ishbel found herself smiling. 'Oh, it's good to see one o' my ain folk!' she sighed.

'Aye, you're hob-nobbing wi' the nobs now. D'you ken what a saik is yet?'

Ishbel was mystified. 'No, what is it?'

'It's what the Morningside folk keep their tatties in.'

'A sack! Oh, Auntie Nellie!' Ishbel burst out, and still laughing, the pair of them set off down the street, arm in arm.

Freddie was welcomed back to the bosom of 55 Squadron with open arms. He found them stationed for the present at Tantonville, one of the better airfields near the front if you discounted dangerous power lines nearby. Freddie was delighted to find himself among friends, notably Matthew

Clark, a young American who had blithely passed himself off as Canadian in order to take part in the war.

'Haven't you owned up yet, Matt, you sinner?' Freddie asked.

He grinned. 'No. It's kind of tricky now America's come into the war, but I guess I'd better remain Canadian for the duration.' He generously offered to stand Freddie a drink at the bar, and the two friends settled down in a quiet corner. Matt lowered his voice. 'Any word from Marietta, Fred?'

Freddie idly sipped the pale French beer. 'No, Matt. That's over and done with.'

The American raised his brows. 'Is it? You hit the bull's eye there, you know.'

There was a chill in Freddie's chest that had nothing to do with the tepid beer. 'What do you mean? She's not—?'

'She is, or rather was before Jerry attacked and we withdrew from St Quentin. She came an' told me the whole story, in tears. Your child should be born now, Freddie, by my reckoning.'

He was greatly agitated. 'Matt, this is terrible! I just got married to the sweetest girl. Marietta and I weren't really in love, we just didn't know whether we'd live to see another dawn with Jerry so close and both drank too much of that blasted cheap wine. You know how it is?'

'I know,' nodded his friend. 'I shouldn't let it worry you. Jerry attacked in strength after your showdown with the Red Baron, and Marietta and her kid are miles behind enemy lines now. You're a lucky guy, Freddie, you've been let off the hook.'

'I feel rotten about this, though. I ought to help her somehow,' said Freddie miserably.

'How can you? You don't even know where she is. *C'est la guerre*, Fred. It happens all the time.' Matt put a comforting arm round his shoulders. 'Come on, pal, stop worrying. Eat, drink an' be merry. Have another beer!'

William Alexander had created a small haven of peace in the smoking room to which he retreated daily after returning home from a long, worrying stint at the shop. There he could smoke and down a stiff whisky without interruptions from his womenfolk, and let his frayed nerves untangle. His normal course of relaxation was not working this evening, however, because of the letter which had arrived on his desk that morning. Frowning, William slipped the envelope out of his breast pocket and stared at it. Judging by its crumpled state and the Zurich postmark, it had been in transit for months before reaching its destination. It was addressed to: M. Alexander, le magasin Alexander, Edinburgh.

Naturally, he had opened it, though it soon became clear it wasn't intended for him but for Freddie. William's mouth set grimly. He made no apologies for reading his son's mail. It was written in halting English, but the meaning was obvious. Freddie had got some wretched French girl into serious trouble.

Fortunately, she was far away in occupied territory, and was relying on a friend to smuggle the letter out via Switzerland. In William's judgement, the girl's pleas for help for herself and the child could be safely ignored, and it was unlikely the unfortunate incident would cause his erring son problems. He hesitated for a moment, stared indecisively at the blazing fire, then scribbled his son's name on the envelope and underlined it heavily twice before depositing the incriminating letter in his personal wall safe, hidden behind the portrait of his respected grandmother.

Sandy MacArthur got his tractor. It had the power of twenty-five horses, weighed a ton and a half, operated on paraffin, and cost Wotherspoon £300 he could ill afford. Sandy drove the lumbering beast to the fringe of the moorland and pitted its strength and his modifications against a rotted tree stump. The stump came out with a rush, roots and all, as clean as a ploughman's molar in a dentist's booth at the Michaelmas Fair.

'Bravo!'

Sandy looked up, startled. Because of the engine noise, he hadn't heard the horsewoman canter along the moorland track. It was the farmer's wife, the former Hannah Hawkerton. She slid from the saddle and held her horse's head, soothing it, for the din scared the nervous filly. She stared at the tractor in awed delight. 'I say, it's splendid, isn't it?'

He smiled. 'It's no' as bonnie as a pair o' Clydes, but it does the job better.'

Hannah studied the young tractorman curiously. 'Hugh says it was your idea to get the tractor, though he's been thinking along these lines himself for some time.'

'Aye. He's forward-looking, your man.'

She stared at him in silence for a moment. 'You know, you don't talk like a ploughman.'

He lifted his brows, amused. 'How should a ploughman talk, Mrs Wotherspoon?'

Hannah blushed. 'Oh – I don't know.' She put a toe in the stirrup and mounted again. On horseback she felt on level terms. He couldn't note her limp when she was seated in the saddle. She gave a friendly nod. 'I'll not hinder you. There's much to be done clearing the moor.'

'Aye,' Sandy agreed. He watched her ride off until she disappeared into the trees, before turning his attention once more to the challenge.

He was tired out when he pushed open the bothy door that night. He found both his wooden kists up-ended, his Saturday suit and clean drawers and sark lying smeared in a pool of honey, his few precious tools scattered with the oatmeal in the ashes of the fire. The other ploughmen stood glowering, even the young loon. Sandy looked at them.

'What's to do?'

Their spokesman was Geordie Orr, famed for taciturn ill-nature. 'You ken fine what's to do, MacArthur. You took the Horseman's Oath,' he growled.

'Aye, I took it. And stand by it.'

There was a dangerous murmur from the others. Geordie Orr thrust his face close to Sandy's. 'You were pleading wi' Wotherspoon to bring thon fiendish contraption to the farm. My Clydes have been aff their oats a' day, wi' the noise an' stink o' it. We're warning you to keep your backside aff the tractor in future.'

Weariness overcame Sandy. He knew very well how they felt, and could sympathise, but there was little he could do for them. He spoke kindly. 'It's the way ahead, Geordie. Folk are crying out for food wi' the blockade, an' that means more land in production. More work than the big Clydes can manage, even wi' the Horseman's Word whispered in their lugs. Geordie man, it's progress and it'll no' stop for you, nor for me.'

'Aye, it will stop!' thundered the older man furiously. 'It'll stop the morn, or I'm warning ye, Sandy MacArthur, you an' your kists will be oot the bothy and into the muck in the cattle-court.'

But Wotherspoon had a way of scenting trouble before it started, and it was Geordie Orr who went tramping from the farm within the week, his bundle under his arm. The happy atmosphere in the bothy was gone, though, and although Sandy played the melodeon and the others joined in on jew's harp and spoons, the old camaraderie was lost.

Ishbel had been having problems in Edinburgh. It was wearisome to be waited on hand and foot, with nothing to do. Time dragged, even though her mother-in-law did her best to occupy her.

'Do you sew, Ishbel?' Eleanor asked, and was encouraged by her daughter-in-law's immediate interest.

'Oh, yes!' she replied eagerly. 'It's funny you should say that, Mrs Alexander, because I was just thinking I could help in the shop wi' the alterations. That poor wee woman looked as if she was over the back.'

Eleanor was shocked. 'Oh, I couldn't allow that, my dear!'

'I wouldn't disgrace you, Mrs Alexander,' said Ishbel proudly. 'I've been well schooled in stitching and dressmaking. Mam was lady's maid to Lady Hawkerton before the war, and made all her ladyship's gowns. I used to help Mam sew, and it had to be done well, because Lady Hawkerton was awful pernickety.'

'I'm sure she was, dear,' said Eleanor gently. 'But it was embroidery I had in mind. You can't work in the shop. That's quite impossible. Apart from being beneath your station as Freddie's wife, our workpeople wouldn't like it. They would consider you were taking bread out of their mouths, and would be up in arms. We could have a horrid strike on our hands.'

Ishbel blinked back tears. She felt useless and frustrated, for she knew in her heart she had much to give, if only they would let her work. Eleanor patted her hand. 'Come, cheer up, dear. If you are keen to see how a lady can be helpful, I'll give you a lesson in debt collection. It's a problem in these hard times, but one must not offend one's customers with vulgar demands for money. That would never do!' She rose purposefully and rang for her maid. 'Go put on your hat, Ishbel. We are going out.'

The chauffeur drove them in the landaulette as far as a certain Corstorphine residence, but when Eleanor and Ishbel alighted, they got no further than the noble portico.

'I regret her ladyship is not at home,' said the maid blandly.

Eleanor handed over her visiting card. 'Kindly tell her ladyship that Mrs Alexander called, and will be at home on Tuesday afternoon.'

They walked away, with Ishbel fuming indignantly. 'The wife's keeking through the screens watching our every move, Mrs Alexander. What cheek! She's been in all the time.'

'Oh, I know,' said Eleanor calmly. 'But she has my card, and she knows fine her account's long overdue. Hopefully she'll be shamed into paying it, and will be round for tea and scones next Tuesday, nice as ninepence.'

And she was.

But despite such lessons in diplomacy, Ishbel remained

listless and unhappy. Dorothy decided to introduce her to the local Ladies' Voluntary Aid centre, where well-to-do women gave of their time to help the war effort. Ishbel and Dorothy were given large basketfuls of dried sphagnum moss collected by schoolchildren on the moors, and wads of material from which to make field dressings.

'It's better than knitting endless scarves and balaclavas, anyway,' decided Dorothy cheerfully. 'I'm no knitter, though I believe the boys at the front welcome the mountains of knitting – to clean their rifles!'

There was a scent of moorland in the soft, dry moss. The remembered scent rose into Ishbel's nostrils as she plunged her hands deep into the basket, and she was desperately homesick. What am I doing here, amongst these aimless women? she asked herself. Outside, the late-August sun shone and the grain would be ripening fast; the barley yellow and hard to the teeth and bowing its head to the binder, the oats still a little green, though that improved the quality of oat straw for the beasts.

The tears were running fast by now, and she clenched her fists helplessly in the dry moss. 'It's no use, Dorothy!' she sobbed. 'I've tried, but I don't fit in. I long to be home on the farm helping with the hairst, being useful again.' She looked up mistily at the older woman. 'Oh, Dorothy, I must work. Can't you understand?'

Dorothy sighed. She'd seen this coming. You couldn't cage an independent spirit like this for long. Her own dull domestic routine was not for such as Ishbel whose birthright was to work hard, love passionately, and be loved with passion in return. Aye, and to suffer for it! Dorothy envied her.

She smiled gently at her sister-in-law. 'Of course I

understand, dear. We mean well, but you must live your own life. I shall drive you home tomorrow,' she promised, then laid a hand urgently on Ishbel's arm. 'But don't forget, this is my brother's home and you're needed here too, Ishbel. Perhaps you've no idea how badly the Alexanders need you, but we do.'

Freddie Alexander was swaddled so heavily in warm clothing he could hardly move. All other operational members of 55 Squadron were in the same cocooned state. On the ground, they sweated in the humid evening air. At 14,000 feet it would be a different story.

He laid a hand affectionately on the drab fuselage of the De Havilland 4 aircraft he'd be flying that night. He'd formed an attachment to the two-seater plane in days spent familiarising himself with it. 'She's not as comfy as my Silver Ghost, Bert, but she'll do the job,' he remarked.

Bertram Jones, his observer and gunner, was busy loading drums of ammunition for the Lewis gun into the cockpit. 'You should've brought that blasted motor car with you, you swank about it so much,' he grinned. 'Alexander Keiller, of Dundee marmalade fame, brought his motor to the Western Front. They say the seats convert into comfy beds too.'

'So I've heard. Wish I'd thought of that. His car was built to his own specification, of course, in Berwick.'

Freddie climbed stiffly into the cockpit and settled himself in the pilot's seat. Neither man was deceived by the casual chat. Their nerves were taut as violin strings.

Recently, British men and women had become incensed by frequent impudent air-raids in broad daylight on undefended British cities, and General 'Boom' Trenchard had ordered the war to be taken to the enemy. Freddie's squadron was bound for Mannheim that night to deposit their load of bombs. Providing they escaped fierce ack-ack fire and swift German fighters that buzzed like angry wasps around the laden bombers . . .

Chocks pulled away, Freddie turned his attention to the discipline of flying. It required all his concentration for they flew in battle formation, Freddie on the starboard wing of the group, a mere wingspan and a half from his nearest neighbour. This was his first show since being wounded, and he was determined to make it a good one. They climbed steadily, higher and higher, into rarer, colder air. He could feel the rush of it bite like fire into unprotected skin round his goggles and mask, and still they climbed, higher than he'd gone in practice flights. Higher, it seemed, than he'd ever gone before.

He realised with horror that he couldn't feel his feet. He couldn't feel the rudder bar beneath the soft soles of his flying boots, nor move the numb and sluggish muscles in his damaged leg. His faulty circulation couldn't cope with the searing cold up here. In this state, he was a liability to the others. Heartsick, he gave the thumbs-down signal to Bertram, before firing the green Very light that meant 'Forced to return'.

Freddie side-slipped out of formation and banked in a wide, turning arc as the others droned on into darkness. Then he and his observer were alone high over enemy territory, left to find their way home as best they could, hampered by inadequate navigational aids and Freddie's numb and useless legs.

Donald Mackie had his lass back again, and his life had

regained its purpose. He walked with her as they used to, down to the river arm-in-arm. 'You'll find changes, Ishbel,' he warned. 'Sandy MacArthur sticks closer to Wotherspoon than a sheep tick, and he's persuaded the man to buy a tractor. Sandy works wi' the smith a' the hours God sends, contriving new machinery for working the land.'

'Does he though?' said Ishbel thoughtfully. She was impressed. She hadn't known Sandy had it in him.

Donald whistled to the dog, ranging ahead. 'They've made a start on the moorland. It's to be cleared and limed to produce mair crops. When the moorland goes, where does that leave me?'

That was a worrying thought which hadn't occurred to Ishbel. Surely Wotherspoon wouldn't put her parents out of the gamekeeper's tied cottage? That dour man was maybe fit for it, but ... 'Hannah's married to Wotherspoon, Pa. She'll see you're not put out,' Ishbel said.

He stared moodily ahead. 'Aye, maybe.'

She longed to cheer him. Remembering the generous allowance Freddie had given her, she searched her pockets and came up with a sovereign she'd stashed there cannily for a rainy day. She offered it to her father. 'Here, Pa. Buy yoursel' a bogie roll and a pint o' beer.'

He drew back as if she'd struck him. She'd never seen him look so angry and mortified. 'Keep your rich man's siller! I'll buy my ain drink and baccy, thank ye!'

He turned his back contemptuously and limped off along the moorland path, whistling to the obedient dog. Ishbel stood with the rejected money in her hand, feeling ashamed. She hadn't intended to offend her father's fierce pride, but she'd been away from reality too long, living in the easy lap of luxury. She'd forgotten how charity could wound a man. Tears ran slowly down her cheeks as she watched him go.

'Oh, Pa, I'm sorry!' she whispered.

The harvest was in full swing and Ishbel flung herself gladly into the hard work. The good weather showed signs of holding. All Wotherspoon's binders were in use, each machine pulled by a team of three Clydesdales. Sandy MacArthur alone sat on the tractor, with one of his new-fangled cutting contraptions linked to the power take-off. Heaven had smiled on Wotherspoon and the yield of grain was heavy, but the tractor worked faster and put in longer hours than the sweating horses. If Sandy noted the baleful looks and muttered curses of the ploughmen at mid-yoking, he paid no heed, and ate his bannock and cheese alone. He paid no heed either to Ishbel.

The crops were thick and the sheaves fell from the binder close together, and therefore were more easily gathered. Normally men gathered them for it was heavy work, but men were in short supply now the army was scraping the bottom of the barrel. Ishbel and the other women were gatherers that year, setting the sheaves in stooks to dry in the wind and take their chance with the weather. Nobody could relax until the carts carried the harvest home, dried and golden, to the stackyard. Catriona laughed when her daughter trailed home sore and weary at lowsing-time. 'Och, lassie, in my young day crofters' wives in Lewis thought nothing of building stooks for their men. You should try carrying a load o' damp peats!'

'No thanks!' declared Ishbel, lowering herself gingerly into the chair.

But she rose blithely with the lark, aches and pains

forgotten, for strenuous work in the open gave her deep, dreamless sleep, and for that she was grateful. Anxiety for her husband was never far from her mind, and she wrote to him nearly every day. Freddie's letters were not so frequent, but she knew his squadron was constantly on the move. 'Like a raggle-taggle bunch of tinkers we are,' he wrote . . .

Near the end of the harvest, Ishbel filled a coggie with water as usual and flung in a handful of oatmeal before calling a cheery goodbye to her parents. Trudging along the path to the fields, she found she could sing again. It seemed a long time since she'd had the heart for singing, and her voice in the clear air sounded all the sweeter.

Sandy heard her song above the idling of the tractor, and the purity of it was like a knife in his breast. She was placing the coggie carefully amongst docken leaves to provide a cool, soft drink at mid-yoking when he trundled by. She stopped singing and straightened, meeting his cold glance.

'You've gone up in the world, Sandy MacArthur!' she shouted defiantly.

'So have you, Ishbel Alexander!' he shouted back, the first words they'd exchanged for many a long day.

Catriona was happier that morning than she'd been for weeks. Wotherspoon had asked her to make supper for the harvesters now the hairst was nearly won, and he'd seen to it she had beef, tatties and flour to make beefsteak pie, and a little over besides. She'd been in her element all morning, cooking and baking. The but and ben was hot as an oven with the fire in the range going full blast, so she opened the outside door wide. She stared blankly at the uniformed

100

laddie standing in the yard propping up a red bicycle. He held out a buff envelope and asked her, 'Are you Mrs Frederick Alexander?'

'Lord save us!' Catriona put her hand to her heart, staring at the telegram. She put out a trembling hand. 'I'll tak' it to her.'

'Will there be an answer?' asked the lad timidly.

'Likely no'.'

Catriona hauled off her apron and dashed out. It was a fair step to the fields, and she sobbed and panted as she hurried along. Oh, she'd seen tragedy coming months ago, in the strange, fey way of island women. Poor Freddie! Ah, the poor lad. She hadn't wanted him for Ishbel, but you couldn't help liking him. Her heart ached for his poor mother, but all the same, deep down, a small treacherous voice rejoiced: 'This will give Sandy his chance!' In time, when Ishbel got over it she'd turn to Sandy, and their lives would progress as the Good Lord intended.

She found Ishbel setting up stooks with the others, the fields dotted all over with the drying grain. Catriona waved to attract her lass's attention, and she came over, black-haired and bonnie, a golden, sun-kissed glow on her skin. Mutely, Catriona held out the telegram.

Ishbel turned pale. 'Oh, Mam!' she whispered. But she was a brave one. She took the envelope steadfastly and ripped it open, scanning the terse message. Then she crumpled the telegram in her fist and broke down in tears.

Chapter 5

Catriona took her weeping daughter in her arms. 'Oh, my lass! It's little comfort, but you're no' the only one nursing a sair heart today.'

But Ishbel pushed her mother away impatiently. 'Mam, Mam, it's no' what you think! They're sending Freddie home to be an instructor. He wants me to meet him in London.'

Her mother was furious. 'Och, fancy him giving us a turn like that, sending a telegram! He'll have a good piece o' my mind when I get hold of him!'

Her mother's annoyance couldn't dampen Ishbel's spirits. The sun shone more brightly, the golden harvest scene was the most beautiful she could ever remember. She flung back her head and laughed. 'Oh, Mam, how else could he tell me?'

'He could have sent a postcard. That would've been almost as quick and no' near so alarming,' said Catriona sulkily.

'Wi' a nice view o' the trenches, I suppose!' Ishbel hugged her mother. 'Oh, come on, Mam, smile. Freddie's safe. That's all that matters.'

The lass's radiant happiness made Catriona want to bury her face in her hands and mourn for a tragedy. It was a fey emotion she couldn't explain, but she managed a smile. Aye, well, it's a relief to find I'm no' a spey-wifie forecasting doom for the young folk, she thought thankfully.

London was a far cry from Wotherspoon's stackyard where the golden sheaves were stacked and the harvest safely home. Ishbel said as much to Freddie as they left King's Cross station arm-in-arm, in the midst of a hustling crowd of passengers newly arrived on the Aberdeen express. He laughed. 'Not such a far cry really, my darling. These good people hope to be safely home too, before the grey-out.'

'What on earth's that?'

'The dimming of poor old London's bright lights, in case the Zeppelins pay us a visit tonight.'

She shuddered, and he looked down at her fondly. 'Don't worry, love. The show goes on regardless. There's *Chu Chin Chow* at His Majesty's, or Wee Georgie Wood and Company at Victoria Palace if you prefer. One of these nights I'll wangle tickets for us.'

Ishbel's eyes shone. Oh, she did love the theatre, and how well and handsome her husband looked in uniform! Her heart swelled with pride as she noted the admiring glances women cast in his direction. Freddie didn't seem to notice. He was perfectly at home in the capital, stepping to the edge of the pavement and jauntily hailing a cab.

'The best introduction to London is by cab, my love,' he said, slinging her modest baggage in beside the driver and ushering Ishbel inside a dark, leathery interior.

'But isn't it expensive?' she protested, round-eyed.

'Who cares?' grinned Freddie, and proceeded to kiss his wife soundly in that haven of blissful seclusion.

The married quarters allotted to instructors at the Flying Combat School in Hounslow were quite basic, but Ishbel was thrilled with everything. Running water at the turn o' a tap, and their own home at last! They could settle down to married life without interruption from well-meaning relatives. Oh, she missed her own folk dreadfully, of course. She missed the farm and her friends, and the work she'd enjoyed, but she set about making new friends and soon discovered that life was never dull with Freddie.

There was a good view of the airfield from the window of the flat. Ishbel watched charabancs arrive two or three times a week with fresh batches of recruits, young lads not much more than schoolboys who'd completed ten weeks' elementary training and were granted a place in flying school to strive for Flying Standard 'Y'. Her kind heart went out to these boys. 'Oh, Freddie, they shouldn't be away from their mothers, the poor wee chicks,' she remarked sorrowfully.

He looked grim. 'My dear, whcn I've finished with 'em, they'll have mastered basic combat tactics that'll make sure they return safely to their mothers, much sadder and wiser but fully fledged.'

She knew he was a good instructor, patient yet firm with the young lads. He was ruthless in weeding out students who did not meet his exacting standards. 'I'm in the business of saving lives, Ishbel,' he told her. 'You hear a lot of tosh about daring young men in flying machines, but I won't pass a young chap fit to fly if he's too cocky. Over-confidence spells danger to himself and the squadron.'

Leaning her elbows on the window sill, she would watch him instruct youngsters in a monotonous repetition of 'circuits and bumps', taking off and landing on the grassy airstrip until Freddie was satisfied his pupils had mastered the controls of the slow Shorthorn trainers. As she watched, her heart sang with pride in her man. She was blissfully happy because she knew he would never fly on active service again. His damaged circulation made flying at high altitudes too hazardous.

Despite the deprivations of war and news of fierce fighting once more at Passchendaele, Christmas and New Year celebrations at the Combat School were the merriest Ishbel had known, and in the springtime she discovered another reason for celebration. She was going to have a baby.

Freddie was delighted when she broke the news, although he confessed to being apprehensive. Childbirth was a mystery to him, and he considered it a risky and dangerous procedure. 'Darling, will you be all right?' he asked anxiously.

Ishbel laughed heartily. 'Of course I will! It's a perfectly natural process, Freddie, and the doctor assures me I'm a very healthy specimen.'

He was reassured for the present, and began cautiously examining his own emotions at the prospect of fatherhood. 'I say, I hope it's a boy, Ishbel. I'll teach him to drive.'

She hid a grin. 'Not right away, darling.'

'The sooner the better.' He had a faraway look as he lay on the sofa, relaxing. 'You know, I always dreamed of designing a car one day, Ishbel. Not any old car, you understand, but a perfect car. One that goes faster and safer than all others. Maybe when my son's a man we'll build it together and start a new industry in Scotland. Imagine that, Ishbel, Frederick Alexander and Son.'

'Or daughter, dear,' she reminded him gently, chuckling.

The early months of 1918 were notable for new beginnings. On the first of April the Royal Flying Corps was dismantled and the Royal Air Force was born. The founders of the new force had at long last persuaded the high heid yins in Government of the aeroplane's useful role in warfare.

Freddie was enthusiastic when he told Ishbel the news. 'Although mind you, darling, April Fool's Day is not an auspicious day to choose for the inauguration,' he observed. 'However, one can't expect much from the idiots who elected to choose Elijah as the patron saint of aviators. You may remember the old boy was taken up to Heaven in a chariot of fire, which I can assure you is every aviator's nightmare!'

'Och, heid bummers have no imagination at all, Freddie,' agreed Ishbel comfortably.

However, that summer her husband paid a visit to his London tailor and was measured for new khaki breeches and service jacket, with pale blue and gold insignia of rank.

Ishbel gave a horrified shriek when the tailor's bill arrived some days later. 'Five guineas for a jacket and two pounds fifteen shillings for breeks. That's daylight robbery!'

'No, it isn't. It's the going rate. Don't get in a flat spin, Ishbel,' Freddie warned. He and his wife didn't see eye to eye upon the subject of money. Freddie spent cash without giving it a second thought, while Ishbel's thrifty upbringing made her examine every penny before parting with it.

Tears sprang to her eyes. She was weepy these days because of her condition, and was easily upset. Faced with

Freddie's rash expenditure she felt hard done by for she had only ten shillings left to see them through the week. She stamped her foot. 'I scrimp to save your siller, Freddie Alexander, and you go out and spend money like water. It isn't fair!'

Freddie hugged her. 'Cheer up, my love. You know what you need? A night out and a slap-up feed. How much money have we got?'

'Ten shillings, but Freddie—'

'Excellent! I've got fifteen bob stashed in my flying jacket for a rainy day. Go and put on your glad rags and we'll dine at the Royal Aero Club. I'll give my new uniform a spin and show 'em scruffy old Freddie can be a model of sartorial elegance when he shrugs off the greasy old leathers.'

Seated at a table, waited on hand and foot by orderlies later that evening, Ishbel decided the change of scene had done her good, even if they starved for the rest of the week. She wore a new dress she'd designed and sewn cunningly to disguise a thickening waistline, and was pleasantly aware of admiring glances coming her way from other RAF officers dining with their womenfolk.

They had just finished the meal and were lingering over coffee and liqueurs when a tall young airman paused by the table and hailed Freddie with a delighted slap on the back. 'Freddie, old pal, I was hoping to bump into you somewhere!'

He leaped to his feet and began pumping the young man's arm. 'Matt, it's good to see you're still alive and kicking! Sit down, old chap, have a drink and meet Ishbel, my beautiful new wife.'

The American smiled and shook hands with Ishbel while

the introductions were made. When fresh drinks arrived and they'd settled down to chat, Freddie noticed for the first time how thin and gaunt his friend looked. 'I say, Matthew, you haven't been wounded, have you?' he asked anxiously.

'No, I've had Flanders fever, or Spanish 'flu if you'd rather. It's raging across the Channel amongst our boys, and I had it real bad. I've been in hospital bored stiff most of the time, but I guess I was lucky, being out of it. Warfare does not improve, Freddie, and Fritz has some ace sharp shooters in the sky – notably a guy called Hermann Goering, easily identified by his black an' white fighter, usually at the head of Jerry's Death Squadron. Not to mention Big Bertha making life miserable.' He grinned at Ishbel and explained, 'That's a monster field gun, by the by, ma'am, called after Herr Krupps' wife. And, Freddie, did you hear a Canadian buddy of mine ended the Red Baron's infamous career at last? That guy won't bother you no more.'

Matthew Clark had been studying Ishbel admiringly. Freddie had not exaggerated his wife's claim to beauty. Matt had heard it rumoured Scots lasses were bonnie, but this must be the pick of them all. Lucky devil!

Ishbel was interested in this unusual character with the infectious grin. 'So you're Canadian, Matt?'

He grinned. 'Just for the duration, ma'am. After that I revert to a Yank from New York.' He turned to Freddie. 'By the way, have you driven on the Brooklands circuit yet? Seems a pity not to. I wouldn't mind a go myself. I have a pal who owns a sixty-horse Napier that can easily touch ninety on the straight. I can arrange somethin' for you if you fancy a spin.'

Freddie's eyes lit up, then he caught sight of Ishbel's apprehensive expression and the eager light faded. He shook his head. 'Sorry, Matthew. No racing for Freddie. I'm a reformed character since Ishbel whispered in my ear I'm due to be a father sometime in November.'

'Gee, congratulations!'

Matthew met Freddie's eye with brows raised speculatively. Freddie shook his head slightly. Both men were thinking of a lovechild of Freddie's whose existence Ishbel did not suspect. Matt tightened his lips. He hoped for everybody's sake the little lady never found out. He gave an easy smile. 'I guess you're wise to opt out, Freddie. There are no fortunes to be made motor-racing. It's a rich man's game.'

Freddie looked at him seriously. 'I *am* a rich man, and so are you from what you tell me. When the war's over I bet we could win against the best in the world, Matthew, providing the car was good enough. And I could ensure it was good, given time.'

Matthew nodded thoughtfully. 'Sure. It would take a lot of dedication and dollars, but I guess we could do it.'

Ishbel looked uneasily from one to the other. She saw they had forgotten about her for the moment, and as usual the men's obsession with speed alarmed her. Then Freddie laughed and slipped an arm round her waist, breaking the spell. 'But that's enough day-dreaming. Back to reality, Matthew. First of all, we've got to win the damned war.'

There were changes on the farm. Sandy's tractor had proved so successful Wotherspoon had splashed out and bought another, which the young loon drove expertly, scorning to learn the horseman's lore like the rest of the long-established ploughmen. Sometimes the big Clydes kicked their hooves idly in the stable most of the day, with little work to be done bar carting neeps.

The greater part of the moorland was tamed by the summer of 1918, and Sandy had been occupied digging trenches in the boggy ground for field drains. He was proud of the digger he'd devised to operate from the tractor's power take-off. It was his own invention, and so successful he was tempted to patent it. He grinned to himself as he headed back to the yard at mid-yoking to refuel at the paraffin pump. Who ever heard of a horseman inventing anything?

He was puzzled to find a cattle-float in the yard when he arrived, and his horses being led up the ramp. Wotherspoon was supervising the operation, and Sandy left the tractor ticking over and walked across.

'I didna think the horses were needing shoeing?' he said.

The farmer gave him a level look. 'They don't. One's going to pull the St Cuthbert's milk cart in the city, the other's going for a brewer's dray. They'll be weel cared for, Sandy, else I wouldn't let them go. The poor beasts are wearied with you on the tractor all day and no work for them.'

Sandy felt the blood leave his face and drain from his heart. His horses, his bonnie Clydes! Oh, he'd never thought to lose his bonnie pair, but what the man said was true. The willing beasts needed work, and he himself had taken it from them. Big Bob turned his long, mournful white face towards his master and gave a low, sorrowful nicker. Sandy wheeled away without a word and strode to the stable. He couldn't bear to watch.

A grown man shouldn't start greeting like a bairn.

He stood in the empty stalls clutching the dandy brush he'd used to sort his horses every day, and the tears dripped down his chin and on to the strippit Kirkcaldy sark that he wore, making dark patches like sweat. He thought about the tractor and its din and smoking stink, the dead mechanical thing! His thoughts turned bitter against himself and the tears ran faster.

'Sandy?'

There was a gentle hand on his shoulder, and he turned quickly in his shame to find the farmer's wife at his back. No use dragging a hand across tear-stained cheeks. Too late for that. She'd seen.

'Is it your horses?' Hannah asked gently.

'Aye. They're going. And it's a' my fault,' he choked huskily.

'No!' She gripped his arms, pulling him round to stare into his face. 'It's just progress. It had to happen. The horses will have a good working life, be well cared for. Hugh made sure of it.'

Tears had left him weak and shaken. Staring at the farmer's wife, he felt a bond growing between them, a strange, strong thing; a man who had wept, and a woman who had watched with compassion. He felt quiet and at peace, without shame. He touched her cheek gently. 'You're a good woman, Hannah. Kindly.'

They stood close together, hands raised to one another. They didn't notice the darkening of the light as Wotherspoon stepped through the doorway and stopped dead.

They were young, of an age. He felt jealousy stab him in the breast. She had never reached out to hold him like that.

He had never dared caress her cheek. 'MacArthur, your tractor's running, using up my guid siller. Get on bye to your work, man!' he shouted harshly, and watched the two of them pull guiltily apart.

Hannah spun round and looked at him with wide, clear eyes, and the look was scornful and cool, and nearly broke his heart.

Catriona came running to Donald in the cottage garden in a great state of excitement, waving Ishbel's latest letter. 'Donald, Ishbel's to have a bairn!'

He'd been digging in the vegetable plot. Now he leaned on his spade. 'Michty! When's it due?'

'November, she says.' They looked at one another in fear, remembering Catriona had nearly lost her life when their lass was born. 'The doctor says she's fine, though,' she added tremulously.

Donald stabbed the spade into the earth. 'She'll hae to come home now. None o' our folk gets born across the border,' he declared firmly.

'There's always a first time,' Catriona said. She'd missed her daughter sorely and hoped the happy event would bring her back home, but Ishbel had a mind of her own and you couldn't count on it.

Donald was happing-up the growing potato foliage to ensure a good crop in his plot. Wotherspoon had provided the seed, which was only right since Donald had laboured long gathering tatties in cold, dreich tattie-fields at the back-end of the year. There was little else for him to do, with the moorland gone and his old gundog laid to rest. They'd kept the cottage so far, but lived in constant fear of losing their home.

'Look who's coming,' muttered Donald.

Catriona shaded her eyes and turned pale. 'Lord save us!'

Wotherspoon came down the drive and stopped by the garden wall. He leaned on the coping and doffed his cap politely to Catriona, before addressing himself to Donald. 'I've been thinking about your situation here,' he began without preamble.

Donald braced himself. This was it, the ending they'd been dreading and expecting. 'Oh, aye?' he said.

'There's no call for a gamekeeper on a farm,' Wotherspoon said.

'I ken that, Mr Wotherspoon,' Donald agreed. Catriona moved closer to her man, gripping his arm so hard it hurt, though he hardly felt it.

The farmer cleared his throat awkwardly. 'On the other hand, there's vermin to be kept doon. Hordes o' rats plaguing the place, and rabbits by the thoosand, not to mention the odd fox or two stravaiging round hen-houses bold as brass. There's plenty work for a man, if you'd care to tak' on vermin-trapping.'

Donald stared at him in silence for a full minute. 'It's a comedown, Mr Wotherspoon. I'll dae it though, and thank ye kindly for the opportunity,' he said proudly.

Wotherspoon nodded. 'By the by, you'll need a dog.' He reached into the bulge in his jacket and brought out a wee terrier. 'This yin comes from good ratting stock. He'll serve ye weel.'

Donald held the warm, little body close to his breast and fondled the dog's silky brown ears as he watched the farmer retrace his steps towards the fields.

'Me, a rat-catcher! What do you make o' that man,

Catriona?' he asked, shaking his head slowly.

'I'd say don't be deceived by the sour facie. There's warmth in Wotherspoon, though he hides it,' answered his wife thankfully.

If you can't beat 'em, join 'em! That was one of Auntie Nellie's maxims, and no' a bad one at that, thought Ishbel as she kept an eye on the stopwatch. Her hands were freezing, her whole body felt like a lump of ice, although she was big and heavy with the bairn, and wrapped up to the nose in furs. She shouldn't be standing in a concrete service pit in her condition, waiting for her speed-mad husband to complete a lap of the racing circuit, but here she was, sharing his interest as best she could. She heard the irritable, girning roar of the engine approaching, then Freddie rocketed into view and drew up in the pit with a squeal of tyres. The now familiar stench of hot oil and rubber and over-heated metal reached her behind the barrier.

She clicked the stopwatch. 'Four minutes thirty-five seconds.'

'Hey, not bad! Must've gained a few seconds across the Byfleet banking.'

She looked at him, this begoggled, grimy-faced man she loved so dearly. Miserable and chilled with standing around for most of the October afternoon, she decided enough was enough. 'Freddie, I want to go home,' she said.

He grinned, teeth very white against black, oily grime. 'Righto, sweetheart. I'll return this baby to its owner and be with you in a tick, then we'll go home.'

'I mean really home. Back to Scotland.'

Freddie slipped off the racing goggles and looked at her

seriously, eyes ringed white against blackened skin. He didn't want to go back to Edinburgh, not yet. His skill on the racing track was improving, and he had innovations in mind which would make the Napier go faster and better. But he loved his wife dearly. She'd been an absolute brick, fostering his growing interest, patiently timing his performance on the circuit for hours on end without complaint.

'I could arrange a transfer,' he said slowly. 'Lloyd George and General Haig have sorted out their differences over the use of tanks, thank God, and the Kaiser's big push on the Western Front is fizzling out. We have supremacy in the air, Ishbel, and I've a feeling the end's in sight. My job at Hounslow isn't so essential these days. We can go home to Scotland if you really want to, my darling.'

She flung her arms round his neck and kissed him, dirt and all. She knew the sacrifice he was prepared to make for her, and loved him all the more for it. 'Oh, Freddie, you are a darling!' she cried tearfully.

'I know,' he grinned.

'It's a lovely wee dog, Pa!' exclaimed Ishbel in delight a few weeks later when introduced to her father's terrier. Foxy rolled over and displayed a well-rounded pinkish tum, basking in her admiration.

Donald beamed. 'Aye, he's a grand wee tyke, brave as a lion.'

'And you're secure now, Pa. Wotherspoon won't put you out.'

'My pride's dunted by the come-down to a rat-catcher, but pride's easy mended, lass,' Donald nodded.

'Are you staying with us 'til the bairn's born, Ishbel?' Catriona asked eagerly. Judging by the state of her daughter, it would be very soon. It was Freddie who answered.

'No, Mrs Mackie. We're going on to Edinburgh for the birth. Ishbel will have better attention in the city.'

Catriona busied herself energetically poking the fire for it was a cold, raw November day. She didn't want her son-in-law to see the hurt in her eyes. Who could give better attention to the dear lass than her mother and the good doctor who'd saved both their lives nearly twenty years ago? she thought sadly.

Ishbel was in a strangely lethargic state. The cumbersome weight of her body sapped her energy, and having broken the long car journey to visit her parents, was quite agreeable to pressing on to Edinburgh, if only she could rest there. Freddie had secured a transfer to an RAF training base just outside the city, and blown all their savings on a Napier, a car to which he'd grown attached. The journey from Hounslow had been far from comfortable, although it had been done in easy stages. Freddie had had to cope with punctures and breakdowns caused by bad roads, and Ishbel ached with weariness.

When they'd said goodbye to her parents and were heading at a decorous pace towards Edinburgh, she rested her head on Freddie's shoulder and closed her eyes. 'Remember how frightened I was the first time you took me out, Freddie? Thirty seemed a disgraceful speed then.'

'I'm taking it canny today, love, I can tell you!'

Dozing a little, she became aware of strange sensations, new and disturbing. She opened her eyes wide and sat up with a jerk. 'Freddie, speed up. I think the baby's on its way.'

'What?' He gave his wife a shocked glance and blanched.

Without another word, he stabbed his foot hard on the accelerator and the car shot forward.

As it transpired, there was no need for haste. Eleanor Alexander summoned aid immediately the young couple arrived, and Ishbel was packed off to bed with Dorothy and Florrie in attendance. The elderly Dr Campbell examined his patient, decided there was no call for his presence just yet, and went off to snatch a few hours' sleep. And so the long tense night of waiting began.

Freddie was sure she would die. They wouldn't let him near her, though he tried to sneak into the bedroom several times. He hung around outside the door while Florrie and Dorothy bustled in and out, but his entry was barred by a midwife with the shoulders and vocal range of sergeant-majors he had known. He tried to doze in bed, but was roused by strange sounds and hasty comings and goings. It was dawn when he suddenly sat up in bed abruptly. There were complications! She was losing their baby – she was losing her life! He was out of bed, hovering white-faced in the lobby, when the doctor came out rolling down his shirtsleeves. Freddie could tell little from his expression. 'Doctor, is she . . . ?'

Dr Campbell patted his shoulder. 'They're all well, son.'

Freddie's jaw dropped. 'All?'

'Aye. Two fine wee boys. I had a suspicion it was twins whenever I set eyes on her,' the doctor said, beaming.

Ishbel was up two days after the twins' birth, happy and sparkling. She sat in a chair by the bay window nursing her babies, while Freddie looked on proudly. 'What'll we call them?' she wondered.

'How about Peace and Plenty?'

Ishbel laughed. 'Oh, Freddie, don't be daft!'

'Not so daft. Listen!' The sound of church bells came to them through the tightly closed windows. 'The Armistice has been signed, my darling. It's over. Peace at last,' he said softly, kissing her.

There were tears in her eyes. 'Oh, Freddie, I should be glad, but all I can think of is your brother and all the other lads who won't be coming home.'

'I know,' he said gently. 'But we have to look to the future, and these little lads are ours. They're as like as two peas, A and B. How about calling them Adrian and Brian?'

Ishbel considered the suggestion. The more she thought about it, the better it sounded. To her fond eyes, the twins were individuals already. The firstborn was bigger, more vigorous in his demands. He was Adrian. The second was smaller. Involuntarily she hugged the little one closer, for he seemed more vulnerable and in need of protection. He was Brian. 'They're lovely names, Freddie. They suit the babies perfectly,' she decided happily.

Freddie left the RAF in April 1919. He'd had enough of peacetime flying and was content to settle down to family life. He returned to the shop, much to William Alexander's delight, while Ishbel remained in Edinburgh at her in-laws' house, caring for the babies.

For a time she was perfectly happy. Her pleasure in her two little boys was shared by the Alexander grandparents and by Donald and Catriona. Dorothy drove Ishbel out to the farm frequently that year so that the doting couple could watch their grandchildren grow. 'Aye, they're

Mackies all right!' decided Donald, as Adrian set off
crawling, heading for the door and the world outside.
Brian, meanwhile, hauled himself shakily to his feet,
hanging on like grim death to his grandfather's breeks.
Catriona gave a little shriek and retrieved one grandson
just as he reached the doorstep and was launching out into
the yard.

'Michty, you have your hands full!' she told Ishbel,
laughing.

Ishbel hugged Brian, who had toppled over and landed
on his bottom in Foxy's dinner dish. 'Better that than
empty hands, Mam!'

But as the months passed Ishbel realised all was not well
with Freddie. He came home from the shop with furrowed
brow. At first he'd shared whisky and cigars with his father
in the smoking room, relaxing while they talked, literally,
'shop'. Now he'd taken a dead set against that routine and
made straight for the nursery to play with his two toddlers.
Ishbel made no comment but watched her husband with
growing concern. The outburst she'd been expecting
happened one Saturday afternoon when he came striding
home early.

'Blasted women!' He slammed the parlour door.

Fortunately, Ishbel was alone, Eleanor and the twins
taking a nap. 'You'll waken your mother, dear, not to
mention your bairns,' she warned mildly.

He calmed down, slumping moodily on the sofa. 'I
ordered one hundred perfectly good felt hats, brown, navy
and green, and the customers complain they're dowdy and
won't buy them. Honestly, Ishbel, what do women want?
Have they forgotten the war? Markets are depressed all

over, and factories closing right, left and centre. Those hats were all I could get.'

She went and sat beside him and held his hand. 'Darling, women don't want perfectly good hats, they want perfectly beautiful hats. They want to forget the dowdy clothes we all wore during the war. Why don't you hand the hats over to Doris, and ask her to trim them in her own individual style, with flowers and feathers and ribbons and bows? They'll sell like hot cakes, I'm sure.'

He sighed wearily. 'Yes, of course. Why didn't I think of that?' He was silent for a long moment, head bowed, then looked up at her. 'It's no good, Ishbel. I'm no shopkeeper.'

She was startled by the stark misery in his eyes. 'Darling, maybe if you were to persevere . . .' she began, suddenly frightened.

'No. It's no use,' he said hopelessly. Then his expression changed and he gripped both her hands. 'Listen, Ishbel, I've had an offer from the chap who sold me the Napier. He's developing a faster prototype, and they're looking for someone to drive it at Le Mans. I have driving experience and plenty of money, so I'm just the chap he needs.' His eyes shone. 'Oh, darling, it's what I want to do more than anything, but it means months spent on racing circuits tuning and improving the car, complete dedication to the job. How can I possibly leave you and the boys for months on end?'

'You can't leave us,' she said quietly. Her secure world was falling apart. She'd always known Freddie was no businessman, but he was her dear husband and his unhappiness was hers. Ishbel was quite clear in her mind what she must do. 'We're a family. If you go, the boys and I go with you.'

He gaped at her. 'But you've no idea what that entails! I'll be moving around racing circuits doing trials, Ishbel, living in digs and second-rate hotels. The race track's no place for a woman with young bairns!'

'I don't care. Whatever happens, we'll stick together,' she said stubbornly.

Freddie was silent, but there was hope in his eyes. 'It wouldn't be for long, Ishbel. Maybe two, three years, 'til the car proves itself in one of the big races. Then I could get all this out of my system and settle down to work in the shop when the boys are old enough to go to school.'

She smoothed the wavy fair hair lovingly off his brow and kissed him. 'Aye, two or three years, my love. That's not long,' she agreed.

Freddie's decision left his mother horror-struck and his father devastated. Eleanor lost no time seeking out Ishbel. 'Surely you can make him see sense, my dear?' she pleaded. 'I know Freddie will listen to you, Ishbel. You must make my son abandon this foolish plan.'

She sighed wearily. 'Freddie and I discussed it thoroughly, Mrs Alexander. It's the only path to take if he's to be happy. I've decided the bairns and I will go with him.'

'What?' Eleanor shrieked, she was so shocked. 'You must be daft! I won't permit it.'

Ishbel's eyes glinted dangerously. 'I'm sorry, ma'am, but you've no say in the matter. The boys go with us. We're a family.'

Eleanor's lip trembled pathetically. 'And are we not your family too? Don't we deserve consideration, or are you too selfish to consider the wishes of Freddie's parents? It would seem so!'

Ishbel's eyes filled with tears. 'Oh, Mrs Alexander, please don't make this parting more difficult than it is already.'

'I am glad you find it difficult. I find it tragic,' said her mother-in-law stiffly, rising and leaving the room without a backward glance.

Ishbel fared little better with her own mother. Catriona refused to see her daughter's point of view, and was deeply concerned for her grandchildren. 'Bairns need a settled life at their young age, Ishbel. Wee boys shouldn't be traipsing round the countryside like tinkers. I don't know what you're thinking about, you and that daft young husband of yours!' she grumbled.

'The bairns will be fine if they're with us, Mam. Being together is what matters. They'll be loved and weel cared for, I'll see to that,' she declared stubbornly.

'Well, I think it's a disgrace taking weans to dangerous places polluted with motor cars and poisonous fumes. I'll not know a moment's peace,' Catriona wailed.

The twins stared solemnly at her. They knew something exciting was in the wind, and watched their grandmother anxiously in case she stopped it happening. The wee boys had an uncanny way of uniting at crucial times like this, and somehow becoming not two little boys but one. When that happened, Catriona wasn't sure which was which. She went down on her knees and hugged them to her breast.

'Why you greetin', Gran?' asked one of them.

'I'm no' greetin', son, I've got the cold,' Catriona sniffed. 'You'll no' forget your poor auld granny an' grandpa when you're away, will you, Adrian?'

The little one stared at her solemnly. 'No' Adrian, Gran, me's Brian.'

The twins' new existence, spent following their father round the race circuits of Britain and Europe, was so exciting they scarcely had time to become fretful. Ishbel, Freddie and their sons moved from English boarding-house to French pension and Italian villa, while Freddie and a team of skilled mechanics perfected the car's performance.

Living in cramped apartments, there was nothing for it but to take the boys with them to the racing circuits. Patiently, Ishbel stood by and tried to keep the twins out of mischief in the service areas. Freddie loved having his small sons close by when his car roared into the pits, and far from resenting the presence of the little ones, the mechanics did their bit in cheerfully instilling rough and ready discipline. As Freddie began steadily winning races with the Napier, the presence of his pretty wife and bairns became essential to the superstitious team who believed they brought luck. Freddie was delighted. 'Who said bairns and motors don't mix?' he said laughingly to Ishbel, his boys perched beside him in the cramped driving seat.

She smiled fondly but nursed secret reservations. The twins worshipped Freddie. Adoration shone like a light from two identical small faces as their hero sped by in his dark green racing colours, waving to them as he went. Somehow the scene troubled her, though she couldn't say why.

Ishbel herself had absorbed a great many of the salient points of motor racing. She knew most of the ailments which beset racing drivers, the cramps, fevers and chills which racked the men's bodies. As for the cars, she had heard all about broken rear springs, cracked cylinder heads and deadly splinters of flint from doubtful road surfaces which could do untold damage to both man and machine. In self-defence she herself learned to drive quite expertly, an accomplishment of which Freddie was extremely proud.

As the months passed, Ishbel sat perched with the boys on the pit-counter in all weathers and locations, patiently timing Freddie's trial laps. Sometimes her sons were on the verge of fretful tears with boredom, sometimes they were up on tiptoes with excitement. It was a hard, vagrant, grimy existence, and sometimes Ishbel wondered why she put up with it. One look at her husband's absorbed, dirty face supplied the answer.

She'd never seen Freddie so happy, and his happiness was worth all the hardships. Freddie was deeply involved in his sport, relaxed and calm behind the wheel, but even so he never failed to tell Ishbel how much he needed her. 'I love to have you and the boys waiting in the pit when I come in, darling. You're my lucky mascots,' he declared. When he kissed her, the sacrifice of a normal, humdrum existence seemed a small price to pay to be with her man and their bairns.

Money was a worry, though. Ishbel suspected Freddie was recklessly spending his personal fortune. When she tackled him on the subject, he merely laughed. 'My dear, you mustn't stop to count the cost of working up to the Le Mans Grand Prix. When you're good enough to be in that league you must prove your car's the best, and so are you. In other words, racing's become an obsession.'

She shivered. 'Freddie, I hate that word!'

'You worry too much, sweetheart,' he said cheerfully.

'Besides, I have a rich American sponsor to help me out.'

'You mean Matthew Clark?'

He grinned mysteriously. 'Could be. You wait 'til my little green British car comes racing past the flag tomorrow. Imagine the boost that'll give the British car industry, Ishbel! If I win my first Grand Prix, I promise I'll retire gracefully and turn my attention to honest toil and the twins' education.'

Her spirits rose high for she'd timed him at practice and been astounded by the speeds he had attained. She was convinced there were few who could catch him. One more race and then we go home! she thought happily.

The scene at the little provincial market town of Le Mans, astride the River Sarthe, was an incredible one next Saturday afternoon. It was more like a fairground than a racing circuit, with marquees fluttering with flags, show-men selling their wares, and conjurors and fortune-tellers their skills. There were hot dog and waffle stands, ice cream barrows and peep-shows, when the motor racing palled. The fields surrounding the circuit served as vast car parks, bordered with scented pinewoods. The warm air thrilled with noise and excitement.

Ishbel sat in her usual seat on the pit-counter with the twins perched beside her, watching the traditional start; the cars, engines dead, lined up at the pits, the drivers on foot at the other side of the road, tensely awaiting the starter's signal to sprint forward.

They were off! The little boys bounced up and down yelling with excitement as their father vaulted into the driving seat and raced off, one of the first to go.

It was going well, and the atmosphere in the pits was

jubilant. Freddie was leading as he roared in for a wheel-change, and the team set to work with a will. He was dusty and grimy as he hastily kissed his family and grinned with a flash of very white teeth in a black face. 'A three-minute wheel-change. Not bad. Just watch me go!' He shot off with a wave, leaving his sons cheering and Ishbel laughing, dirty smudges on her lips where he had kissed her, stop-watch in her hand.

The stop-watch had become an essential part of Ishbel's existence. It was her reassurance as she timed Freddie's laps. Now the minutes ticked by, heralded by the scream of tyres and the revving of tortured engines as Freddie's rivals passed one by one in a swirl of dust. The boys grew restive after a while. 'Where's my daddy gone?' Adrian demanded.

'He's very late,' one of the mechanics muttered anxiously, while Ishbel frowned stupidly at the stop-watch. He should have finished the lap by now. What had happened to him? A breakdown, that wretched piston rod again, or—? Seized with a sudden dread, she pushed the boys towards the head mechanic. 'George, look after the bairns for me?'

She heard the children shouting plaintively after her as she went, walking at first, then running fast, shoving her way through the festive crowds, eyes fixed in horror on a point far down the track. The straw bales lining the bend of the circuit were scattered in all directions and oily black smoke rose thick and menacing into the blue sky.

Chapter 6

Nearing the scene of the crash at the Mulsanne turn, Ishbel found her way barred by a white-faced official. She tried to push past. 'Let me through!'

Somebody whispered, 'It's his wife!'

The official became even more agitated. 'Madame, I am sorry, but you cannot.'

'Let me through, I want to see my husband!' she cried desperately.

He was a kindly man, deeply distressed. He held her by the shoulders. 'Madame, you must be brave. There was an oil spillage on the circuit. Others were alerted, but there was no time to warn the leading driver. After the fast Mulsanne straight your husband's car skidded at high speed going through the turn and there was a serious accident, I am afraid.'

'No!' Ishbel froze. She knew an oil spillage was the hazard most feared by racing drivers. Wheels lost traction and the car became unsteerable. Freddie would have had no time to manoeuvre, but even so she still allowed herself to hope. He'd crashed during races before and come out unscathed; he was adept at whipping the car round to meet obstacles with the rear end of the vehicle, much the safest way to hit. He was cool-headed, skilful. Surely he would be all right?

The crowd milling round fell silent, moving aside to allow a laden stretcher to pass. A motionless figure swathed in blankets lay on it, but a mop of tousled fair hair and the grimy features were instantly recognisable. With a heart-broken cry Ishbel dodged beneath the official's restraining arm and ran to her husband. The stretcher bearers paused, startled by her sudden appearance.

Shocked, Ishbel noted Freddie's unnatural pallor. She was filled with a terrible foreboding of disaster as she stooped to kiss him. 'Freddie, oh, Freddie, my darling, please speak to me!' she sobbed.

He stirred, opened heavy eyelids and looked at her with sudden recognition. He moistened dry lips and whispered, 'Ishbel, always remember, no matter what happens – since I met you – there was only you.'

There was something preying on his mind, she could see the worry and anguish mirrored in his eyes. 'Freddie, don't worry. I love you no matter what happens,' she cried, desperate to drive away the awful haunted look and reassure him that even if he was crippled for life, she would care for him devotedly. Perhaps she succeeded. With a ghost of the merry, twinkling smile she loved, Freddie's eyes closed.

The stretcher bearers moved Ishbel gently aside and hurried off towards the waiting ambulance with their burden. She longed to follow, all her instincts urged her to go with the grievously injured man, but she remembered the distressed little boys she'd abandoned to George the mechanic's care. She stopped in her tracks and covered her face with her hands. 'My bairns. I can't leave my poor wee bairns!' she wept. Compassionately, a race official took her arm and led her away from the scene.

* * *

Freddie Alexander died peacefully from his injuries later that day, in the foreign land he and others like him had fought to set free. Ishbel remained dry-eyed when they told her the dreadful news for she could not weep. Somewhere beyond bleak reality, a beloved, remembered voice sang softly.

'Goodbyee, don't cryee,

Wipe the tear, baby dear, from your eye-ee!'

But she could not weep. She held Freddie's wee, distraught sons in her arms and listened to the bairns' bewildered grief as they sobbed pitifully, and still she could not weep.

'Mam, I want my daddy! Where's Daddy gone?' they wailed in unison.

'Hush, my wee lambs. Daddy's at rest. He's gone up to Heaven.'

That silenced them, and they stared at her. 'Like flying in an airyplane?' Brian said.

'Yes, darling,' Ishbel nodded. 'Into the blue sky, into eternal sunshine, just like flying in an airyplane.'

And then, strangely, she found she could cry.

When Ishbel's telegram arrived in Edinburgh with the shocking news, William Alexander dropped everything and left for Le Mans. He allowed himself no time to think on the long, wearisome journey, his emotions were too confused. What a tragedy for his dear son to survive the war only to suffer a pointless death like this, in a racing car! William gripped the rail of the cross-Channel ferry and his eyes stung with tears. Why hadn't his wife put her foot down and stopped the foolishness before it came to this?

William was fond of his daughter-in-law and admired her spunk when standing up to Eleanor, but oh, how he wished Ishbel had used her influence more wisely!

William met his daughter-in-law in the apartment Freddie had rented, and they hugged one another speechlessly. It was a comfort to have one of her husband's folk with her, but Ishbel was shocked by the change in William. She'd remembered him affectionately as a dapper elderly gentleman, but today he looked doddering and old, bowed with worry and sorrow. She led the old man gently to a chair and he sank down with a grateful sigh. The little boys stood well back, curiously eyeing this stranger who was their grandfather. To them, he seemed incredibly aged.

'Ishbel, lass, how bleak the future seems now Freddie's gone! I always hoped my son would settle to the shop given time, and now it's too late. Ah, Ishbel, I can't see the future clear, but I doubt if I can go on,' William admitted wearily. After a moment, he roused himself and glanced at her kindly. 'What's your financial situation, my dear?'

She lifted her chin proudly. 'I've paid all that Freddie owed. There are no debts, Mr Alexander.'

He nodded. 'That's a blessing. My son had access to the considerable sum he inherited from his grandfather, of course, as well as his officer's gratuity. You and his wee laddies will be well provided for, fortunately.'

Ishbel hesitated. Money hadn't been important to Freddie. Improving the safety and performance of motor cars had been his aim, and he'd considered money well spent when invested in his dream of a perfect car for ordinary folk. Despite all her efforts to scrimp and save,

132

she'd had a severe shock when the state of Freddie's finances had been revealed to her after his death. His father might as well know the truth. 'I'm sorry, Mr Alexander, but there's very little of Freddie's fortune left,' she told him.

'What?' he cried sharply. 'Don't tell me he squandered it all?'

Ishbel felt duty bound to speak up in Freddie's defence. 'It's only by driving a car to the limit you can search out its strengths and weaknesses, Mr Alexander. Freddie took risks with his money, aye, and with his life too, so that others might benefit. Motor racing's a dangerous, costly sport, and you might as well ken this – Freddie was on the brink of bankruptcy when the accident happened. If he'd won, then it might have been different, but as it is, we'll no' get a penny back.'

The old man groaned. 'I can hardly believe this!'

'It's true all the same.' Ishbel pressed a hand to her head, which had begun to throb. She felt ill and sick, and longed to be alone for a minute or two to compose herself. 'We both need a cup of tea, Mr Alexander. If you'll excuse me, I'll boil the kettle.' Quietly, she left the room.

When his daughter-in-law had gone, William sank his head in his hands. To discover Freddie had frittered away a fortune was the last straw. In his misery, William had forgotten the two silent little boys. He jumped when a small hand timidly touched his knee. He opened his eyes with a start and stared into two identical, concerned little faces. 'You never spoke to us at all. Don't you want us to come to Ed'burgh with you. Grandfather?' asked one of them forlornly.

Impulsively, William hugged them both. 'Och, of course

133

I do! You can help to cheer us up. That'll be your job. There's a rocking horse and train-set in the attic that belonged to your uncle and your daddy when they were wee boys. Those will be yours when you come home.'

Their eyes brightened, and for an instant he caught a glimpse of Freddie, a brief resemblance to his dead boy. His sad heart warmed, and he couldn't hide the tears that rolled slowly down his cheeks.

'I will not see that woman, Dorothy!' Eleanor Alexander declared stubbornly.

Her daughter sighed wearily for this row had been raging since Ishbel and her sons had returned to the capital. 'Mother, you can't lay the blame for Freddie's death at Ishbel's door. You know how stubborn the dear man was once he'd made up his mind.'

'She could have made him see sense if she'd wanted to. He thought the world of her. It's no use your standing up for her, Dorothy. This tragedy is all Ishbel's fault.'

Dorothy could see she would never win. Her poor, sorrowing mother had broken down completely and taken to her bed. Eleanor needed somebody to blame for this terrible tragedy that had crushed them all, and she had a particularly ferocious bee in her bonnet concerning Ishbel. Dorothy put an arm round her mother and helped her sit up against the pillows. 'Here's a sleeping draught Dr Campbell left for you, dear. You'll feel better now the funeral's over.'

'That's another thing!' Eleanor said, dabbing her eyes. 'Women in our position don't stand with menfolk in the cemetery, parading our emotions for all to see. Has Ishbel no pride?'

'I believe she has her fair share of it, Mother,' remarked Dorothy drily.

'Och, you were aye on her side.' Eleanor swallowed the milky liquid with horrible grimaces. 'How can I sleep with that awful banging going on?'

'It's just the twins playing on the rocking horse.'

Nothing could please Eleanor. She scowled. 'That's disgraceful! Hasn't their mother told those bairns this is a house of mourning?'

It was unfortunate Ishbel chose that moment to tap on the bedroom door bearing a tray of tea and biscuits. She had been very worried about her mother-in-law's collapse, and since most of the domestic staff had been paid off, and Florrie the cook-general balked at stairs, Ishbel welcomed an excuse to comfort Freddie's mother. They had scarcely exchanged a word since Ishbel's return to Edinburgh.

'I brought your tea-tray, Mrs Alexander,' she said.

'Then you can just take it away again. I'm going to sleep.' Eleanor closed her eyes tight and turned her face to the wall.

Perplexed, Ishbel set down the tray and looked helplessly at Dorothy, who shook her head and whispered, 'I'm sorry, dear, but it would be best if Mother slept. She'll be better tomorrow.'

'Oh, no, I won't!' cried Eleanor. 'I'll never be better. My boy would be alive today if it wasn't for her.'

Distressed by the unfair accusation, Ishbel moved swiftly to the bedside. 'I couldn't stop Freddie, and wouldn't if I could! He did pioneering research work on that car, and loved every minute of it. He was happy right to the very end, doing work he loved for the good of other motorists...' She broke off, choking on a sob.

Eleanor fixed her with a furious glare. 'Happy? Ishbel, that work, as you dare call it, killed my son!'

'No, it didn't! A spillage of oil on the track killed him. It was just a terrible accident. Nobody's fault.'

The sleeping draught was beginning to take effect, but Eleanor struggled against it, shouting: 'You could have prevented it. He would have listened to you, and you know it. He would be alive today if you'd spoken up. It's all your fault!'

Ishbel backed away. 'No! Oh, please – no!' There was a hard grain of truth in the accusation, and the pain of it struck deep.

Eleanor realised she'd inflicted grave wounds and struggled with her conscience. Her drowsy mind tried to work out some form of reconciliation, but it was beyond her. She gave up, closed her eyes, and sank thankfully into oblivion.

Ishbel fumbled with the door handle and ran out on to the landing where she stood for a moment at the head of the stairs, gripping the banisters. Dorothy hurried after her sister-in-law and laid a comforting hand on her shoulder.

'Ishbel dear, Mother's sick. The doctor's concerned about her mental state. She doesn't know what she's saying.'

'I think she does. Freddie would've stayed at home if I'd asked him to. You ken fine, Dorothy.'

'My dear, Freddie was no shopkeeper. Of course he would have stayed, because he loved you, but my poor brother would have been an unhappy, frustrated man.'

'But he would be alive!'

It was true. Dorothy was lost for words as Ishbel walked blindly away. She headed for the nursery, where a rhythmic thudding told of her sons' pleasure in their father's discarded toys.

Brian had been riding across green fields, the horse leaping fences and ditches in its path. When his mother came in, he was brought back to earth with a bump, to find himself back in a gloomy house with blinds drawn and creepy shadows everywhere. He slid off the rocking horse's rump and landed beside his twin who was lying on his stomach watching a clockwork train go round and round. Without conscious thought, Brian knew Adrian was on a similar journey, stoking the engine's boiler with coal, steaming fast towards London on the LNER line, hoping to beat the speed record. The twins did not require verbal communication. They knew pretty well what the other was thinking, and Brian thought their mother was more upset than usual. Alerted, Adrian glanced up and scrambled to his feet.

'Get your caps on, boys. We're going out,' Ishbel said.

She must get out of the house and take her boys with her, or she would break down completely. She wasn't welcome in Freddie's home. She had to plan for a future filled with so many unexpected complications she didn't know where to turn.

'Can we go on the bus, Mam?' Adrian asked eagerly when they reached the street.

'Yes, if you want to, dear.' Ishbel hadn't thought where they might go, but she longed to be with her own folk. If that meant a bus fare, then it couldn't be helped. Besides, life hadn't been much fun for the poor wee boys lately.

'Can we go up the stairs and sit outside?' Brian asked,

jumping up and down excitedly at the bus stop.

'Aye, it's a braw afternoon,' she agreed.

Sitting on top, the breeze tugging her hat, Ishbel handed over a penny ha'penny and two ha'penny fares to the conductor, who doled out tickets with a suitably mournful expression, mindful of the black triangles sewn on his passengers' sleeves.

'Are we going to Princes Street?' asked Adrian, as the bus trundled along.

'Aye, and down Leith Walk.'

'Florrie says there's to be electric trams in Princes Street soon, but she's no' keen on thon things,' Brian added, swinging his legs.

'Why no'?' demanded his twin curiously.

''Cause if you were to put one foot on the overheid wire and the other foot on the tram rails, you'd frizzle up, Florrie says.'

Ishbel found herself laughing. 'Och, Florrie's a gasbag!'

The twins leapt loyally to their friend's defence. 'No, she's no'! Florrie's seen a gasbag, Mam. There was a gasbag on top of a bus on Waverley Bridge during the war, Florrie says. They filled a big bag with coal-gas to make the bus go, 'cause nobody had petrol,' explained Adrian, who, like his father before him, knew all there was to know about propulsion.

'Nobody would get on it they were that feart it would blow up,' added Brian happily.

With such interesting diversions, the journey to Leith passed quickly, and Ishbel and the boys alighted in the independent port which had been dragged reluctantly over the city boundary in 1920. Walking along, she was struck by how rundown the buildings and shops were, and pitied the groups of gaunt men hanging aimlessly around street corners. It saddened her to see such deprivation. Where was the land fit for heroes Lloyd George had promised his returning soldiers?

Auntie Nellie was delighted when she found Ishbel and the weans on her doorstep. She folded them to her bosom.

'Oh, the bonnie weans! They must miss their daddy sair, Ishbel. Poor Freddie, fancy killin' himsel' at the racing! I've aye said toffs have mair siller than sense, Ishbel dear.'

When they were inside the spotless apartment and Nellie had occupied the little boys with a set of building blocks kept for the amusement of visiting bairns, she and Ishbel settled down for a good blether.

'I'm to get spliced again, Ishbel,' Nellie confided. 'He's a nice man, a fishmonger frae Newhaven. Quiet-like, but we get on fine.'

Ishbel was delighted. She kissed her aunt's cheek. 'I hope you'll be very happy, love. You deserve it.'

'Aye, well—' Nellie studied her niece pensively. You couldn't expect the poor lass to look well, after what she'd been through, but she looked really ill, too skinny, and with dark smudges under the eyes. 'What will you do wi' yoursel', Ishbel?' she asked quietly.

'I don't know, Auntie Nellie. I'm at my wits' end.' Ishbel paused and her eyes filled with tears. 'Oh, Auntie Nellie, I'm near three months gone wi' another bairn!' she cried in despair.

Nellie drew in a breath. 'The Lord save us! Och, the poor, wee, fatherless mite! One blessing, you'll no' be short o' a penny or two. Your man was well heeled, wasn't he?'

'The money's near all spent,' sighed Ishbel. 'I'm not welcome in the Alexanders' house. They think Freddie's accident was my fault. They could be right.'

'Oh, lassie, for God's sake dinna torture yoursel'!' Her aunt put an arm round her, and Ishbel rested her head wearily on the comforting shoulder. 'What'll you dae noo?' Nellie asked quietly.

'Go back to Mam and Pa on the farm. Maybe once the baby's born I'll see the way clear,' Ishbel said listlessly.

Going to the country was a dream come true for Brian. From the door of Grandpa's cottage he could run into the open air, day or night. He could work the handle of the old pump in the yard, and a stream of pure cold water sloshed over his boots. He was given important jobs to do. Grandpa said everyone must bring a log from the woodpile when they visited the outside privy to save Granny work. That's why Grandpa had sited a woodpile at that strategic point.

Adrian wasn't so keen on the change of lifestyle. Adrian liked buses and cable cars and Grandfather Alexander's big house. He liked hissing gas mantles and the gas fire in the hallway that lit with a fearsome 'Plop!' when Florrie set a wax taper to it. He liked the big car Grandfather drove to the shop every day. He liked riding in it, swanking a bit. Granny and Grandpa Mackie's cottage was a bit of a come-down after such luxury.

Still, Adrian liked the four new green tractors with all their fascinating bits and pieces which were kept in the old cartsheds. He'd had a peep at them through a crack in the door, but the only snag was the Grumpy Man wouldn't let the twins near them.

Oh, that Grumpy Man! The little boys shivered when they thought about the Grumpy. He was tall, very nearly a giant, and he never smiled. They'd met him an hour or two after they arrived.

When they'd reached Granny and Grandpa's cottage by train and horse and cart, the twins had gone racing off to explore the wide fields while the grown-ups blethered. They'd found hayricks and climbed them, sliding down with whoops and squeals of delight, dragging handfuls of sweet, dry hay after them. Then the Grumpy had appeared, waving a stick and shouting angrily. They'd been terrified, running back to Granny's cottage as fast as their legs would carry them.

'That man's a Grumpy,' Adrian declared, with feeling.

Wotherspoon did not regret giving the wee city laddies a fright they'd remember. The hay crop had been too hard won to be scattered by thoughtless bairns. They were lucky lads, he thought as he patiently sorted the tumbled ricks. When he'd indulged in the same caper as a wee loon, his harsh father had fetched him a crack on the lug that had dulled his hearing on one side to this day. Wotherspoon went on his way. He was keeping an alert eye open for his wife. Hannah had gone riding on the black mare, a mettlesome beast, and he was growing anxious. It seemed she'd been out of his sight longer than usual.

Soon after Hannah had set out, the black mare had gone lame. Hannah slid from her back and walked the horse slowly back to the stables. She was gently examining the strained fetlock when she realised she wasn't alone. The stables had once been a bustling place, filled with the contented sounds of Clydes tired after a day's work and the cheery chaffing of horsemen sorting their gear, but now the horses were gone, and it lay deserted and silent.

141

Hannah turned in surprise. 'Why, hullo, Sandy.'

Sandy MacArthur came to the stables when he needed peace to think, for there was no peace and precious little privacy in the bothy. He wanted to think long and hard now Ishbel was back on the farm and widowed. He wasn't pleased when he found the farmer's wife there, though he greeted her politely enough.

Hannah studied the young man astutely. A pleasant friendship had grown between the two. A companionship shared by lonely folk, nothing more, but enough to permit her to ask a bold question. 'Sandy, will you go courting Ishbel now she's widowed?'

He smiled. 'I wish I knew the answer to that, Hannah.'

She moved closer. 'Do you still love her?'

He stirred impatiently. 'Och, love! Love's a hard struggle for a man like me!'

'And a woman like me,' she agreed sadly. She felt in the mood for confidences, and he was a nice lad who'd understand the dilemma. 'I thought I'd never love Hugh Wotherspoon, Sandy, our marriage was just a partnership to save Papa's land, but strange as it may appear, I *do* love him. He's not as he seems. He's thoughtful of me, so caring and kind.' Her head drooped against the mare's flank, and she sighed. 'But he doesn't love me. As you say, love's a hard struggle, sometimes.'

Sandy was heart sorry for her. He knew how painful rejection was. He reached out and pulled her close for comfort. Presently he felt her warm tears against his cheek, and bent his head and kissed her tenderly for pity.

A hand grabbed him by the braces and jerked him back. He was shoved hard against the limewashed wall, Wotherspoon's fist on his chest, the farmer's angry red face inches from his own. Sandy's jaw dropped, and for once in his life he was afraid. He'd never suspected there was such passion in the man.

'Get your gear and go!' Wotherspoon snapped.

Sandy recovered. He'd done nothing wrong, only comforted a sad and lonely lass. His conscience was clear, but . . .

'I'll go, if that's what you want, Wotherspoon.'

'Aye. It is.'

Hannah had been standing as if turned to stone. Now she came alive, hauling wildly at her husband's arm. 'Hugh, don't!'

He paid no attention bar taking his fist from Sandy's chest. 'Get oot o' my sight, MacArthur! Be away from my place by nightfall or I'll no' be responsible . . .'

Sandy dusted off his crumpled shirt. 'I'm going, dinna fash yoursel', Mr Wotherspoon.'

Without a backward glance, he strode out of the stables that had once housed his bonnie Clydes.

Hannah was beside herself with distress. She screamed at her husband: 'Why did you do that? There was no need. For heaven's sake, Hugh, why did you send the poor man away?'

He looked at her, all anger spent, tired and defeated. 'Because I love you, Hannah. I love you so much I canna abide to see another man touch you. I'm a clumsy auld fool that canna speak of love for you, Hannah, my dear lass. That's why I sent that glib young man away.'

'Ah, Hugh!' Tears in her eyes, Hannah flung her arms round her husband's neck and kissed him.

Once again, Catriona's hopes of finding a steady lad for her widowed lass were dashed. It was a sair disappointment when Sandy MacArthur left the toun suddenly without a word to anybody. Nobody knew for certain why he'd gone, though there were rumours. It was whispered in the toun he'd taken fright when Ishbel Mackie came back widowed with two gentry bairns the spitting image o' their da, and another one on the way. Catriona tightened her lips. It could be true. Times were hard, and it was a brave man, or a wealthy one, who would take on a widow and three weans.

Ishbel knew what they were whispering, and Sandy's desertion hurt. Not that she'd wanted a renewal of his courtship, because the loss of Freddie was still a raw and aching void in her life, but she would have welcomed friendship. She'd been given her old job in the dairy while she awaited the birth of the baby, and as the weeks passed she became a dab hand at making the special cheese for which the farm toun was famed. Wotherspoon had a ready market for the delicacy amongst commercial travellers in Edinburgh railway hotels. Ishbel also resumed her friendship with Hannah, who was glowing with happiness these days.

When Ishbel commented on her looks, Hannah laughed. 'Does my contentment show? Then you can blame it on a husband who loves me, and the baby we're waiting for so eagerly, due in the spring. Isn't that a perfectly beautiful time to have a bairn?'

Ishbel was delighted for her friend's sake, but while Hannah and her husband prospered, the laird and his lady in the Big House grew poorer and shabbier as they struggled to settle their debts. More priceless paintings and antique silver went quietly to the saleroom in a vain bid to heat and maintain peeling, echoing apartments now the wounded officers had gone.

Wotherspoon had certainly mellowed. Ishbel suspected her father was not a successful rat-catcher, yet he was kept on. As a sporting man, Donald's attitude to vermin was wrong, it seemed to his daughter.

'I'll no' use poison an' traps. It's only fair to give the wee beasties a chance,' he declared stubbornly. Fortunately, Foxy the terrier had no such squeamish inhibitions, and energetically preserved his master's reputation, and his job.

Freddie's little daughter was born on a dreich day early in December. The steam threshing mill was set up in the stackyard at the time and all hands were on call to see the grain threshed and bagged. There was a wheen of folk around that day, for fourteen hands at least were needed for a good thresh. Wotherspoon was keen to sell his store, for good grain was scarce and prices soaring in the shops. A stone of flour cost nearly one and six to the housewife, and the price still rising.

Catriona was heartily glad of the diversion which kept Donald and her grandsons out of the way for most of the day, the little boys enthralled by a marvel of belts, pulleys and connecting rods churning away with a steaming, fantastic roar which covered any untoward sounds from the cottage.

The steam mill moved from toun to toun, mostly by night, guided by a cheery, sooty-faced crew usually well fortified with drams. Catriona and Ishbel had watched the mill arrive at the stackyard in a shower of firework sparks in the wee sma' hours, while Ishbel timed the slow pains and waited. Her thoughts were sad and lonely at this time, thinking of the man she'd loved and lost, but she kept sorrow to herself as the weary hours dragged on.

'Oh, a wee lass, Ishbel! A darling!' cried Catriona delightedly much later, as the midwife handed her the healthy, wailing baby. Lovingly, she washed her tiny grand-daughter and dressed her in a flannel gown she'd made and embroidered with hope in her heart. Oh, how she'd prayed her daughter would be given the comfort o' a daughter! And the prayer had been answered. 'There, lovie.' Catriona proudly placed the wee mite in her mother's waiting arms and stood back, dabbing her eyes with her apron.

This one was an Alexander, Ishbel decided as she examined her little daughter. Even with a thatch of dark hair the colour of Ishbel's own, the tiny features reminded Ishbel poignantly of Freddie's. She kissed the little one's cheek, and remembered the story he'd told her once about Elspeth the widow-woman who'd founded the Alexanders' fine business, long ago.

'She's an Alexander, Mam. I'll call her Elspeth after the first o' the tribe. I think Freddie would have liked that.'

Catriona nodded. 'Aye, weel, it's an auld-fashioned name, but the wean has an auld-fashioned look. It suits her.'

Ishbel was on her feet quickly after the birth, but as she nursed Freddie's daughter she found her thoughts turning anxiously to his family. She had Freddie's bairns to comfort her, but the Alexanders had nothing. Ishbel remembered the big, gloomy house with the dark blinds drawn at every window, and shivered.

As Christmas approached, she had a word with her mother. 'Mam, would you look after the bairns for a few hours while I take a trip to Edinburgh? Now the weather's turned sour I want to buy combinations for the boys.'

Catriona frowned. 'You're splashing oot, aren't you? What's wrong wi' knitted semmits?'

'Nothing, but their semmits aye hang out the back o' their breeks, the monkeys! They'll catch their death of cold this winter.' She gave her mother a significant look. 'Besides, I want to find out how Mrs Alexander is.'

'Ah!' said Catriona, shaking her head. 'That poor wifie. I've been wondering about her mysel'.'

When Ishbel descended from the train at Waverley, she found Edinburgh putting on a brave tinsel show with Christmas 1922 not far off. But ranks of hunger marchers drawn up on the Mound told a more depressing story. Ishbel watched the procession move off into a bitter wind with banners held high. Their hope was to reach London and lobby Mr Bonar Law, the ailing Prime Minister who'd ousted Lloyd George recently, but she wondered how many would have the stamina or the boots to do it.

Sobered by the sight, she turned away.

Hesitantly, she made her way to the big shop on its dominant site in Princes Street. She spent some time studying the windows before plucking up courage to go in, and was perplexed by the dowdiness of the goods on display.

'Standard suits for gentlemen for £2 17s 6d, readymade from patterns and materials as purchased by His Majesty King George V recently in London', a notice said of the dark navy and brown pinstripes displayed. Another window showed outmoded gowns and hats in dull colours, alternating with sensible, dreary and most unflattering ladies' vests and knickers in thick wincyette. She remembered the black satin and lace underwear she'd drooled over in Paris shops, and smothered a smile. Perhaps not suited to 'East-windy, West-endy', but, oh, how smooth and luxurious against the skin!

Knowing it was unlikely she'd be recognised, unless by William Alexander himself, Ishbel took a deep breath and went in. Once she had been a raw country girl awed by the luxury of the place, but she'd travelled widely since and had a yardstick of beautiful European shops by which to measure Alexander's. She made her way slowly from department to department, a small frown furrowing her brow. Something was very wrong. The whole shop needed a good clean and a lick of fresh paint, which was understandable after the rigours of war and recession, and the dowdy goods on sale could easily be perked up with more judicious buying. What was wrong with the place seemed more fundamental, though she couldn't put a finger on it. She was still frowning when she stopped to buy combinations for the twins and found herself in a quandary over sizes.

'Should I take a larger size for four-year-old boys growing so fast, do you think?' she asked the young assistant.

The bored young woman smothered a yawn. 'Please yoursel'.'

Ishbel bought the combinations, but she was tight-lipped. A shop is only as good as its staff, she thought, and every one of those behind the counter looked depressed and disinterested. She stood hesitating for a moment, then made her way towards the lift.

The cheery little lift boy Ishbel remembered had gone, replaced by a tall, lanky youth. He had a melancholy look, but brightened when she asked to be conveyed to the offices. 'I ken who you are, you're Mrs Freddie!' he cried triumphantly. 'D'you no' mind me, wee Archie? I've been here since I left the school.'

'Archie! But you've grown so tall!' Ishbel smiled, studying him. Looking closer, there were still traces in his skinny frame of the cheery wee lad.

'Och, aye. I shot up so fast my ma was fair demented keeping me in breeks,' he grinned, then became serious. 'We're all sad about Mr Freddie. Devastated. The heart's gone oot o' this place.'

Ishbel stepped out of the lift on the top floor thoughtfully. Archie was right. The heart *had* gone out of the place, and that had caused its serious decline. Oh, if only she could start that heart beating strongly again, for Freddie's sake!

The door at the end of the corridor was open. Ishbel could see her father-in-law seated behind a desk, and hear his voice raised in heated argument.

'I'll no' do it, McPherson. It's too risky wi' trade slumping,' William was saying.

'But Mr Alexander—' The elderly man facing his employer had a desperate look, but turned when he noticed Ishbel framed in the doorway. Her father-in-law saw her at the same moment, and stood up. 'Ishbel, my dear, you're back!' He waved his store manager impatiently away. 'That'll be all, McPherson.'

The silver-haired man straightened and gave Ishbel a

quick, rueful glance as he walked out. William came round the desk and embraced his daughter-in-law. 'Bonnie as ever, my dear! How are the bairns?'

'Thriving. Your wee grand-daughter's a charmer.'

He sighed. 'Yes, I read your letter to Dorothy. I wish I could see Freddie's wee lass, but Eleanor—' He shook his head and sat down wearily. He looked much older, haggard and drawn with worry.

Ishbel's heart went out to him. 'Are things no better at home?'

'Better? Ishbel, they're worse if anything,' he cried bitterly. 'My wife's bed-ridden and poor Dorothy has her hands full looking after her. I've struggled on my own to keep the business going, but I'm at my wits' end. Trade wasn't too bad when Freddie was with us, but after he left there was a slump. Sales have gone from bad to worse. I can't go on, my dear. To be frank, I've lost the will.'

He paused for a moment as if making up his mind, then sighed. 'Ishbel, I've decided the shop must be sold. The family will get a fair price for the value of our good site, but I fear all my loyal salesfolk will be put on the dole. There's nothing else for it. It's the end of the road for me.'

Her mind was working fast, planning ahead. 'Maybe it's the end of an era, but shouldn't that mean the start o' a bold new one? Please, Mr Alexander, won't you let me help?' she begged eagerly.

Chapter 7

'You?' William Alexander's brows rose. 'What could you do?'

Ishbel warmed to the subject. 'Well, I know what fashionable women wear, and I've helped Mam design and sew gowns for a society lady. Freddie had an eye for style in menswear, so I know quite a bit about men's clothing. Then of course there's bairnswear—'

'Exactly!' he broke in. 'You have three young bairns to look after. I thank you for the kind offer, Ishbel, but I don't see how you can possibly help.'

'I could work in the shop.'

William was shocked. 'Work? My dear Ishbel, it's not done for a lady in your position to work.'

She felt desperate. How could she make the man see sense? 'Mr Alexander, I'm a widow with a young family to support and little siller to do it. Years ago, Elspeth Alexander was in the same plight. It's no' beneath my dignity to follow that woman's path and work.'

Normally mild-mannered, William could be mulish on matters of principle. 'No, Ishbel, I won't see my daughter-in-law serving behind a counter. I appreciate the offer, but it's out o' the question.'

She moved forward to the edge of the desk. 'Listen,

don't sell the shop just yet,' she pleaded. 'Let me help you in the office for a while. Tell me what you want done, and I'll make sure your orders are carried out.'

He smiled and shook his head at her naivety. 'My dear lassie, do you think my staff would take orders from you?'

'Why shouldn't they?'

'Because I'd have a strike on my hands in a jiffy if a woman dared order them around,' William said grimly.

His attention was diverted from the argument by a muffled sound outside the room. He turned towards the door, then rose swiftly and dragged it open. His startled floor manager almost fell into the room, down on hands and knees with an ear to the keyhole.

'Aye, McPherson, eavesdroppers never hear good o' themselves, they say,' William remarked drily. 'You may as well join the discussion, since you've overheard the most o' it!'

He held the door wide and the elderly man dusted off his knees and trod sheepishly into the office. William seated himself behind the desk and steepled his fingertips. 'Well, Adam, would *you* take orders from a woman?'

Adam McPherson eyed Freddie's young widow. They said she had spunk, and by God, it was spunk that was needed. He'd worked hard to save the shop, the only workplace he'd known since he was a wee lad sweeping the warehouse floor. Bold measures were required, Adam was convinced, but old Alexander's canny ways thwarted him. Mrs Freddie gave him an appealing look, and Adam made up his mind and spoke out.

'I'd take sensible orders from Felix the Cat, if it was for the good o' the store, Mr Alexander.'

'Hmm.' William drummed his fingertips on the desk top, scowling. 'You're one o' the old school, but there's a rebellious element in the workforce nowadays, Bolshies and suchlike, and I doubt if a woman could handle them. I haven't slept easy in my bed since the Russian Revolution gave agitators their head.'

Adam McPherson put his fists squarely on the desk and leaned over it. 'Mr Alexander, I'm near as old as you so I'll speak out. The world's changed since we were laddies working our apprenticeship together in this shop. There's a wild daftness abroad and a lack of decorum, and who can blame the youngsters with a whole generation of disciplined men gone to the graveyard? It takes a young mind to understand bright young things. We need fresh ideas to bring a new generation to the shop. I think you should give the lass her chance to help us, Mr Alexander. I promise you, I'll back her to the hilt.'

Ishbel held her breath, watching her father-in-law biting his lower lip doubtfully. At last William relaxed and smiled at his old friend and colleague. 'Very well, Adam, I know fine you have the future of the shop at heart, like mysel'.'

He turned sternly to the young woman. 'Ishbel, you'll have six months' working here to prove yoursel'. I hope you've considered what you're doing? You'll live in my house with your bairns, but you'll make other arrangements for the care of them because I'll be working you hard in this office from morn 'til night. You'll have very little time for mothering when you enter a man's world, I promise you,' he warned grimly.

It was a hard decision for a devoted mother, yet she hailed it as a victory for her sex and felt elated. 'You won't sell the shop in the meantime, will you?' she insisted.

'No-o,' he answered grudgingly. 'I'll no' sell – unless I'm forced to.'

Ishbel left the shop in a daze. The full impact of what she'd done hit her and she felt chilled. What have I let myself in for? she wondered. Oh, I must have gone daft, she thought, as she considered the conditions her father-in-law had laid down.

She must leave the farm and the loyal support of her parents, to live in a house where she was not welcomed. Once there, she must entrust her baby daughter and growing boys to another woman's care. Tears blurred her sight. How could she make such sacrifices? Being an intelligent woman, however, she could see through William's scheme. He hoped to make the decision so difficult and the work so hard, she wouldn't stick to the job. The thought stiffened her backbone. Well, we'll see about that! she thought.

There was a one-legged war veteran turning the handle of a barrel organ at the edge of the pavement, shivering in the bitter wind blowing nor'-easterly straight from the Forth. Ishbel glanced at the poor soul with pity, and the man met her compassionate gaze and ducked his head in shame. She searched in her purse and dropped a florin in his cap before walking on. At least she had the offer of a stout roof over her head, and a job. She was luckier than most in these hard times.

In Lothian Road she paused for a moment outside a barber's shop, intrigued when an elegant lady with neatly bobbed hair made a triumphal exit from that exclusively male domain. A new start? Ishbel pondered. Och, well, why not? Widow's weeds did not become her, and she knew that although Freddie had loved her beautiful, long dark hair, he would have been scathing of her dowdy looks today. She would always mourn him but life must go on, and she fancied a new, smart image to bolster her morale. Ishbel made her way purposefully into the barber's.

Dorothy Alexander answered the door when Ishbel arrived at the Alexanders' mansion some time later. Her sister-in-law gave a delighted cry and hugged her. 'Oh, Ishbel, it's just wonderful to see you!'

After this emotional greeting, Dorothy stood back, wiping her eyes, and Ishbel saw how thin and careworn her once plump little sister-in-law had become. Her heart ached for Dorothy. 'I called to ask how your mother was, love.'

Dorothy sighed. 'There's not much improvement. She's lain in bed so long the muscles have wasted, and she can't walk now. I doubt if Mother will ever leave her bed again, Ishbel, and to crown it all, dear old Dr Campbell's retiring and a new man will take his place. Mother is quite devastated. She has Dr Campbell under her thumb, and fears another doctor may not prove so docile.'

'I'm so sad for your mother. She was such a live-wire.'

'Yes,' Dorothy agreed. She stared at Ishbel curiously. 'I say, you look different somehow.'

Ishbel gaily removed her bonnet. 'It's the hair. I've had it bobbed.' She giggled. 'D'you know, Dorothy, since I had it done, I feel like a giddy goat!'

Dorothy laughed heartily. 'I must try it myself some-time.' The laughter faded and she sighed. 'I haven't laughed for a long time, Ishbel. There's been precious little to laugh about since you left.'

155

Ishbel laid a hand on her arm. 'Dorothy, you told me once your family needed me, do you remember?'

'Yes, my dear. I meant it.'

'I went to the shop this afternoon to buy combinations for the boys. I was so shocked by its rundown state I offered to help your father. He's reluctantly agreed to take me on for six months' trial. I have my doubts as to the wisdom of what I've done. What do you think?'

Dorothy was overjoyed. 'Oh, my dear! You don't know what a relief that is to me! I've been watching my poor father kill himself with work and worry. You'll take a load off his shoulders, I'm sure. This is wonderful news.'

'That's the good news!' said Ishbel ominously. 'Now for the bad. Your father insists I live here with the bairns, and I don't know what your ma will say to that! Also, he's ordered me to find someone to care for my weans while I go out to work.'

'Look no further,' Dorothy beamed happily. 'Auntie Dorothy will do the needful, ably assisted by dear old Florrie who has a weird and wily way with weans.'

Ishbel was taken aback, overwhelmed by the generous offer. 'But, Dorothy, the boys can be a handful, and the baby's awful fretful these days. I don't have enough milk to satisfy her, and she's colicky on the bottle.'

Dorothy laughed. 'My dear, having put up with dear Mother's tantrums for months, a colicky baby will be a picnic!'

Catriona was in a tizzy. She was struggling to come to terms with her daughter's shocking decision while the baby girned and grizzled against her shoulder. To stretch her nerves even tighter, her husband played with his latest acquisition, a gramophone. Donald had proudly humped it home that morning, having paid an out-going cottar five bob for it. Five bob they could ill afford, mind you! It was an odd-looking contraption, consisting of a turntable covered in red felt and a loudspeaker mushrooming from the base like a huge varnished lily. Half a dozen precious records went with it, one of them cracked, and you wound the machine up by means of a handle at the side.

Long-suffering Catriona thought if she heard 'Tea for Two' from *No, No, Nanette* once more, she'd hit somebody – and she knew who it would be.

Of course the little boys were glued to this marvel. 'Grandpa, play "Tiptoe Through the Tulips" again!' ordered Adrian.

'Hey, sonny, that's the cracked one!'

'I know. It's the funniest, Grandpa.'

So of course, Donald, the big bairn, played it. The twins rolled around on the floor laughing when it came to the 'T-toe-T-toe-T-toe' bit, and Catriona gritted her teeth and prayed for patience.

'What were you saying, love?' she asked Ishbel, rubbing the sleepy baby's back.

'I'll need a really smart outfit for the shop, Mam. Something like this.' She pointed, and the two women pored over the magazine Ishbel had bought in the city with this purpose in mind.

'I could make that from one of your old winter frocks,' Catriona decided. 'It's just a case of lowering the waist and lifting the hem. Women have nae shape anyway these days – just like laddies, straight from the neck down. It's nae wonder you can't buy decent whalebone corsets for love nor money,' she grumbled.

Donald was tuned in to the women's conversation, indignant at the shearing of his lass's long, raven locks. 'Nae shape and nae hair. My lass's bonnie hair cut short like a wee laddie! Did you ever see the like, Catriona?'

'You must admit it's neat, Pa!' Ishbel protested.

'Aye, so's a bald heid,' growled Donald, and defiantly put on his favourite record, 'Tea for Two'.

'I don't want to wear combinations,' girned Brian, who had a bad cold and was feeling miserable and hard done by.

'Wheest!' hissed his grandmother, who was glaring fiercely at the gramophone. 'You must wear them now your mammy's gone an' spent good money buying them. You can't walk about Grandfather Alexander's hoose wi' the tail o' your semmit hanging out o' your breeks.'

Brian started to sob in earnest. 'I don't want to live in Grandfather Alexander's hoose and wear combinations. I want to stay here wi' Foxy an' my grandpa an' my mammy's mammy.'

Catriona and Ishbel exchanged worried glances, and Donald lifted the sad little boy on to his knee and cuddled him. 'You'll get on just fine wi' your daddy's folk, son. You'll go to a grand school in Edinburgh and be taught to speak pink like the gentry, an' your auld granny an' grandpa will have to mind their p's and q's when you come to visit. Now how about a nice cup o' cocoa, and away to your beddie?'

So Brian was petted and comforted and settled in the little bed under the eaves he shared with Adrian, the bad cold eased by Donald's thick working sock wrapped lovingly round his throat, and a liberal rub of eucalyptus oil on chest and back.

* * *

Catriona decided Ishbel's departure required her co-operation, and volunteered to accompany her daughter and the weans when they flitted to Edinburgh. Indeed, it wasn't much of a flitting, only an old carpet bag and the clothes they stood up in. Catriona had studied Ishbel's magazine thoroughly on her own account, and by dint of cutting the brim off her old Sunday bonnet and adding a spot of trimming here and there, had fashioned a cloche hat that would pass muster wi' Morningside. Furtively, she'd adjusted her own waistline downwards and eased three inches off her skirt. Fortunately her ankles were still good, thank the Lord. After splashing out secretly on a pair of brown lisle stockings from the Co-op van, she felt like the bee's knees.

They set off for Edinburgh by train the day after Christmas. Christmas Day had been an ordinary working day on the farm as usual, but Catriona had tried to make it special for the bairns' sake. She'd made a pot of soup, the kale sweetened and enriched by hard frost, followed by a clootie dumpling with a threepenny bit in it, which she suspected Donald had swallowed.

Today, the wee boys clutched net stockings filled with sweeties, cheap toys and games, which their mother had bought in Edinburgh in a fit of reckless extravagance. The twins could hardly bring themselves to open this wonderful cornucopia of goodies, delicately picking out dolly mixtures through the white net and savouring each tiny bite as the train chuffed along. Catriona nodded contentedly in one corner of the compartment, while baby Elspeth lay fast asleep opposite, cradled in her mother's arms.

Ishbel was plagued with doubts at the thought of leaving

her children every day, even in kindly Dorothy's care. But I'm near penniless, and must work at something, she thought. She rocked the baby in her arms. This little one would never know a father's love. It seemed tragic that Elspeth must be deprived of a mother, too. Ishbel stared unhappily through the carriage window, but saw little of the passing scene, for it was blurred with tears.

Catriona's courage nearly failed when they reached the door of the Alexanders' mansion. It was much grander than she'd expected. She backed away when Dorothy answered the bell. 'I'll away home now I've seen Ishbel and the bairns safe and sound, Miss Alexander,' she said nervously.

Dorothy laughed and grabbed her arm. 'I'm afraid you won't get off so easily, Mrs Mackie. My mother's looking forward to meeting her old friend, and you'll stay the night as planned. I'll drive you to the station tomorrow morning.'

Ishbel was glad of her mother's support as Dorothy led the way upstairs to Eleanor Alexander's bedroom. The boys were unusually quiet. The house was familiar to them, but held dark memories.

Dorothy paused outside the door, whispering, 'You'll see a big difference in her, but she's much brighter today and looking forward to your visit.' Raising her voice to a cheerful pitch for the invalid's benefit, she opened the door and ushered them in. 'Here they are, Mother!'

Eleanor Alexander had made an effort that day. On her carefully waved white hair she wore a grey silk toque as popularised by the stately Queen Mary, and matching silk bedjacket trimmed with pale blue ostrich feathers. Dressing up had exhausted her and she could barely raise a smile for the apprehensive little group that gathered round the end of the bed. Months ago she'd regretted the harsh words spoken to her daughter-in-law, but for the life of her couldn't think of a way to heal the breach, short of saying 'Sorry'. That small word stuck in Eleanor Alexander's throat.

'So you have a little girl?' she said abruptly.

'Yes, Mrs Alexander. She's called Elspeth.' Ishbel was shocked by the change in her mother-in-law. The listless invalid moved her to pity. She brought the baby to Eleanor's bedside and drew aside the shawl to let the old lady study the sleeping baby's face.

Eleanor stared down at the tiny creature. Dark-haired, beautiful, but not like her mother. More like George and Freddie and those twin boys whose resemblance to their father and uncle was heartbreaking. How can I have bairns in my house who remind me constantly of my dear lost lads? she wondered and turned her head away from the baby. 'This'll mean more work for Dorothy. I'm against the scheme!' she said dourly.

Ishbel was hurt by her mother-in-law's indifference, but tried to have patience. 'Mr Alexander needs help in the shop, and I'm willing to do what I can. Dorothy offered to look after the bairns. It was her idea, and she says she's pleased to do it. I'd never impose upon her good nature otherwise, Mrs Alexander.'

'Florrie will help too, Mother,' put in Dorothy anxiously, terrified lest her mother vetoed the arrangement. Dorothy longed for children, and this was a chance to savour the joys of mothering at second hand. She was over forty, in everyone's eyes a hopeless spinster, and sometimes when the night was dark and she lay sleepless, Dorothy shed bitter tears for her barren life.

The baby wakened with a fretful whimper and Dorothy turned eagerly to her sister-in-law. 'Is she needing to be fed, Ishbel? Come downstairs, I'm longing to show her to Florrie.'

'Can we come too, Aunt Dorothy?' asked Adrian, edging towards the door. The hot, stuffy room with its sad, elderly invalid was not to his taste, and he longed to escape.

'Kiss your Grandmother Alexander first, boys,' ordered Catriona. She'd been consumed with pity at sight of her old friend, so changed from the brisk lady she remembered with affection. Catriona nudged her reluctant grandsons forward to the invalid's bedside.

Adrian bravely planted a kiss on the dry old cheek and shot out of the door after his mother and sister. Brian hesitated, staring fascinated at the figure seated in the richly appointed bed. Somehow the aged woman reminded Brian of his daddy in heaven. It was rude to stare, but he couldn't help doing so open-mouthed. Grandmother Alexander glared at him with blue-grey eyes that were like faded memories of his father's. 'Well, get on with it, boy!'

He moved closer. 'Mammy made us wear combinations to come and live with you, and I don't like combinations. They itch something awful,' he confided to those well-remembered eyes. With amazement he watched a wee spark of amusement light in them.

'East-windy, West-endy, my lad!' Eleanor retorted. 'You'll be glad of itchy combinations when you go skating on Blackford pond. Your father and uncle usually had a holiday from school to go skating, and there's skates in the attic. Now, you'd best get on with the kissing and get it over with,' she said with the merest ghost of a smile, presenting her cheek.

He kissed the pale cheek gingerly and found it fragrantly soft, scented with the same vanishing cream Granny Mackie bought from the Co-op van, when she could spare a bob.

Left alone, the two older women relaxed. They studied one another and found their friendship still held fast. Eleanor took off the toque and sank back wearily against the pillows with a heavy sigh. 'Aye, Catriona, I've gone far down the hill.'

'Can you no' walk a step or two, love?'

'No, I've been too long in my bed. I doubt if I'll leave it now.' Eleanor lay quiet for a moment, pleating the linen sheet nervously between her fingers. 'I've been too hard on your lass, Catriona. It was cruel to blame Ishbel for my boy's accident. I'm – I'm sorry.'

Catriona sat down beside her, taking the restless hand in hers. 'Och, Ishbel knows fine you were beside yoursel' wi' grief at the time, dear. She bears you no grudge. Dinna fash yoursel', Eleanor.'

'But how can she work in the shop, Catriona? It lets the whole family down for Freddie's widow to have to earn a living. Besides, she knows nothing about shops,' complained the sick woman.

'Och, it's changed days, love. Ladies drove ambulances in the war and were even clippies on the buses. It gave the younger ones funny notions,' Catriona answered. 'Ishbel has a good heid on her shoulders. When she was at the school she was the quickest o' them all at figuring, and her nose was never out o' a book. Ishbel and the laird's crippled lassie were a right pair o' wee bookworms. She'll help your man all she can, and by what she's let slip, the poor soul's sair needing help.'

'Oh, I feel so useless!' mourned Eleanor. 'Poor Dorothy, I give her so much work, and now she has Ishbel's wee bairns to look after too.'

Catriona's eyes twinkled. 'If you were to ask me, Miss Dorothy looked pleased as Punch at the prospect. I wouldna worry about Dorothy and the bairns. They'll get on fine.'

Eleanor lay quietly for a time, her thoughts far away. 'Catriona,' she said presently, 'what about the young man who was keen on Ishbel before Freddie stepped in? Will he come courting now she's widowed?'

'You mean Sandy MacArthur?' Catriona sighed. 'It's unlikely. He did a moonlight flit when Ishbel came back to the farm wi' two young bairns and another on the way. I dinna blame him, mind you. It's a brave man that'll take on a burden like that, these chancy times.'

After Wotherspoon's summary dismissal, Sandy MacArthur went straight to the bothy and changed into his Saturday clothes. He bequeathed his two kists to the tractorman, then stuffed spare clothing, the melodeon and a few working tools into his old kitbag. With that strapped to the carrier of his bike, he left the farm toun for good. The sizeable sum he'd gathered in savings had been cannily consigned to an Edinburgh bank months ago, but the bankbook made a comforting bulge in the inside jacket pocket of his Saturday bicycle claes. Sandy had ambitious plans which he still hoped would earn him wealth one day to wave in Ishbel Alexander's face. His feelings for her were a confused mixture of love and hate. He must just put up with the confusion, for he was a proud man. One thing was sure – I'll never go seeking Ishbel Alexander again, he vowed.

Sandy had planned for departure, though it had come sooner than expected because of an innocent kiss. Without a backward glance at fields he'd walked in all weathers with his bonnie Clydes, he settled down to cycle steadily along the Edinburgh Road.

On reaching the city he changed course a little for he'd an important mission before attending to his own business with a blacksmith friend in the Corstorphine district. Sandy headed for the St Cuthbert's stableyard. He settled down patiently to wait and presently was rewarded by the sight of a finely caparisoned young Clydesdale stepping briskly homewards, harnessed to the Co-operative bakery cart. His Bertie, in gleaming condition and happy in his work! There was moisture in Sandy's eye as he watched his bonnie horse trot by. Reassured, he cycled on.

The sickly smell from the brewery led him by the nose, and after some searching, Sandy dismounted at the stables. There was a coachman hosing down the wheels of a shining dray, and several Clydes poking their long white faces curiously into the yard above stable doors. Sandy had a good look around, but none of the horses was Big Bob.

He questioned the coachman for news of his lead horse, and the man pushed back his bonnet and scratched his head. 'Oh, that one! He didna tak' to the team in the dray. I persevered wi' him for a good while, but in the end he had to go. I'm told the boss sold him at the Perth horse market to Harry Watt, a carter frae Dundee, for the jute trade.'

Sandy went sadly on his way. Big Bob, his faithful auld

friend, sent to pull a jute cart in hilly Dundee! What a come-down for the brave beast. Something must be done. He felt heavily responsible for the horse's plight. Though he knew in his heart the future lay with machines on the farm, as a ploughman he'd taken the Horseman's Oath and that put heavy responsibility on him to ensure no cruelty or harm befell his horses. Big Bob's fate wouldn't let Sandy rest easy. He must see for himself the Clydesdale was working happily and treated well. Heartsore, Sandy headed the bicycle towards the westering sun and the hill above the village of Corstorphine, now absorbed into the hungry, spreading city.

Adam McPherson was as good as his word. He assembled the staff at 8.30 on Ishbel's first morning and introduced her with a few kind words. 'And I'm sure you'll extend a hearty welcome to Mrs Freddie, and join me in assuring her she can depend upon our help and good wishes in her new job,' he said, fixing the workforce with a challenging eye.

There were Bolshies everywhere. There was a scatter of polite applause from old timers but the younger element remained ominously silent, and someone muttered audibly, 'Management spy!'

It was the loneliest moment of Ishbel's life. She stood beside old Adam and watched the men and women who were the lifeblood of Alexander's disperse to their posts. Most looked sceptical and unfriendly. They didn't want a member of the Alexander family working in their midst, least of all a woman member. She couldn't blame them.

The manager took her arm and led her across to a stately lady whose greying hair was regimented into Marcel waves. 'This is Clara, our head buyer, Ishbel. She'll show you the

166

ropes.' He left the two women together. He was throwing the lass in at the deep end, eager to test her mettle.

Ishbel smiled at the elegant creature. Fortunately, she knew her own shining cap of dark, bobbed hair suited her, and the dress Mam had created skimmed her slim figure flatteringly and was the height of fashion. Ishbel's confidence soared, but Clara's expression remained frosty. 'One thing you must always remember, Ishbel, Alexander's remains at the forefront of quality and fashion in this city,' she said.

'That will change, I hope,' Ishbel smiled, eyes twinkling. 'My intention is to put Alexander's far ahead of everyone else.'

Clara blinked. 'I don't know how that can be done.'

'Maybe by keeping an eye on Paris and London, and on American fads. You'll be visiting London regularly in your job, of course?'

The older woman turned beetroot red and looked decidedly uncomfortable. 'Er – well, no. That's hardly necessary when our stockists know just what we want.'

'Oh, but don't you study the catalogues?' said Ishbel in surprise. 'There are lovely new lines in dresses, and gorgeous crêpe de chine underwear.'

'Quite unsuitable for Edinburgh's climate!'

'East-windy, West-endy?'

'Exactly. Now, if you will excuse me?' And Clara went quickly on her way.

Ishbel had an objective in mind before heading towards the top floor offices. She walked past counters where staff stared unsmiling or awkwardly refused to meet her eye. There was a pervading atmosphere of gloom. Morale was

low, she thought, and who could blame them? Rumours
were obviously rife, and no doubt they expected notice of
dismissal any day. She ran a finger along a shelf and
grimaced at the dust. The place could do with a good clean.
What were the early morning cleaners up to? Ishbel
resolved to be there next morning at 5.30, to find out for
herself.

She reached the Children's Department and found the
bored young assistant still yawning drearily. 'Why are you
bored?' Ishbel demanded.

'Eh?' The girl's jaw dropped. She studied Ishbel warily
and decided she wasn't in for a telling off. 'Och, I'm the
oldest o' seven bairns and I was put here 'cause they
thought I'd know all about bairns' clothes. Well, so I do,
Mrs Freddie. I've helped Ma do the washing and ironing
and mending. But I jumped at the chance to work at
Alexander's so's I could get away from all that.'

'You had something else in mind?'

The girl paused, then went on with a rush. 'It's perfume
I'm interested in. My ma says I'm aye sniffing.' She covered
her mouth and giggled. 'Och, I don't mean colds in the
heid! No, flowers and suchlike. Sometimes I buy a wee
bottle o' Californian Poppy out o' Woolies on the sly. My
ma says to me, "Jeannie, you've a nose for scent like a
tinker's pup."'

'Well, a good nose shouldn't be wasted.' Ishbel smiled at
the girl, who looked alert and pretty when talking on her
favourite subject. 'I'll see what can be done for you,
Jeannie,' she promised.

William Alexander put his head in his hands and groaned.
For the past few weeks, since his daughter-in-law had

entered his employ, he'd heard nothing but gripes and grumbles from his staff. The head buyer's elderly mother had just left his office in venomous mood. She was a grim old tyrant who objected strongly to being left on her own while her daughter Clara, who'd been quite biddable until she came under Ishbel's influence, staged a revolt and traipsed off to London. On top of that, he'd dealt with a cleaners' deputation earlier in the week, claiming Ishbel had gone through the store like a dose of liver salts early one morning, giving them all the fright of their lives. He'd noticed a big improvement in the cleanliness of the store since, but still!

Then there was tearful Mrs Bingham from Perfumery to be comforted and placated. She'd been seconded to the Children's Department on orders from Ishbel, and considered the move demotion. Enough was enough! William went in search of his daughter-in-law.

She was sitting in the next-door office that had once belonged to Freddie, engrossed in a circular which appeared to contain little but grocery items. The sight infuriated William. He'd shared McPherson's hope that a fresh young mind could light on something to make trade pick up, but instead Ishbel seemed bent on wrecking what little they had. She glanced up from lists of foodstuffs and smiled at him, bright and eager, eyes sparkling.

'Mr Alexander, couldn't we open a new department for high-class grocery products? "Delicatessen" they call it. Isn't that a lovely word? It means exotic things like pickles and Indian chutneys, or freshly sliced boiled ham and farm cheese like I used to make at Wotherspoon's. Oh, and I can see wee pots of Scottish jam and marmalade for foreign visitors to take home, and maybe Edinburgh Rock in tartan packets. Mr Alexander, couldn't we . . . ?' She faltered in mid-sentence, catching sight of William's thunderous expression.

'Ishbel, I never heard such nonsense! Have you gone daft? Groceries and sweets in a high-class clothing store?'

'But in America . . .'

'Och, America!' he scowled, dismissing that vast country with a scornful wave of the hand. 'They have their problems in America, with drink prohibited and the law broken every minute of the day. Don't hold America up to me as an example of progress! My staff are upset enough already, thanks to your new ideas. Mrs Bingham is offended because you shifted her from Perfumery to Bairnswear and put an inexperienced lassie in her place.'

'Mr McPherson agreed!'

'I thought the man had mair sense.'

'Mrs Bingham's a kindly soul wi' no sense of smell but a lovely way wi' bairns. She'll be an asset to the Children's Department once she settles in. And Jeannie's a bright youngster wi' a keen nose for perfume. She'll do well in Perfumery,' declared Ishbel staunchly.

William tore his hair. 'Ishbel, you're inexperienced and I expected mistakes, but enough's enough. You'll have to go.' He'd never enjoyed arguments and came out in a cold sweat now. His stomach was heaving because of the unpleasant scene and he didn't feel well, but he was determined Ishbel would not get the better of him.

She was distressed and angry. Working in the big store had been a fascinating experience. The possibilities were endless. She'd read every retail and marketing publication she could lay hands on, and just when she was seeing the path ahead more clearly, her father-in-law wanted her to leave. It nearly broke her heart. 'You promised to give me six months!' she protested angrily.

'Six months? By that time you'll have me in the bankruptcy court!' cried William, temper flaring.

'You're breaking your promise. I thought you prided yoursel' on integrity, Mr Alexander!'

The jibe struck deep and he clenched his fists. 'So I do, damn you! But can't you get it into your heid it's ruin we're facing? All because – of you—' William gasped out the words wrathfully, clutching at his chest. His heart pounded, and the room was spinning. Turning ashen, he fumbled for the edge of the desk and dropped to his knees with a groan. Ishbel screamed and ran to his aid, cradling the old man in her arms as she called frantically for help.

William lay staring up at her as the scene became increasingly misty. He knew he was ill, very ill, but even so was aware of a glimmer of triumph. 'Have to sell now, Ishbel. Nothing else for it,' he whispered thickly, before slipping quietly away into the mists which were invading his mind.

Chapter 8

'This is a sad day for Alexander's, Ishbel,' sighed Adam McPherson as his sick employer was carried to the waiting ambulance. 'Mr Alexander gave everything he had to keep the shop going, even his health, poor man. Aye, I fear we're seeing the last of a grand institution in this city.'

Ishbel flung on a coat, ready to follow her father-in-law to hospital, then paused in the doorway. The shop assistants were huddled in concerned groups around the store, and she could read despair on every face. They knew they faced the prospect of unemployment, and there were precious few jobs to be had in Edinburgh. She turned to the store manager. 'The show must go on, Adam. There are customers waiting to be served so get everyone back to work, will you, please?'

He stared at her thoughtfully for a moment, then went off quietly to do her bidding.

Ishbel lost track of time as she sat waiting in the hospital corridor, but eventually a white-coated doctor appeared from the ward and advanced towards her. He looked grave. 'I'm afraid the poor gentleman has suffered a complete mental breakdown, Mrs Alexander. I'd say he's worn out with work and worry, like so many businessmen these days.'

She choked back tears. 'But he'll recover, won't he?'

'Oh, yes. He'll recover – after a fashion.'

'What does that mean?' she demanded sharply.

'It means he must retire. He shouldn't have any stress or worry whatsoever, or else I'm afraid...' The doctor shrugged eloquently. He noted Ishbel's distress and patted her shoulder. 'Never mind, his physical condition is good. He should be quite fit to potter around for the rest of his life, although quite frankly, I suspect the brain function has been damaged by a slight stroke.'

This was terrible news and Ishbel was in despair. What about the shop? There was no hope for Alexander's now, and nobody to keep the shop going. It must be sold as William had predicted.

'May I see my father-in-law?' she asked in sadly subdued tones. At least she could comfort the old man who must be devastated by this cruel blow.

'Of course,' agreed the doctor kindly, leading the way.

William did not need comforting. He lay peacefully asleep, his expression blank as a baby's. Ishbel took his hand and spoke his name gently and the old man opened his eyes with a start and recognised her. He seemed surprised, blinking at her. 'Why, Ishbel, what are you doing here?' He looked around with a puzzled air. 'Where am I?'

'You're in hospital, love. You've been working too hard, and now you must rest and leave everything to me.'

He yawned widely. 'Yes, must rest. Must leave everything to Ishbel,' he murmured obediently. The grip of his thin fingers slackened and he drifted quietly off to sleep again. Ishbel stood looking down at him in dismay. If William had lost his sure grip on the business, what then?

She returned to the shop via one of the electric trams whose arrival in Princes Street Florrie had feared. Florrie wasn't the only one who'd voiced misgivings. There had been a stushie in the press, and great alarm expressed lest unsightly overhead wires spoil the look of the capital's most famous street. They needn't have bothered, Ishbel thought as she alighted. The wires had been skilfully set in place along elegant central pillars, and all this achieved in one remarkable overnight operation.

Adam McPherson pounced on Ishbel when she appeared and hustled her into the little buckie he called an office. 'What's the news of Mr William?'

'Not good, I'm afraid.' She told him briefly the future the doctor had outlined and her own concern. 'So you see, Adam, the shop will have to close. There's no Alexanders left to keep it going.'

He looked at her steadily. 'There's you.'

'Me?' She laughed incredulously. 'My father-in-law gave me the sack before he was taken ill. He insisted I was upsetting staff and ruining trade.'

'The staff needs upsetting! Do 'em a world o' good,' retorted Adam. 'And as for trade, it's picking up. There's a more optimistic air in this shop, I feel it in my bones.'

'But that's got nothing to do with me!'

'Maybe no', but if you don't keep going we'll never know for sure, will we?' he argued.

Ishbel was silent. Faced with this crisis her inexperience seemed daunting. The thought of taking over from William flung her into a panic. 'I couldn't do it on my own!' she cried.

He patted her arm reassuringly. 'Of course not, Ishbel. But I'll be right behind you. So will the staff.'

'Oh, will they?' she said doubtfully. She'd encountered only suspicion and resentment so far from the staff of Alexander's.

Adam laughed. 'Don't you worry, lass. They know which side their bread's buttered. And if they don't, I'll tell 'em!'

Baby Elspeth was too young to care, but the twins missed their mother. She'd always been there when they needed her, but they couldn't shake off the bad memory of another time she'd rushed off and left them, and their happy world had crashed around them. They'd lost a wonderful father that awful day, and now it seemed they were losing a mother. She left the house before they were awake, and didn't return until they were ready for bed.

They missed easy-going Granny and Grandpa Mackie and the freedom of the countryside, but there were compensations. Grandfather Alexander's illness had disrupted the household and the twins had more freedom to explore the district. Florrie was not fleet of foot, and the park was as far as she could manage while pushing Elspeth's pram. Auntie Dorothy could walk for miles when occasion demanded, but she was fully occupied looking after the baby and her two invalids. The little boys covered remarkable distances exploring Edinburgh, especially after an unexpected visit from Great-auntie Nellie.

It wasn't what you'd call a formal visit, for Nellie came to the back door dressed in Newhaven fish-wife's costume, with a full creel of fresh herring slung on her back. Nellie

176

was on the lookout for Ishbel, but in her niece's absence she and Florrie struck up an immediate rapport over a cup of tea. While the two women cooed and clucked over the baby, the twins inspected their colourful relative with open-mouthed wonder. Nellie brought with her a strong smell of fish, a tang of the sea, and a taste of adventure.

'I never thought I'd see the day I was a fish-wifie, ken, Florrie,' Nellie confided with a laugh. 'But when I married my second hubby last year his business was in the doldrums, dealing just wi' poor folk in Newhaven and Leith, so I persuaded him to let me hawk fish in the West End.'

'Guid idea,' nodded Florrie. 'Though mind you, Morningside's no' what it was.'

'Aye, I've noticed. Curtains on the windaes, and nae sheets on the beds.'

'Aye, they're hard times,' sighed Florrie. 'Here's Mrs Freddie working for a living to keep her fatherless bairns. The wee laddies are awful wearied without their ma, and them no' at the school yet.'

Auntie Nellie smiled kindly at the boys. 'Never mind, you can come an' help your Auntie Nellie sell caller herrin' to the rich folk.'

'What's caller herrin'?' asked Adrian curiously.

'They're fresh herrin', lovie. My man was out wi' his boat last night seeking a shoal o' the silver darlin's, and these are them in the creel. You'll no' get much fresher than that!' laughed Auntie Nellie.

When Nellie visited the house after that first time, the twins accompanied her on her round and picked up much colourful information about the city on the way. Brian had inherited his father's musical ear, and listened enthralled to a peal of eight fixed bells in the belfry of St Andrew's church in George Street, which Auntie Nellie swore chimed out the fish-wives' age-old chant:

'Wha'll buy my caller herrin'?'

The sound fired his lively imagination with thoughts of the sea, and of the ships that left Granton and Leith docks to steam away to distant lands whose shores the little boy could only imagine.

Eleanor Alexander braced herself for her first visit from the doctor who'd taken dear old Dr Campbell's place. When Florrie showed in a young man who seemed hardly out of the schoolroom, Eleanor nearly fell out of bed in horror. Dr Michael Burton informed her cheerily that he was an Englishman, and hailed from London.

'What brought you to Edinburgh?' asked Eleanor truculently.

'Your city's always been a centre of medical excellence, Mrs Alexander.'

'Oh, aye, Burke and Hare, the body-snatchers!'

Dr Burton laughed. 'I was thinking of the less criminal element. Dr James Simpson who discovered the benefits of chloroform, for example.' He sat down beside her in friendly fashion. 'Now, what's your problem?'

Eleanor snorted. 'That's for you to tell me!'

He gave her a thoughtful look. 'Oh, I don't think so. I've studied Dr Campbell's notes on your case very thoroughly, Mrs Alexander, and I've reached the conclusion there's nothing wrong with you.'

Eleanor shot up in bed in great agitation. 'Don't be daft! D'you think I'd be lying here in this bed if there's nothing wrong?'

He was unperturbed. 'You could be. That's why I'm asking you, what's your problem?'

She blinked and spluttered, not sure whether to order him out of the house or burst into tears. Fancy being landed with a cruel, tactless youngster after kind Dr Campbell's sympathetic ministrations! She shouted at him irritably, 'I can't walk. That's my problem!'

His expression was kind and his eyes compassionate. 'If that's the only problem, then it can be solved. You could walk again if you really want to, Mrs Alexander.'

Eleanor was agitated and confused. She wished the fresh-faced young man would leave so she could indulge her misery and sob into her pillow. 'Dr Campbell did his best to cure me and failed. What makes you think you'll fare better?' she demanded pettishly.

He stood up. 'I didn't offer to cure you myself, ma'am. I said you could walk again if you really want to. That's up to you, isn't it?'

He took his leave, but turned in the doorway and smiled gently. 'Think about it, Mrs Alexander. I'll look in again very soon.'

An epidemic of grass sickness that spring carried off all but two of Wotherspoon's remaining Clydesdales. Grass sickness was a deadly scourge that struck suddenly and swiftly. Some said it came over from France after the war with the Yeomanry horses, and took hold first in the soldiers' camp at Barry Buddon outside Dundee before spreading rapidly north and south. It was the loss of the horses, more than anything, that speeded the arrival of tractors on the farm.

Grass sickness was uppermost in Catriona Mackie's thoughts when she opened the door to frenzied knocking and found Wotherspoon standing on the doorstep looking wild-eyed. The man was more distressed than she'd ever seen him. 'Catriona, can you come? It's Hannah!'

She put a hand to her heart. 'Is it the bairn?'

'Aye. The midwife's with her, but the woman needs help. The doctor's out on call and no' to be found,' Wotherspoon told her.

When she'd hurriedly banked the fire and closed the door behind her, the man set off at such a pace Catriona could hardly match it. There was little conversation until the farmer paused outside the farmhouse door. The man's expression was so distracted she drew back in alarm.

'We longed for this bairn, Catriona, we wanted it sair, but if it comes to a choice between mother and bairn, save Hannah, for God's sake! Save my dear lassie for me.'

She was shocked by the depth of the man's suffering. She'd seen fathers-to-be in a state before, but this was beyond reason. She patted his arm gently. 'Och, it'll no' come to that, Mr Wotherspoon. They'll both be fine, you'll see.'

'You haven't seen her. You haven't heard her!' he groaned, staring at Catriona with tortured eyes. 'Hannah was never strong, it was just the brave heart of her made you believe she was. She should never have had a bairn. I should never have let it happen. I blame mysel'. I'll always blame mysel' to the end o' my days.'

Catriona felt a chill strike her, infected by the man's abject despair. She left him without a word and hurried into the house. She stood listening apprehensively at the bottom of the stairs. It was quiet, then a sound filtered from an upstairs room which she recognised as the healthy cry of a newborn infant. Catriona closed her eyes thankfully for a moment. At least one o' them's alive! she thought.

The bedroom was almost unbearably hot, the capable midwife tousle-haired and grim-faced. The kitchen-maidie who helped in the house was crouched nearby, cradling a wee scrap of humanity wrapped in a towel. There were tears on the lassie's lashes and the horror of what she'd seen reflected in her eyes. She hugged the baby and it gave another strong, mewing cry.

The only peaceful sight in the disordered room was Hannah. She lay pale and quiet, scarcely breathing. Catriona looked at the midwife questioningly and the exhausted woman gave her head a sad little shake. Looking down at the dying young mother, Catriona's heart grew heavy with grief. She took Hannah's hand gently and spoke her name, and after a moment Hannah opened her eyes and her pale lips twitched into a smile.

'It's a girl, Mrs Mackie. Oh, I wanted a wee girl so much!' The effort of speech was too much for her failing strength and her eyes closed wearily. 'Hugh? Is Hugh there?' she whispered.

He had followed Catriona upstairs. He stood in the doorway, blind to everything but the state of his wife. His grief as he took in the situation was terrible to see, and the women looked at one another in distress then stole quietly away with the newborn infant. The man hadn't spared a glance for his bairn.

Wotherspoon knelt beside Hannah and raised her hand to his lips. She opened her eyes and smiled. For a moment she looked radiant, her eyes shining with love and joy. 'We have a daughter, my dearest!'

'Thanks be to God,' he said, heavy-hearted. He bent and kissed her, and she clutched his hand with sudden, feverish urgency. 'Care for her, Hugh. Look after her for me. Promise?'

'Aye, sweetheart, so I will.'

Hannah lay back against the pillows with a contented little sigh, and drifted into a peaceful sleep. Wotherspoon knelt beside his dear wife until gloaming darkened the room and the chill of a long night crept in, then he cradled his head on his arms and wept.

Lady Hawkerton arrived at the farmhouse after the funeral. The maidie nervously showed her ladyship into the parlour, and Hugh received his mother-in-law formally. He'd never got on with Hannah's mother, although they'd been civil enough to one another in the past. Nothing had been said, but Wotherspoon knew her ladyship considered him a poor match for her only child.

So here they were, he thought, an unlikely pair united in their grief for a lovely lass. He ordered the maidie to bring tea and sat her ladyship down kindly in the best chair.

When the tea was served and they were alone once more, Lady Hawkerton set down her cup. 'I'll come straight to the point, Mr Wotherspoon. I shall engage a nurse for my grandchild and raise and educate her myself in the Big House.'

Hugh Wotherspoon froze rigid. He hadn't looked at the bairn since Hannah died. He couldn't bear to look at it, and yet he knew it wasn't right to blame the innocent child for the loss of the dear mother. He hadn't thought beyond the morrow, or dared to contemplate the lonely future, but – to hand over Hannah's bairn to this autocratic woman? A nice enough woman in her own gentry way, but the bairn was his bairn and if Lady Hawkerton laid hands on it, he'd rarely see it. Knowing her ladyship, he suspected his daughter would be brought up to be scornful of her father and his way of life. Besides, there was a promise given to a lass he'd loved with all his heart.

'No,' he said. 'I thank you for your concern, my lady, but I'll care for my bairn mysel'.'

His mother-in-law turned beetroot red. 'You can't do that. You're a man!'

'Woman, I have two hundred head o' cattle, flocks o' sheep wi' lambs on the hill and pigs breeding in the sties. I care for all the laird's land and it prospers. Are you telling me I can't care for a wee bittie bairn?'

She set her teacup down with an agitated clatter. 'You talk like a common farm labourer. My grand-daughter deserves better than that.'

Wotherspoon stood up. 'Ma'am, if this argument goes further, we'll likely insult one another, and I seek nae quarrel wi' you. I'll look after my ain. You're very welcome to visit whenever you please, but for now I'll ask ye to leave.'

She swept out icily, and he closed the door gently behind her. He wasn't sure if he'd acted wisely, but what was done, was done. Hesitantly, he made his way to the kitchen.

The maidie had taken a great fancy to the baby. She was rocking the wee one in its cradle with one foot while tending to the supper, crooning a nursery rhyme to it the while. She stopped when he came in and stared at him. Her name was Bunty Mutch, a wandering Aberdeen lassie who'd come in wi' a wild team o' harvest lasses at the back-end of the year. Hannah had taken a fancy to her, and Bunty Mutch had stayed behind when the others moved on. She'd cooked and kept house for Hannah, and cleaned out the men's bothy once in a while. He studied her thoughtfully. 'If I were to offer fifty pounds a year and your keep, would you stay and mind my bairn and undertake no' to flit off gin the hairst?' he demanded sternly.

Her eyes widened. 'Aye, I would.'

'Richt you are then,' he grunted. He turned to go, but Bunty called him back.

'Mr Wotherspoon, you havena named the bairn.'

Neither he had. He went cautiously to the side of the crib and peered in. Oh, it was like a knife turning in his heart to look at his daughter, and yet a pleasurable pain. A wee, sleeping face with a look of Hannah, but an individual wee lass, a new little person in her own right. He felt the pain ease a little.

'Joanna. That's to be her name,' Wotherspoon decided.

Dorothy Alexander had her hands full, but that was better than empty. Her father had changed greatly since his breakdown and the slight stroke in February 1923. During lucid spells, William attended the shop and created havoc for Ishbel and old Adam with mischievous glee, but mostly he was content to follow a fascinating new hobby, the crystal wireless set. The household became accustomed to anguished roars when vibrations from a boisterous game or slammed door dislodged the fragile cat's whisker from its position. William himself had been known to wander off absentmindedly with headphones still on, hauling the whole precious apparatus off the table.

The change in Dorothy's mother was gradual, but more heartening. The marked improvement in Eleanor's mobility had something to do with the arrival of the new doctor, though Dorothy wasn't clear how he'd worked the miracle.

Her own introduction to the young man had been unfortunate.

Dorothy had been carrying baby Elspeth when she met Dr Burton on his way upstairs. He paused with a friendly smile. 'How do you do, Mrs Alexander?'

'It's Miss Alexander,' Dorothy corrected with a smile.

He eyed the baby thoughtfully. 'Ah, I see!'

Dorothy blushed scarlet. 'No, you jolly well don't! This is my sister-in-law's baby, not mine.'

He laughed heartily. 'Well, that'll teach me not to jump to conclusions, won't it?' He continued on his way, still chuckling. Dorothy stared after him, bemused. He was the youngest, merriest member of the medical profession she'd ever met.

Ishbel soon discovered that any high-falutin ideas were best abandoned when attempting to run a shop profitably. It wasn't so easy introducing new ideas, for these invariably cost money and meant going cap in hand to the bank. She decided the wisest course was to build on what Alexander's had: a reputation for excellence.

More easily said than done in the present depressed economic climate, though. Bonar Law, the iron merchant from Glasgow, struggled on until May 1923 when ill-health forced him to hand over the reins to Stanley Baldwin, whose comfortable policy was, 'When in doubt, do nothing'. Such changes at the top made for nervous trading throughout the land.

Ishbel strove to keep up with current fashion trends. High-necked and low-waisted dresses were in evidence in Edinburgh that summer, and younger women joyfully flung off corsets. Hemlines rising almost to the calf showed beautiful opaque silk stockings. Doctors looked askance at a fashion for high heels, predicting these would produce abnormalities in unborn babies. Ishbel laughed, and stocked the shoe department with the highest heels she could find.

Cocktail parties were all the rage, and were thought of as very daring and not quite respectable. Ishbel frowned when an invitation to one such arrived on her desk in late summer. It came from an Edinburgh firm of motor dealers, tempting shop-owners with a new range of delivery vehicles. She handed the invitation across to Adam McPherson.

'Here, Adam, this is more your line.'

He looked shocked. 'No' me, Ishbel. I'm tee-total.'

'We could do wi' a new delivery van, though,' she remarked thoughtfully. 'Maybe I could wangle a discount if I went?'

'I wouldn't count on it, wi' motor sharks,' warned Adam.

A few weeks later, Ishbel found herself crammed into a room with a crush of people all talking at the tops of their voices. In one hand she held a bright pink concoction of gin and heaven knows what else, and in the other a bite-sized sandwich. Her feet ached in their high heels after a day spent in the shop, but there were no seats to be found anywhere. She popped the sandwich in her mouth, sipped discreetly and grimaced, wondering how soon she could decently escape.

Ishbel and Sandy MacArthur were more or less forced together by the tight press of bodies around them. The shock of the unexpected meeting stunned them both. 'Sandy! What are you doing here?' she gasped.

He lifted his glass to safety above the mêlée. 'I might ask

you the same. I've started a wee business o' my ain in Corstorphine making farm machinery.'

'Have you?' She was impressed. He wore a good suit, and wore it well. He was a handsome man, standing out from the crowd. The chattering throng milling round pressed her close to his chest, and she felt her pulses quicken. She stepped back hastily. 'I'm working in Alexander's shop. I was hoping for discount on a new van.'

Sandy grinned. 'You'll no' get it here, lassie, only a sair heid.'

She hadn't seen him grin for a while. She remembered a merry wee lad who'd been her childhood sweetheart, and that brought to mind another dear friend lost forever. 'Oh, Sandy, it was so sad about Hannah,' she said sorrowfully.

'Aye, a great tragedy.'

A jazz band struck up. The noise was deafening, and they had to shout to make themselves heard. The din was giving Ishbel a headache. She longed to be alone with Sandy for a while, to talk quietly as they used to do. There were so few she could call her friends. She rested a hand tentatively on his sleeve. 'Sandy, could we—?'

'Coo-ee, here I am!' A pretty young woman pushed her way towards Sandy, edging Ishbel rudely aside with an elbow. The bright young thing looked up at him archly, red lips pouting. 'Sandy, let's go. This is so boring!'

'Aye, so it is,' he agreed. He looked at Ishbel with a grin. 'My latest secretary,' he explained, as his companion dragged him away. The crowd pushed in around Ishbel, many feet tapping to the beat. They'd be dancing next, if only they had room. Ishbel poured the colourful drink quietly into a nearby aspidistra and made her lonely way home.

* * *

The twins started school that autumn. When the boys were older, Ishbel intended sending them to the school Freddie and his brother had attended, but meantime a small private school served the purpose. Eleanor Alexander approved of the establishment, and being just round the corner it meant less to-ing and fro-ing for Florrie and Dorothy. Ishbel was happy with the arrangement, and returned with an easy mind to the many problems demanding her attention.

Adrian and Brian were not so happy. The battle with their teacher, Miss Dixon, began on the very first day. 'You boys will be in the Mixed Infants' class with the other little ones,' Miss Dixon announced, shepherding them along.

Adrian stopped dead. 'I'm no' an infant!'

'You are a very small boy, my dear.'

'But I'm no' an infant. My sister's an infant. She's just a wee baby.'

Miss Dixon bent down to the indignant little boy, long nose inches from his. 'While you are in my school, you are an infant!'

The twins tramped gloomily after their teacher, but brightened when shiny slates and long grey slate pencils were doled out round the desks. 'Now,' said Miss Dixon, 'I will show you little ones how a pencil should be held, then I will come round the class to see if you are doing it properly.'

Brian was confident. He and Adrian had been scribbling busily since an early age. Their mother had encouraged them to draw and paint. He held the cold grey pencil between finger and thumb and itched to get started on the empty slate. He knew his ABC and could read a little and count quite a bit. Grandfather Alexander had plenty of time for small boys. Grandfather was funny and vague, but

Brian and Adrian spent a great deal of time with the old man, being read to, playing Snakes and Ladders, or just listening to scratchy music and voices on the crystal set.

'What is this? What are you doing?' A shadow fell over Brian and he looked up open-mouthed as the teacher towered darkly over him. He was puzzled and frightened by her disapproval.

She tapped the hand holding the pencil. 'Do you know which hand this is? This is your left hand, the *wrong* hand. I don't want to see you using this hand, little boy. I shall be very strict about it indeed.'

She transferred the slate pencil firmly to Brian's right hand. It felt wrong, his hand awkward and clumsy when he tried to move the pencil. It refused to do his bidding, and he was on the verge of tears. He looked up with brimming, pleading eyes. 'B-but p-please—?'

Miss Dixon was strict with the little ones but not unkind. She knew there was a school of thought which said left-handed children should not be forced to use the right hand, but she strongly disagreed. Left-handed adults were at a severe disadvantage in so many ways, and surely it was best to correct the disability at an early age? She hardened her heart to the little boy's heart-rending sobs. This treatment was for the child's own good. His brother, fortunately, was not afflicted. She wagged a finger sternly at Brian. 'Now remember, I shall be watching you!'

Donald Mackie was delighted when Ramsay MacDonald became Prime Minister in January 1924. 'And him born in Lossiemouth, Catriona, wi' his mother a poor unmarried lassie scratching a living from the land!' Donald cried jubilantly. 'Here's a man at last who knows what it's like to wonder where his next penny's coming from. Oh, we'll see great changes for the better now!'

Catriona was highly suspicious of politicians, but she'd seen photographs of the new Prime Minister in the *Illustrated London News* and been impressed by his bearing and shiny top hat. She rested her knitting in her lap for a moment. 'He's a real handsome man, that Ramsay MacDonald. He must be the most handsome man in the whole House o' Commons.'

'Och, well, he's a Scot, so he would be mair presentable than most, wouldn't he?' said Donald complacently. 'They say King George has taken to MacDonald better than to Baldwin, and the King and the Socialist ministers get on fine. Fancy a farm laddie being chummy wi' a king! It's changed days, Catriona.' Donald puffed at his pipe and stroked Foxy, who lay comfortably stretched across his lap.

'Aye, and fancy our daughter in charge of a posh Edinburgh shop. It's a funny auld world!' agreed Catriona, resuming knitting.

Donald sighed. 'I wish Ishbel hadn't done it. We haven't seen her for months, and I miss my daughter and her bairns sair. You know, love,' he went on sadly, 'sometimes I wish she was just a poor cottar woman on the farm, married to a good working man and looking after her bairns and her auld ma and pa.'

There were times when Ishbel shared her father's sentiments for life in the shop was not easy. The Alexander family's welfare depended upon the firm's success, and more responsibility rested on Ishbel's slim shoulders as William Alexander became increasingly vague and forgetful. Sometimes she longed to be rid of it all and carefree, but there were invalids, growing bairns, hard-working Dorothy and Florrie as well as the loyal staff to be considered. She was forced to soldier on.

In that distressing time of year after Hogmanay, Ishbel felt particularly low after recovering from a feverish cold. The customary dip in trade after the festive season appeared even worse that year, and she was at her wits' end, puzzling how to reverse the trend. She suddenly recalled the ill-fated cocktail party she'd attended, and the many fashionable young ladies and gents who had been there. Such events had become increasingly popular this winter in the city, and the only steady increase in trade had been in the evening gown department.

Ishbel spent the rainy morning sketching, a skill she'd recently perfected as a way to get her ideas across to her staff, then went in search of Doris who was a dressmaking wizard. She spread the sketches in front of the little woman.

'Cocktail wear, evening wear and head-dresses, Doris, not to mention gowns for tea-dances. Could we summon up enough to put on a fashion show in the tearoom once a week, do you think?'

Doris fumbled with her spectacles. Ishbel was surprised. 'I didn't know you wore specs.'

The little woman looked shame-faced. 'Och, I don't really need them,' she assured Ishbel hurriedly. 'You get these in Woolworth's. You test your eyes wi' the card, then it's sixpence for each lens and sixpence for the frames.' She peered at the sketches. 'Aye, we could put on a grand show. I'd just need to make one or two alterations to our existing stock to fit your drawings, then manufacture fancy head-dresses out o' bits an' pieces.'

'Good! When you're ready, we'll put a discreet notice in the papers advertising afternoon fashion shows. Oh, and Doris, the Egyptian look is ever so popular since they discovered Tutankhamen's tomb, mind!'

'Oh, aye? Toot an' Come In! I'll remember,' Doris chuckled.

With their mother busily occupied from morning 'til night and the rest of the family absorbed in their own affairs, it was small wonder nobody noticed Brian's misery. Nobody noticed the lively little boy had become listless and withdrawn. Nobody noticed, because Adrian protected his brother nobly.

Adrian was always there, his brave little chest stuck out and small fists clenched when Brian needed protection. When questions needed answering, Adrian was there to answer them and nobody noticed how quiet Brian had become. In the night, when his brother sobbed on and on into a damp pillow, it was Adrian who hugged and comforted him until he slept exhausted in Adrian's arms. Nobody noticed the damage well-intentioned Miss Dixon was inflicting upon a sensitive, left-handed boy. Only Adrian knew, only Adrian rebelled fiercely on his brother's behalf, and spent hours standing wearily in a dark corner of Miss Dixon's classroom, facing the wall.

Miss Dixon had rarely encountered such awkward pupils. She'd had left-handed children before, but most had taken readily to correction. The Alexander boy remained obstinately caurry-fisted despite her sternest efforts, while his brother became more rebellious and unruly as the term wore on. The final straw came the day Miss Dixon in desperation tied Brian's left hand behind his back. Adrian promptly kicked her shins hard, and spent the morning shut in the broom cupboard in darkness. When the children burst thankfully out of school that afternoon, Adrian put a comforting arm round his sobbing brother. 'Dinna greet, Brian. That's an awful wifie, a real Grumpy yin.' He stuck out his chin dangerously. 'Och, we're no' goin' back that school!'

Brian wiped his nose forlornly on his sleeve. 'We have to. They'll m-m-make us.'

'No, they'll no'. We'll hide from them, until they say we don't have to go. I've got my dinner piece in my schoolbag, 'cause I couldn't eat it in that smelly cupboard. It's a big jammy piece, too. I bet we could hide for ages,' said Adrian excitedly.

The two little boys trailed along the road, arms round one another. Brian warmed to Adrian's idea. 'We could be like R-Robinson Crusoe in the pant'mime we saw at Christmas, an' m-make all our own things,' he said thoughtfully. His eyes lit with hope. 'Adrian, I know someplace we can go where n-nobody will ever find us. Come on!' He grabbed his brother's arm and the two little boys set off down the road, running.

Doris rose nobly to Ishbel's challenge and produced a stunning collection of gowns and head-dresses. Ishbel spent a hectic day interviewing models to show off the various styles and discovered there was more to the fashion business than she'd anticipated. She worked late in the shop making sure of the smallest detail so that everything would go without a hitch on the first day of the new venture. Nothing less than perfection would do.

It was dark and gaslamps lit in the street outside

Betty McInnes

Knoxhall House when she alighted wearily from the tram. To her surprise, she found Dorothy waiting for her. It was raining, and the little woman was soaked to the skin and shivering. She ran up to Ishbel and clutched her arm. 'Have you seen the boys, Ishbel? Did they turn up at the shop?'

Ishbel stared at her with an awful foreboding of disaster. 'The boys? No, I haven't seen them. Dorothy, what's happened?'

It was a miserable February night. Droplets of sleety rain mingled with tears ran down Dorothy's cheeks. 'They didn't come home from school. Nobody noticed they were missing until it began to get dark, and then Florrie and I went out looking for them. They haven't been seen since they left school, and we can't find them anywhere!'

194

Chapter 9

The twins were lost! As panic gripped her, Ishbel was reminded of the tragic accident that had robbed the boys of their father. She imagined she heard the whine of cars on the race track and the roar of the crowd, then her nerve steadied. Panic wouldn't find lost bairns. She said quite calmly, 'We must notify the police, Dorothy.'

'I've done that. I told the bobby on the beat and he promised they'd start searching right away.'

Dorothy's teeth were chattering, and Ishbel put an arm round her. 'Let's go inside, dear, you're soaked to the skin. If you've searched the house and grounds there's nothing we can do meantime.'

Even as she spoke, Ishbel recalled with dread the fascination Blackford pond held for the twins now it was frozen over. She'd taken them there only last Wednesday, early closing day. At the pond, the little ones had watched the antics of older children enjoying a skating holiday from school. They'd begged to slide on the ice, but she hadn't allowed it in case they were knocked down by bigger boys. What if they'd sneaked back on their own to slide? It didn't bear thinking about, with a thaw setting in.

Her thoughts whirled around in panic. Both little boys had seemed unnaturally subdued recently. She herself had been preoccupied with plans for the fashion show. Now she wished she'd taken time to probe the reason behind those unusually glum wee faces. She was sure the incident at the pond had some bearing on their disappearance. 'Oh, Dorothy, I should be at home caring for the bairns myself!' Ishbel cried in an agony of remorse.

Dorothy stopped dead, her face drained of colour. 'You blame me? You think I've neglected your children?'

Ishbel was astounded by the accusation. 'Of course I don't blame you, dear. I'm grateful for all you've done. You and Florrie have been just wonderful.'

'Well, I blame myself. If anything has happened to the twins, I'll just lie down and die!' Dorothy sobbed, shivering violently.

'Don't talk daft!' Ishbel said sharply. Dorothy's behaviour was alarmingly out of character, and the little woman did not look well. Ishbel tugged anxiously at her sister-in-law's arm. 'Come inside before you catch your death of cold, love.'

Dorothy resisted all Ishbel's efforts to guide her into the house. 'No, I must look for the boys. I must go on looking, Ishbel. I must go on!' Her voice faded to a whisper, and to Ishbel's horror she suddenly slumped to the ground.

Ishbel struggled to lift her. The weight proved too much for her, and she was forced to drag the unconscious woman up the steps and into the hallway. Once inside, she dropped to her knees beside Dorothy, calling desperately for help. Her mother-in-law appeared, followed closely by Florrie, who had come puffing up the back stairs to see what all the fuss was.

Eleanor Alexander could walk with the aid of two sticks now. She'd taken Dr Burton's words to heart and was recovering strength slowly, bringing her formidable will-power to bear upon wasted muscles. She rapidly took in the situation and began issuing crisp orders. 'Get her into the parlour, Ishbel. There's a good fire in there, and she looks half frozen. Florrie will help.'

Between them, they carried Dorothy into the warm room and laid her on the couch. Eleanor bent over her sick daughter anxiously. 'Oh, dear, this to happen on top of everything else!' she cried. 'We must send for the doctor, Ishbel. I warned Dorothy she'd make herself ill going out so soon after that bad dose of 'flu. She wouldn't listen, of course, and I didn't insist because we were so worried about the boys. Any news of them?'

'No, nothing.' Ishbel buttoned her coat. 'I'll fetch the doctor, Mrs Alexander. It isn't far to Dr Burton's house.' She welcomed the task. It was better than sitting around waiting for news.

Eleanor wrung her hands. 'Oh, how I wish we'd one of those new-fangled telephones. What a blessing at a time like this!'

But Ishbel was already hurrying on her way. Outside, the miserable night took on a nightmarish quality, icy sleet stinging her face cruelly, her feet slipping treacherously on the slushy pavement as she hurried along. She pressed on doggedly, pausing briefly now and then to peer into dark corners in the vain hope her boys were hiding there. When at last she reached Dr Burton's door and gasped out the whole story, the young doctor wasted no time, he grabbed a bag and ushered her towards his car. She hung back unwillingly.

'No, doctor, I won't come with you. There's somewhere I must go first.'

He gave her a keen glance. 'Where?'

'To – to Blackford pond.'

His expression became grim. 'That's not far out of the way. Get in. I'll take you.'

Ishbel didn't argue. She sat huddled in the passenger seat in silence until he stopped the car beside the pond. He turned to her.

'What now?'

She clambered out. 'Leave me and see to Dorothy, Doctor. I'll be all right.'

Before he could protest, Ishbel walked off into the night, heading for the deserted pond with its treacherous covering of ice. She stopped when she reached the edge, staring across the dark expanse of ice with tears cold on her cheeks. At that moment she longed for the impossible, the comfort of Freddie's arm around her and his shoulder to lean on. She had never felt so lonely and frightened.

A light flashed suddenly on to her face, blinding her for a moment. Her dazzled eyes caught the sheen of silver buttons and a large figure loomed up beyond the beam. The bobby recognised her and smiled. 'Aye, it's you, Mrs Alexander! I checked the pond whenever I heard your wee laddies were missing, and the ice is still thick and hasnae been broken anywhere on the surface, which is a good sign. I don't think the bairns came this way. They're weel-kent wee faces, and nobody claims to have seen them when I asked round the doors.' He took her arm and turned her gently from the pond, steering her towards habitations and lights. 'Away home and have a nice cup o' tea, ma'am. You leave the searching to us,' he ordered kindly.

Ishbel nodded and went obediently, feeling oddly comforted. By coming here she had faced up to her greatest fear and it appeared to be groundless. Now she could only wait and pray.

Dorothy had the strangest dreams as she lay semi-conscious all that long night. The dreams centred around a man. She was burning, and he cooled her burning skin. She was chilled to the marrow, and he warmed her. Often, fierce pains gripped her chest so that she could hardly breathe and feared she was dying. She stretched out her arms to him with pitiful, moaning cries of fear and he was there, holding her, gently easing the pain and letting her breathe again.

Wondering hazily at the miracle, Dorothy drifted at last into a deep, dreamless sleep, only to waken hot and feverish in daylight, relishing the cool sponge that gently soothed the heat of her naked body.

She opened her eyes languorously, focused slowly upon young Dr Burton wielding the sponge, and promptly wished she were unconscious again. She grabbed for the bedclothes in dismay and hauled them modestly beneath her chin. 'Stop that at once. Go away!' she croaked.

He grinned. 'You're obviously feeling better, Miss Alexander, though your temperature's a mite too high for comfort yet. So, if you'll permit me . . . ?' He dipped the sponge in the basin and reached purposefully for the blankets.

She pulled the covers tightly under her nose. 'Florrie will do that. Have – have you been here all night?' she asked in a small voice.

'Yes. Your condition was giving cause for concern, to use the medical jargon. You were running an extremely high temperature. One can't take chances with pneumonia,

Miss Alexander, but I believe you're over the worst now.'

'Pneumonia?' she whispered, shocked. That was a very serious illness, often fatal. The doctor looked exhausted after his battle for her life, dark stubble shadowing his chin. The sight provoked her to tears. 'You shouldn't have stayed. You – you shouldn't have bathed me. Ishbel would have done it,' she sobbed.

'Your sister-in-law is worn out with worry about the boys, and I gave her something to help her sleep. Besides, it was my job to get that temperature down, and you were in no fit state for false modesty. I'm your doctor after all, Miss Alexander.'

She turned her head away. Yes, he was her doctor, but that didn't make her chaotic emotions any less confusing.

'Any word of the twins?' she asked presently.

'They haven't been found yet, I'm afraid.' He rested a cool hand on her forehead and frowned. 'We must watch that temperature. Since your modesty is offended by my ministrations, I'll leave you now and send Florrie to carry on the good work. But don't think you're out of my clutches yet, Miss Dorothy. I'll be back!' he warned with a smile.

One of the crew of the lighthouse tender *Pharos* ran a duster down the gleaming brass rail of the companionway. A sooty deposit from Granton gasworks offended his eye though the rest of the ship was spotless, as usual. Spick and span, *Pharos* was preparing to head out of her berth in Granton harbour at the top of high water, making for the Bass Rock and May Island to offload stores and mail for the lightkeepers.

It had been a wet, bitterly cold night, and pausing in his polishing to survey the dour sky just after daybreak, the sailor doubted if the day would improve. He was on the point of heading for the galley, where hot tea was on the go when his eye caught a slight movement ashore. He went to the rail to see better. Straining his eyes, he saw there was a poor wee stray doggie crouching miserably behind a stack of lobster pots close by the harbour wall. The man blinked as the gloomy light of day strengthened, and he saw there were two wee stray heads peeping out. He scratched his head in amazement. 'Well, blow me down, I believe it's bairns!'

The twins' escape plan had gone sadly wrong. They'd reached the harbour quite easily, but had no chance to steal aboard the lighthouse ship in daylight. When darkness fell, the little boys had spent a miserable night huddled together behind stacked lobster pots which had afforded some protection from the wet. Though they would not have admitted it, they were relieved to be discovered by gruff, kindly men and carried aboard ship. Wrapped in cosy blankets in the warm saloon, their chilly fingers stretched round steaming mugs of sweet cocoa, they faced a gentle inquisition from captain and crew.

'Our teacher's a Grumpy, we dinna like the school, and we're running away to sea on your ship,' explained Adrian stoutly.

The captain fingered his chin thoughtfully. 'Aye, well, son, that's easier said than done now. There's nothing I'd like better than to welcome you two braw lads aboard, but I'm no' allowed to have wee laddies working on my ship unless they can read an' write an' do algebra. I'm thinking you'll have to bide at the school a wee while yet.'

'We're no' needing to go far, just to a desert island like

R-Robinson Crusoe,' piped up Brian. 'There's plenty of desert islands in the firth of Forth, so you could just drop us aff at one. The lighthouse ship sails to m-m-most of them, my Auntie Nellie says.'

'Which Auntie Nellie would that be now, sonny?' enquired the captain innocently.

The twins told him in concert, proudly supplying Auntie Nellie's address above the fish shop in Newhaven. The captain gave one of his crew the wink, and the man grinned and slipped quietly away. The little boys didn't notice, for they'd started drowsily reciting a tally of islands located in the wide mouth of the Forth, as taught by their cheery great-aunt. 'There's Cramond an' Inchcolm, Inchkeith, Inchmickeray...'

'Fidra, the Bass Rock, and the Isle of May,' the Mate finished for them softly. But the little boys didn't hear the ending of the rhyme. Warm and comforted, they had drifted happily off to sleep.

'They'll never go back to that school! Never!' stormed Ishbel.

She could hardly contain her anger when the full extent of her little boys' ordeal was revealed to her. She listened to Adrian's story of Miss Dixon's treatment with growing horror. Brian's halting account of the teacher's persecution almost broke her heart. The outcome could so easily have been tragedy, and she hugged her sons tearfully and thanked God they were safe.

With the boys tucked up in bed and seemingly none the worse for their ordeal, Ishbel gave vent to her anger. Fuming, she paced the parlour floor while Eleanor eyed her anxiously. William Alexander, though present, was far away in a world of his own, headphones on, listening to the wireless.

Eleanor was feeling guilty. The private school had been her idea, and had seemed an excellent solution to the boys' schooling at the time. Ishbel had enough on her plate managing the firm virtually single-handed.

'Oh, that Miss Dixon! Fancy tying a wee boy's arm behind his back because he was born left-handed!' Ishbel cried indignantly. She found it hard to forgive herself for the harm done to poor Brian. She should have noticed what was going on and put a stop to it.

Eleanor sighed. 'Don't be too hard on the woman, my dear. She thought she was helping him overcome a handicap. She meant well.'

Ishbel spun round, eyes flashing. 'Handicap? Brian's caurry-fisted like many other folk. That's no handicap to a healthy bairn, but now my wee one's so confused by that stupid woman's meddling, he can hardly speak without stammering.'

'Oh, my dear, he'll get over that.'

'Never! He's at an impressionable age. I've a good mind to report Miss Dixon for cruelty and have the school closed down.'

'No!' Eleanor protested in horror. That would cause a sensation in the district, and the threat only added to her list of worries. Poor Eleanor lived in a constant state of anxiety. She had only to look at her husband to be worried about the future. Sometimes when she spoke to him, William would stare at her in puzzled fashion as if she were a stranger. It gave her a lost, lonely feeling.

'What'll you do about the boys' education, Ishbel dear?' she asked, hoping to steer her thoughts along a safer path.

'Nothing until autumn, then they'll be big enough to go to Freddie's old school. It's a fair distance across the city for wee ones to travel, but we'll manage it somehow. I want them to spend time with Mam and Pa on the farm this summer. I want them to run wild.'

'Everyone needs discipline, Ishbel. Especially bairns,' observed Eleanor reprovingly.

William had been twiddling knobs on the wireless and now he cried out excitedly, 'I say, it's Moscow! Come and listen, Eleanor. Can you imagine? Moscow!'

She limped to her husband's side and obediently fitted on the headphones. A gabble of meaningless sound filled her eardrums, then a blare of military music that made her wince. She smiled gently at William, who was grinning with childish delight. 'Aye, dearest, it's Moscow. Isn't that just wonderful?' She hoped her husband wouldn't notice her eyes, brimming with lonely tears.

Ishbel noticed, and pity for the old folk cooled her anger as nothing else would. They were dependent for their comfort upon her success in the shop, and had become very dear to her. She crossed the room and fondly kissed William's cheek, then took Eleanor's hand and gave it a comforting squeeze.

'Give me the headphones, love. I want to listen to Moscow too,' Ishbel said, smiling at her delighted father-in-law.

Freddie's Silver Ghost lay unused in the garage. The last chauffeur had left to seek more lucrative employment long ago. When the family required transport, they used Dorothy's little black Morris. Ishbel had driven it herself on occasion, but with autumn not far off and the boys' schooling in mind, she decided she must have a car of her own. Money was the problem. She only drew a small wage from the shop, enough to cover her simple needs and clothe the bairns. She went out to the garage and surveyed the Silver Ghost thoughtfully. It had been Freddie's personal property, so it was legally hers to dispose of.

Callum, the resident gardener and handyman, a war-wounded ex-soldier, paused beside her. 'Thon's a big braw motor, Mrs Alexander. Pity to see it mouldering awa'.'

'Do you think it would fetch the price of a new Austin, Callum?'

He lifted his cap and scratched his head. 'I could ask around, if you like. I daresay there's plenty of folk in Edinburgh would jump at the chance o' a swanky vehicle like that. They might even have siller to buy it.'

Ishbel smiled. 'Very well, Callum. Spread the word it's for sale, will you?'

Two or three weeks passed and Ishbel had forgotten all about the conversation when Florrie poked her head round the study door one evening.

'There's a man to see ye about the car.'

Ishbel looked up with interest from a pile of invoices she was checking. 'Show him in, Florrie, will you please?'

Florrie disappeared and presently returned with a stranger. Ishbel stood up abruptly, scattering the papers. No, not a stranger!

'Sandy!' she said flatly.

'Aye.' His expression was as cool as ever as his gaze travelled slowly round the shabby room. She wondered what he was thinking.

She tried to keep calm. 'You've come about the car?'

'Aye. When I heard Freddie Alexander's Silver Ghost

was up for sale, I couldna resist the temptation. What are you asking for it?'

'The price of a new Austin saloon.'

'Around two hundred pounds? You could get a bit mair.'

'From you?' She studied him with surprise. As before at the cocktail party he was well dressed in quiet good taste. A far cry from his old Saturday bicycle clothes, she thought.

His lips twitched as if he guessed at her thoughts. 'Aye, from me. You'll get your siller, dinna fash yoursel'.'

'I'm no' worried on that score.'

'Then you ought to be. They tell me you're a braw business woman, so why sell a Rolls-Royce at less than its worth and ask no questions about the buyer?'

She looked away, suddenly remembering Freddie and that first journey they took together that was the start of everything that happened after. 'The car has too many memories for me, Sandy. The time's come to let them go.'

'I see. Your memories come cheap,' he said deliberately.

She turned on him with a flash of anger. 'Why must you be so hurtful? Can't you forgive and forget?'

'It's no' so easy for me. My memories are golden and can't be bought.'

I mustn't lose my temper, she thought. That's what he wants, to humiliate me. She clenched her fists until the nails dug deep into the palms. 'I told you what I'll take for the car, Sandy. The price of a new Austin. Take it or leave it.'

'I'll tak' it, subject to inspection o' the car's condition,' he decided cannily.

'Very well, I'll arrange that with Callum.'

He nodded and prepared to leave then paused, looking at her. 'I dinna ken if you've noticed, but I'm on my way up the ladder. You'll get your new Austin, Ishbel. I'll see to it.'

She followed him to the front door. For a moment they stood face to face in the doorway, and she felt again the warm attraction he'd always had for her, all the more compelling because they were no longer in love.

She touched his arm appealingly. 'Can't we be friends again, Sandy, for old times' sake?'

She felt his arm tremble at the touch. 'Kiss and make up?' He smiled grimly. 'Naw, I'm sorry. My young lady doesn't approve o' fickle conduct, and neither do I.'

Ishbel stepped back and glared at him, her temper fiery as ever. 'You'll never forgive me for jilting you, will you? I'll tell you something, Sandy MacArthur, it's only your pride that's dunted, and you know what they say about pride. It goes before a fall. Mind you dinna fall off the top o' the ladder, when you reach it!' She slammed the heavy door in his face.

The crash of his dismissal rang in Sandy's ears as he strode away. He was angry, but not with her. Angry with himself most of all for hurting her. Far from being the triumph he'd planned, Sandy suspected that riding in Freddie Alexander's Silver Ghost would be cauld comfort to him now.

Dorothy took time to recover from pneumonia. It was summer before the damage to her lungs finally healed, and Dr Burton remained attentive during that time. One fine summer day she washed her hair and put on a pretty muslin dress to sit in the sheltered garden to await his visit. Little Elspeth was toddling now, a bonny, curly-haired little girl who followed her aunt everywhere when not being nursed and petted by Florrie, who doted on the pretty bairn.

'Daisy-chains, darling!' cried Dorothy happily, settling

Elspeth on the rug beside her. The large garden was a handful for Callum, who did what he could, and there was a fine crop of daisies on the lawn this summer. Dorothy picked them, threading the heads carefully through the stems while Elspeth watched. 'There, sweetheart!' Dorothy finished the little necklace and presented it to the toddler, who immediately began eating it.

'No! No, lovie! You wear it. Like this, see?' She draped it around her own head, like a crown.

'The loveliest bonnet I ever did see,' remarked Dr Burton.

Dorothy was startled. How long he'd been standing watching her daft antics she didn't know. She blushed. 'Oh, there you are, Doctor, I was just amusing the bairn.'

Uninvited, he sat down on the rug. Elspeth was delighted and began untying his shoelaces. He watched the child abstractedly. 'You're better now, Dorothy. I came to tell you I shan't be calling again.'

Had the sun gone behind a cloud? The sky seemed just as clear and blue, yet a cold shadow had passed over the garden. 'I see. Then I must thank you for your kind attention during my illness, Dr Burton,' she said primly.

'I don't think you quite understand. I'm leaving Edinburgh for good,' he said.

She couldn't hide her distress. 'But why? I thought you were happy here!' She was almost in tears. She wanted to keep him near. She only wanted to know he was in the city, to see him sometimes. Some precious times.

He sighed. 'I am happy. Very happy. But I've made the gravest mistake a doctor can make. I've fallen in love with a patient. I don't dare to hope she loves me. I have to take the honourable course and go.'

208

Dorothy snatched off the ridiculous crown of daisies and threw it petulantly on the grass, furious with the woman who had sent him away. 'Well, really, that young woman's hard to please! I'd give anything to be young enough to – to—' Dorothy stopped, aghast at what she was saying so rashly.

He gripped her wrist. 'To what? Dorothy dear, speak up for Heaven's sake! It's you I love. I love you.'

'No!' She felt numbed with incredulous joy, and at the same time swamped by a bleak misery of grief because this crazy union could never be. 'You can't love me! That's ridiculous. You're a young man and I'm an old maid.'

'You're not listening to a word I'm saying! I love you. How many times do I have to say it? I love you. Is there any hope for me?'

She faced him furiously. 'I'm forty-two, dumpy and plain. You can't possibly love me. It's quite impossible!'

'Oh, Dorothy, you're wonderful!' he laughed. 'What has age to do with it? I'm thirty-five, you're beautiful, and I love you. Dorothy, don't you care for me a little?'

Dorothy sat motionless. She'd never told a lie in her life, but she must tell one now for Michael Burton's sake. She loved him dearly and didn't care what gossips said about her, but Michael was a different matter. If he was really set on courting one of his patients who was seven years his senior, popular opinion voiced in Edinburgh's tearooms would likely ridicule and ruin the young doctor's promising career. She must nip this love affair in the bud and send him away. It was the only course open to her.

She lowered her eyes and carefully picked a daisy. 'Your first decision was the only honourable one, Michael. Perhaps you should leave the city.'

'Dorothy, are you saying you don't love me?'

She couldn't look at him or she might weaken. 'I'm begging you to go. Please!' she whispered.

He tied the tangled shoelaces and stood up. For a moment his hand rested on her bowed head. 'I'm sorry I embarrassed you. I wouldn't have spoken up, but I thought just now that you – well, anyway, goodbye, dear Dorothy.'

She didn't move until he had crossed the lawn and the garden gate closed behind him, then she took the drowsy little girl in her arms and hugged her close to her breast for comfort.

It was not merely a spirit of revenge that had prompted Sandy to buy Freddie Alexander's car. He had a purpose for it: a round trip of over one hundred and twenty miles. At the back-end of the summer he was leaning one day on the rail of the busy little ferryboat carrying himself and a load of cars and lorries across the Forth at the spot favoured nine centuries ago by Malcolm Canmore's queen. His engineer's brain appreciated the mechanics of the railway bridge across the wide river, but his thoughts were elsewhere, roaming with a willing Clydesdale taken from its farming tasks to pull jute carts in Dundee.

It was a grand day for motoring, the hairst being gathered on all sides as Sandy passed through the fertile Carse of Gowrie. He narrowed his eyes thoughtfully as he drove by fields where three and more horse-drawn binders worked, and an army of labourers set up stooks. There was business to be had here, selling the farm machinery his efficient factory was producing in ever-increasing quantities. He'd look into it. This could mean another step up the ladder.

Smoky Dundee appeared as a dark smudge on the east against a clear sky, at the widening of the River Tay he'd followed down from Perth. The city was in the grip of recession, and some of the mills lay silent after busy war years making sackcloth. Others rumbled on relentlessly still, making the pavements shake beneath his feet when he reached the Dens Road stables. He'd seen plenty jute carts coming and going on the hilly Victoria Road, laden and unladen, but none of them was pulled by his distinctive old friend, Big Bob. Hope still ran high, though.

The farrier he asked frowned thoughtfully for a minute or two, then his brow cleared. 'Och, him! Bobbie. He was a cantankerous deevil when harnessed in a cart. Tram cars! Man, the beast couldna stand the sight o' them. Kicked in the side o' the Maryfield tram one day at the terminus, an' that was the feenish. The boss packed him aff tae the Aikie horse fair where naebody would ken about his ill nature. It was a dour auld farmer frae Dundreich in the Mearns that bought the beast for less than its worth, they said.'

Sandy returned despondently to the car. A dour auld farmer frae Dundreich in the Mearns! That harsh and trying soil that bred hard men and sent many a willing beast to an early death. Poor Bob. Poor loyal, bewildered Big Bob. There was a sore lump in Sandy's throat and his eyes were misty as he let in the clutch and the regal car purred smoothly on its homeward way.

Life was either valleys or hills, Brian thought. Valleys were the quiet, peaceful times; on the farm with Granny and dear old Grandpa and wee Foxy, or at home listening to the wireless with funny, muddled old Grandfather Alexander while struggling to do homework with Adrian. It was the hills you remembered long afterwards, though, and today was quite literally a hill.

The Scottish War Memorial had been built within the Castle, high on a hill, and King George V and Queen Mary had attended the dedication service two years ago in 1927. Today was 11 November 1929 and the twins' class had been allowed to attend the ceremony of Remembrance at the War Memorial. The two-minute silence marked by guns and Reveille had brought tears to Brian's eyes, though he was a big boy of nearly twelve now.

Adrian lingered with the rest of the crowd in the Memorial after the service. Adrian liked crowds. He liked joining things like the Boy Scouts and the Ovalteenies. Brian's tastes were different. He sneaked quietly away to have a look at the half-moon battery and Mons Meg, his particular favourite. The cannon was ancient. It had burst the last time it was fired many years ago, which seemed a satisfying revenge upon those who'd manufactured such a massive weapon of destruction.

He rested his arms on the battlements and looked over the little cemetery below reserved for soldiers' pets. It was a clear day and he could see for miles, as far as Auntie Nellie's fish shop in Newhaven. Auntie Nellie didn't hawk fish any more because her canny husband had prospered catching the silver darlings and had a high-class business supplying railway hotels. Not as good as Mum's, of course, thought Brian proudly. Alexander's was the very best shop in the capital. That wasn't just Brian's biased opinion either. Everyone said how much the shop had changed for the better since his mum took charge six years ago.

An odd, small sound surprised Brian and he looked hurriedly over his shoulder. His mouth dropped open for he'd never seen a man crying before. This was Mr Holland, his own class teacher, sobbing as if his heart would break. Brian was alarmed and upset. Mr Holland was jolly nice, and had tried hard to help Brian overcome a slight stammer.

'S-sir?' he ventured nervously.

Mr Holland looked up with a start, furtively wiping his eyes. 'Brian! I didn't notice you there. I'm sorry, but the ceremony got through to me. I fought in the trenches, though I don't like to think about it much.' The young man shuddered. 'It was very horrible, the war.'

'There won't be another one, sir. That's the last, else they wouldn't have bothered building a War M-memorial,' Brian reasoned.

Mr Holland smiled shakily. 'Well, I hope you're right.'

Brian cast around anxiously for a way to cheer his disconsolate teacher, and recalled a ditty that had taken his fancy in the class copy book. 'Listen to me, Mr Holland, I've been practising, like you said. *"The Pickwick, the Owl and the Waverley pen, They come as a Boon and a Blessing to men,"*' Brian enunciated slowly and carefully.

'Jolly good! Spoken without a single hiccup. You *are* coming along, old chap!' The teacher placed a hand on the youngster's shoulder and they walked companionably towards the sombre crowd gathered on the castle hill that chilly morning.

Down below the Castle, the two-minute silence ended and traffic began to flow on Princes Street. Ishbel sailed serenely on her rounds through the departments of Alexander's busy store. In recent hardworking years she'd progressed a long way from the worried novice who'd taken

213

over reluctantly from her sick father-in-law. She and Mr McPherson had introduced some innovations while retaining the shop's Edwardian charm and the family firm had forged ahead and prospered well, despite difficult trading in years of post-war depression.

There was a pert American lady at the jewellery counter today, Ishbel noted. Rather unusual in November, especially since the Wall Street Crash in October had left many wealthy Americans impoverished and shell-shocked. Ishbel paused to watch the American hold a pair of ornate ear-rings to her neat little ears. 'Say, are these real or junk?'

Ishbel impressed on her staff that no matter what, even if the ceiling fell on you, you smiled. The sales assistant smiled. 'They're perfect replicas of real gems, madam, as worn by Her Majesty Queen Mary.'

'You don't say!' breathed the customer, suitably awed.

Ishbel walked on towards the perfumery counter. Jeannie reigned supreme here, the best perfumery assistant they'd ever had. She crooked a finger mysteriously and leaned over the counter. 'There's a Yank seeking a word wi' you,' she whispered.

Ishbel frowned. 'It's not a complaint is it, Jeannie?'

'Could be, though I don't think he's the girning sort. He's a real matinée idol, this big yin. The dead spit o' Douglas Fairbanks. I directed him to take the lift up to your office.'

The American's visit worried Ishbel. She hoped to establish trade links with America soon, and didn't want the delicate negotiations hampered by complaints from dissatisfied American customers. She nipped anxiously into the lift and was ferried upwards by Archie. The big man waiting patiently outside the office rose eagerly when she appeared and held out a hand. 'Ishbel, it's great to see you! Remember me? Freddie's pal, Matthew Clark.'

Ishbel laughed with relief. 'Matthew! Oh, I'm so glad to see you!' she cried as they shook hands warmly.

She ushered him into the office and seated him with a dram of whisky to hand. He lifted the glass and toasted her. 'Cheers, Ishbel. I'm sure glad I found you in the store. I guess I owed it to you to speak to you first.' Matthew set the glass aside and leaned his arms on the desk, continuing in a different tone, 'Ishbel, I was devastated when I heard Freddie had been killed. Such a waste of a wonderful talent. He was a great guy.'

'Yes, he was,' Ishbel agreed. She still didn't care to talk about the accident. Memories were too painful, and this visitor brought many poignant moments to mind. 'What brings you to Scotland?' she asked curiously.

Matthew hesitated, watching her thoughtfully. 'Did Freddie tell you I sponsored him while he was developing the racing car?'

'Sponsorship was mentioned, but he didn't name names. I thought it might be you.'

'Yeah. Freddie and I had an agreement. I loaned him money to develop and patent a new engine on the strength of his IOU. That's the way he wanted it, Ishbel. He said the car manufacturer would pay sweetly for the patent after the race, and he'd pay me back with interest. Of course, when he died I didn't press for payment. I didn't need the money.' He paused for a moment. 'Until now, that is.'

The room went so quiet she could hear her own heartbeat. She moistened her lips. 'How much, Matthew?'

'Half a million dollars. I got the IOU right here.' He fumbled in his waistcoat pocket and produced a document which he laid on the desk between them. Ishbel recognised Freddie's dashing signature. Her brain did a rapid calculation. £125,000. An impossible sum which would cripple the business if she honoured Freddie's debt.

She sat so motionless, pale with shock, Matthew reached for her hand and held it. 'Ishbel honey, I hate to do this to you, but I must. I lost everything in the Wall Street Crash.'

Chapter 10

Ishbel knew all about the Wall Street Crash of October 1929. Panic selling of shares on the American stock market had rocked the financial markets of the world, and not least Edinburgh's stolid merchant bankers. Harrowing tales of despair and tragedy filled the newspapers as American millionaires and small investors alike watched vast fortunes and life savings become worthless in the space of a few hectic hours. She could understand Matthew Clark's dilemma. He was a victim of circumstance too.

'Oh, Matthew, I'm so sorry!' she said.

'Yeah.' He stood up resolutely. 'I just wanted to put you in the picture first, Ishbel. Now, if you'll excuse me, I have to speak to the boss of the firm. I guess there's some hard talking to do.'

She stared at him, surprised. 'Matthew, I don't think you understand. There's nobody else. I'm in charge.'

His expression was comical in its consternation. 'You're kidding! A woman running this classy store?'

Ishbel frowned. 'Why not? Women over twenty-one have the vote, and even flappers have a say in running the country. It makes me mad to see hungry men marching to London demanding work, and I hear the situation's no better in your country. I'm sure women could do better.'

'You think so?' he said scathingly. 'Nancy Astor's an American woman in your British Parliament, and she's done nothing but pick fights with that cheeky guy with the American mother, Winston Churchill. Sorry, Ishbel, but I'll settle this account with Freddie's father. I prefer to deal with men.'

'It's out o' the question,' Ishbel told him. 'My father-in-law's far from well, and I'll not have the old man bothered with this worry. If there's an account to be settled on my late husband's behalf, you'll discuss it with me, Mr Clark, or go on your way out o' my office.' The man's high-handed attitude annoyed her. If offending him meant a legal wrangle, then so be it.

He sat back and studied her narrowly. She thought she detected a gleam of amusement in the thoughtful eyes. 'OK, Mrs Alexander. You win. Let's discuss how I'm to get my money back. Half a million dollars is a heck of a sum for your business to pull out of thin air in the present economic fix. How will you do it? A bank loan? Okay. So what's your collateral?'

Ishbel stood up, determined not to be browbeaten. 'Come, I'll show you.'

Matthew followed her obediently to the lift, and said nothing until they were descending to the lower floors with Archie in command. 'Pretty ancient poky rattle-trap elevator this is,' Matthew remarked pleasantly.

Archie spun round. 'Hey, it never gives ony bother. This lift's never been out o' service since way back afore the war.'

'Okay, son, I believe you. I guess Noah had something similar, in the ark.'

'I wouldna be surprised if he had. This lift was the first o' its kind in Edinburgh.' Archie slid open the door on the ground floor with an insulted clang of metal.

Matthew Clark stepped out and stood looking around, hands in pockets, chin jutting thoughtfully. Ishbel felt justifiable pride in the scene. She'd worked hard and used much imagination during the past six years.

The shop had an air of restful elegance which she'd struggled to foster from the start. The assistants wore pleasant, helpful smiles. She knew their feet were killing them and many had personal problems to face at home, but no matter what they smiled, their cheerfulness bolstered by the generous bonus scheme she'd instituted.

Adam McPherson went by on his rounds, immaculately turned out as usual, pink carnation in the buttonhole of his frock coat. He eyed Matthew speculatively as he passed, and lifted his brows questioningly at Ishbel before going on his way. Adam guessed something was up.

'Hmmm. I guess this place has possibilities,' Matthew said.

Ishbel glared, insulted. 'What d'you mean, possibilities?'

'It's not exactly geared to the thirties, is it?'

Ishbel was ready for battle. 'Listen, we've weathered depression, recession, unemployment and a nine-day General Strike that had my floor walkers out driving the trams in Princes Street wi' medical students acting as conductors. We're profitable, fashionable, and our luncheon and tearooms are packed to the doors every day o' the week. Could you do any better under difficult conditions?'

He grinned. 'Okay. I get the point. So this is your collateral. When do I get my money?'

This man has a talent for flooring you, Ishbel thought

resentfully. 'I'll have to think about it. Take legal advice,' she said sulkily.

'Sure. You do that.'

'Coo-eee, Matt!' Their discussion was interrupted by the American lady Ishbel had spotted earlier. She hurried towards Matthew and angled her pretty head to show off the ear-rings dangling beneath the peek-a-boo hat. 'Look what I bought, honey. As worn by Roy-al-tee!'

Matthew looked anguished. 'Polly, I warned you to go easy!'

'Relax. They're paste. Didn't cost more'n a couple of dollars. Besides, we're not bust yet, are we? Did you get the money?' she asked eagerly.

'I'm still working on it.' Matt caught Ishbel's eye and made the introductions. 'My wife Polly, Ishbel Alexander, Freddie's widow.'

Polly's handshake was hearty, her smile engaging. 'Say, I like this quaint old-fashioned store, Ishbel. It's cute.'

'Thank you, Mrs Clark,' Ishbel said, her smile wearing thin.

Polly wrinkled her nose. 'Mrs Clark! You Scots are so formal. Tell me though, Ishbel, as one of the British public, d'you think a film actress like me has any hope of becoming a star, saddled with a plain ol' name like Clark?'

'Lilian Gish did it with much worse,' Ishbel replied cannily.

Polly patted her arm. 'Lilian was silent, honey. It's talkies now.'

Ishbel decided it was safer to take the initiative when dealing with Matthew. She smiled sweetly at the American.

'Matthew, I wonder if you and Polly would care to come to dinner tomorrow evening and meet the family? That will give me time to seek legal advice on the problem.'

Matthew gave her a narrow look, but Polly beamed. 'Why, that's kind! Real neighbourly of you. Sure, we'll be there, won't we, Matt?' And of course he was forced to accept the invitation.

Americans! When little Elspeth Alexander heard Americans were coming to dinner, she could hardly contain her excitement. The wee seven-year-old danced around the kitchen until Florrie's patience was exhausted. 'I wish ye'd stop birlin' aboot. I'm tryin' to put on a show for they foreign Americans coming,' she complained, up to her elbows in flour.

Elspeth hopped from foot to foot. 'I'm putting on a show, Florrie.' She'd just begun dancing classes and had mastered a basic step, the pas de bas. She wore new dancing pumps with elastic criss-crossed round white anklesocks, and felt like the bee's knees. 'Florrie! Watch me doing my paddy-baas!' she commanded.

'I see you. You'll loup right into the soup ony meenit,' warned Florrie, thumping away at pastry destined to top an enormous steak and kidney pie.

The wee girl paused, out of breath, and flung herself down on the raggie rug Florrie had made to keep her poor old chilblains warm on the stone flags.

I'll do paddy-baas and my curtsey for the Americans, Elspeth planned. The teacher said mine was the best in the whole class. She rolled over on to her back and looked up at the clothes pulley slung from the roof above her head, where damp clothes were airing. I'll sing 'Rose Marie' for

them, she decided. Elspeth knew by listening to Grandfather's wireless that 'Rose Marie' was King George V's
favourite.

Elspeth had heard the man with the plummy voice on the
wireless relate that the poor king had been awfully ill that
summer. He'd had to go to the seaside to get better. He'd
chosen Bognor, and loved the town so much he honoured it
when he was well again. It was called Bognor Regis now,
and that was a happy ending of which Elspeth approved.

In a clear, little voice, she began singing softly: '"Oh,
Rose Marie, I love you, I'm always dreaming of you . . ."'

Busy as she was, Florrie paused to listen with delight.
The glorious wee voice, pure and true as a choir-boy's in
chapel, brought tears to her eyes with its beauty. But the
wee imp broke off after a few more bars and was on her feet
with a change of mood. 'Och, no, I'll sing a funny one,
Florrie. "Horsey, keep your tail up!"' And she was off,
singing in a different key, feet clip-clopping on the flags like
a comical wee pony. Oh, she was a scream this bairn, a real
comic! Florrie thought, shaking with mirth. Sobering up,
she gave her charge a wee spank on the bottom as she
trotted past. 'Away an' wash now, lovie. Your ma wants
your best dress on an' your white hair-ribbons in. They
must be awfy important folk, the Americans.'

'Florrie, maybe they're film stars!' whispered Elspeth,
eyes shining.

'Aye!' she breathed.

Polly Clark did not know what to expect when she arrived
at Knoxhall House. Her first impression was of ancient
gloom, which was not Polly's scene. There were no bright
lights, modern wallpapers or chrome furniture to be seen,

but the old-fashioned furnishings grew on you. Polly displayed modern elegance herself, her own gown having a slim skirt almost to the floor at the back but showing good ankles, silk stockings and high-heeled slippers at the front. She also wore modified Clara Bow makeup and ropes of artificial pearls.

She had hesitated anxiously over taking the cigarette holder and matching cigarette case, then stuffed them in her bag. She wasn't a smoker, cigarettes made her cough, but women smoking them looked daring and thoroughly modern, and Polly wanted to put on the style to impress the Alexanders. The family represented a lifeline for Matthew. She smiled and laughed and chatted charmingly all through the delicious dinner until her jaws ached. All the same, it sure was true what they said: Never act with children and animals.

The Alexander children were present at the meal. Also present was a dog, a terrier named Foxglove, Foxy's baby daughter, Polly was informed shyly by Elspeth, the smallest Alexander child. Foxglove was curled up with her nose resting on the high-heeled satin slippers Polly had eased off below the table because her feet were killing her. Every time Polly reached out a toe to retrieve a slipper, Foxglove growled menacingly and the little Alexanders giggled into their damask table napkins.

Gosh, but they were beautiful children, Polly thought admiringly. Talk about Jackie Coogan in *The Kid*! If Griffith or Cecil de Mille set eyes on those handsome twins – wowee, they'd have plans! Polly liked children, but the little charmer in the hair ribbons was something real special. She made Polly feel like a ham actress, yet she wasn't much more than seven years old and hardly opened her mouth. She didn't have to; the expressive eyes said it all. That kid is a natural, thought Polly.

'Your Prince of Wales is quite a star in the States. He's tremendously popular with Americans. All the girls love him,' Matthew was saying.

Mrs Eleanor Alexander looked anxious. 'Oh dear. I don't think Queen Mary will approve of that.'

Some imp of mischief, or perhaps that second glass of wine, made Polly burst into song: 'I danced with a man, who'd danced with a girl, who'd danced with the Prince of Wales.'

The kids turned and stared, the dog growled horribly under the table, and Matt fixed her with a warning glare. The old family servant hovering in the background reached over Polly's shoulder and sympathetically poured a large cup of black coffee. She sighed. Matt and old man Alexander had lit cigars so she bravely took out the cigarette holder and lit up defiantly with best Turkish.

Ishbel had kept conversation light until the meal was over and coffee served when she judged the time right to discuss the crisis that had arisen in the family. She wanted Freddie's children to be part of it. They were his bairns and had a right to know the pickle their father had got her into. It might serve as a warning.

Choosing a suitable moment, she looked round the table. 'We all know why Matthew and Polly are here. Matthew was a good friend to my husband when Freddie needed help. Matthew loaned him a substantial sum, and when things went tragically wrong, generously did not press the family for immediate payment. Now Matthew himself is in need of our help. I think we're all agreed

Freddie's debt must be honoured in full, with interest. But £125,000 is a lot of money. I've been forced to take legal advice.'

There was heavy silence. Eleanor Alexander sighed. It was all too much for her. 'Ishbel, I think the business should be sold, my dear, and Freddie's debt paid out of the proceeds. We'd manage somehow.'

'No!' Ishbel struck the table lightly with a fist, and they all sat up in surprise. She had spent a sleepless night working out a plan after a day-long consultation with the firm's lawyers. 'There is a solution,' she went on. 'No' a perfect solution perhaps, but a working solution. If Matthew agrees to it, that is.'

He eyed her cautiously, blue smoke curling upwards from the tip of the cigar. 'What have you in mind?'

Ishbel smiled and reached for old William Alexander's hand. The old man had contributed nothing to the conversation, but she knew he understood his son had got the family into debt. She'd explained the situation to him beforehand, gently and simply. 'Mr Alexander's share of the working capital amounts to over £125,000, roughly the same as mine. My dear father-in-law has agreed to relinquish his share temporarily to Matthew as security for the loan to Freddie.'

'What? But, Ishbel!' squeaked Eleanor indignantly.

She ignored the interruption. 'On the understanding that Matthew works in the shop until the debt is repaid. If he agrees to that, he's to be paid a monthly salary, and a proportion of the shop's profits paid regularly into a separate high-interest account, until that amount reaches a sum honouring Freddie's debt, wi' interest added.' She turned squarely to the American who hadn't uttered a sound. 'At that point, Matthew, my father-in-law's capital will revert to the family, and you can decide whether to bide in the business or take your money and go.'

There was a long silence when she'd finished. Cigar smoke hovered above Matthew's head as he thoughtfully considered the proposition.

Yeah, he thought. He liked the sound of it. The way things were in the States at the moment, he'd be one of a million broken, white-collared unemployed. The Alexanders were offering him a chance to do work he'd enjoy with a negotiable salary and profit-sharing thrown in. I've nothing to lose, he told himself.

'Okay,' he nodded. 'I like the scheme, Ishbel. I guess it will work. You can count me in.'

There was, however, a huge snag, which Ishbel could see right away. 'We'd have to work together, Matthew.'

'Oh, I guess we'd manage that,' he said airily.

William Alexander sensed the atmosphere of relief. He beamed at Matthew. 'You know, I got America on the short wave once. I thought it was Bratislava at first, with a call-sign just like a glockenspiel, but no, it was an American dance band. Oh, was I excited! It was the middle of the night and I wakened Eleanor, but I'm afraid she . . .' The old man shook his head and laughed happily to himself.

Ishbel was filled with doubts now that Matthew had accepted her plan so enthusiastically. She could see control of the firm slipping out of her grasp. 'If you're set on this course you'll have to bide in Edinburgh for some time, Matthew,' she warned.

'I love Edinburgh!'

Polly gave a wail. 'What about my acting career? Cecil de Mille was interested.'

'Talent can flourish any place, Polly,' he said cheerfully. 'There are plenty of theatres in Edinburgh, my love.'

'Sure, but Edinburgh ain't Hollywood!' she mourned.

Donald and Catriona Mackie were delighted to be given charge of their grandchildren for the Christmas holidays. Ishbel arrived in a flustered state, driving her Austin saloon. 'There's a new man come in, an American, and he's causing ructions in the shop, Mam,' she explained in a hurried aside to Catriona. Her efficient daughter looked ruffled, Catriona noted with surprise.

'Could you no' stay for Christmas, Ishbel, and to hang wi' that wretched shop?' begged her father eagerly.

Donald wasn't so fit these days. Rheumatics bothered his wounded leg, and though he suffered pain stoically, the limp had worsened. He longed for his daughter's pleasant company on a slow dander with old Foxy. He longed to hear all Ishbel's news, and feast his eyes on her bonnie face. To have her near him for a day or two would make Donald's Christmas just perfect.

She kissed him lightly. 'No' possible, Pa. We're working flat out wi' the Christmas rush, and I've to keep an eye on Matthew, the new man. He's a real fly one.'

Catriona smiled at her crestfallen husband. 'Never mind, lovie, we have the bairns an' their wee doggie to keep us cheery.'

Ishbel kissed her mother hurriedly. 'Thanks for taking them at such short notice, Mam. Grandfather Alexander's down wi' the 'flu, and the bairns will have more freedom here than in Edinburgh. It'll give the old man peace and quiet to recover too. Now, I must fly!'

'Everyone's fleein' since Charles Lindbergh flew the

Atlantic in thon wee airyplane. Man, who but a daft American would attempt a reckless caper like that?' grumbled Donald, but he found he was talking to thin air. His daughter had gone.

The twins had moved up into senior school, and considered it beneath their dignity to write a letter for their wee sister to send up the chimney to Santa Claus. Catriona volunteered for the task.

'We'll take the dogs for a walk, Granny,' Brian offered helpfully.

He delighted in the freedom of the countryside, but Adrian was more restless. He kicked a stone moodily into the undergrowth as they walked along the muddy track. 'Blast! I'll miss the Scout meeting. They were going to teach us tracking an' making signs, an' how to follow animal spoors.'

'We can teach ourselves tracking,' Brian laughed. 'There's rat, rabbit an' fox tracks everywhere. I don't think Grandpa can be a very good rat-catcher. Maybe we can start by tracking Foxy and Foxglove. They've disappeared.'

The boys heard the dogs yapping excitedly in the distance. 'They've got something cornered,' yelled Adrian. 'Come on!'

Crashing through undergrowth, they broke out into a clearing bounded by a high stone wall. The dogs were leaping up and down at the base, barking wildly, and an indignant little girl was perched on the parapet above. She called out when she saw the boys, 'I say, are these your dogs? If so, kindly remove them.'

The boys whistled to the dogs and clipped leads on the

228

little terriers. Then they stood below, looking up at the girl. 'What on earth are you doing up there?' Adrian demanded.

'This is my grandmother's house. I'm Joanna Wotherspoon,' the child replied with dignity.

Adrian laughed. 'Och, you're the Grumpy man's daughter!'

'My dad's a very nice man, you cheeky boy! Bunty says I can twist my daddy round my pinkie. Bunty's my nurse. I don't have a mother, you see. She died.'

The child wore a felt hat firmly secured under the chin with elastic, and a matching coat. Her legs were clad in thick black woollen stockings. The wee, thin legs dangled down over the wall. Brian smiled and held out a hand. 'Come on, Joanna, I'll help you down.'

'No, you won't. I shall come down by myself, thank you. Turn your backs and cover your eyes, both of you,' she ordered.

They obeyed, grinning widely. There were scrabbling, slithering noises, then a thud. 'You may look now,' Joanna said.

She was smaller than they'd expected, a thin, wiry child, dark-haired, with solemn brown eyes. 'Don't tell my daddy I was visiting my grandmother, if you please,' she requested. 'They can't stand one another.'

'Was that why you were climbing over the wall?' asked Brian.

'Yes. Dad's working by the gate.' Joanna hitched up the black stockings, which had a large hole in one knee. 'I'm going now. I'm pleased to have made your acquaintance, but kindly keep your dogs leashed on my land in future.' She nodded regally then ran off towards the farmhouse, the black stockings wrinkling in concertinas round her skinny ankles.

The boys looked at one another. 'D'you ken what happens to girls that wear black woollen stockings?' asked Adrian.

'No, what?' said Brian curiously.

'Nothing!'

And the two boys went laughing uproariously down the track.

Dorothy Alexander had time on her hands now Elspeth and the twins were at school all day. Eleanor Alexander had made a good recovery and willingly taken over the care of her husband. The old couple shared a peaceful contentment which was heart-warming to see, going for short walks or listening to the valve-operated wireless set Ishbel had bought for William when she'd had electricity and a phone line installed in Knoxhall House.

Dorothy didn't know what to do with her newfound leisure. Her thoughts would very often stray wistfully to the young man she'd sent away from the city for his own good. She'd had no word from Michael Burton these five years, and calmed the ache in her heart by telling herself she was glad of it. She wished she could train as a nurse, but that was out of the question at her age. As a last resort, Dorothy joined the local branch of the Red Cross as a voluntary worker.

At first she contented herself with hospital visits, arranging flowers for patients, running errands and tidying lockers, like the other ladies of her class, but that very soon palled. Then Dorothy ranged further afield.

She boldly penetrated the overcrowded slum areas in the Old Town. Conditions in the ancient high lands and tenements sickened and angered her. Historic places, once home to the highest and lowest in the land, had been shamefully abandoned to misery and disease. She plunged bravely down smelly, hilly wynds and dark vennels and poked into the blackest and filthiest of closes, shining her bicycle lamp into verminous corners. By such tactics Dorothy came across some sickening sights and alarming situations, but in her own small way did a great deal of good.

Pitiful whimpering led her deep into an ill-lit cellar one day. The lamp revealed three tiny children huddled together, hugging a sadly flea-bitten dog. 'Wir mammy's awfy seek, an' the man telt us tae get oot o' his road,' the eldest sobbed.

'Oh, did he indeed?' said Dorothy grimly, dealing out generous jammy pieces to bairns and dog alike from a knapsack she kept for such emergencies. 'You bide here 'til I tell you. I'll be back!' She left the lamp for comfort and resolutely picked her way up a green and rotting staircase right to the stairhead, following the sound of a woman moaning in pain and a man's voice, shouting.

Dorothy reached the top and rushed into a dimly lit interior. A woman lay weak and collapsed on a makeshift bed covered with old newspapers, a man bending over her shouting at the top of his lungs while holding a tiny newborn baby in both hands. He glanced over his shoulder. 'Thank God somebody heard! Are you a nurse? Well, can't be helped. See to this woman, will you? The baby's not breathing.' He turned away and began working feverishly on the motionless little body.

Dorothy rolled up her sleeves and did what she could to make the mother comfortable. The woman opened her eyes weakly and whispered, 'How's the bairnie?'

Dorothy hesitated, but at that moment she heard a gurgling cry, and then another, much stronger. She smiled her relief. 'Your bairnie's fine.'

'It's a boy,' the man said, and handed the squalling baby gently into its mother's arms. Then he and Dorothy looked at one another for the first time and received the shock of their lives. 'Dorothy! This is the last place I expected to find you,' cried Dr Burton.

'Maybe that's why you chose it,' she answered sadly.

He sighed. 'You're quite right. I worked in leper colonies in Africa and India until Mr Gandhi staged his non-violent revolution and there was unrest. I came back and worked in London for a bit, but couldn't stay away from Edinburgh. I had to be near you, Dorothy. I thought working in the slums would be the safest place, because it's a region no lady would visit, and besides the folk here most need help.' He tended the exhausted young mother, the baby cradled in her arms, and tucked a ragged coverlet around them, before straightening and looking directly at Dorothy. 'Seems I was wrong though. What on earth are you doing here?'

'The same as you, Michael. Trying to forget somebody I love,' she admitted. 'I should never have sent you away into misery and danger, saying I didn't love you. That was dishonest, but I only wanted to save you from ridicule.'

He looked astonished. 'Ridicule, for loving you?'

'Yes, a dumpy little old maid seven years your senior. Can you imagine the meal malicious gossips would make of that?' She turned away from the bed, searching the squalid room for some means of washing the baby and keeping it warm.

He touched her and took her in his arms. 'Dorothy, do

you seriously believe I care tuppence about gossip?'

'You should. It can ruin a man's career.'

He laughed heartily. 'Not here in the slums, it can't! These poor folk are only too glad to see a doctor. Any doctor.' He became serious again. 'Dorothy, look at me!' he said softly.

Hesitantly, she lifted her eyes. The light from the guttering candle showed how he'd suffered in the intervening years. He wasn't a young man any more, he was middle-aged, thin and drawn and saddened. And she had done this to him, with her foolish lies and prim ideas! 'Dorothy, my feelings for you haven't changed,' he went on. 'If I go down very uncomfortably upon bended knee, will you marry me?'

Dorothy's laughter burst from her in a great surge of joy and happiness. 'Oh, Michael, there's no need to strain a ligament, because I love you dearly and the answer's yes. If you've no objection to marrying a mature woman, why should I care a button what folk think?'

He rested his cheek against hers for a moment before kissing her. 'Well, you know what they say about age, Dorothy dear, it's only a question of mind over matter. If you don't mind, it doesn't matter.'

The new mother watched impassively, with dull resignation. Her mind was already ranging ahead, wondering how her bairns were to be fed and clothed now there were four.

Once the family recovered from the shock of Dorothy's sudden romance, everyone was highly delighted. The happy couple were married quietly in June 1930, and took up residence in the lodge of Knoxhall House. The pair of them swiftly became a formidable force, agitating for reconstruction of deplorable slums, and campaigning for help for poor folk living miserably in the historic Old Town.

Dorothy's newfound happiness only served to highlight Ishbel's isolation as joint head of Alexander's. Since Matthew joined the firm a power struggle had taken place, and she found she must keep her wits constantly about her to answer his searching questions and fend off criticism.

Matthew and Polly had moved into the vacant caretaker's flat at the top of the building. 'My penthouse suite', Polly called it. This was practical but had some drawbacks. No matter how early Ishbel arrived at the shop, Matthew beat her to it.

She suspected he prowled around after hours too, scheming and planning. He was reasonably polite and amiable, but these were early days and she guessed Matthew was biding his time until he had the measure of her and the business. Any day now the American would launch an attack. It was time for the Alexander family to stand united.

Usually, Sunday evening after supper was a happy time in Knoxhall House. Ishbel and the children would relax, listening to the radio while the old folks dozed by the fireside.

'The Palm Court of Grand Hotel' was one of their favourite programmes, broadcast for an hour on Sundays. The children enjoyed it almost as much as 'Children's Hour' with Uncle Mac and Larry the Lamb. Then Elspeth got out her colouring book and crayons, while the boys leafed idly through back copies of *Adventure* and *Wizard* comics.

In the Palm Court of the illustrious hotel, Albert Sandler

would play violin and Peter Dawson might sing songs such as 'The Road to Mandalay' in a reassuringly deep and British voice. In the background you could hear the genteel chatter of refined Grand Hotel guests as they clattered coffee cups and tinkled brandy glasses.

All the same, thought Brian, not for the first time, it was jolly bad manners to chatter and chink brandy glasses while somebody was performing. Grandmother and Grandfather were sound asleep as usual, and Peter Dawson had just launched into 'Drake is in his Hammock' when Brian's mother stood up and held a warning finger to her lips, before ushering the children quietly through to the drawing room. She closed the door and faced them. The children looked at one another. Something was up!

'I wanted to talk to you in private, about the shop,' she said.

All three groaned inwardly. The shop spelled boredom.

'I've never spoken to you about the future of Alexander's,' Ishbel hurried on, 'but now I must, because we're facing – well, an American invasion. This could ruin everything our shop stands for – high quality and service. I'm fighting hard as I can, but I need your help. The shop is your future too, you know.'

They were silent. Adrian had thought about his future often. It was a golden path leading straight to St Andrew's University by the cold North Sea. He'd gone on a trip to the ancient university town once with the Scouts, and watched enviously as the red-gowned students strolled past. They'd seemed so confident and dashing, and Adrian had greatly fancied the life. It had never entered his head to work in the shop when he grew up. The idea left him quite cold. 'What do you want us to do?' he asked blankly.

'Just a Saturday job, sweeping the floors and tidying up. Just being there,' Ishbel said eagerly.

A Saturday job! Brian's spirits plummeted into his slippers. He roamed far afield on Saturdays, weather permitting, and saw all sorts of exciting things. He'd seen the huge Graf Zeppelin, when the airship flew over the city last year. Sometimes he took a sandwich in his pocket and climbed to the summit of Arthur's Seat, where he stood with the wind whipping his hair and the River Forth spreading out into the wide North Sea right before his eyes, with the Bass Rock and even the May Island visible on a clear day. It was easy to imagine a shadowy King Arthur standing there long ago, surveying his threatened kingdom. If the weather was bad, Brian took the easier path to the penny matinée at the Picturedrome, to watch Tom Mix or laugh at Charlie Chaplin's pathetic wee tramp or Harold Lloyd's crazy exploits dangling from skyscrapers. But to work in the shop, shut away in a dusty warehouse – no!

Elspeth spoke up. 'What'll I do in the shop, Mam?'

Ishbel laughed and hugged her. 'Nothing much just yet, sweetheart, you're too young. But the shop's your future too. Always remember you're named for the brave lady who laid the foundations for it years ago.' She looked hopefully at her sons. 'Well, boys, what d'you say?'

Their young faces were guarded and she couldn't tell what they were thinking. Ishbel felt a moment of panic. She needed the support of her children, but they seemed like strangers. 'You'll get paid, of course,' she added in desperation.

Her boys stared at her speculatively. 'How m-much?' asked Brian.

* * *

236

'What the heck d'you call these things?' Matthew Clark flung a pair of gentleman's underpants on Ishbel's desk, rather like a knight flinging down a gauntlet.

'Long johns,' she answered.

'I never seen anything so antiquated in my life.'

'You've never stood at the top of Waverley Steps in a January gale, Mr Clark!'

'They're wool! Itchy, prickly, brings me out in goose bumps. Ain't you heard of artificial silk or celanese? We doped aircraft canvas with cellulose acetate varnish way back during the war, for heaven's sake!'

'We don't deal in cheap stuff,' retorted Ishbel.

'Oh, sure! Pink, white or beige bloomers. Beige! I ask you, what sort of colour is that? I guess it was invented to go with that awful coffee you serve up in the tearooms.'

The battle was on. Matthew Clark had gained confidence and was showing his teeth. 'And another thing,' he continued, 'we got to do something about new elevators. Yours is ancient and in the wrong place for what I have in mind, which is a complete reorganisation of the various departments.'

Ishbel's cheeks glowed with anger. 'Tell me, do you intend to bankrupt this store?'

'No, honey. Only drag it into the twentieth century,' he replied sweetly.

Elspeth had begged to accompany her mother and brothers to the shop that Saturday morning and was present in the office during this altercation. The little girl grew weary of the fierce argument raging over her head. She tugged at Ishbel's sleeve. 'Mam, may I go an' look round?'

'Certainly, lovie.' Ishbel beamed. She was secretly

delighted by the little girl's interest. Maybe wee Elspeth held the future of the shop in her hands, she thought hopefully. The boys were certainly not so keen.

Polly was surprised to find the little Alexander girl at her door when she answered a timid knocking. The child stared at her shyly. 'Please, are you a film star?'

Polly's bosom swelled. 'Well, honey, I guess so. Almost.' She drew the little one into the flat. Luckily she had a bottle of lemon soda and a box of chocolate crackers, which she produced. 'Do you like movies, Elspeth?' Polly asked.

'Oh, yes. I wish I could grow up to be a film star like you.'

Elspeth and Polly took stock of one another over the lemon soda. Polly was delighted to find a kindred spirit in this gloomy desert, and warmed to the child. She cupped Elspeth's chin in her hands. 'You have lovely violet eyes, that's good.'

'Is it?'

'Yes. Pale blue eyes register blank on orthochromatic film, you know, honey. In the early days of silent movies the cameramen made a frame of black velvet and poked the lens through it if the star had pale eyes, and that fixed the problem.' Polly laughed happily. 'You'd never guess the tricks they get up to in the movies! I played a part in a silent movie for D. W. Griffith once, an' he dumped a whole load of white gravel round my feet to cast a reflection on my face, then Billy Bitzer the cameraman took a shot right into the sun to make it seem like a halo round my head. Nobody dared do it before, but it came out real swell. Pity the film was a turkey,' she sighed regretfully. 'And hot! Gee, you'd never guess how hot Aristo arc-lights can be when you're wearing furs. No wonder Chaplin headed for the snows of the Sierra Nevada when he was filming *The Gold Rush*.'

Elspeth listened round-eyed and open-mouthed. Talking to Polly gave her a tantalising glimpse of a more exciting world. She sighed. 'I want to act in movies like you, but my mammy says I've to work in the shop when I grow up 'cause I'm an Alexander. Working in a shop's awful boring, but Mam says there's an American invasion of our shop and Alexanders have to fight it. Do you think there's been an American invasion?' Elspeth asked her new friend anxiously.

'I guess so, love,' said Polly, hiding a grin. Matt working at full steam sure had that effect.

What a sin though, condemning this great little girl to a boring future without so much as a by-your-leave, Polly thought indignantly. Serve 'em right if someone upset their cosy little plan. She studied Elspeth thoughtfully. The child had potential, no doubt about that. 'If you really want to be a movie star, Elspeth, you gotta start young.'

'I can sing a bit an' do paddy-baas,' she volunteered eagerly.

Polly folded her arms. 'OK. Pretend I'm Cecil de Mille. Convince me.'

Chapter 11

The battle of the elevators raged for weeks. It was small wonder the staff got wind of it and uneasy rumours spread. Ishbel found Archie the lift boy waiting outside the office one morning. He was a bright lad, yet he'd stubbornly resisted Ishbel's attempts to promote him to junior management. 'Naw. I like working in the lift. I'd rather bide there,' he'd declared.

'But don't you want to rise in the world, Archie?' she asked.

He'd grinned. 'I *am* rising in the world, missis. Up an' doon, a' day!' But Archie's usual cheery grin wasn't in evidence this morning. He looked glum.

'They're saying you're doing away' wi' the lift, Mrs Freddie. I'll be oot o' my job.'

'They're blethering, Archie. I give you my word we'll never dispense with the old lift. It's well-placed for invalids and elderly folk visiting the shop,' she declared.

He cheered up. 'Aye, so it is. Och, they had me worried for a meenit. I'd never get another job.'

'Of course you would, an intelligent lad like you. I wish you'd agree to become a floor walker, Archie. You could be an assistant manager in no time.'

To her amazement, he looked positively terrified at the

241

prospect, backing away. 'Naw! No' me, ma'am, I like the lift.' With that, he bolted.

Ishbel stared after him, puzzled.

Still thoughtful, she went into the office. As she'd half expected, Matthew had beaten her to it. Their offices adjoined with only a sliding partition between, which Ishbel closed and Matthew kept open so that he missed nothing. 'Good morning, Ishbel!' he greeted her cheerfully.

'Not so good!' She dumped a load of order sheets on her desk. 'I've just assured a leal member of my staff he won't lose his job. Rumours are rife, thanks to you.'

Matthew smiled. 'OK, let's scotch rumours and get on with the plan. I got a revised estimate today. The elevator manufacturer will survey the site, supply all necessary mechanical parts, and the installation can be done by an approved local firm. That knocks more than five hundred pounds off the total. What d'you say?'

Ishbel sat down and stared at him. The problem was, she agreed the store would benefit from better access to the upper floors. The staircase and lofty galleries with a beautiful cupola soaring above were spectacular, but she sympathised with customers puffing up so many flights to reach the upper departments and the luncheon and tearooms situated on the top floors. The small existing lift obviously could not cope with the numbers.

Never let it be said Ishbel Alexander stood in the way of progress! she thought resignedly. 'Very well, Matthew, we'll go ahead,' she decided. 'We must spend precious capital to do it, and I hope you're prepared for months of disruption and loss of trade.'

He acknowledged victory gracefully. Over the next few

weeks he produced carefully drawn plans and spread the blueprints eagerly before Ishbel. She was impressed. He had not been wasting his time while prowling round the shop. 'I've drawn up a four-year plan, Ishbel, starting with installation of elevators and improvements to stairways and fire escapes.' He pointed to the plan. 'I suggest we can keep disruption to a minimum if we utilise this unused storage space to house the elevators. That way we can work behind scenes until we're almost ready to unveil the scheme to the public.'

'Ah, but you can't hide noise!'

He smiled. 'Sure, I agree. Tell the guy who plays the grand piano in the tearooms to play fortissimo!'

His enthusiasm was infectious, and she found herself warming to the project. 'The success of this venture will depend on who's doing the work, Matthew,' she pointed out. 'Can you really trust local mechanics to handle it?'

'Don't worry. I've asked around an' found the very best.' He rolled up the plans, then looked at her. 'Thanks, Ishbel.'

She raised her brows. 'What for?'

'Letting me win. I didn't think you would.'

There was a well-established Scottish custom which almost drove Matthew wild. That was early closing day on Wednesdays. 'A whole afternoon's trading wasted!' he grumbled.

'It's all very well you girning,' Ishbel retorted. 'Shop assistants work hard for long hours. They're entitled to time off to relax with their families and enjoy some fresh air.'

He glared accusingly at the work piled high on her desk that sunny Wednesday afternoon. '*You* don't take time off.'

'Ah, but I'm the boss.'

'Glad you think so,' Matthew remarked drily. He strode to the window and stood looking out, restlessly jingling loose change in his pocket. 'It sure is a lovely day! I envy your little shop assistants filling their dusty lungs with fresh air.'

'Take Polly for a walk,' suggested Ishbel, nobly making a start to the order sheets.

'Polly don't walk. At least, only as far as a cab. Besides, she's got herself a job. She's out this afternoon coaching little kids at Elspeth's school in acting and voice production.'

Polly's efforts with the school children had impressed Ishbel. Elspeth gave glowing accounts of rehearsals for the forthcoming school play, and Ishbel was surprised to learn her daughter had been given a leading role. Fortunately, despite a growing number of dancing, singing and music lessons, Elspeth's interest in the shop had not waned, much to her mother's delight. Elspeth never missed a Saturday visit to the store.

'The children all love Polly. They think she's a real film star,' Ishbel remarked warmly.

'Yeah, kids take to Polly. Pity she can't have any,' he said with a hint of sadness.

'Oh, Matthew. I'm so sorry,' said Ishbel softly.

He shrugged. 'San fairy Ann.' He hesitated, then glanced at her hopefully. 'Say, I want to explore the city, but I hate walking on my own. Looks so kind of aimless. Why don't you walk with me?'

She laughed. 'We'd probably talk nothing but shop, and argue. That's all we do these days.'

'Then it's time for a change.' He crossed the room and leaned on the desk. 'I'd really appreciate your company, Ishbel. What d'you say?'

She sat quite still for a moment. She'd fought hard, since fate had thrown them together, and perhaps she'd fought hardest against his charm which he was quite capable of using as a deliberate weapon. Now, for the first time, she let herself be swayed. She glanced wistfully out of the window at the splendid view of the castle perched on its rock. 'It *is* a lovely day. Please don't tempt me, Matthew.'

'Heck, you ought to be tempted. It does you good to give in to temptation once in a while.'

Privately, she doubted it, but against her better judgement allowed herself to be persuaded.

September can be a beautiful month in Edinburgh when the mellow sun shines warmly on old stone and breezes blow soft and gentle from the Pentland Hills. Ishbel had forgotten how beautiful it could be. Perhaps she had forgotten many simple pleasures since she came to the city. When she and Matthew left the shop, she lifted her face eagerly to the sun. Her skin was pale, untouched by sunlight these days. She imagined she could smell all the scents of autumn in the countryside. Her heart grew heavy with a wistful longing, and she sighed. 'I always loved the busy hairst time. The hard work stacking the sheaves, and the joy of bringing the crops safely hame.'

Matthew looked down at her. 'You're a country girl at heart. I guess you always will be,' he noted observantly.

Ishbel was annoyed by her lapse into nostalgia. She was

showing far too many weaknesses which gave him ammunition for battle. She laughed lightly. 'Och, farming's a gey hard way of life, Matthew, and I wouldn't want it for me or my bairns. Now, where do you want to go?'

'How about Princes Street Gardens?'

'No. Not there,' she said too quickly.

'Memories?'

'Yes.' She turned away, unwilling to let him witness yet another weakness. She could not walk with another man in that warm and pleasant spot where she and Freddie had kissed. That would seem like a betrayal of her dead husband's memory. Tears stung her eyes. Would the past never fade?

'Where do you suggest?' Matthew asked gently.

She thought for a moment. 'You get a grand view from the Calton Hill. My Auntie Nellie used to take me when I was a wee lass. I've never forgotten it.'

'No bad memories?'

'Och no!' she laughed, spirits rising as they walked. 'Only fond memories, of cheerful wifies beating carpets on the hill at the spring cleaning. The fluff from dusty carpets was like a haar coming in from the river.'

'Well, it ain't springtime, so we ought to be okay,' Matthew smiled. He felt good, young and carefree. He tugged the trilby to a rakish angle and tucked his companion's hand under his arm.

Matthew paused when they reached Register House and studied with interest the statue of the Duke of Wellington on a prancing war horse. Walking on, he spotted the distinctive ruins on Calton Hill and stopped in his tracks. 'I never saw such a city for hills! How come you got the Acropolis on top of this one?'

Ishbel smiled. 'Ah, they call that Scotland's pride and penury. It was meant to be a grand monument to the men who died in the Napoleonic Wars, but they ran out o' money halfway through.'

'I'm glad they did. It looks better as a ruin.'

Matthew discovered he had great affection for the foggy east coast city, aptly nick-named Auld Reekie. A sense of history surrounding him gave him a comfortable feeling. He felt at ease walking the stone-flagged sidewalks with Ishbel Alexander.

Matthew was used to adapting his pace to his wife's high-heeled trot. Walking with Polly was no great pleasure for an active man, but Ishbel walked with a graceful stride which fitted well with his own. He suspected she could walk on for miles if the need arose, conquering summits and glens. Gee, I would love to conquer those heathery summits with Ishbel one day, he thought to himself. At work, she drove him wild with annoyance when she calmly vetoed his schemes, but he couldn't deny he was finding her company stimulating today.

A slight furrow in his brow, Matthew glanced down at the woman walking by his side. He'd been so preoccupied with their power struggle he'd hardly noticed the neat, straight nose, the smiling curve of lips which could curl scornfully and reduce him to frustration with a few biting Scots words. The determined set of the chin he already knew, for that signalled trouble.

They paused for a rest halfway up the steep path. Matthew leaned his arms on top of the dyke while Ishbel stared westwards across the city. It always seemed more peaceful on Wednesday afternoons. The breeze stirred the trees in the Gardens below, where once she'd strolled with

Freddie. If she closed her eyes, she could almost imagine she was eighteen again and he was by her side. Her senses quickening, she could smell the faint aromatic scent of the hair-oil he'd used, feel the warm pressure of his arm against hers. Ishbel opened her eyes with a start. It was Matthew who leaned beside her, his arm resting against hers. She shivered. Such a vivid daydream! Why did Freddie seem so close to her today?

As for Matthew, he was happier and more relaxed than he'd been since Wall Street collapsed. He smiled at his companion. 'D'you realise we're in harmony for once? Not a cross word, and we haven't even mentioned the shop.'

She laughed. 'Och, Matthew! You just broke the spell.'

'Did I?'

Smiling, he leaned back against the wall and looked at her. An odd thing happened. The image of the working woman he saw every day blurred and she appeared to him in a different light, the sun warming her skin with a golden glow. She was beautiful.

Matthew was badly shaken. He'd noticed she was attractive – what man wouldn't? – but the emotions her sun-kissed beauty roused in him now were deep and frightening. He swallowed uneasily. 'I guess the spell's still intact, Ishbel. It's this place, this city.'

'Aye. It's the magic of Edinburgh.' She laughed a little unsteadily because the look in his eyes unsettled her. Silently, he held out his hand, and Ishbel hesitated before resting her palm gingerly in his. His long fingers clasped hers, disturbing yet comforting in their strength, and not for the first time she realised how much she needed a man beside her. She'd been alone too long.

They scrambled up the hillside together hand in hand,

laughing breathlessly. It was a difficult path they'd chosen, uneven and steep. Like my life from now on, I guess, thought Matthew.

Donald Mackie had a new interest, which Wotherspoon fostered. Bee-keeping had become a popular pastime in the area, and the farmer was quick to recognise that clover honey sold in attractive jars could provide a useful source of income in these difficult times. Edinburgh stores would snap them up, no doubt. Meanwhile the busy bees would pollinate two fields of prime raspberries and strawberries Wotherspoon cultivated specially for big Edinburgh hotels.

The farmer generously replaced Donald's ancient straw hives with six smart timber ones from a well-known source in Wormit, Fife. With Wotherspoon's blessing, Donald ordered bees of a calm disposition from France to occupy the new hives, and took delivery of his wee workers when they came north by rail. There was no prouder man in the Lothians than Donald when he fitted the bee-keeper's veil over his old bonnet and puffed smoke at his bees to render them calmer still while he collected the first combs of golden honey.

Even when caring for additional hives, Donald found most seasons relatively troublefree, but on sultry summer days a sharper watch on the bees was required. They became restive in thundery weather, and might swarm from over-populated hives after the queen. At that vulnerable point a swarm might be lost to any wily bee-keeper in the vicinity who could capture the queen and pinch the lot. That threat kept Donald on his toes all summer, eyes wide open and shotgun handy.

One hot, thundery summer day, anxious thoughts were

going through Donald's head as he tended his bees. He kept an eye on a menacing sky opaque with heat and all his attention on the throbbing hives. The wee creatures were tetchy.

'How do you do, Mr Mackie?' enquired a voice.

He turned with surprise to find the farmer's young lassie standing behind him. 'I'm fair to middling, thank ye, Miss Joanna. How's yoursel'?' Donald answered, smiling. Joanna was an old-fashioned wee soul, with old-fashioned ways which stemmed from being too much in the company of her father, grandmother and the Aberdeen kitchie-maid.

'I'm sorry to interrupt you at your work, Mr Mackie, but I was wondering if your grandsons are visiting at present?' she asked in her precise way, the dead spit of her ladyship in the Big House. Her grandfather the laird had faded quietly away some time ago, leaving his wife a lonely widow living in mouldering splendour. They said Wotherspoon did what he could to support the old lady, but she was proud, and the Big House a burden.

Donald shook his head regretfully. 'No, I'm afraid I haven't seen the laddies for a wee while, Miss Joanna. They work in the shop on Saturdays and school holidays, so they've little time to visit their old grandparents, more's the pity.'

Her face fell. 'Oh, I see. I have gifts for them. They were helpful when I became trapped on top of a wall some time ago and I should like to give them a small token of my appreciation and thanks.' She held out two little parcels carefully wrapped in Christmas paper. 'Would you be kind enough to give these to your grandsons when next they visit?'

'Surely,' he said obligingly, frowning at the two differently shaped packages. 'Which is which?'

She looked non-plussed. 'I liked one boy better than the other, but I don't know which, they are so alike. One gift is very precious, and I should like the nicest boy to have it.'

'Very well.' Donald tucked the two small gifts into his pocket. 'I'll have them toss for it, shall I, miss? That gives a fifty-fifty chance it'll work oot.'

She gave a brilliant smile that transformed her plain wee face. 'What a very good idea, Mr Mackie! Thank you so much.'

'Now, Miss Joanna, you'd better away for I've an idea the bees will swarm, and that's a gey alarming sight for a young lady to witness,' he warned.

Joanna looked at him solemnly. 'I'm not afraid. I'm not afraid of anything.'

Matthew had arranged for a local contractor, Allsop and Company, to install the elevators, and work began later in the year on the ambitious project. To begin with Ishbel had little to do with the reconstruction of the shop. She was anxiously monitoring a revolutionary new invention recently introduced into the store. Daringly, she had ordered five hundred of the new fasteners to replace buttons on all Alexander's gowns. The chairman of ICI had named these 'Zip' fasteners, because of the odd noise made when opening and closing them.

Ishbel was seriously concerned that her lady customers might not take kindly to the labour-saving device, but to her relief she discovered they were more than delighted. For those ladies who could no longer afford a lady's maid, 'Zip' fasteners did away with much awkward squirming and struggling with button-hooks on back-fastening gowns. Hard times hit all, as Doris remarked.

Very soon, however, building work began to intrude upon Ishbel's daily round. Most activity took place behind brick walls in the storeroom as she and Matthew had agreed, but even so dust settled over everything and sales assistants and customers grumbled. A bedlam of hammering and drilling went on all day.

At last Ishbel could stand it no longer. She walked purposefully into the storeroom, where a complex structure of steel girders was rearing upwards, enclosed by solid concrete walls. More wooden shuttering for concrete work was being hammered into place as she approached, and Ishbel sought out the foreman. 'Couldn't that work be done when the shop's shut? My customers are complaining.'

The man scratched his head. 'I'd need to ask the boss.'

'Ask him!'

Ishbel stood tapping her toe while the foreman retired behind scaffolding. Presently he returned, accompanied by a familiar figure. Ishbel sighed resignedly. 'Och, so it's you, Sandy MacArthur. I might have guessed. Still climbing the ladder?'

Sandy wiped oily hands on a rag. 'What's the problem?'

'The noise you're making. Can't you hammer after hours?'

'Oh, certainly, ma'am, but it'll cost you in overtime.'

'I'm getting so's I don't care!'

'You really want it that way?'

'Sandy, I want peace and quiet at any price.'

'Righto. I'll see to it.' He would have turned on his heel and left her, but she detained him.

'What are you doing here?'

'My firm amalgamated wi' Allsop's a wee while ago. Didn't you read it in the papers? Sir Stewart Allsop hasn't been too well, so I'm in charge o' this job seeing as how I'm engaged to his daughter.'

She stared blankly. 'I didn't know you were engaged.'

'Och, Sarah didn't want a fuss made.'

She touched his arm. 'I'm happy for you, Sandy,' she said, but in truth her emotions were mixed. She was glad he'd found somebody else to love, but it made her feel even more alone.

'Thanks,' he said gruffly. 'You want peace and quiet, Mrs Alexander, I promise you'll get it.'

True to his word, an eerie hush fell over the whole building, which lasted for approximately five minutes, then Matthew's ringing tones were heard echoing throughout the store. 'Hey, what the hell's goin' on? What's the holdup?'

Ishbel rushed behind scenes, and found Matthew and Sandy facing one another angrily. The American rounded on her. 'Ishbel, this guy says you ordered him to stop. Is this true?'

'Aye! Something had to be done, Matthew. Customers have been complaining.'

'Let 'em! We're working on a tight schedule for this job, and you've wrecked it sticking your nose in.' He clenched his fists and lifted his hands high in frustration. 'Just what I might expect from a bossy woman!'

Ishbel was furious. 'You listen here! It's lucky someone considers our customers, or we'd have none. You're a typical, selfish male, Matthew Clark, with little regard for other folk.'

He spluttered. 'Why, you stubborn little—'

Sandy caught his arm. 'Wait a minute. There's no call to insult Mrs Alexander. She has a point. We could easily do the noisier work before the shop opens and after hours. It wouldn't affect the cost a' that much.'

Matthew shook off his hand angrily. 'You stay out of this. I can get someone else to do the job.'

'Aye, you can,' agreed Sandy calmly. 'But you canna trust them to do complicated engineering work like this properly. I'm the best engineer you'll get hereabouts.'

Matthew paused, scowling. 'I know, damn' you. I checked.' The two men eyed one another. Matthew decided reluctantly it was stalemate, and shrugged. 'Okay. Muffle the hammers.'

He turned to Ishbel, already ashamed of the angry outburst. 'Honey, I'm sorry I lost my rag,' he apologised. Impulsively, he bent his head and kissed her gently on the lips, no more than a butterfly touch brushing her mouth yet a very public gesture which Sandy watched with disapproval.

Ishbel caught her breath shakily at the unexpectedness of the caress, and found herself blushing. 'I – I forgive you, Matthew,' she muttered, as she spun on her heel and hurried back to the safety of the shop.

Polly Clark was enjoying herself more than she would have believed possible in a city where she'd once thought there would be no fun. Every movie that came to the nearby Alhambra, she had already seen twice in the States. If she hadn't become involved with Elspeth Alexander and her little school friends, she would have been driven to distraction.

The child was so talented Polly could hardly believe it.

254

Sing, dance, act . . . the enchanting kid could do them all. She flung herself enthusiastically into the task of coaching Elspeth, who responded with a devotion that warmed Polly's heart.

The choice of an adaptation of *Peter Pan* for the annual school play gave her protégée a chance to shine. When Elspeth's overworked teacher heard glowing accounts of Polly's credentials from her pupil, she begged the American lady to direct the production of the play. This Polly did with glee. Casting Elspeth in the leading role proved a stroke of genius. The child was magic – light as a feather as she moved across a darkened stage, so that you really thought Peter Pan was flying through a midnight sky. She contrived to be comical, yet there was a pathos about her performance that touched every heart. The moment Elspeth stepped on stage she became the little lost boy who never grew up.

Elspeth was excited about the part. Her heart beat fast when she thought about acting in front of her mother, who had no idea she could act and sing so well. 'You will come, won't you, Mam?' she begged Ishbel anxiously, a few days before the performance.

'Of course I will, lovie.' Ishbel smothered a yawn. Amateur dramatics had never appealed to her. She would attend the school performance for Elspeth's sake, of course, but she would probably find it embarrassing, she knew, watching the children fluff their lines.

She felt tired, for the shop took all her time and energy. She had become much more absorbed in the business since Matthew Clark arrived. He infuriated her with his grandiose schemes and scathing criticism, surprised her sometimes with his perception and kindness, and

when he set out to deliberately charm her, she found
him . . .

Ishbel wakened out of the reverie to find her daughter
had been questioning her. 'What was that, dear?'

'I said, did you know a statue of Peter Pan appeared in
Kensington Gardens during the night, and London children think it was put there by fairies? It wasn't really, you
know, Mam. J. M. Barrie just wanted children to believe in
fairies.'

'What a lovely idea!'

'Yes, wasn't it? Polly told me. She tells lovely stories. I
love Polly so much, Mam, 'cause she's never too busy to
talk to me.'

'I'm glad, Elspeth,' yawned Ishbel sleepily, and didn't
heed the danger signal.

Catriona had never used a telephone in her life, but she was
attempting to use one now. She hadn't known where to
turn when Donald collapsed suddenly as he was getting up
that morning. She'd made him as comfortable as possible
then hurried to the farmhouse where they had a telephone.
Miss Joanna was leaning helpfully over her shoulder at that
moment, instructing her in its use. To her surprise,
Catriona found herself talking to her old friend Maggie
Birse, telephone operator and post-mistress in Dalkeith.

'Maggie, Donald's taken a bad turn. Could you get the
doctor to him?' she gasped.

'Oh, mighty, aye! Dinna fash yoursel', Catriona, I'll see
to it for ye. The doctor's just away up the street to the
butcher's bairn.'

'Could you maybe tell my daughter for me as well,
Maggie? Ishbel works in Alexander's, the posh shop in

Princes Street. I dinna ken the number. I'm sure it would help Donald if she would only come,' sobbed Catriona.

'I'll look it up in the book, lovie. Away home to your man now,' said the comforting voice.

Joanna seized the receiver and bawled into the mouthpiece, 'Mrs Birse, tell the Alexander boys to come too! Mr Mackie wants to see them. He told me so.'

Bunty Mutch had been standing by listening to this drama unfold and dug her charge slyly in the ribs. 'Och, Joanna, own up. There's mair than Mr Mackie keen to see those lads!'

When Ishbel received her mother's message, she paused only to pick up the twins from school as instructed and put Dorothy in the picture, then she drove fast towards Dalkeith. The boys sat grim-faced and silent, but she was glad of their company. 'Oh, I've neglected your poor grandfather!' she cried tearfully. 'I'll never forgive myself if anything happens to him.'

She wiped away tears. An echo of a hollow promise made to him once came back to haunt her. She'd sworn never to neglect her darling pa, but she had neglected him. The shop occupied all her time, and Matthew occupied all her thoughts. What's happening to me? she wondered in bewilderment, and pressed her foot hard on the accelerator.

Catriona hurried to meet them when they arrived at the cottage, a wealth of relief in her smile. 'Ishbel, he's no' too bad. It's his heart, but your pa's sittin' up in bed giving me cheek already. It's just been a warning to take things easier, the doctor says.'

Ishbel hugged her mother. 'Oh, thank God!' she breathed as she hurried inside to see her father.

Donald thought it well worth while being ill to have his family round him. He sat regally holding court in the box bed in the kitchen, comfortably propped up with pillows. Ishbel held his hand, and he was soon beaming with pleasure. 'Pity wee Elspeth didna come,' Donald remarked regretfully.

'Oh, Pa!' Ishbel covered her mouth in dismay. 'It's Elspeth's school play tonight and I quite forgot! It went clean out o' my head when you were taken ill. It's lucky I asked Dorothy to see to her. She'll go, but I do hope Elspeth won't be too disappointed if I don't turn up.'

'Och, she'll understand when she hears her auld grandpa's sick,' said Donald comfortably. He turned to his two grandsons. 'By the by, I've gifts for you two from a young lady.'

Adrian looked interested. 'Which young lady, Grandpa?'

'Miss Joanna, auld Wotherspoon's lass.'

'Ah, the girl in black woollen stockings!' Adrian winked at Brian, and the pair of them burst out laughing.

'I'm past noticin' lassies' legs, but if you look in my working jacket, you'll find your reward for helping a damsel in distress.' Brian delved into the pocket and drew out two little parcels. 'Mind now, one of them's precious, the lassie told me,' Donald warned.

'Which one?' demanded Adrian eagerly.

'I dinna ken. You'll have to toss for it.'

Donald lay back contentedly and watched the fun. The two boys tossed sixpence, and Brian was allocated a long, flattish parcel. He ripped off the paper and his eyes grew round. 'Gosh, I've got the precious one! It's a fountain pen. I've always wanted a fountain pen.'

'There's a note on it,' Adrian said, disgruntled. He took

258

the scrap of paper and read it out. '"We are not permitted to use fountain pens at my school, so I hope you may find this useful. P.S. Do not tell my grandmother if you please, as she gave it to me for Christmas."'

He looked up. 'You lucky duffer, Brian. Now let's see what I got.' He tore the wrapping paper from the oddly shaped package and his face fell. 'It's a pin cushion! A rotten old pin cushion!'

'Och, the lassie meant well. Likely she made it herself,' said Catriona.

Adrian wrinkled his nose in disgust. 'I know, but – I mean to say – a pin cushion! That's a fat lot of use to a chap.' He tossed the gift on the floor and examined Brian's pen with interest.

Brian stared at the rejected little gift. Maybe Joanna did make it herself. She'd be awfully hurt if she saw it lying there. On impulse, he picked it up. It was made of red velvet in the shape of a rather uneven heart, and trimmed with black lace. There were pins carefully stuck into the top, forming the words 'I RESPECT YOU'. Brian grinned. He could imagine the child deliberating long over that cautious little message. Feeling somewhat foolish, he slipped the little heart quietly into his jacket pocket.

Satisfied her father's illness wasn't so serious as they'd feared, Ishbel and the boys returned to Edinburgh that night to let him rest. She promised to visit more regularly, but feared that would prove a difficult promise to keep. There were so many demands upon her precious time.

When Ishbel arrived home, Eleanor told her that Dorothy had brought Elspeth back after she'd performed in the school play.

'How did it go?' Ishbel asked.

'I don't know, to be quite honest,' replied her mother-in-law. 'Dorothy was loud in her praises, but Elspeth kept very quiet. She didn't say much, just ate her supper and went off to bed good as gold. I expect she was quite exhausted, the wee soul.'

Ishbel felt uneasy listening to this account. It didn't sound like Elspeth. She was a little chatterbox, and full of energy. Oh dear, had the performance been a disaster, and was Dorothy merely trying to cheer her downcast little niece? Anxiously, Ishbel hurried upstairs and crept into her daughter's room.

The nightlight candle burned brightly in its saucer of water and its yellow light showed Ishbel that her daughter was wide awake, fully dressed in Peter Pan costume. Elspeth lay on top of the covers, eyes fixed dreamily on the starlit night beyond the window. Ishbel sat down and took her hand. 'My darling, I'm so sorry I missed the play. Grandpa was taken ill, and I had to go to him right away.'

Elspeth showed some animation. 'How is he?'

'He's fine, love. He's just been doing too much.'

The child lay quiet and Ishbel stared at her, perplexed. 'How did the play go?' she asked nervously.

'Polly got two curtain calls. I got six.'

'Elspeth, that's wonderful!' Ishbel was amazed at such success. Curtain calls at the school play were unheard of. 'Oh, I wish I'd been there, darling!'

Elspeth slowly turned her head and stared up at her. 'You know, Mam, I thought I'd break my heart if you didn't come to the play tonight, but Polly was there and I found I didn't really care about you. You're never there

260

when I need you anyway. If you don't bother about me, why should I care?'

Every cruel little word hurt. Ishbel cried out tearfully, 'Elspeth love, you're wrong. I do care! I love you, but the shop...'

'I don't want to hear about the shop!' Elspeth blazed at her. The child turned her back and tugged the covers fretfully over her shoulders. 'Goodnight. I'm tired and I want to go to sleep now, if you don't mind.'

Ishbel left the bedroom in deep despair. It was small comfort to remember that William Alexander had warned her years ago of the dangers she faced in abandoning the role of mother when entering a man's world.

Chapter 12

Reconstruction continued throughout 1931, but Ishbel successfully avoided Sandy MacArthur. This was not difficult, since Matthew supervised renovation and replanning of the various departments himself. Apart from keeping a strict eye on what her partner was up to, Ishbel was left in peace to attend to the daily running of the store.

Fashion shows held in the main tearoom once a week had proved popular. Perhaps they took everyone's mind off the depressing length of the dole queues which increased as the 1930s began and showed little sign of decreasing after a General Election in October 1931 which made Ramsay MacDonald head of a coalition government. Fortunately, Alexander's weathered the storm and profits remained healthy, with hopeful signs of an upturn in trade in 1933. Ishbel decided this was due in part to her head buyer Clara's judicious choice of artificial silks and celanese to keep prices down, and to Matthew's daring marketing strategy.

He had plans for a modest 'grocertaria' once access to upper floors became easier on completion of stairways and elevators. This was an American idea which Ishbel cautiously approved. Customers would select packaged grocery items from well-stocked shelves and pay at a manned cash desk, thus saving time and money. When it was finally set up, she planned to give that department a Scottish flavour with Wotherspoon's bottled fruit and farm cheese, both of which had won favour in Edinburgh hotels. For the rest, jars of her father's clover honey, her mother's prized bannocks, and packets of Edinburgh rock should prove popular with tourists.

'When we open the furnishing department in '34 we must think seriously about hire purchase,' Matthew said.

'The never-never? Och, that'll no' catch on wi' thrifty Scots,' Ishbel asserted confidently. 'There's plenty of jokes about the never-never, Matthew. "One more payment and the furniture's ours, then we can throw it all out and get new stuff."'

'Sounds like good business,' he remarked idly.

'The road to ruin!'

Matthew sighed. 'OK, if you refuse to take reasonable risks, we must follow old H.J.'s policy with what we have.'

'Who's he?'

Matthew looked incredulous. 'You never heard of H.J.? The old boy was America's king of ketchup before he passed away. Nothing but perfection would do for him, and from humble beginnings he built up an empire. I guess he taught me that quality control is the key to success.'

'I agree. Alexander's aye had a name for quality.'

'Sure, apart from that beige hot water they serve in the tearooms an' call coffee,' he remarked scathingly. 'Say, Ishbel, why don't we aim to produce a perfect cup of coffee? I've noticed your Edinburgh ladies love coffee, cake and a chinwag more than anything. OK, let's make our coffee and cake the very best in town.'

Ishbel was amused. 'If you can do that, Matthew, I

promise you wifies will be queued out the door.'

She'd had her doubts, but after weeks of dogged trial and error, he'd succeeded. Many a hardened tea-jenny had been wooed from the national beverage on to Matthew's special American blend, accompanied by individual portions of Wotherspoon's fresh whipped cream served to the discerning coffee-drinker in tiny silver pots.

Later in the year, Ishbel made her way towards a fashion show in progress. She paused to let one of the models pass while running an expert eye over her outfit. Ishbel approved it. French fashion houses had decreed a more romantic look for the coming season, with hat brims dipping seductively over the eyes, curves in evidence and skirt lengths well below the knee. The age of the brassière had arrived, and Ishbel had made certain of a good stock of these welcome innovations and corsets to go with them. Boyish figures, Eton crops and the Charleston had had their day, although a few ageing flappers and faded bright young things still clung grimly to old ways.

The elegant model whispered to Ishbel in passing, 'Mrs Alexander, my corns are fair killin' me in these fancy shoes.'

Ishbel smothered a grin and went on her way. Her sharp ears picked up the sound of Sandy's workmen still engaged in major reconstruction work, but the muffled noise was drowned by the happy buzz of many voices. The valiant maestro at the grand piano was still playing *fortissimo* as instructed. Seeing Ishbel, he grinned and struck up President Franklin D. Roosevelt's election theme song, 'Happy Days Are Here Again', mindful of Alexander's American connections.

Ishbel walked through the packed luncheon and tearooms with some pride, because she regarded these as her own most successful enterprise. A delicious aroma of freshly made coffee percolated to her nostrils, and she blessed Matthew for it. A selection of fresh cream cakes was going the rounds on glass and chromium trolleys, trundled by smiling waitresses in spotless uniform. No wonder fashionable Edinburgh ladies congregated here daily in droves.

A woman seated in a corner by herself hailed Ishbel. 'You're Mrs Alexander, aren't you? I've been wanting to meet you for ages, I feel I know you so well.'

Ishbel was puzzled. She'd never seen her before. 'I'm afraid I don't recall—'

'Oh, you don't know me, my dear!' the woman laughed. 'You may never even have heard of me. My name's Sarah Allsop.'

Ishbel sat down abruptly on a vacant seat beside her. 'Sandy's fiancée?'

'That is correct.' Sarah took a slow sip of coffee whilst studying Ishbel intently. She replaced the cup carefully on the saucer. 'Ah, now I begin to understand!'

'What?'

'What it is about you that breaks a man's heart.'

Ishbel frowned. 'That's not a comfortable thought, Miss Allsop.'

'Lady Sarah, actually, but I don't pull rank.'

'You talk like my late husband,' Ishbel said, arrested by a sudden memory of maimed officers with mutilated faces.

'Ah, yes, Freddie Alexander. A terrible tragedy. I was considered as a possible bride for Freddie until you came along. He was a most attractive man.'

'Yes, he was.'

'I liked him. I might have married him if I'd had the chance,' Sarah announced calmly. She leaned her elbows on the table and stared at Ishbel. 'And now I discover you were Sandy MacArthur's childhood sweetheart. Our paths seem fated to cross, Mrs Alexander. Alarm bells rang madly when I heard Sandy was working for you. I hope you don't intend to steal my man?'

Ishbel stiffened. 'There's little risk o' that, Lady Sarah. Sandy canna stand me.'

'You think so?' murmured Sarah.

'I'm sure of it.' Ishbel stood up. 'If you'll excuse me, I'll go on my rounds. I'll take this opportunity to wish you every happiness. Sandy's a braw lad.'

'They don't make 'em much brawer,' agreed Sarah. 'That's why I will fight tooth and nail to keep him.'

'Is that a threat?' Ishbel asked quietly.

Sarah laughed merrily. 'Bless you, no! Nothing so dramatic. Just a friendly warning. I thought you ought to know.'

Ishbel's Auntie Nellie and her man had prospered in the fish trade, and on their retirement had sold the business and bought a new bungalow in Burntisland, a busy small port just across the Forth. It was a pleasant trip in the train over the railway bridge, and an even more enthralling expedition by red-and-black-funnelled ferryboat, the paddle steamer *William Muir*, which plied to and fro across the river between Burntisland and Edinburgh, depositing commuters at Granton Harbour. Brian had rebelled vigorously against working in the shop and had taken to visiting Auntie Nellie and hcr man sometimes on

Saturdays, while Adrian had been picked for the school rugby fifteen. Ishbel's united front seemed to have crumbled dismally.

Brian liked Jock, Auntie Nellie's husband. He was a quiet man with thoughtful eyes which glinted shrewdly in his weatherbeaten face. Jock never said much, but then he didn't have to. Auntie Nellie chattered enough for two.

'Mercy, here's you, and here's me with hardly a bite in this house!' she said when Brian turned up in Burntisland one Saturday. She took out her purse. 'Jock, away with Brian to the baker's and let the laddie choose what teabread he likes for his tea.' There was method behind the command. Nellie could quite easily whip up a fine batch of homemade scones in no time, but she suspected the fatherless lad and the childless man had a need for one another's company.

They headed for the seafront as they usually did. There was time enough for teabread. 'Adrian and I joined the c-cadets,' Brian said.

His companion glanced at him. 'Did you want to?'

'N-not particularly. Adrian did, so I thought I'd better, but I got around the guns and soldiering bit by volunteering for the b-band. I'm learning to play the p-pipes.'

'Man, you'll be popular at the Burns suppers!'

The harbour and shipyards were busy with all sorts of craft. Big ships, small ships, two or three trawlers in for repair. They walked slowly along the quay. The sea scents rose to them from the fishing boats, the rugged, salty smells of ropes and nets and tarry wood. Jock removed the pipe from his mouth. 'Aye, mony's the time I've been on boats like these, with phosphoresence lighting the sea on calm autumn evenings. We ca'd it "the burning fishing" then.' He smiled to himself, seeing the lad's rapt expression. 'Y'see, Brian, if you chap the gunwale wi' the anchor shaft, the fish will answer to ye.'

'Och, Uncle Jock, you're p-pullin' my leg! Speak, you m-mean?'

The elderly man laughed. 'Och, no' exactly, son. It's like this. First you'd maybe spot a spittle on the surface o' the sea, a clean jump by one or two herring, quiet-like, no' a great ploudering in the water like saithe jumping. Or you might see a gannet prowling in the sky and suspect there was a shoal beneath him. Aye, he kens a thing or two, the fly Solan goose! So then you lean over the side and chap wi' the anchor shaft on the gunwale, and the fish will give an answering start. There's a blue flash comes off the herrin' shoal like a wisp o' smoke in the water, no' to be confused wi' darting mackerel that leave gleaming trails like comets, or dopey dogfish curled in upon theirsels like sleepy pups. If you have the eye to see, you ken if it's a worthwhile play o' the silver darlings, and where to shoot your net. It's just as simple as that.'

Brian looked out across the grey sea in silence. He couldn't tell the old fisherman of the emotion that gripped him then, nor explain his awe at the great mysteries of the sea, because once a foolish woman had crippled his tongue. He felt small and insignificant, a novice in the ways of that cruel master. But he wanted to learn. 'When I l-leave school, I will go to sea,' Brian said quietly.

His companion sighed. The patient old countenance showed no elation. 'Aye, son. I thought you might.'

On Sundays Sandy MacArthur was often bored and restless

with no work to be done. He wasn't one for the kirk, more's the pity. Maybe he'd had too much kirking in his youth, and found cinema seats more comfortable as a young horseman. Besides, apart from many other irritants, there had been a persistent worry nagging at the back of his mind for a good while.

Sandy was finally forced into action one Sunday morning in early spring, when the first shivering lambs had appeared on the cold, bare foothills. He drove the Silver Ghost out of its garage and headed for the Allsops' Corstorphine mansion. Sarah came out to greet him.

He bent down to kiss her. 'I'm away to the Mearns. Come wi' me, lass?'

She smiled. 'You mean to carry me off and have your wicked way with me? How exciting, Sandy!'

'Well, I wouldna mind, love, but I'd planned to be back in the evening.'

Sarah sighed. 'Just my luck. Anyway, I can't, darling. I promised to drive Father to the kirk. He's not getting any better, and finds the kirk service a great comfort. I'd hate to disappoint him.'

He put his arms round her waist. 'You're fell devoted to your father, aren't you? More than to me?' She was straight as a die, and Sandy knew he'd have an honest answer to a question that had bothered him.

'I'm devoted to you both, Sandy, but in different ways. Can you live with that?' She looked up at him quizzically. 'Now a question for you, my fine lad. Everything my father owns will be mine one day as his only child. I'm quite a prize, and you're an ambitious man. Was it ambition that made you propose to me?'

Sandy hesitated. That was a tricky one, and he wanted to

be honest with himself let alone the lass. 'When I was a horseman sitting on my kist in the bothy wi' not much more than bicycle claes to my back, I swore I'd be a rich man one day,' he admitted. 'It was a big step up when your father offered to amalgamate his building firm wi' my engineering business, but it wasn't ambition that drove me to propose, Sarah. I fell in love wi' you right from the start.'

She stared at him steadily. 'What about Ishbel Alexander?'

His expression hardened. 'Ishbel had her chance and muffed it.'

Sarah put her arms round him and kissed him fondly. 'Away you go to the Mearns, you conceited man. I've my bonnet to put on and my nose to powder for the kirk.'

Sandy set out on his own, heading for the bridge across the Forth at Kincardine. At first he was preoccupied, but gradually his spirits lifted as he motored along. Freddie Alexander's beautiful old car ate up the miles now the foolish 20 mph speed restriction had finally been abolished. Strange, but he still thought of it as Freddie Alexander's car, although the man was long dead. No wonder Ishbel had wanted shot of this car, for memories clung to it like ghostly cobwebs. Had Freddie held her in his arms and kissed her here? Sandy changed gear jerkily. The smooth mechanism didn't care for rough treatment. The car shuddered.

He passed through Kinross with a glance for the grim castle in the loch that had once imprisoned the Queen of Scots, and drove on towards Perth through a bare winter landscape. Folk were assembling for the kirk and the showy car attracted attention. For the first time, Sandy felt embarrassed to be seen in it. He wasn't the showy kind.

Fortunately, when he reached Forfar and skirted the loch Malcolm Canmore's queen had made her own, there was nobody hanging about in the snell wind. There was a dusting of snow on the Grampian foothills, and he headed for that.

Keen frost had bleached colour from the pastures as Sandy drove through the arch erected for Victoria, a later queen who'd discovered the joys and sorrows of the Highlands. Beyond Edzell and Fettercairn lay harsh, hilly land, and he found the Dundreich farm sign without much difficulty. It proved to be a grey farmhouse and steading set in a grey landscape, and Sandy's heart beat fast and eagerly. He scanned all round the place, but there were no signs of life bar a few ewes gnawing at neeps, and no sign of Bob, his horse. He raised the rusty knocker and chapped on the door.

The farmer was a spare man, with hardship etched deep into the furrows in his skin. 'You bought a horse, a Clydesdale, at the Aikey horse fair some years ago,' Sandy said.

'So I did. A willing enough big beast at the ploo. Too willing, in this hard soil. When it went lame the fourth time I got rid o' it. Vet's fees is scandalous, ken? Near ten bob a time.'

A chill passed over Sandy. 'I would've come sooner, but I've a business to see to. What did ye do wi' the horse?'

The man looked uncomfortable. His gaze wavered. 'I sellt it to MacPhee the tinker for ten bob.'

'Where's MacPhee now?'

The farmer shrugged. 'Wha kens? Could be you micht find him in Blairgowrie at the berries next summer. Or in Carse o' Gowrie at the tatties at the back-end o' the year.

Maybe he's wintering in the quarry at Kirriemuir or the woods up by Inverquharity. Maybe he's no'. Wha kens?'

'Aye, wha kens?' nodded Sandy sadly. He thanked the man and turned to go. The farmer clutched his sleeve.

'It was either that or the knacker's cairt for the auld horse. You understand the choice, don't ye? You hae the look o' a horseman someway, and I'm a horseman mysel'. I just wanted the beastie to hae its chance.'

Sandy looked at him, and for the first time both smiled. 'Aye, sir. I understand,' Sandy said kindly.

The gulf between Ishbel and her daughter had widened as Elspeth grew older. The situation distressed Ishbel, but she comforted herself Elspeth was at a difficult age, and she was hopeful relations would improve given time. Ishbel was encouraged by the interest her daughter still showed in the shop. Elspeth never missed a Saturday, and disappeared into the busy store for hours on end. Ishbel had all her hopes pinned on Elspeth, because to her lasting disappointment the twins had shown no interest in their heritage.

'I took my harp to the party, but nobody asked me to play,' sang Elspeth to Polly that Saturday morning. Every Saturday, she headed straight for Polly's flat and the two spent the day together, shopping in Princes Street, enjoying a light lunch, and taking in a movie matinée in the afternoons.

Polly wiped away tears of mirth. 'Honey, you're as good as Gracie Fields any day! What a talented mimic you are, my dear.'

Elspeth grinned and flopped down on a chair. Oh, how

she loved dear, generous Polly! She couldn't imagine life without her to run to with troubles and triumphs. Polly was her dearest friend.

'You gotta get your teeth fixed, sweetheart,' Polly remarked kindly. 'I guess they'll put braces on, but don't you fret. I wore the durn things for months, and see what pretty teeth I got.' She proved the point with a dazzling smile.

'I'll tell the dentist next time I go, Polly. My mother doesn't bother,' sighed Elspeth forlornly.

'Now don't you be saying that! Of course she does.'

Elspeth jumped up and hugged her. 'I wish you were my mother, Polly, I do love you so!'

She sat motionless. It had been a huge pleasure coaching Elspeth and the other little lasses. The school had welcomed her help and paid a fee which was very welcome, but more importantly the task had filled a void in Polly's life, a void she'd hardly known existed. Working with the children had become an absorbing interest which kept her happily occupied while Matt clawed their fortune back from the Alexanders.

It was only now she realised the danger, with this beloved, talented girl's arms trustingly round her neck and her own heart full to bursting with overwhelming maternal love. She knew where it was leading. Straight to disaster for Elspeth and her mother, and heartbreak for Polly herself.

After some heart-searching over the next few days, Polly decided there was only one practical solution to the dilemma, a solution she must face bravely. At the first opportunity, she tackled Matthew. 'Matt, darling, when can we go home?'

274

'Edinburgh feels like home to me, honey,' he answered mildly.

She gave him an exasperated glance. 'But it's not our home. When are we goin' back to the States?'

'There's a trade depression in the States worse than here, honey, despite all Roosevelt's best efforts. Things are real bad, with the dollar low and stocks and shares at rock bottom. There's unemployment and hunger and beggars in the streets. They're even setting up soup kitchens for the starving. We're better off biding our time, Poll. When Freddie's debt is cleared, we can choose to quit or stay.'

She frowned. 'The store's doing well. Why don't they pay up and let us quit right now?'

'Because they can't,' he said with a hint of exasperation. 'Ishbel agreed to make major alterations on my advice and spent capital to do it. I can't suddenly demand my money and leave her in the lurch, can I? It wouldn't be fair, honey.'

'That's her lookout. What about my movie career?'

Matthew hesitated. 'Polly, I'm sorry about that, I guess.' He looked so guilty she quickly pressed home the advantage.

'I could've been a real movie star by now!'

Polly didn't honestly believe she'd have been so lucky, but if it made Matt feel guilty, so much the better. She was a hard-headed product of Brooklyn, and having viewed Elspeth's talent had formed a lower opinion of her own ability, which seemed kind of meagre by comparison. She might have done OK in silent films, but those days were over and like Clara Bow, despite 'oomph' and 'it', the Brooklyn accent didn't come over too good in talkies. Polly was intelligent enough to accept she might not make it to the top as a glamour baby. So what?

She had other plans. She worked well with kids, and there were plenty of talented kids in the States she could tutor. She could make a darn' good living training budding actors and actresses, delivered into her hands by pushy parents. She was good at encouraging real talent and sparing the feelings of little turkeys. Besides, she loved kids, even though she couldn't have any herself after an appendix operation went wrong.

'Hollywood. That's where I oughta be,' she said aloud.

Matthew became nervous when his wife mentioned stardom. He suspected Polly didn't have that elusive star quality, and he wasn't trusting solely to intuition either. He'd deliberately intercepted and destroyed the result of her Hollywood screen test. It had been quite brutally frank, and he'd bribed her agent to make up a more glowing and encouraging rejection. Maybe it was dishonest, but he couldn't stand by and see his wife's heart broken. It was lucky in a way Wall Street had crashed when it did, and they'd headed for Scotland soon after.

He put his arms round her persuasively. 'We'd be crazy to quit now, Poll. Another year or two will earn us half a million dollars. Please be patient a little longer?'

'Okay, I'll try,' she sighed. Immediately she'd agreed, she was scared. She had a premonition she'd made a fatal mistake by not sticking to her guns, but when Matt was persuasive, she was like putty in his hands.

The twins acquired bicycles at thirty shillings apiece that spring and their mobility increased. With the bicycles, they developed an interest in angling, for now they could reach well-stocked burns on the outskirts of the city and come home with a basketful of trout. Both boys had been studying hard for school exams, and cycling and fishing provided both fresh air and relaxation. Dalkeith was within cycling range, and they delighted their grandparents one day by turning up out of the blue.

Catriona fussed over the two young lads while Donald beamed proudly. 'Aye, so you've taken to the fishing like your auld grandpa, I see.'

'Brian's better than I am. He has more patience,' admitted Adrian generously.

'Och, I'll need to show you how to busk flies for the casting if you're really keen,' said Donald.

'You will not!' broke in Catriona severely. 'You've already pinched all the feathers off my best hat for that ploy.'

Donald winked at Brian, who grinned. 'I'd a t-talk wi' Uncle Jock about sea-fishing, Grandpa. He kens a lot about f-fish.'

'So he should, and him a weel aff fishmonger,' sniffed Donald, who was somewhat envious of his sister Nellie's second choice.

Catriona had rolled up her sleeves and was busy baking. It was grand to have hungry laddies to bake for. She paused a moment. 'I'll never understand why Nellie and her man flitted to Burntisland. It's an out-o'-the-way place after Edinburgh. Nellie likes the bright lights.'

'Uncle Jock says she bursts a wee p-paper bag at one o'clock every day to mind her o' the one o'clock gun, and she's f-fine pleased,' remarked Brian.

Donald laughed. 'Och, well, there's humour in the man. That's aye something.'

'Are there salmon in the river?' asked Adrian eagerly.

'I daresay there might be one or two, this time o' year. Away and look while your granny's making your tea.' Donald sat back. He would fain have gone with the lads, but it was beyond him since his bad turn. His hand stole down and gently fondled the snoozing old terrier's lugs. Aye, and beyond poor old Foxy too, Donald thought sadly. Age doesna come to man alone.

The twins stood on the river bank and studied the water. It was a grand reach of the river close by their grandfather's house, with rushing white water tumbling over rocks and dark, swirling pools below.

'Do you know you are trespassing, and if you intend to fish you will be poaching?'

The two youths spun round and stared at the owner of the voice. They recognised her at once, though she had grown and matured since they last saw her perched high upon a wall. Joanna Wotherspoon at thirteen was worth a long look. She wore breeches and stockings and stout shoes, a red tartan shirt tucked into her belt, and should by rights have resembled a young boy, but did not. The boyish clothing merely accentuated her dawning femininity and charm. Brian was afflicted by an odd, choking sensation, as if his heart had stopped beating. He had to breathe deeply to set it going again. Adrian recovered more quickly. He smiled the engaging smile that brought girls flocking to him in droves.

'We're not poachers, and if we're trespassing we'll leave, of course. But couldn't we stay and talk to you?'

'We-ell, perhaps.' She wasn't taken in by smooth talk, Brian noted. She looked amused.

'We never thanked you for the gifts you sent,' Adrian said.

She wrinkled her brow, puzzled. 'What gifts?' Then she laughed and turned pink. 'Oh, those! What a little idiot I was. Tell me, who got the pin cushion?'

'I did. I'm Adrian.' He jerked a thumb at Brian. 'He's Brian. He got the fountain pen, but he couldn't write with it very well. He's caurry-fisted. Left-handed, you know.'

'Oh dear, that must be awkward for you?' Joanna looked hopefully at the other twin. He just stared at her in thoroughly glaikit fashion, then swallowed once or twice as if the cat had his tongue. Joanna felt piqued by the rejection of her friendly overtures. The brothers looked identical, but one was nice and friendly while the other was really just a tumfie. That word came from Bunty's expressive Aberdeenshire vocabulary, and, meaning an awkward person, fitted this boy to a T, Joanna thought. She turned back to Adrian with relief. 'I was only teasing about trespassing. It's my father's land, but you may visit as often as you like.'

'Thanks, you're a sport.' He reached for her hand and squeezed it. Shyly, Joanna disengaged the hand and backed away. For an instant, Brian glimpsed a leggy, awkward child in wrinkled black stockings, and was captivated by her innocence. She wasn't pretty or pert like other girls he'd admired, but he knew he could never forget her.

'I am pleased to have met you, but if you will excuse me, I must leave you now and help my father,' she said formally, then turned and ran, lightly, gracefully, sure-footed over grassy tussocks.

'Wowee! She'll be a peach when she's ripe,' breathed Adrian.

Brian said nothing for speech was beyond him. Tucked away at the back of the dresser at home he'd hidden a pin cushion, a little red heart with its shy message: 'I RESPECT YOU'. Brian stared after Joanna Wotherspoon and his heart beat out its own painful message of first love. I love you, Joanna. I love you!

The exterior of the lift shaft had been clad in walnut veneer. Mighty expensive but worth it, Ishbel thought as she surveyed the luxurious effect. The storeroom walls had been finally removed during the long holiday weekend, new carpets laid throughout, and now the elevators were revealed in all their gleaming glory.

Despite the holiday the shop was a scene of frenzied activity, and most members of staff had nobly given up their short break to help rearrange disrupted departments and stock shelves. Little Mr Wilkie from Men's Outfitting scuttled past Ishbel, barely visible beneath a pile of gentlemen's polo neck sweaters and Fair Isle pullovers, as popularised by the Prince of Wales, but Mrs Bingham, who reigned supreme in Children's Wear, paused to examine the new elevators. She clutched to her bosom an armful of small breeks, semmits, combinations and liberty bodices destined for new quarters.

'Wait 'til Archie gets an eyeful o' those, Ishbel! He'll never be content to ride in his poky old lift again.'

'I don't know, he seems attached to it,' she said doubtfully. 'That bright lad puzzles me, Mrs Bingham. I've tried to promote him time after time, but he refuses.'

The older woman looked surprised. 'You mean you

don't know about Archie, my dear? Why, the poor soul can't read or write, and he's bitterly ashamed of the fact. Written words don't make sense to him, he told me. It's not the laddie's fault, there are many folk afflicted in the same way. He knows he could never be a manager, of course.'

'Ah, I see!' said Ishbel, as light suddenly dawned on the problem. The saleslady bustled off as one of the elevator doors slid open and Matthew looked out. He'd been behaving like a bairn with a new toy since the elevators became operational, riding up and down, testing them. 'Going up, madam?' he called to her invitingly.

Ishbel laughed light-heartedly. She could afford to be magnanimous, for this wonderful asset to the store had been introduced largely due to Matthew's tenacity. She stepped gaily into the spacious elevator.

'Tearoom, please, and I hope you know how to work this thing?'

'I'm getting the hang of it. Look here, I'll show you. Just press that button for Fourth Floor.' He pulled Ishbel close to the control panel, guiding her hand with his. The moment the door slid shut and they were alone, Ishbel realised that this seemingly innocent excursion was a serious mistake. They were too close, the enclosed space too intimate. Matthew knew it too. She heard his sharp intake of breath as his hand tightened on hers. The lift started its smooth upward journey. The mechanism was virtually silent and Ishbel imagined she could hear their two hearts thudding madly in unison, like Sandy's muffled hammers.

His face was close to hers. 'Ishbel, I gotta confess, I can't help it but I've fallen in love with you,' he whispered.

'Matthew, you – you can't.' Her protest sounded small and agonised in the confined space. She saw the light of passion shining in his eyes and knew he wanted to kiss her. Oh, how her body ached for his kiss, but her common sense, her thoughts, were appalled by what was happening.

'Matthew, don't! We can't,' she breathed as he took her in his arms, trying to push him away in a last desperate attempt to retrieve a situation slipping out of control. If he kissed her, she knew all was lost. She would succumb. She'd fought hard, but she'd fought in vain. She'd fallen in love with Polly's husband.

'Oh, Ishbel, my darling, please,' Matthew whispered, his mouth searching, caressing her lips.

Her arms slid round his neck. 'Matthew, I love you too. God knows I don't want to, but I can't stop myself.' Then she was in a wild state of tears and passion, sobbing with joy and moaning with distress even as they kissed hungrily. It had been so long since she'd been kissed, so many lonely years since she'd responded willingly to a man's fierce loving. She closed her eyes and surrendered to overwhelming emotions. These were Matthew's hands caressing her body, Matthew's lips on her neck. This was the final defeat of all she'd stood for, the ultimate weakness. And she didn't care.

He recovered his wits first. He held her close, groaning. 'Oh, my God, Ishbel. I never meant this to happen.'

She rested her head weakly against him. 'Ah, neither did I!'

He stroked her dark hair. 'I guess I've wanted to kiss you for years. I've been mad at you, irritated by you, but God knows how hard I fought against loving you,' Matthew sighed. 'I lost the battle. Right or wrong, I love you.'

She looked up at him, her eyes wide and frightened. 'Matthew, what about Polly?'

He groaned wretchedly. He didn't like to think about Polly. He cared about her. She was his wife, unsuspecting, trusting him; the innocent victim of their love. 'I don't want Polly to know about us. Please, not yet, Ishbel!'

She pulled away, and her chin came up in a determined gesture he recognised. 'I won't indulge in a furtive hole-in-the corner affair, Matthew. I couldna live wi' the guilt o' that. I'd despise myself to the end of my days. If we truly love each other, Polly will have to be told.'

His thoughts were confused for the elevator was near their destination. 'Not yet, Ishbel. Let me decide the best time to tell her. Please, darling?' he begged.

'All right,' Ishbel agreed reluctantly.

She could feel their conveyance slowing and coming to rest after the short, fateful journey. Matthew moved away from her side as the door slid quietly open and they found themselves facing an empty tearoom.

Not quite empty. Sandy MacArthur was close by, neatly coiling a length of electrical cable. He stopped what he was doing when Ishbel and Matthew appeared and studied the pair with a furrow in his brow. To her chagrin, Ishbel turned a guilty beetroot red, a fact which Sandy noted with raised eyebrows. Matthew stepped out of the elevator and Ishbel followed hesitantly.

'Just been – er – checking the elevator,' Matthew said.

'Oh, aye?' Sandy reached into his pocket and silently handed Matthew a clean handkerchief.

Matthew frowned at it. 'What's this for?'

'To wipe the lipstick frae your mouth,' Sandy said contemptuously.

Chapter 13

Lipstick traces and Ishbel's guilty manner had confirmed Sandy's worst fears. He'd suspected for some time the American found Ishbel Alexander attractive, but he'd hoped she had more sense than to encourage the man. Sandy strode furiously through the empty tearooms with the heavy roll of cable slung over one shoulder, seething with a fine mix of emotions.

Of course it was none of his business what she did, but Sandy would have felt differently about the affair if this had been a decent, honourable, unattached man. A married man with a wife living on the premises, though! Och, that was a scandal which would make Ishbel a social outcast in this douce city if ever it came to light. So-called righteous folk could be cruel. Aye, thought Sandy grimly, and you didn't have to look far for evidence o' that. Just look how the Prince of Wales's popularity had plummeted since rumours spread about his association with a married American woman, Mrs Simpson.

Sandy fought against a sense of sorrow that hurt most of all. This affair wasn't worthy of Ishbel who was an honest and good-hearted lass. He'd never doubted her integrity though she'd hurt him cruelly when she fell in love with another man. Sandy decided he must do something to bring her to her senses before it was too late.

'Cereal? Or would you like Scotch porridge?' asked Polly.

'Hmm?' Matthew turned his attention to his wife with an effort. Since falling in love with Ishbel, he'd found it increasingly difficult to converse with Polly. Call it guilt or estrangement, there was an increasing strain in their relationship. Poor Polly was doing her best to please, but it didn't help. It just made Matthew feel worse. She'd tracked down a packet of Post Toasties locally, because he'd said he preferred them for breakfast. Slowly but surely, American wheat flakes were ousting oatmeal with a younger Scottish generation. He tried to look delighted. 'Oh, cereal, please, love.'

Polly tipped a liberal helping into a plate and placed it in front of him. Nobody could accuse her of being a talented cook, but she went one better: she could organise good cooks to produce a sparkling menu, which was a talent in itself. She and Matthew enjoyed a beautifully cooked dinner every evening, sent up to the flat from Alexander's kitchens.

Perhaps 'enjoyed' wasn't the word, Polly thought as she toyed with her own breakfast. It was becoming harder to find common ground on which to talk with Matthew, and that distressed her. Maybe a vacation would help, she thought. 'Seems a pity to be in Scotland without seeing more of the country, Matthew. How about taking a vacation this summer? Over the sea to Skye sounds kind of romantic, don't you think?' she suggested hopefully. She wasn't keen on small boats, unlike Bonnie Prince Charlie, but was prepared to make sacrifices. Atlantic liners were more her scene.

Matthew looked up quickly. 'Vacation? That's impossible, Poll. I'm much too busy just now.' The thought of leaving Ishbel was too painful to be considered.

Something snapped in Polly. She wasn't usually pettish, but she couldn't take this treatment any more. She flung her spoon down, scattering cereal everywhere. 'You're always too busy to go anyplace! I hate this durned store. I wish we'd never come to Scotland. Why didn't we weather the storm in the States?'

'You would've been first to moan when we had to pull in our belts,' Matthew retorted angrily.

'Are you saying I'm extravagant?'

'I'm saying you've got expensive tastes. We both have. We need that half-million dollars.'

Her eyes brimmed with tears. 'Aww, Matt, it's only money. Why don't we settle for less an' go? Why don't we go back home?'

He stood up fiercely, sending a plate skidding across the tablecloth. 'This is my home! You go if you want to, but I'm staying. I like it here.' He stared at her defiantly then stormed out of the flat. When he'd gone downstairs, Polly laid her head on her arms amidst the ruins of breakfast, and sobbed.

Ishbel found that working with Matthew had become difficult and dangerous since they'd fallen in love. Secretly, she'd felt more at ease when they were at loggerheads. Every word, every glance, was charged with an emotion which must be carefully guarded in case any of the staff noticed, and Polly got wind of what was going on.

Not that there *was* anything going on. A stolen kiss in the elevator once, tender glances when their eyes met, a pressure of the hand now and then; that was the sum total of their romance, and the strain was telling.

Meanwhile, the shop ran smoothly now major reconstruction was completed. Trade picked up at the beginning of 1935, and old Adam McPherson decided to call it a day. Although well past retirement age, Adam was fresh-faced and spry, and the shop had been his whole life for many years. Ishbel was upset at the prospect of losing her dear old friend and manager. 'What on earth will you do with yourself when you retire, Adam?' she asked him curiously.

He grinned. 'Och, Mrs McPherson'll think o' something. What with papering and painting and doing the gairden, I'll no' have a meenit. When I do have an hour or two to mysel' on a Saturday, I'll be away to Tynecastle on the tram, cheering on my team.'

'Oh, Adam, how can we ever replace you?' she cried mournfully.

The old man looked thoughtful. 'I've been pondering that for a wee while. How about your head buyer? Clara would be my choice for the manager's job.'

'Clara?' Ishbel was astounded. Clara had finally stood up to a domineering mother and insisted upon living her own life, and been much happier and more agreeable since. She'd proved to be an able and imaginative buyer, popular with London fashion houses and wholesalers alike, but . . .

'She's a woman, Adam,' Ishbel protested.

He laughed and dug her playfully in the ribs. 'Och, lassie, I thought you'd be the last to discriminate!'

* * *

Predictably, Matthew was opposed to Clara's appointment. 'Heck, Ishbel, you know my opinion of bossy females,' he grumbled.

'It was never high,' she agreed, 'but I thought I'd forced you to change your mind.'

He squeezed her hand. 'You're not bossy, you're unique. This woman will be up front, meeting the public, dealing with queries and complaints and staff problems an' heaven knows what. It's an important job which old Adam did well. My choice would be little Stan Wilkie from Men's Outfitting.'

'Of course it would, because the dear, mild-mannered gent could be kept under your thumb,' remarked Ishbel shrewdly. 'No, Matt, we must have someone who's not scared to voice an opinion, and if Clara can stand up to her domineering mother she can stand up to anyone, even you. Besides, she's proved she can keep staff in order without raising hackles. Adam McPherson believes she can do it, and I agree.'

Matthew sighed. 'OK. So that'll leave us without a buyer. What then?'

'Jeannie from Perfumery shows great promise. She's been to London with Clara several times, so she knows the ropes. Besides, the lassie has style and an eye for what youngsters wear. I don't intend Alexander's to end up wi' a dull, elderly image, and I want to see more young folk shopping here. With a little training, I think Jeannie could fill the gap and bring in a younger clientèle.'

'OK, honey, on your own head be it!' he declared ominously.

And so Clara, much to her amazement, assumed old

Adam McPherson's mantle when he retired, clutching a fine presentation clock to mark the time, and a hefty cheque to keep him and his good lady in comfort for the rest of their days.

One of Ishbel's problems was what to do with Archie the lift boy. He was an intelligent lad despite his handicap, and she was determined to create a more responsible position for him. She suspected an improvement in Archie's self-esteem could work wonders.

As it happened, there had been teething problems with the new elevators, and engineers sent by the manufacturer had been operating the system on a trial basis for some weeks. Now they declared themselves satisfied, and Ishbel prepared to advertise for lift boys. Before she did so, she sought out Archie, who still trundled up and down in the antiquated lift that had served the shop faithfully for many years. He was looking gloomy, but brightened when he saw her. 'Goin' up, Mrs Alexander?'

'To my office, thanks, Archie.' When the door closed, Ishbel turned to him. 'Archie, the time's come for you to give up this job.'

He turned pale. 'Is this the sack?'

'No, no!' she laughed. 'It's promotion I have in mind.'

He turned whiter still. 'Mrs Alexander, I've tellt ye 'til I'm tired, I dinna want to be promoted.'

'I know you don't, but I'm promoting you just the same. I've advertised for lift boys, and somebody has to select the lads, and train them and keep an eye on them. I want the lifts kept spotlessly clean and running smoothly. We need an elevator manager, Archie, and the natural choice is you, with all your experience.' Ishbel held her breath. If he refused the offer, she didn't know what to do.

But Archie gulped emotionally. 'Fancy me, a manager! My teacher said I'd never get on, Mrs Alexander, I was such a dunce at the school.'

'It'll mean four pounds a week, Archie.'

He whistled. 'Michty! Four pounds. I'll be able to pop the question to my young lady at last. We've been courtin' five years withoot much hope o' getting spliced.'

Ishbel laughed. 'She's a lucky lass.' The lift reached their destination and Ishbel stepped out. She smiled at her new elevator manager. 'We'll see about a new suit for you. I'll arrange something with Men's Outfitting.'

Archie's eyes glowed. 'Imagine me in pinstripes, wi' my tie in a Windsor knot and a bowler to walk oot wi'. What a toff!' Dreamily, he closed the lift door and sank blissfully out of sight.

Smiling, Ishbel pushed open the door of the outer office. The smile faded abruptly. Sandy was inside and her spirits sank to her shoes after one quick glance at his grim expression. She hadn't seen him since that last embarrassing encounter in the empty tearoom.

'Here's Mrs Alexander now,' said Ishbel's secretary with ill-disguised relief. Sandy had a countryman's patience, and had been waiting doggedly for some time.

'Can I have a word wi' you in private?' he demanded.

Ishbel showed him into the inner office, after assuring herself Matthew was safely occupied elsewhere in the building. She indicated a chair and sat down behind the desk.

'What can I do for you?' she asked in businesslike tones.

'You can stop carrying on wi' a married man!'

Angry colour flooded her cheeks. 'How dare you! Besides, if I choose to be friendly with Matthew, it's none o' your business.'

'Huh! More than friendly – kissing the man!' He leaned towards her. 'It *is* my business when I see the lass I grew up with makin' a fool o' hersel'.'

'I am not!' she cried indignantly. 'Have you come here to insult me?'

'No. Only to set you straight. Any other way will lead to misery.' His manner was cold and calm, and only served to infuriate her. She jumped up.

'Don't you preach to me, Sandy MacArthur! I ken why you asked Lady Sarah to marry you. You're climbing the ladder, and don't care how you do it.'

'*You* hae the cheek to accuse *me* of social climbing, and you ditched me for a wealthy man! Well, set your mind at rest. I love Sarah, rich or poor.'

'And I love Matthew, married or no'!'

Sandy had risen too. He leaned on the desk, his angry face inches from hers. 'Then I'll tell you this for nothing. You're heading for disaster! Him as well as you.'

His warning left her shaken. She nervously twisted the gold wedding ring she wore. It had never left her finger since Freddie placed it there on their wedding day. She wasn't angry any more, only deeply saddened. She crossed to the window and stared out. 'I loved Freddie,' she said softly. 'If he'd been spared, I would have been a faithful wife to him all my days. But it's a gey lonely path being a widow when you've known such happiness. You long for someone to love, for someone to care. I pray to God you never know the heartache o' that state, Sandy.'

'I do know it,' he said. 'Your rejection near killed me

when I was a weaker man. How do you think his wife feels, Ishbel? Worse than a widow, I'll wager.'

She lifted her hands to her ears, distraught. 'Oh, hush, man! Do you think I'm heartless?'

Sandy put a hand gently on her shoulder where it curved to the slender neck. 'Lass, I ken better than most you have a kindly nature, but your heart rules your heid. It always did. I want to save you grief, but this affair's none o' my business, as you say. If I've caused you distress, then I'm sorry.'

She buried her face in her hands. 'Sandy, don't be nice to me! Don't apologise. I can't bear it!'

He stepped back hastily, then turned on his heel and quietly went out, leaving Ishbel to her own troubled thoughts.

Edinburgh was en fête and Princes Street dressed overall in red, white and blue on 6 May 1935, the Silver Jubilee of King George and Queen Mary's reign. The bearded sailor king and his queen were astonished by the fervour with which their subjects celebrated the anniversary. The ailing king in particular was much affected by the wealth of genuine affection which came his way. He wrote in his diary that night with a sense of wonder: 'I am beginning to think they must like me for myself . . .'

The weather was kind on the school holiday declared in honour of the Jubilee, but the twins decided to go their separate ways. Now in their seventeenth year, the boys had grown tall and handsome. Their hair, though fair in child-hood, had darkened to a few shades lighter than their mother's, but retained their father's attractive curl and what Florrie called 'a coo's lick' on the crown. These attributes afforded the two youths much anguish, for curly hair was unfashionable at the moment and required liberal doses of brilliantine to curb its appearance.

Brian eyed his subdued hair anxiously in the mirror before wheeling out his bicycle and heading towards Dalkeith. His spirits alternated between high hope and nervous despair. He had not told anyone of his plans, not even his twin, who had other fish to fry in Form 4, a saucy little black-eyed Susan who'd captured Adrian's roving fancy and was attending a Jubilee party in the school playing fields. In Brian's jacket pocket nestled a lumpy, heartshaped pin cushion trimmed with black lace.

Catriona hugged her grandson silently to her bosom when the lad arrived. She wasn't given to displays of emotion, but was worried about her husband's fragile health and found it a comfort to see one of her own folk. Somehow it lightened the burden she carried, alone and uncomplaining, day after day.

Donald peered hopefully into the yard. 'Has your mammy come wi' you, son?'

''Fraid not, Grandpa. She's b-busy in the shop wi' a daft Jubilee sale.'

The old man sighed. 'Ishbel's aye too busy to visit her auld pa,' he mourned.

The young lad had become aware of something vital missing from the room. 'Where's Foxy?'

Donald furtively wiped away a tear. 'I laid him to his rest beneath the apple tree, but I miss my wee pal sair.'

Brian felt his own eyelids prickle. He placed a hand on his grandfather's shoulder awkwardly. Catriona bustled around them like a purposeful sheepdog, herding them out of the room. 'Away and take a breath o' fresh air, the pair o' ye, while I make the tea,' she ordered kindly.

The old man and the youngster went obediently. Donald rested one hand on his grandson's shoulder, his stout stick in the other, for he felt doddery today.

'Where would you l-like to go, Grandpa?' asked Brian. Impatience boiled up inside him, a longing to see the lass he loved, but he hadn't realised his grandfather had grown so old and shaky, and pity calmed the urgency of young love.

Donald smiled. 'There's a saying: "Tell your troubles to the bees, and they'll give your heart its ease". Let's walk to the hives, lad. It's no' too far.'

It was slow progress to the dry-stane dyke on the edge of the clover field where the green-painted hives sheltered. The wee winged workers were busy that pleasant May day, and Donald and his grandson stood listening to the sounds of their industry. 'It calms, gives peace. Don't you feel it, Brian?' the old man whispered softly.

He had been thinking about Joanna, wondering if she would be home, in agony in case she wasn't. Calm? Peace? He hardly knew the meaning of the words. 'I don't feel peaceful. Anything but,' he confessed.

Donald propped himself against the wall and studied the lad shrewdly. Aye, he recognised that lovelorn look. He wasn't so old he couldn't mind the joys and anxiety of courting. And he'd won his Catriona, awkward young colt though he'd been! Catriona frae the Far Islands, still beautiful, ever faithful. He wished he could have given her an easy life, been more than just a common soldier, a gamekeeper, a rat-catcher, a nothing.

Och, well! He sighed and turned attention to the youth. 'Who's the lass, Brian?' he asked kindly.

'What?' Brian stared, amazed by such perception. 'It – it's Joanna Wotherspoon, Grandpa.'

Wotherspoon's lass! thought Donald. Well, well, now there's a union to ponder. He gave the lad a gentle prod with the stick. 'You're in luck, man. Joanna's home frae a lassies' boarding-school for the weekend. If you try the farmhouse, you might be lucky.'

Brian's heart leaped, but he hesitated. 'Will you be all right, Grandpa?'

Donald grinned. 'I'm fine. I've told my troubles to the bees. I'm at peace.'

Brian set off at a run, but slowed nervously as he approached the farmhouse, feet positively dragging as he walked up the path. This was awful cheek, but he'd been planning the escapade for weeks. Summoning up courage, he grasped the door knocker and banged loudly.

Wotherspoon happened to be passing in the hallway when he heard the summons. He raised his brows a thoughtful fraction when he saw who was there. 'Aye. What can I do for ye?'

Oh, heavens, the Grumpy! thought Brian, petrified for a moment. Then his hand brushed the pin cushion in his pocket, and he gained courage from the talisman. 'Is M-Miss Joanna in, please? I have something for her.'

'Have ye now? You'd better come in.' Wotherspoon stood aside. Brian glanced around curiously. The interior was austere but very clean and bright, with plain white-washed walls and a red-patterned carpet spreading a feeling of warmth throughout. He wished he could pause to study the many fine paintings on the walls. They were striking watercolours and oils, a mixture of still life and landscape. 'My daughter has a fancy for pictures. I'm afraid I indulge the lass,' Wotherspoon remarked.

Brian gulped. Grumpy the man might be but little escaped him, and there was a glint of amusement in the cool, shrewd eyes that reminded Brian of old Jock the fisherman and was oddly reassuring.

'A gentleman to see you, Joanna,' Wotherspoon announced mildly, opening the door of a large, pleasant living room. Brian walked in and her father quietly withdrew. That surprised Brian. Such tact was unexpected. Not that she was unchaperoned. Bunty Mutch, the kitchie-maid promoted to nurse and now elevated to housekeeper, sat by the window where the light was better, working away at a treadle sewing machine. She stopped and stared at Brian with a hint of suspicion.

Joanna was seated at a table sketching a glass bowl filled with pink tulips. From where Brian stood, the watercolour seemed pretty good. She jumped up, looking pleased and welcoming.

'Why, hello! Which one are you?'

'I'm Brian.'

She looked sceptical. 'Oh, you're teasing me! Brian wouldn't have the courage to come here. Brian is a tumphie.'

Bunty snorted with mirth. 'Och, Joanna!'

'What's a tumphie?' he asked.

Joanna grinned. 'Never you mind. If you were one, you wouldn't be asking.'

'I brought you something.' He rummaged in his pocket and produced the pin cushion, which he balanced on the palm of one hand and held out to her.

Joanna laughed triumphantly. 'Ah, I knew you were

teasing me! Adrian got the pin cushion and Brian the fountain pen. I never forget details. So you're Adrian!' she declared triumphantly.

Bunty shook her head, sighing. 'Trust you to take up wi' a twins!'

'Yes, doesn't it make life interesting, dear Bunt?' Joanna smiled at Brian. 'Come and sit down on the couch, Adrian, and tell me all about yourself. Are you on holiday too?'

'Aye, because of the Jubilee.' He sat down cautiously, leaving a respectable three feet between them. Joanna wore an emerald green cotton dress with a demure white lace collar. Her long legs were tanned and bare, ending in low-heeled black shiny pumps. Brian thought he'd never seen anyone so beautiful.

'We were given a long weekend off school, and a little silver tin with sweets in. Three cheers for dear old King George and Queen Mary!' enthused Joanna.

Bunty gave her charge a stern look. 'If Her Majesty saw your bare legs, the poor woman would throw a purple fit. She canna stand women wi' bare legs. Even Suzanne Lenglen had to cover up at the tennis.'

'Yes, I know.' Joanna cheerfully clasped her fingers round one bare knee and studied Brian with frank curiosity. 'Have you left school yet, and what are you going to be?'

'The answer's no, and I don't know,' Brian laughed. He found it easy to talk, his heart so light the words ran freely off his tongue. It helped greatly because she believed he was Adrian. When would he stop hiding behind his brother, his brave protector? 'I may go to sea. It all depends,' he said.

'Depends on what?'

He wanted to say, 'Upon you. If you love me, if you want me, I'll stay ashore forever and never leave you.' But he couldn't say that, not yet. He felt awkwardness creep over him, tripping his tongue. 'Up-upon exam results. N-nothing less than ship's captain will do for an Alexander, and that takes b-brains and a-a-application.' He was beginning to falter and stammer. It was time to leave. He made a show of glancing at his wristwatch, an acquisition of which he was proud though his mother considered it rather caddish. He stood up. 'I say, I must go. My grandfather will be w-wondering where I've g-got to.'

Joanna looked regretful. 'You will come back again sometime, won't you?'

'In the summertime, Joanna,' he promised.

She followed him. 'Thank you for bringing back the pin cushion. It was a daft present to give a boy.' Joanna picked up the little red heart from the table and examined it. She could remember making it years ago, with this nice boy Adrian in mind. She recalled agonising for hours over the message written in pins. She stopped and stared. I LOVE YOU, it read. Funny, but she didn't remember writing that. What a naughty little minx she must have been!

Brian left the farmhouse in a daze. He didn't know whether to be happy or humiliated. A tumphie? That sounded like a silly ass! Well, he was indeed a silly ass to hide behind his bolder brother, but she'd liked him for himself this time, he was sure. He began to run for sheer youthful delight, pounding along the track through fields where a thick green flush of wheat and barley showed; tidy fields, clean and weedless. Grazing cows with calves at hoof raised their heads curiously in the clover field, chewing and watching with wary brown eyes. Brian could see no sign of his grandfather as he reached the dyke. He checked his reckless progress and leaned over the wall, breathless and smiling. 'Grandpa, I met Joanna. She was there!'

And then he saw him. The old man lay peacefully on the grass in the lee of the dyke as if asleep. 'Grandpa!' Brian gasped in horror, then vaulted the dyke and knelt beside him. Gingerly, he touched Donald's cheek, felt desperately for a pulse, listened for a heart-beat – but in vain. Brian sat back on his heels in anguish and sorrow. He remembered the last words Donald had spoken: 'I am at peace.' The memory seemed poignant.

Brian felt tears threaten, but he wouldn't cry. Crying was for bairns, and he had a man's responsibilities suddenly thrust upon him. He rose slowly, looked down sorrowfully at the old man he'd loved so dearly, then hurried off to summon help and give what strength and comfort he could to his grandmother.

Polly had spent a dreary afternoon alone in the flat while Edinburgh celebrated. It was little comfort to know she'd chosen this course in a noble cause. Elspeth had pleaded with her to attend the Jubilee celebrations in the school playground. Polly sighed regretfully. It would've been fun. She would have been the life and soul of the party, surrounded by adoring youngsters. She would have worn the blue velvet with fox furs and a Garbo hat, because the girls expected her to dress like a film star.

But no! She'd pleaded a headache, and told the fib for Ishbel Alexander's sake. I sure hope that woman appreciates the sacrifice, Polly thought as she leafed idly through a *New York Times* her aunt had sent. Reviews of Broadway shows only served to increase Polly's boredom and frustration. She should be over there.

She flung down the newspaper and stood up restlessly. Why was she alone, for heaven's sake? Where was Matthew? They hardly spoke to one another any more. Today there was a Jubilee sale in the store, and she hadn't seen him all day. Surely a sale didn't require such close attention? Women knew what they wanted and made sure they were first to grab it.

Polly glanced at the clock. Nearly five. Why not get dressed up this evening and go out with Matthew to celebrate Royalty's Jubilee? She wanted to dine and dance the night away like they used to. She wanted his arms around her tonight. Purposefully, Polly left the flat and went in search of her husband.

She became aware of an odd little sound that grew louder as she descended the stairs. She couldn't place it, but it sounded kind of harrowing. When she reached the offices it was louder, though. It came from the inner sanctum and it was someone crying. Concerned, Polly pushed open the door.

Matthew was framed in the doorway. Framed was the word, she thought, stunned. She had caught him in the act of kissing Ishbel Alexander, murmuring soft endearments, holding her in his arms as if he'd never let her go. Ishbel was crying. Softly and hopelessly, she was sobbing as if her heart would break, and that was the sound Polly had heard. The sound that had led her here in time to witness this incriminating scene, to have her faith in her husband shattered for good.

'Matthew!' she whispered brokenly. She clung to the doorframe. She felt weakened, nothing left inside where her heart should be, only emptiness. 'Oh, darling!' she mourned, as if he'd died. She could have borne bereavement better than betrayal.

Matthew released Ishbel and spun round to face his wife. 'Polly, Ishbel just had bad news. Her father died suddenly.'

'Oh, I'm sorry. I'm sorry I barged in.'

Polly spoke the truth. She was bitterly sorry. She pitied the sobbing woman, but Matthew's guilt was even worse. One of his most endearing qualities was his patent honesty. He'd never cultivated a poker face like some. Now the guilt stamped all over his countenance appalled her. She turned blindly and walked out.

Matthew was devastated. To be caught like this ruined his intention of breaking the news gently to Polly. Ishbel was even more distressed. 'Oh, Matthew, please go after her. Try to make her understand.'

He gave her a worried look. Her outburst of sorrow at news of her father's death had alarmed him. 'Darling, will you be OK?'

'Yes, yes, Matthew. Go on,' she insisted.

He set off anxiously in pursuit of his wife.

Polly had returned to the flat and was standing staring out at the spectacular view across the city. The westering sun shone, flags flew in the breeze, the city was beautiful. Polly looked on it with loathing. This was not her home. It never would be.

She heard Matthew come in. 'Polly – darling—' he began awkwardly.

'How long has this been going on, Matt?'

He wished she wouldn't act so cool. He wished she would holler and shout and throw things at him. Matthew ran his fingers through his hair in a distracted gesture. 'Heck, Polly, I always said women shouldn't work, and this mess we're in proves it, I guess. If only Ishbel had stayed home an' left the running of the shop to me, I would never have fallen in love with her.'

She leaned her forehead wearily against the window-pane. 'But it's happened. Oh, Matt, let's go home now, before it's too late to pick up the pieces.'

He didn't know what to say. How could he leave Ishbel, the woman he loved and admired? Besides, this shop was his baby, and he wanted to stay and watch it grow and prosper. Yet he cared deeply about Polly's future welfare. He wanted his wife to be happy, but was that possible?

Hesitantly, Matthew went to her and put an arm round her shoulders. 'We can't leave right now, Poll. Things are still tough in the States, and we'll need every dollar Freddie owed me to start over again. Give me another few months, then the debt will be paid and we'll decide what's to be done about us. Try to trust me, Polly?'

Trust him? She felt like laughing in his face at the irony, or breaking down and howling. No! Polly felt her backbone stiffen; she was no pushover. If she stayed, Ishbel Alexander would find she'd a fight on her hands. 'OK, Matthew. Get our money back, then we'll work it out,' she agreed.

Ishbel found the silence oppressive after Matthew had gone. It served only to heighten her inconsolable grief. She left the office and hurried downstairs through the shop, barely acknowledging the greetings of sale-weary assistants tidying the counters after a hectic afternoon. Walking quickly, she left the premises and crossed Princes Street, dodging tramcars decked in bunting for the Jubilee.

She hesitated uncertainly, then walked up the Mound with a group of revellers, pausing at the spot where, as a little girl, she'd watched a Punch and Judy show with Pa. Memories of him were vivid, as if he walked beside her with his uneven gait as she continued on her way to the old High Street through lofty tenements and steep, narrow wynds he'd known as a boy. With scarcely a glance, Ishbel passed the spot where another widow-woman had once rented a lockit booth and started an industry.

Odd, but she felt her father very near and alive in the neglected closes where a few brave flags fluttered. Ishbel became uncomfortably aware she looked sadly out of place in her smart, fashionable clothing. Inhabitants of dark premises glared out and muttered angrily beneath their breath. In her stylish costume she didn't belong here, amidst squalor and rundown buildings where one ought to roll up one's sleeves and help. She couldn't blame them for harbouring resentment. But *where do I belong?* she wondered.

Wandering on, Ishbel reached the tenement where Donald and Nellie and the rest of the lusty brood had lived. She stared up mistily at a window Donald had once pointed out proudly, where he'd had his beginning. Tears threatened again, but she choked them back for there were bairns playing all round her in the wynd. Familiar snatches of bairns' rhymes drifted to her ears. Little lasses skipping to a chant most suitable for Jubilee Day:

> *'I'm a Girl Guide all dressed in blue,*
> *See all the actions I can do.*
> *Salute to the King an' bow to the Queen,*

*Turn my back on the bold sailor boy.
One – two – three – oot!'*

There was a rumbling and rattling behind her, and a warning shout. 'Hey, wifie, get oot the way!'

Ishbel skipped sideways, and a homemade cartie shot past her with a wee boy on it and his even smaller brother tucked in behind, rattling off recklessly down the hilly wynd.

She found herself smiling. The spirit that had fostered Pa and Auntie Nellie was still there in these bairns, still alive and kicking. Strangely, the thought gave Ishbel great solace and comfort.

Chapter 14

Eleanor Alexander could not concentrate on the crossword puzzle she'd planned to finish that Sunday afternoon. Crossword puzzles were the latest craze to take Morningside ladies by storm, and held precedence over whist at the moment. There was much discussion and consultation of dictionaries in drawing rooms these days.

'I worry about your mother now she's on her own, Ishbel,' Eleanor said, laying down the paper.

'Yes, I'm worried about Mam too,' Ishbel admitted. 'It was kind of Wotherspoon to let Pa stay in the cottage under pretext of catching vermin, but I'm afraid he wasn't very good at the job, poor darling. I'm not sure what will happen now.'

'Surely your mother won't be put out of her home?'

'I hope not,' Ishbel frowned. She'd made a point of visiting her mother regularly, but had been unable to break through the unnatural barrier Catriona had built round herself. She was resigned and quiet, and to the casual observer would seem to be coping well with her grief. Only Ishbel knew differently.

She stood up restlessly and went to the window, staring out at a garden dripping under a sudden downpour of summer rain. Her greatest fear was that her mother would insist upon moving out of the tied cottage now Donald had gone. To stay on would be to accept Wotherspoon's charity, and Ishbel knew that would go against the grain. Catriona had hinted as much on Ishbel's last visit. 'I have no right to live in the cottage now, Ishbel. No right at all,' she declared in such dull, lifeless tones it had frightened her daughter.

'Wotherspoon would never put her out voluntarily. If only Mam would swallow her pride!' Ishbel sighed.

Eleanor smiled sympathetically. 'Pride's not a bad fault, my dear. It can often save the day.'

'It won't help this time, I'm afraid,' said her daughter-in-law.

Old William had been listening to the wireless as usual, tapping out a beat on the arm of the chair. 'Ssshh!' he cried suddenly. 'This is Henry Hall and his orchestra.'

Eleanor looked interested. 'You mean that young man who used to play at Gleneagles Hotel, dear? We went there once on holiday in the twenties.'

'We had afternoon tea and strawberry tarts, Ellie,' beamed the old man.

'Trust you to remember!' laughed his wife. 'I said at the time Henry Hall would go far. Mind you, he's not quite so famous as that other lad from Helensburgh, Jack Buchanan. Thon's a real heart-throb!'

'They all go far, don't they?' remarked William.

'You're right, lovie, far as London and New York usually,' Eleanor replied drily. 'Pity they wouldn't bide in Scotland for a change, then we might have some shows worth seeing in Edinburgh.' She picked up the crossword and frowned at it. 'Six down. What's "split with beheaded force", seven letters? D something . . . ?'

'Divorce?' suggested Ishbel.

'Why, good for you!' Eleanor smiled and wrote busily.

Ishbel returned to her seat and picked up her sewing. Divorce! She shivered at the dreaded word. Would it come to that if she persisted in her love for Matthew? She could see nothing but trouble ahead for herself, for Matthew and for Polly, the innocent wife who must suffer most in this emotional tangle.

Catriona Mackie unlocked the door of the bothy and went quickly inside. She closed it behind her then turned and rested her back defensively against the flaking paint. She drew in a painful breath and shut her eyes. To live here, in this awful place!

She forced her eyes open. Well, it was her choice, her own suggestion to the farmer when she'd heard Wotherspoon was advertising for another tractorman with wife to tend the dairy. She'd no right to occupy a good family cottage with Donald gone. Her pride wouldn't permit it. With all the other cottages tenanted, only the bothy lay empty, all the horsemen and horses gone, bar one old cart horse.

When she'd suggested the switch to Wotherspoon, the man had protested vigorously, but she'd been determined and dug her heels in, and here she was. She hadn't told her daughter. It was difficult enough speaking to Ishbel while resentment still froze Catriona's lips. She brooded daily on her resentment, and it kept growing. Why, oh why, hadn't Ishbel come to see her father during those last precious weeks and days? Donald had longed so much to see his beloved lass, and Ishbel had stayed away. That needed time to forgive.

Catriona took a hesitant step into the single room. Well, the walls and roof were sound, and the broken windows had been fixed for her. The dirt and muck of years could be swept up, scraped off, scrubbed out. The walls lime-washed, curtains put up at the windows.

She rolled up her sleeves, tied on her pinny and reached for the brush. All that day Catriona laboured doggedly, and when she fell exhausted into bed that night, she knew one thing for sure. The place would never be home. It hadn't been built to be home, only bare lodging for homeless men hired for a six-month, to move on at Martinmas to another farm toun and another cheerless lodging. Catriona buried her face in the pillow, and for the first time since she'd lost her beloved Donald, the tears came flooding in a torrent of despair.

Ishbel had guiltily avoided Polly since the incriminating scene in the office. It was easy enough to fall in love, Ishbel thought sadly. Love crept upon you stealthily before you realised what was happening. Love was so wonderfully absorbing you thought of nothing but the loved one and your own longings, until one day your eyes were opened and you saw the anguish of the innocent injured one. Then the situation wasn't so wonderful!

While Ishbel struggled with guilt and remorse, Matthew and Polly's marriage was going from bad to worse. He had moved into the spare room, and was up and away in the morning before Polly wakened, returning late to partake of a lonely evening meal delivered from the shop's kitchens. Polly was rarely in. To combat unhappiness, she had flung herself energetically into amateur dramatics.

Polly had begun attending the nearby kirk on Sundays

for comfort in her present dilemma, and it wasn't long before her talents were recognised and she became involved with the kirk dramatic society. They were rehearsing *Dear Brutus*, a J. M. Barrie play which had run successfully in London's West End. Polly was content to prompt and stage manage, since all the parts were allocated. Save one, that is.

'We need someone to act the part of a child, a girl aged about eleven or twelve,' the minister's wife told Polly worriedly. 'It's one of the most important parts in the whole play, and none of the little girls in Sunday School could handle it. Our ladies are all much too long in the tooth to be convincing, I'm afraid.'

Polly smiled. 'Don't you worry, ma'am. I guess I know someone who'll fit the bill.'

And so Elspeth Alexander got the part, and began rehearsing excitedly for her first real stage show.

'Oh, Polly, it's such a wonderful play!' enthused Elspeth when she visited Polly that Saturday to run through her lines. 'It's so funny it makes me laugh, and so sad I want to cry.'

'I know. It's about being given a second chance in life. I guess that can be fun, though it's more likely to be disappointing,' said Polly. She sighed as she spoke, and Elspeth studied her anxiously.

She sensed a change in Polly, a sadness that wasn't there before. She knew someone had made Polly unhappy. The future wasn't very clear to Elspeth yet, but she had a notion Polly needed her. It was rather wonderful to be needed like that, to help someone you love to be happy again, she thought. So Elspeth went to Polly and hugged her. 'I'm your second chance,' she told her softly. 'I'm your daughter that might-have-been, just like the girl in the play.'

Polly's eyes brimmed with tears. 'But you'll be taken away from me soon, dear girl. You're only a magic dream that happened to me once. When I leave Scotland you'll stay behind, get on with your life, forget about poor old Polly, and I guess that's how it ought to be. I'm the might-have-been, honey baby. Not you.'

'No! When you go, I'm going with you,' Elspeth cried.

Polly smiled. 'We'll see, Elspeth. We'll work it out somehow.' She couldn't help a twinge of triumph that gave no lasting satisfaction. There was a rough justice in this. Ishbel had stolen her husband, and it looked like Polly had stolen Ishbel's child. Could you call that quits? she wondered.

Exams over, results satisfactory, summer holidays begun, Brian whistled as he wheeled his bike out of the garage. He'd soon be learning to drive, then he'd cover the miles to Dalkeith in no time instead of a long hard slog on the bike. Worth it, though, if he saw Joanna!

'Hey, where are you off to? As if I can't guess!' Adrian appeared at his elbow, and Brian groaned inwardly.

The twins looked at one another speculatively in a way that did not require words. 'You've got it bad!' Adrian said.

'Yes,' Brian admitted tersely. He couldn't talk about his love for Joanna. It was too deep and personal to be shared even with his twin. 'You haven't seen her lately. She's a real peach now,' he added proudly. Adrian immediately looked interested.

'Maybe I should come too. Keep an eye on you, wee brother.'

'Huh! You're only ten minutes older. A measly ten minutes!' grunted Brian bad-temperedly. He waited, scowling, while Adrian fetched his bike. The two lads set off, cycling in silence through the outskirts of the expanding city where bungalows were springing up like mushrooms, on to the Dalkeith road and away out into the fresh, green countryside.

When they reached their grandmother's cottage, they were surprised to find the door locked. That had not happened before. They looked at one another, then Brian hammered loudly with a fist. The key turned in the lock, and a woman they didn't recognise stared out at them. An active toddler was clutching her skirt. Adrian was first to recover. 'Excuse me, but where's our grandmother, Mrs Mackie?'

The woman smiled. 'Oh, Mrs Mackie moved out. She's in the bothy.'

'The bothy!' the twins repeated in unison. They stared at the woman so aggressively she stepped back nervously.

'Sorry, I'll have to lock the door. The wee one's so adventurous, and there's the river close by, ken?' The door closed gently in their faces and they heard the key click in the lock.

Adrian clenched his fists. He felt like hitting someone, and he knew who it would be. 'That Grumpy, that damned Grumpy Wotherspoon! He's put poor Gran out!'

'Come on, let's go see her,' Brian cried, and they mounted the bikes and careered down the track. When they reached the bothy they paused only long enough to prop the bicycles against the wall before barging in. They stopped abruptly on the threshold, silenced.

Catriona hadn't been expecting visitors. She'd had no

time to put on a brave face, straighten her shoulders, sort the room to some semblance of welcome and poke the dour fire to give enough heat to boil a kettle. She was caught slumped in misery and despair. She cried out in anguish. 'Oh, you should have warned me you were coming. I didn't want to be seen like this.'

'Oh, Gran!' groaned Brian. He looked round the room. She'd made pathetic attempts to make it homely, with bits and pieces of furniture from the cottage and curtains at the windows, but it was an ugly, cold, cheerless place.

'You can't stay here!' Adrian protested stormily.

Maybe that was the wrong thing to say. It got her dander up. Catriona straightened her back. 'How no'? The roof's weathertight and the walls are strong. It just needs a lick o' paint.'

'But Gran—!'

She turned on the lads sternly. 'If you want to help, collect firewood and stash it in the shed for me. Meanwhile I'll set the bellows to the fire and get the kettle biled for our tea.' Her stern gaze fell away and she faltered. 'It – it's milder today, so I haven't bothered to keep the heat up.'

They went outside in silence. They knew fine the firewood was an excuse to get rid of them, so she could collect herself and put on a brave show of managing. But she wasn't managing, she was depressed and miserable. 'What are we going to do?' wondered Brian unhappily.

'We're going to knock that mean old Grumpy's block off!' cried Adrian, and was off before Brian could stop him, grabbing the bike and heading boldly for the farmhouse.

'Oh, no!' groaned Brian. He mounted and raced after his brother, heart and legs pumping madly.

Adrian was already thundering on the door when Brian

caught up with him. There was a pause then Joanna Wotherspoon opened it. She was wide-eyed, startled to see them both standing there.

'Where's your father? We want to speak to him!' Adrian demanded.

Joanna's eyes sparked with resentful anger at his tone. 'Well, you can't. He's gone to market.'

'Then you can tell him we won't stand for the way he's treated our grandmother, putting her into the bothy. He's a cruel old skinflint, tell him!'

She stepped forward furiously. 'Don't you dare say that about my dad! Anyway, it was your grandmother's idea to live in the bothy. My father was dead set against it, but the silly old woman won't listen to reason.'

'Don't you insult our gran!' warned Adrian dangerously.

'I'll say what I like, when it's the truth,' she shouted. She glared from one twin to the other. 'Which one are you?'

'I'm Adrian.'

Her lip curled. 'Oh, are you?'

'You tell your dad—'

'I'll tell him nothing! Except that you are the rudest, most horrible boys I ever met. Goodbye!' The door slammed in their faces with a resounding crash.

Adrian stared at the closed door for several long moments, then looked at Brian and grinned. 'You're right. She *is* a peach.'

Sandy MacArthur had been withdrawn and preoccupied for most of the long warm summer following the Silver Jubilee. Sarah had noticed his moodiness, though she wisely kept her own counsel and said nothing. She also kept a shrewd eye upon Allsop & MacArthur's business affairs, and presently noted a worrying imbalance.

'Darling, shouldn't we be building more bungalows? Private housing is much in demand, but we're not getting our fair share of orders,' Sarah remarked one day.

They were out walking near ancient Corstorphine kirk on an invigorating Sunday afternoon. The east wind blew in their faces with the first chilly hint of cold weather to come, and Sarah tucked her scarf more cosily round her throat and clung tighter to Sandy's arm. He was frowning.

'Och, I don't approve of wee houses strung out like ribbons along main roads. Why don't they build like they used to, in communities? I liked the farm toun, Sarah. The cottages looked bonnie grouped together, and folk were neighbourly and looked after one another. You couldna be snooty in a farm toun.'

'Yes, but people living in town enjoy their bit of garden, and want their own little bungalow. Why shouldn't they have what they want?' she argued.

Sandy paused to stare upwards at the heavy branches of the aged sycamore that had stood on this corner for more years than anyone could remember. There was building going on, even here. He felt angered. 'You can give the townsfolk what they want, my love, I'll stick to farm machinery. Clayton produced the first combine harvester a few years back, but mine could be better. I'm an engineer, no' a brickie!'

She dropped his arm and moved away, looking at him. 'But you mustn't ignore the building side, Sandy. Allsop's reputation is at stake! My father's not fit enough to handle it now.'

'Then what's wrong wi' you buckling in? You have a good head on your shoulders. We could get married quietly

316

and you could help run that side o' the business.'

'But my father needs me at home!'

He waved that aside. 'The man has servants galore to care for him. He does not need you, he just refuses to let you go. He's waited on hand and foot, and I've never seen him lift a finger to help. What's to hinder you working? Ishbel Alexander does.'

The wind felt cold against Sarah's cheeks. She shivered. 'It always comes back to her! You still admire her.'

His mouth set grimly. 'Not since she took up wi' the American. That did it. I thought she'd mair sense.'

Sarah took his arm and they walked along a paved street that had once been boggy marshland and given rise to Corstorphine's ancient Celtic name: 'the white mist that lies in the hollow'. It was still damp and cold in the dip of the land where the sluggish stream flowed. She rested her head against his shoulder. 'You're a hard, ruthless man, Sandy MacArthur.'

'So I am, dearest, or I couldn't have climbed that blasted ladder,' he laughed.

He could not see her expression or he might have been more concerned. Sarah's brow had furrowed doubtfully, and there was a troubled look in her eye.

Matthew came into the office to find Ishbel with her head in her hands. He crossed the room swiftly and put an arm round her. 'Honey, what is it?' he asked in concern.

'It's my mother. I've felt miserable since the twins told me Mam had moved into the bothy. She's unhappy too, but pride won't let her shift. I've argued with her 'til I'm tired, and Mrs Alexander sent word to Mam she'd be delighted to have her company. There's plenty of room in that big

317

house, but Mam won't budge. I worry about her in that freezing cold wee place, wi' winter coming on.'

Matthew looked thoughtful. 'D'you think your mother would listen to me? I can be a mighty persuasive guy.'

'She might, Matthew.' Ishbel considered the suggestion hopefully. Her mother needed care, but more than that she needed lively company to jerk her out of the deep melancholy into which she was slowly sinking. She needed a fresh purpose in life, and wouldn't find it sitting huddled in Wotherspoon's bothy. Ishbel had tried reasoning with her, but they invariably ended up arguing. Perhaps Matthew would have more luck. It was worth trying.

'It's Wednesday afternoon, and I guess the countryside will be beautiful in the fall. Couldn't we drive over and see your mother right now?' he suggested eagerly.

Ishbel hesitated. She had made an effort not to be left alone with Matthew, nor to be seen walking out with him. So far, no rumours concerning the love affair had reached her ears, but Ishbel suspected she'd be last to hear what her shop assistants were whispering. It was risky driving with Matthew, yet she longed to be with him, just this once.

'Very well, we'll go,' she decided recklessly. 'But what is Polly doing this afternoon?'

His expression changed and he sighed. 'Polly don't tell me her plans any more, but I guess she has a rehearsal in the church hall. That's usual on Wednesdays.'

There was much more traffic on the roads these days, and Ishbel smiled as she drove along, remembering how terrified she'd been when Freddie touched seventy on this self-same stretch. It was a built-up area within the city boundaries now with a thirty-mile speed limit. Recent legislation demanding that new motorists take a driving test would have pleased Freddie who had often complained about the many idiots let loose upon the roads. She chuckled to herself. 'You know, Matthew, I never sat a driving test in my life. Freddie taught me to drive when we were on the racing circuit. He was a very strict instructor. I'm surprised our marriage stood the strain,' she smiled.

'He taught you well.'

She changed down for the hill, and the Austin saloon soared up the incline like a bird. She took her eyes off the road for a moment and smiled at her companion fondly. 'I think Freddie would approve of my loving you, Matthew. He seems very near when we're together. I like to think he understands.' She turned her attention to the road, her mood changing. 'But sometimes I feel as if he's trying to warn me this love of ours can't last. Too many people are getting hurt. Oh, I can't explain the strange feeling, my darling, but it's like a shadow hanging over us.'

'It's because Polly's unhappy,' he said soberly. 'I guess we both hate hurting her. Freddie would understand about that, because he was a caring guy. People can get hurt mighty bad, by circumstances beyond their control.'

At that moment, Matthew was remembering another woman Freddie had loved once, poor Marietta who had borne his baby under such desperate conditions. He was tempted to tell Ishbel the whole story, then decided against it. Freddie was dead. Better to bury the dead past with him.

Ishbel stopped the car at the head of the drive before they reached the Big House, where Lady Hawkerton still lived alone in faded grandeur. Matthew climbed out and filled his lungs with the damp, mossy scent of woodland carpeted with red and gold leaves. More leaves floated down from the golden glory of the boughs above and gently touched his broad shoulders. He took Ishbel's hand. 'And you grew up here? No wonder you're beautiful.'

Being Wednesday afternoon and her daughter's half-day, some sixth sense had alerted Catriona and she'd made a supreme effort to make the bothy look more homely. When she finished the chores, she'd drawn a good supply of water from the tap lagged with straw on the outside wall, and washed herself, shivering, in icy spring water. Still, it made her skin tingle and glow, and she felt better for it. Her usually high standards had been slipping badly, she thought, ashamed.

The fire was burning brightly in the black-leaded grate and Catriona more like her old self when Ishbel and the American walked in. Catriona stood up defensively at sight of the tall man who seemed to dominate the small space. Their eyes met across her daughter's head. He had a direct way of looking, with no smiles yet. A canny man, assessing the situation. No' like poor dear Freddie, who jumped in merrily with both feet. She frowned. Now why did Freddie leap immediately to mind?

Ishbel decided it was best not to beat about the bush. 'Mam, I've brought Matthew Clark with me to add weight to my argument. I thought it was high time you met. I've talked enough about him.'

'Aye, you have.' Catriona held out a hand and he took it. A firm clasp, not ingratiating. Take me or leave me, it indicated.

But his smile was warm. Catriona felt its warmth reach her, and moved back. She didn't want to be warmed. She gestured awkwardly to a chair. 'Won't you be seated, Mr

320

Clark?' She turned to Ishbel. 'You'll have had your dinner?'

Ishbel couldn't help laughing. 'Oh, Mam, you sound like a real Edinburgh wifie. In Glasgow it's "You'll stay for your tea?" and in Edinburgh they say, "You'll have had your dinner?"'

'Och, that's a lot of blethers!'

Catriona watched the man's shrewd glance travel slowly over her billet, taking in the iron bedstead pushed into a far corner, the patchwork cover that represented a married lifetime of pieces and patches beautifully interwoven, rusty nails hammered into the mortar of bare stone walls to hold a horseman's gear, which she couldn't remove though she'd tried hard enough.

'Well, what d'you think o' my wee place, Mr Clark?' she challenged him drily.

The look he turned on her was just as challenging. 'I think it's not worthy of you, ma'am.'

'Huh! I'll warn ye now, ye'll get nowhere by buttering me up.'

'Mam!' Ishbel protested.

The American took no notice of Catriona's antagonism, relaxing into a laugh. 'Any woman who can make a mouse-hole like this look homelike is special. You got the pioneering spirit, Mrs Mackie. Only, it's wasted here.'

'What d'you mean? Surely this is just where a wee bit o' spirit is most needed!'

'No, I guess you're wrong, ma'am. You're needed else-where. By lonely old Mrs Alexander in her home. By your hard-working, overworked daughter in the shop.'

Catriona snorted. 'Och, what would I do in a shop?'

He pointed to the patchwork cover. 'Anyone who can

design an' sew like that is pure gold. You could help poor Doris, our alteration hand. She's losin' her eyesight.'

Ishbel spun round and stared hard at him. 'I didn't know that! She never said a word to me. How do you know, Matthew?'

'I caught sight of the magnifying glass she's hiding, the poor lady. I guess it's my job to notice details like that, honey.'

'Oh, Matthew, you are wonderful!' Ishbel breathed softly. She forgot her mother's presence in an overwhelming rush of love for this caring man.

Catriona's heart nearly stopped when she witnessed her daughter's besotted look. So that's it! she thought. Ishbel had fallen in love with a married man. Oh, this was a far worse shock than when her lass took up with Freddie! This man had a wife. Catriona felt like weeping at this new disaster to hit her family. She must stop the affair somehow. Her brain started working madly. First, she must sink her pride and accept Mrs Alexander's kind offer of a room, then devote all her energies to ending her lass's association with a married man.

'So you see, ma'am, you're sorely needed in town. What d'you say?' Matthew Clark had continued speaking, persuading her to shift. Well, she'd let herself be persuaded, Catriona decided, but not for the reason he thought.

'I'll think about it, Mr Clark. In the meantime, how about a nice cup o' tea?' she said sweetly. There was no harm at all in keeping a fly lad like this on tenterhooks, she thought.

Shortly after Catriona Mackie had thankfully closed the

door of Wotherspoon's bothy for the last time and moved into the Alexanders' braw house, there was another General Election. Poor Ramsay MacDonald, his concentration going, eloquence faltering and credibility sadly eroded, made way for the solidly dependable Stanley Baldwin.

In November, the flags flew in Edinburgh for the marriage in London of Prince Henry, Duke of Gloucester, to Lady Alice Scott. Polly and Elspeth viewed snippets of this grand occasion on the Gaumont News when on a visit to the cinema to pick up tips from the child star Shirley Temple. The two little princesses, Elizabeth and Margaret Rose, were bridesmaids; their grandfather, the old king who doted upon his grand-daughters, looked sadly wan and ill.

Polly watched with alarm the clips of massed torchlit processions marching in Germany. Such fanatical young men, and so many of them saluting the German Chancellor, Herr Hitler! The sight hardened her resolve to go home. She felt threatened, somehow. With all her heart, Polly longed to return to the safety of America.

'I'll not attend any o' the four kirks on Holy Corner, Eleanor,' declared Catriona flatly. 'I'd rather take the tram to the Highland Kirk and hear my own sweet tongue spoken again.'

'Please yourself, dear. You usually do,' smiled Eleanor. Life had improved dramatically since her friend came to stay. Even William seemed brighter, jollied along by Catriona's kindly company.

Catriona decided she'd made a wise decision, moving to Edinburgh. Her energy had returned. She was needed

here, and there was nothing like helping folk for taking
your mind off yourself. She went to the shop by tram three
afternoons a week while Eleanor and the old man were
resting, and helped Doris in the workroom, altering gowns
and happily offering advice.

It was a mixed blessing having her mother in town, Ishbel
thought cautiously. Ishbel's mind was at ease concerning
Catriona's physical welfare, but very little escaped her
mother, and Ishbel dreaded the day Catriona found out
about her love for Matthew.

Fortunately, Christmas 1935 was an extra busy one
for Alexander's, and all hands were occupied with the
Christmas rush. The bright lights of Princes Street shone
through the early darkness with haloes of misty fog, that
frosty season. The reek from thousands of lums was
trapped by the rime and spread in a thick yellowish blanket
across the city. That didn't stop the hardy folk shopping
though, and there was more money about.

The surge in seasonal profits finally wiped out the debt
that Freddie Alexander had owed. Polly had been keeping
an eager eye on bank statements and balances, and when
she checked the accounts at the beginning of January 1936,
she couldn't contain her excitement. Half a million dollars,
plus substantial interest, was theirs. They could go home!

Despite their estrangement, Polly hastened to tell
Matthew the good news. If only they could leave this
country which had woven a spell round her husband, Polly
was sure everything would be OK. He would soon forget
Scotland and the Scottish woman once he was back in the
swing of things in New York. Eyes sparkling, Polly tapped
on Matthew's office door and went in.

He was seated at the desk. He looked up, his eyes

widening apprehensively at the unexpected visit. Polly waved the latest bank statement exultantly under his nose. 'We made it, Matt. Half a million dollars plus interest. It's been a long haul. Now we can go home.'

His expression didn't change. He sighed wearily. 'We talked this all out before, Poll. This is my home. I'm staying.'

Polly was frantic. These days she lived in fear. Fear of what would happen if Matthew left her, fear of those flickering shadows she'd glimpsed, gathering over Europe and this defenceless little country. Her voice rose in agitation. 'Honey, see sense! This isn't your home. How can it be? You're American. You're kidding yourself if you think you could be Scottish, like that wretched woman you've taken a fancy to.'

He was on his feet. 'You have a care what you say, girl!'

'No, I won't, I'll speak up!' Polly shouted at him bravely. 'I'm leaving, Matt. If you have half the sense you were born with, you'll leave with me.'

For a long moment husband and wife stared at one another in a breathless silence. Once they'd been young and frivolous, Matt a dashing young pilot, Polly a talented actress. They'd existed in a crazy, unreal world where everyone had gone a little mad.

But those days were long gone, and what was left now they approached middle-age? Precious little, and they both knew it.

'Oh, Poll, I'm sorry,' Matthew groaned.

'No sense being sorry. That won't help nothin',' she cried tearfully. She had to get out. She would make a fool of herself soon, crying over a past that was dead and gone.

'Polly, listen to me—' Matthew called out, but she'd had

enough. Polly crossed the room quickly and hurried outside. In the corridor she cannoned straight into Ishbel, her mother following close behind.

Ishbel steadied the tearful woman. 'Polly, what's wrong?'

'You should know!' she replied bitterly. 'Freddie's debt is cleared, we're free to go, but Matt won't leave on account of you. You've wrecked my marriage and ruined my life. I hope you're good an' satisfied!' She shoved past and fled to the sanctuary of the upstairs flat.

Ishbel was devastated by the scene. She met her mother's accusing eyes hesitantly. 'Mam, you heard all that. What am I to do?'

Catriona grimly seized her daughter's arm. 'Ishbel, this state o' affairs can't go on. You ken deep in your heart what to do. It must be ended. Right now!'

'Ended?' Ishbel gasped. Mam's code of honour was simple black and white, no wandering from the straight and narrow. But life wasn't so simple. It was complex and contradictory, shaded by patches of grey. How could she end this love affair, hurt Matthew cruelly, wound herself so badly? Never to see him again, never to argue, never to laugh together? How could she end something that was part of her reason for living? 'Mam, I love him!' she said in an agonised whisper.

Her mother's fingers bit deep into her arm. 'He's not yours to love! He belongs to that other poor, suffering woman.' Catriona's expression softened and she put her arms round her daughter and hugged her. 'End it, love. Send this man away. It's what your father would have wanted, Ishbel. Your pa was straight and honest. He'd never willingly hurt another living soul.'

'I know.'

Ishbel kissed Catriona's cheek gently then moved away, heading purposefully for Matthew's office. Quickly, she went in and closed the door. He was standing just as Polly had left him, one hand resting on the desk. He looked drawn and tired and sad, and she felt a sudden surge of pity for him. This was a heart-breaking situation for Matthew too. Maybe he wished he'd never set eyes on Ishbel Alexander, never fallen in love with her. Life would have been simpler. Mam was right. Ending this agony was kindest for all concerned.

He sighed and rubbed a hand tiredly across his eyes. 'Polly is leaving me, Ishbel. Freddie's debt is settled and she's going back to the States. I guess that was the bargain.'

'Aye, that was the bargain, Matthew. Bide or go.'

Something in her tone made him lift his head quickly. 'What's wrong? What is it, my love?'

She met his eyes steadily, with the determined look he knew so well.

'I want you to leave with Polly, Matthew. Go back to the States and make a fresh start.'

Chapter 15

Polly could hardly believe she'd won. She drew deep breaths of relief when she remembered she was going home and Matt was going with her. There was only one snag. How would she get along without Elspeth? And more importantly, how would the dear girl get along without her?

Elspeth had been living in a dream world since her performance with the dramatic society. It had taken place just before Christmas, and her portrayal of Margaret, the daughter that might-have-been, had been highly acclaimed by all who'd seen it. Elspeth was her own sternest critic, however, Polly having impressed upon her she still had much to learn.

'You think you know it all, you're sunk, honey!' Polly had warned.

Elspeth had an unexpected break from school that afternoon, because King George's funeral was taking place in London, and the whole country was in mourning for their sailor king. She sat drinking lemon soda and cookies in Polly's flat. It was a cheerful, warm spot on that dreich January day and Elspeth required cheering and warming, having turned out for a melancholy church parade with the Girl Guides.

'It was so sad, Polly. The bells began tolling at one o'clock, then the guns fired at half-past for a two-minute silence. All the girls were sniffling and sobbing, but I wasn't. I believe in keeping a stiff upper lip,' Elspeth said.

'Yeah. He was a good guy, your old king. Still, you know what they say, honey. The king is dead, long live the king! You got Edward VIII now,' said Polly absently. She was thinking it was high time she told her young friend she was leaving, but she sure hated doing it. Polly took a deep breath and began bravely, 'Elspeth love, I got good news an' bad news, depending how you look at it. Matt and I are leaving for the States pretty soon.'

'Oh, Polly, no!' Elspeth's eyes brimmed and her lip quivered. This departure was the worst crisis Elspeth could remember in her whole life. She ran to Polly and flung her arms round her. 'Please don't go!'

This was just as bad as Polly had feared. She rocked the weeping girl in her arms, her own tears threatening to spill over. 'Honey baby, don't you cry!' she begged. She seated Elspeth on her knee, big girl though she was, and gently mopped her tears with a hanky. 'Listen, I got a plan. It ain't perfect, but it's the best I can do. Why don't you come to the States with us for a holiday? It'd be fun. I could show you around.'

Elspeth considered the startling proposition. A holiday was only delaying the moment of parting, but she jumped at the chance. Oh, if only I could go to America with Polly, what fun it would be! she thought wistfully. But . . .

'I'd have to ask Mam,' she said, her heart sinking.

Polly kissed her fondly. 'You do that, honey. Tell your ma I got friends coming to Scotland in the fall who'll bring you home safe an' sound.'

* * *

Nervously, Elspeth put off approaching her mother until she judged the time was right. Studying her mother anxiously, it seemed to Elspeth she was more preoccupied than usual, but fortunately an ideal opportunity arose next Sunday afternoon. It was a cold, wet day, which made the parlour appear cosy and intimate as she and Ishbel sat by the fireside. The old folk had retired for a nap and Elspeth's brothers were upstairs studying for important exams in March. She decided she'd never have a better chance. She took a deep breath and launched eagerly into Polly's plan for the American holiday. 'Polly says I could travel home with friends in the autumn, Mam. She's thought it all out carefully.'

'I bet she has!'

Ishbel had listened to the outline of Polly's scheme with growing indignation. She certainly would not allow her beloved daughter to go off on this trip with Polly! She loved Elspeth far too much even to consider it. For years she had struggled to support her children and keep the Alexander family together, and the thought of one of them leaving home so young, to go so far, was intolerable.

'Please, Mam, let me go!' begged Elspeth desperately, watching her mother with trepidation.

Ishbel touched her hair tenderly, smoothing wayward curls that reminded her poignantly of Freddie. 'I'm sorry, my darling, but I can't.'

'Why not, Mam?' wailed Elspeth.

'Because I don't want you to go so far away. Not yet, not until the time comes to spread your wings. I love you far too much to let you go off with someone else.'

Elspeth struck her hand away furiously. 'You don't love me at all! You don't care tuppence. Polly does, and she hasn't any children. She needs me!'

'Elspeth, I need you!'

'No, you don't!' she shouted, red-faced with distress. 'You don't need anybody. All you need is the beastly shop.'

'Elspeth!' Ishbel breathed in horror.

'It's true!' the angry girl went on. 'I know why you want to keep me here – it's so I'll work in the shop. Well, I won't, Mam! I wouldn't work in the shop if you paid me a thousand pounds. I'm going on the stage. I want to be an actress like Polly.'

Ishbel was stunned by this shocking disclosure. She didn't know what to say. Elspeth childishly knuckled away tears. 'Ohhh, Mam! Please change your mind?' she pleaded.

But Ishbel's expression had hardened, and her mind was made up. 'No, Elspeth. I'm sorry, but I will not let you go with Polly.'

With a heart-rending cry, Elspeth rushed out of the parlour, slamming the door. A hushed silence fell over the big family house after she had gone. It was an overwhelming silence, Ishbel thought, as if youthful joy and happiness had fled for ever from the quiet rooms.

On Monday after school, Elspeth plodded dejectedly upstairs to Polly's flat to deliver her mother's decision. Usually she walked in unannounced but today she heard Matthew's voice and hesitated. She was rather in awe of him. He was big and handsome and his smile was kind, but Elspeth had never known a father and felt awkward in his presence. She thought of herself as Polly's make-believe daughter, did that make Matthew her make-believe father? she wondered. It was a strange thought. She listened to the rumble of his deep voice, and to her surprise heard her name mentioned.

'Polly, you can't be serious! You can't take Elspeth to America!'

'Why not? Ishbel took you away from me. It's quits.' Polly's voice sounded harsh and angry, and Elspeth was suddenly frightened. She wanted to run, but found she couldn't move.

'Oh, don't start that again!' His voice sounded flat and wearied. 'You think Ishbel and I could help falling in love? Anyway, she made me leave Edinburgh with you, and I guess that was mighty honourable. For heaven's sake, Polly, we're all unhappy enough! Why make matters worse by involving the girl?'

'She's not just an ordinary girl, she's the daughter I never had!' Polly cried tearfully. 'All I want is a little more time with her, in my own country. Is that too much to ask from that woman who stole my husband and ruined my life?'

Elspeth backed away. She had heard enough. Her mother and Matthew were lovers! The awful word pounded like a drumbeat in her head. She tiptoed numbly away from Polly's door.

So that was really why Polly was leaving, not all this rot about debts being repaid! Elspeth felt sickened and angry. Without pausing to think, she rushed downstairs, barged past the startled secretary and burst wildly into Ishbel's inner sanctum. She was on the phone but spun round, startled. She cut short the telephone conversation while Elspeth closed the door and stood in the middle of the room, breathing hard.

'Elspeth, what is it, dear?' Ishbel asked anxiously.

'I know all about you and Matthew,' she said brusquely.

The words washed over Ishbel with the shock of icy cold water. 'Who told you?'

'I overheard Matthew and Polly talking. She's leaving because of you.'

Ishbel gripped the edge of the desk. 'No, Elspeth. Not because of me. Polly always intended to leave when your father's debt was cleared. She isn't happy here.'

Elspeth stamped a foot childishly. 'She *is* happy! I made her happy, and you and Matthew made her sad and ruined her life.'

'I tell you we did not!' Ishbel moved quickly from behind the desk, bending down to her daughter's height. 'Listen to me! I love Matthew. I know I've no right to love him, but it's happened and it can't be undone. I sent him away for Polly's sake. She won in the end, Elspeth, so don't you dare accuse me. I've done nothing to be ashamed of, and neither has Matthew.'

Subdued, Elspeth stared into her mother's dark, angry eyes and her own rage cooled into a state of hopeless misery. She'd read many plays with Polly, in which they'd acted out the fierce and deep emotions of grownup love, and perhaps that gave Elspeth an insight beyond her years. She found she could identify with her mother, and pity her dilemma; she could identify with all the sad actors in this human drama, but that was a painful procedure – much too painful to be endured by a sensitive young girl who had only recently become a woman.

Elspeth began sobbing forlornly. 'But Polly's so unhappy, Mam. She's terribly unhappy because Matthew loves you and doesn't love her any more. If I don't go with her it'll be much worse. She really does need me. Oh, please, Mam, won't you let me go?'

Ishbel stood looking down at the weeping girl, deeply moved by her tears. Elspeth was not usually prone to emotional outbursts, and her distress was all the more disturbing. Ishbel gently put an arm round her daughter and felt such anguished tremors of misery shiver through the slender body she was deeply concerned.

Holding the sobbing girl to her, Ishbel began anxiously examining her own motives. She loved her daughter too much to let her go willingly with Polly, but was she also deluding herself? Am I jealous of Polly because Elspeth loves her so? Is that the real reason I'm dead set against this trip? Ishbel wondered. Am I being possessive and unreasonable, and causing my dear child unnecessary misery?

She cupped her daughter's wan, tear-stained face in her hands, staring down at her. 'If I let you go, Elspeth, will you promise to come back to me?'

She stopped crying, and mother and daughter stared at one another. This was a momentous decision, and Elspeth was well aware of its importance.

'Aye, Mam. I promise,' she answered gravely.

'Then I will let you go.'

'Oh, Mam! Mam, thank you!'

Elspeth slipped her arms round her mother's waist and hugged her, then they stood together quietly holding one another, closer in spirit than they had ever been before.

The twins commandeered their mother's car and began learning to drive in November 1935. They were true sons of Freddie, and required only a few lessons before they were quite proficient, passing the driving test with ease before the New Year festivities took place.

Brian had one aim in mind now he possessed a full driving licence, and that was to make peace with Joanna. Wisely, he gave his brother no hint of his intentions. The twins were in their final year at school, studying hard for Higher Leaving Certificate exams in March. Adrian hoped to be accepted by St Andrews University to read for a degree in mathematics, while Brian had dreams of going to sea as a trainee deck officer and eventually gaining his Master's ticket.

But first, Joanna!

He chose a mild Saturday early in February for the planned excursion. His mother good-humouredly agreed to pay three ha'pence on the tram, and gave her son full use of the car. Brian's heart was singing like a mavis in moonlight as he made his way to the garage. He paused before he reached the old stable block, frowning. He imagined he heard an engine ticking over somewhere. The noise suddenly became a throaty roar as the engine revved. 'Oh, no! It c-couldn't be. Could it?' he groaned, and began running.

He rounded the corner just as his brother drove out of the stable yard. Brian considered flinging himself wildly in front of the wheels in a desperate bid to stop it, but fortunately wisdom prevailed. Adrian shot past, grinning broadly and sounding a triumphant cacophony on the horn. 'Tough luck, wee brother!' he yelled through the open window.

In the way of twins, Brian knew exactly where Adrian was headed. To Dalkeith, to be first to make peace with

Joanna Wotherspoon. Brian had never felt more danger-ously furious, nor more determined not to be beaten. Whirling round, he set off at a run for his Aunt Dorothy's house. Dorothy owned a car, and had a very soft spot for her two handsome nephews.

Adrian whistled merrily as he drove. He'd had a twinge of conscience about leaving poor old Brian in the lurch, but comforted himself he was doing the old lad a good turn. It required an understanding of the ways of women to make peace with a fiery little number like Miss Wotherspoon, and dear Brian was not at his shining best when confronted with the fair sex. Little Joanna had a deal of spunk for a young lass. Given a little more maturity, she'd be an interesting prospect, Adrian thought.

It felt strange driving along the familiar road into the estate, knowing his grandparents were no longer there to welcome him. Adrian swallowed a lump in the throat, but forgot the forlorn feeling when he reached the gateway leading to the old mansion. The high wrought iron gates were closed, and a small, slim figure clad in dungarees was busily at work painting them, perched precariously on top of a tall ladder. Adrian let the car roll to a gentle stop. He wound down the window and rested an elbow on the sill. 'Tell me, do you enjoy roosting?' he called. 'This is the second time I've found you perched high above ground.'

Joanna looked down. 'Oh, it's you, whoever you are. I'm not roosting. I'm repainting the crest and restoring my heritage.'

Adrian climbed out of the car and squinted upwards. She was making a good job of the old metal crest incorporated in the gateway, picking the heraldic arms out in gold and bright colours. 'Well, it's a start, but you've a job on your hands if you aim to restore that mouldering old heap!' he remarked, jerking a thumb at the mansion.

She glared indignantly. 'It's a lovely old house! Grandmother says it will be mine one day, and I've promised her I'll make it beautiful again. I am starting at the gates and working my way inwards.'

Adrian was amused by her optimism. Such a small person, such an enormous task! 'I'm very sorry we parted on bad terms last time we met,' he apologised.

'Oh, I don't bear grudges. I'm glad your grandmother moved out of the bothy,' she replied, carefully completing the family motto in paint which gleamed gold in the sunlight. Joanna admired her handiwork. 'There, that's done.'

She began to descend, hampered by paint pots and brushes. The ladder rocked dangerously and Adrian made a grab for it. 'Hey, watch out!'

Anxiously, he reached up and caught hold of her. She slid down the last few remaining rungs and landed in his arms, paint pots and all. Adrian held her close and was overwhelmed by a tender emotion. Surely a grubby lass in dungarees shouldn't rouse such turmoil in his breast? He'd kissed dozens of eager girls, so why on earth . . . ?

Bemused, Adrian didn't notice his Aunt Dorothy's Morris come shuddering to a halt and his brother leap out. He was oblivious to everything but the girl in his arms until Brian seized him roughly by the shoulder and dragged him round.

'Leave go of her!'

Adrian turned beetroot red. 'Don't be daft. Why should I?'

338

'Take your hands off her or I'll punch you!' warned Brian dangerously. He'd never felt so angry. This was Adrian, his twin, his other half, and at that moment he hated him.

Adrian's eyes widened with shock as he read his twin's sentiments accurately, then his fighting spirit asserted itself and he doubled his fists. 'You punch me, and I'll flatten you!'

'Go ahead, just try it!' challenged Brian.

They would have fought savagely. For the first time in their lives they would have inflicted pain and injury upon one another, but Joanna flung herself bravely between, shoving them apart.

She turned to Brian. 'Stop it! This nice boy didn't mean any harm. I slipped on the ladder and he caught me. Which one are you anyway?'

'I'm Brian. The tumphie. Couldn't you guess?' he growled bitterly.

'You're not! You couldn't be. You're much too angry!' Clutching paint pots and brushes to her chest, Joanna backed away from the two young men. 'Why must you tease me?' she cried out tearfully. 'Why must you always make me so unhappy?' Whirling on her toes, she ducked her head and ran. The brothers stared after her, then without exchanging a word raced to their respective motorcars and drove off angrily in opposite directions.

1936 had begun with change when King George V died, and it seemed set to go on that way. The chilly month of March dragged to a close before the legal details of Matthew's departure were complete. He and Polly had arranged to leave Edinburgh early in April, joining the

Cunard liner *Queen Mary* at Southampton before making the Atlantic crossing. Elspeth would travel with them. Ishbel tossed and turned sleeplessly as the day of departure approached, wondering if she'd been wise to allow her daughter to go.

Matthew sought out Ishbel on the last Wednesday afternoon before he was due to leave. 'You've been avoiding me,' he accused.

'Yes. It seemed safer,' she admitted wearily.

He came so close she could see the pain of their parting reflected in his eyes and etched in careworn lines on his brow.

'Walk with me one last time this afternoon, my darling?' he begged softly. 'Polly is packing. Surely it won't matter if we're seen together, just this once?'

She hesitated, but the temptation was strong. 'Very well, Matthew,' she agreed.

He took her hand, and they went slowly through the beautiful shop they had created together. It was now an important tourist attraction, and had a name for excellence far afield. This afternoon the shop lay empty and silent, ornamental gates closed across the main entrance. Matthew paused and looked round this emporium of fine goods upon which he'd lavished his creative ability for seven years. I guess it grew to be like my own child, he thought, and that's why it hurts so much to leave it.

'How I shall miss this place!' he murmured wistfully, and Ishbel squeezed his hand, understanding the emotion.

They went out through the side door into a blustery, chilly March day with grudging glimpses of sunlight escaping through grey clouds. He looked down at her quizzically. 'Where to?'

'There are bonnie crocuses blooming in the Gardens,' she answered.

He held her arm tightly. 'And no memories?'

'I must learn to live wi' memories, Matthew.'

They crossed the road, dodging the comings and goings of Edinburgh's cheap and efficient trams. The heavy, metallic sound of wheels on tramrails faded away almost to nothing as they descended the wide stone steps leading down to the Gardens. Few folk walked here today in the snell, searching wind beneath leafless trees, and Ishbel welcomed the solitude. She clung to Matthew's arm, feeling his solid strength and warmth, soon to be taken from her forever. Her eyes filled with sorrowful tears she couldn't hide.

'Don't cry,' he begged. 'Honey, if you cry, how can I bear to leave you?'

That steadied her, and she smiled. 'Then we'll laugh, my dear. We'll make this a braw afternoon of laughter. Something good to remember.'

'This is good,' he said, drawing her close in the shadow of the bare trees, kissing her with all the pent-up love and longing they would never share. Crocuses bloomed in a purple, yellow and white carpet round their feet as they clung together fiercely for the last time.

A bobby on the beat walked by, gave the lovers a quick observant glance, for he prided himself he knew most folk of note in the city. He raised his brows beneath the tall helmet when he saw who it was, and discreetly looked the other way. Scandal was not his business, and there were worse crimes in his book than kissing.

The departure of Matthew, Polly and Elspeth was a very

public affair, with the twins allowed off school for an hour or two for the occasion, and even Catriona present. Ishbel felt drained of emotion. She went mechanically through the motions of farewell while the gleaming engine steamed impatiently close by. Matthew's lips brushed her cheek lightly. She looked into his eyes and remembered details of the last stolen hours together. Would she ever forget them? They'd laughed and held hands, kidding themselves the day would never end. She'd taken him to Blenheim Place to share a favourite joke of Auntie Nellie's. She'd made him study the row of single-storey stone houses, and he'd stared at the unremarkable terrace obediently. 'Ishbel, I guess those are just little old cottages. So what?'

'Look at the lums, dear! Count the chimneypots.'

He'd looked more closely. 'My gosh, there must be dozens!'

Then she'd showed him the three hidden storeys underneath, entered from the lower level of Greenside, and he'd laughed heartily. 'Well, what d'you know, my darling? I never knew such a city for hills!'

But the enchanted afternoon had passed all too swiftly, and now they stood on a grey railway platform that smelled of smoke and faintly of fish, shaking hands in formal farewell. Tears threatened, and Ishbel turned hastily to Polly.

'Goodbye. I hope you have a pleasant journey.'

'Thank you. I'm sure we shall.' She was thinking it was odd she and Ishbel had never become friends. They should have been, for they had a lot in common – mainly Matthew. Had they known from the start they were destined to be rivals?

Well, I guess I won, Polly thought, if you can call the

charade of my marriage winning! Impulsively, she threw an arm around Elspeth and drew the girl to her for comfort. Elspeth laughed and hugged her friend. Polly watched pain tighten Ishbel's expressive features at the affectionate gesture. Maybe we're all losers in this game, Polly thought sadly. I guess that's more like the truth.

Ishbel kissed her daughter. She'd be lonely indeed with Elspeth gone, but she let no hint of sorrow spoil her girl's departure. 'Have a lovely time, my lamb. Come back soon.'

'I will, Mam,' Elspeth promised mistily, hugging her.

Catriona enveloped her grand-daughter in a bearhug. 'Mind and wrap up warm, Elspeth dear. They say New York's an awfy draughty place wi' a' they skyscrapers. It's no disgrace to wear combinations an' liberty bodice at your age, mind. I've packed two pairs o' thick black stockings in your bag, to keep ye cosy.'

'Wise move, Gran!' murmured Adrian. Brian spluttered and dug him in the ribs, deadly rivalry forgotten for the moment. The two youths kissed their little sister affectionately.

'Be good, peanut,' Brian said gruffly, ruffling her curly hair. He didn't like this parting. He sensed emotional undertones and didn't approve of his sister's leaving home to go so far away. He was surprised his mother had allowed it. He hated departures; they brought back vague, unhappy memories, buried deep.

Brian concentrated upon the *Flying Scotsman*. Porters began slamming doors, ushering passengers aboard. The streamlined engine was blowing steam like an impatient racehorse on a frosty track. He wished he could travel with them, far from Joanna who despised him.

Ishbel waved and waved as the train pulled out. Her eyes were aching with tears, and somewhere a melancholy little voice was singing:

'Goodbyee – don't cryee,
Wipe the tear, baby dear, from your eyee.'

Am I fated to lose those I love best? she wondered bleakly as the red tail lamp on the guard's van disappeared from sight. Catriona cast an eye over her and took her arm firmly. 'Come, lass, we'd best go to the shop. You must keep an eye on that Clara for the prices the woman's putting in the shop windows these days are scandalous. Near five pounds for a silk coat you could spit peas through, and six bob for a cambric nightie I could run up in half an hour! Folk'll no' stand for it.'

The shop! thought Ishbel thankfully. That's where her salvation lay. Dear Freddie had given her the shop, and Matthew had improved and expanded it until Alexander's had a reputation second to none. The shop was the gift her men had bestowed upon her, and she vowed she would treasure it always.

'She's sent the man away, Sarah!' said Sandy MacArthur jubilantly.

His fiancée looked less than impressed. 'You mean, he escaped in time?'

Sandy eyed her with a frown. 'It's no' like you to be catty,' he remarked.

She put her arms round his neck and kissed him. 'I get fed up hearing about Ishbel Alexander. Why do you think I put my foot down with Daddy, and insisted on working for a living? I wanted to be as good as her, while keeping an eye on you, my handsome lad.' Sarah had been running the house-building side of Allsop's for some weeks now, and handling the business well. Allsop's had secured a fair share of building contracts in the council housing boom, and Sir Stewart Allsop, while grumbling loudly at Sarah's desertion, was secretly pleased and proud. Who needed a son with a clever daughter like that?

'We should get married, Sarah, quietly, wi' no fuss,' Sandy said urgently. But again he noted her hesitation, a reluctance to name the day which was worrying. 'Don't you want to marry me? Don't you trust me?' he asked.

'No,' she said honestly. 'I don't. I think you are quite ruthless when you are climbing that ladder, Sandy. You'll reach the top by hook or by crook. You admitted it yourself. I don't want to be just one of the rungs.'

He laughed. 'Not by crook, my dear, I'm an honest man, polite and kind to the folk I meet on my climb – because they're the same folk I'll pass on the way down.'

She tapped his cheek reprovingly. 'Don't joke about it! And another thing, where do you disappear to occasionally, driving off into the countryside without a word?'

Sandy looked uncomfortable. 'I'm searching for a man called MacPhee, a tinker who ranges far and wide. I havena found him yet.'

'What'll you do when you find him?'

His expression hardened and became the look Sarah feared and mistrusted. 'That all depends,' he said.

1936 proved to be a year of crisis and uncertainty, when by rights it should have been a time of hope and optimism. In December, after months of speculation, the bachelor King Edward VIII renounced his throne for love of Mrs Simpson, an American estranged from her husband. The quiet Duke of York, his Scottish Duchess and their two little daughters found themselves thrust unexpectedly into an unwelcome limelight.

Ishbel was pleased when she reviewed the year's trading, though the most famous hunger march of all time had set out from Jarrow earlier that year, with the firebrand MP Ellen Wilkinson at its head. Britain continued to disarm despite furious protests from Winston Churchill. The man was known to enjoy a good war, so nobody paid him much attention. True, the Italian leader Mussolini had invaded Abyssinia, and the German Chancellor, Herr Hitler, amassed a large army and built wide roads to speed troop movements within Germany, all in defiance of the League of Nations, but most politicians thought that provided a comfortable buffer against the threat of Russian Communism. Everyone was agreed Herr Hitler's brave show of massed flags and uniforms added pomp and colour that summer to proceedings at the Olympic Games, held in Berlin.

Elspeth had not returned that autumn, nor did she arrive in the spring of 1937 in time for the Coronation, as Ishbel had secretly hoped. Elspeth wrote loving little notes to her mother, telling Ishbel she was well and happy and Polly had arranged for her to attend high school in Los Angeles that semester, because: 'Guess what, Mam? Polly and I have been given mother-and-daughter parts in a movie. It's only what they call a "B" movie, but it's funny, and the director was impressed with our performance and may give Polly more work. So you see, I had to stay a little longer. The studio changed my name, by the way. Polly says my new name has more "star quality", whatever that is. Matthew is working somewhere in Washington DC. Polly thinks it's "hush-hush". We don't see him very often . . .'

Ishbel laid down the letter and gazed mistily at a garden bursting with all the glorious flowers of May. How empty life was without Matthew and her lovely girl! The twins had gained Leaving Certificates with distinction and gone their separate ways with an enmity Ishbel found difficult to understand. Adrian was studying at St Andrews University, very dashing in his scarlet gown, Brian had joined the Merchant Navy as a junior officer. Her children were far away, independent and happy, getting on with their lives without her.

Ishbel spent most of her time at the shop. The whole city was festive this May month with preparations for the Coronation, and she wanted Alexander's window display to be particularly eye-catching. She and her mother designed blue and white silk backdrops for the windows, with scarlet gowns on view beside the huge golden crowns suspended in midair. The window dressers were busily at work that Wednesday afternoon, and a crowd of interested spectators had gathered outside to watch.

Supervising the operation, Ishbel paused suddenly, wondering why an image of Freddie had come rushing to mind, the features so fresh and alive she was startled by their clarity. With dread, she recalled a similar incident when she was on the brink of falling in love with Matthew. It had been a portent of disaster then, and it seemed like a warning now. She glanced around with a shiver and nervously ordered the window blinds lowered, shutting out the curiosity of the onlookers. Gradually the image faded.

Eleanor Alexander was a great believer in fresh air and

sunshine for others, though preferring to remain insulated from the beneficial rays herself. The mild weather tempted William to wander around in the shelter of the walled garden, and Eleanor was content to let him go off on his own, knowing Florrie would keep an eye on the old man from the kitchen window. William wasn't strong enough to walk far.

Ishbel and Catriona were relaxing that Sunday afternoon after a strenuous week, and to Ishbel's delight Dorothy had turned up to pay her parents a visit. She and her doctor husband had flitted from Knoxhall Lodge some months ago to more spacious premises near the Botanic Gardens. They needed the additional room, for Dorothy and Mike Burton looked after a succession of foster children. Waifs, strays and orphans, all found a secure home with the happy couple.

'My bootless bairns,' Dorothy said affectionately.

'How many do you have now, dear?' Catriona asked.

'Four at the last count, but we—' Dorothy paused, listening. 'I say, what was that?'

Eleanor cupped a hand round her ear. 'I didn't hear anything.'

'I did,' Ishbel said. 'It sounded like—' She stopped and met Dorothy's eye anxiously.

Dorothy stood up. 'I think I'll go and see if Father's OK.'

'I'll come with you,' Ishbel volunteered.

The two women met Florrie in the garden. She ran up to them. 'Oh, do come quick! It – it's the master.'

'What's happened?' demanded Dorothy sharply. She took Florrie's arm and hustled her along.

The elderly cook began sobbing. 'Och, Miss Dorothy, I dinna rightly ken. Your pa was doddering down the path right as rain last time I looked out. Then I heard voices.'

Dorothy looked up sharply. 'There was someone with him? Who was it, Florrie?'

'Well, there's an awfy lot o' vacuum cleaner salesmen goin' the rounds. Mind you, the old man does mutter to hisself, and he was behind the yew hedge so I couldna see what went on. Then he gave a shout, some blethers about Master Freddie. Near froze my blood to hear him. I went out after a wee while to see if he was all right, and – oh, michty me!' she broke off with a wail. They had rounded the corner of the clipped yew hedge sheltering the garden from the east wind. There was a bench there and William lay slumped upon it.

'Oh, no!' breathed Ishbel. 'Florrie, go and phone for a doctor.'

Dorothy bent over the old man, then straightened slowly. 'It's too late, Ishbel. He's gone,' she said quietly.

Chapter 16

It was a sad house without old William Alexander. Dorothy and Ishbel had decided to make no mention of the mystery surrounding the old man's last moments, though Florrie stuck doggedly to her story that a visit from a vacuum cleaner salesman had brought on William's fatal heart attack.

'Those folk are enough to mak' onybody scream. I've felt like screaming mysel', opening the back door and finding another yin standing on the doorstep,' she declared.

'But not on a Sunday afternoon, Florrie!' protested Ishbel.

'Och, I wouldna put it past them to pollute the Sabbath, they're that persistent,' she said scathingly.

For poor grieving Eleanor's sake, Ishbel thought it best to drop the subject. Florrie's imagination tended towards the dramatic, and William had been guilty at times of arguing quite loudly with himself.

Ishbel wrote to Elspeth at once, breaking the news of her grandfather's death. She had high hopes the sad event would bring her daughter home. William and Elspeth had shared many happy hours listening to the radio together, and there had been a bond of love and understanding between the muddled old man and the bright young girl

351

that had been quite touching to see. In due course, Elspeth replied. After sincerely mourning her grandfather, she went on: 'Mam, I hope you won't be too disappointed if I don't return to Edinburgh just yet. After that first movie, the director wants me to appear with Polly in a comedy series. It's about an American family that adopts a Scottish daughter. Polly's the mother and I'm the daughter, and oh, Mam, I believe it could be a success! At least I hope so for Polly's sake, because she's so thrilled to be working again. She will be writing you with the legal details. Your signature is needed on the contract because I'm still a minor. Mam, I do love you for letting me go, and giving me such a wonderful chance to act in films . . .'

Ishbel laid down the letter and rested her head in her hands. She was filled with despair. She longed with all her heart to have her daughter home again, but if she wrote and demanded Elspeth's immediate return, the starry-eyed youngster would never forgive her for putting an end to a promising career. Polly must know that. This was a game Ishbel could never win.

When Polly's guarded letter arrived with the contract documents, it contained no word of Matthew. The omission seemed deliberate and caused Ishbel much anguish. What had happened to him? Had he found work, and was he well and happy? Ah, not happy! she prayed. Had he forgotten her so soon?

Matthew did not write. Ishbel had decided when they parted it was best not to exchange letters and had made him promise not to. Now she deeply regretted that decision. She had not bargained for the agony of not knowing where he was and how he fared, and spent sleepless nights wondering if he still loved her.

* * *

There were a few tattered flags still flapping dejectedly in the Grassmarket after the Coronation celebrations ended. The inhabitants of some closes lacked the will to bring them down because the memory of celebration lingered as a bright spot in drab lives. There was a scrap of faded red, white and blue caught upon a rusty nail above the door of the lodging house in Feemie's close. The rusty nail was one of several securing a flaking wooden notice board, which read:

CLEAN BEDS FOR WORKING MEN . . . 4d per NIGHT
WITH BRECKFAST   . . . 5d

Euphemia Geddes kept a decent house. Feemie was fussy about the folk she took in, and she'd been very doubtful indeed when confronted by her latest lodger. For a start, she wasn't keen on taking females. Women were fussy about bathing and that sort of nonsense, and were a real scunner to a hard-working landlady. But this woman had somehow touched Feemie's well-seasoned, leathery heart.

She was young, and looked as if a puff o' Edinburgh wind would blow her down the Waverley Steps. When Feemie snorted 'No' likely!' to her request for a bed, the young woman just kept staring at her with huge, suffering eyes and repeated one soft word.

'Please?'

Feemie looked her up and down doubtfully. You wouldn't give tuppence at a jumble sale for her clothes, though they might have been good once. She wore a hat pulled well down over her brow, as if she wanted to avoid attention. Only the eyes stared out beneath the brim, clear and dark and startling in a thin, pinched face.

'We-eel . . .' Feemie dithered.

'I have only little money. Your charge is all I can afford in the whole city,' the lassie admitted.

That should have put the tin lid on it, but to Feemie's surprise it had the opposite effect. She felt a softening of her heart. 'I'd need eightpence deposit. Elevenpence if you're wanting breakfast,' she warned.

The young woman's face lit like the sun coming out in the narrow close and she turned modestly away and fished out a purse hidden in her underclothes. She held out a coin. 'This is one shilling. You call this "bob", yes?'

'You foreign?' demanded Feemie suspiciously, securing the coin. There was no mention of change, so she ignored it.

At that, a grieved look which Feemie wouldn't forget in a hurry came over the lassie's face. 'I do not know what I am,' she said.

Feemie put her new lodger in the wee boxroom next door to her own room, where she could keep an eye on her. Not that she expected trouble from the working men, who were all suitably cowed and wouldn't dare try anything of that sort in Feemie's lodgings. She was genuinely concerned about the skinny lassie, to the extent of ladling an extra dollop of porridge into her bowl and saving the top of the milk for her in an attempt to feed her up. Where the creature disappeared to all day, Feemie had no way of knowing, until one Sunday afternoon her lodger came back in a state of collapse.

'In the name o' a' the Wee Folk!' Feemie declared as she opened the outer door to a feeble knocking and found the young woman lying dazed and fainting on the doorstep. She heaved her over her shoulder and carted her bodily up the stairs, then laid her on the boxroom bed. Her white cheeks were streaked and dirty with tears, and she stared up at Feemie tragically.

'My father is dead!' she whispered.

'Aye, weel, at least you had one. Some folk are no' so lucky,' said Feemie comfortingly.

The lassie closed her eyes, tears sliding through her lashes and dampening the pillow. 'I had hoped so much!' she whispered in such exhausted, defeated tones Feemie was really worried. She'd never had a lodger die on her yet, but there was always a first time. 'Are you needing the doctor?' she asked nervously.

'No. No doctor,' she gasped.

'Well, that's a God's blessing. It's near one-an'-six for a house call.'

Feemie had noted previously that the small hidden purse was becoming thinner and thinner, like its owner. She sat gingerly on the rickety chair and took the fragile, limp hand in hers. 'Care to tell me about it?'

For a moment, Feemie thought she wouldn't get a squeak out of her, then the poor, sick lassie gave a long, tired sigh. 'He was a British flyer. During the war in France he – he shamed my mother.'

'Ah!' said Feemie knowingly.

'My mother wrote to an address she had in Edinburgh, asking him for help, but there was no reply.' The young woman's eyes showed a quick flash of anger. 'My mother forgave him and his family, but I never shall. She married a

German soldier, a good man who cared for me like his own daughter, but then—' She stopped, and began shivering uncontrollably.

Feemie drew the quilt over her. 'Go on.'

'It is not good to live in Germany today, you understand,' she continued, her eyes so huge and dark they sent a shiver down Feemie's spine. 'Even friends cannot be trusted, and sometimes in the darkness there is loud knocking on the door, and in the morning whole families have gone. The knocking came to our door one night. My Vati, he rushed me to the cellar and made me hide in a space he had made beneath the coal. He kissed me and left me, and when I crept out hours later, the house was empty.' She closed her eyes tightly, and tears squeezed out beneath the lids.

Feemie pressed her hand in comfort. 'So you came to Scotland amongst decent folk, seeking your real pa?'

'Yes. I am named Fredrika for him, and so I thought why shouldn't he help me? It is only right. I am proud, but when I reach Britain after many months wandering, there is nobody else to turn to,' she said hopelessly. She turned her head wearily and looked at Feemie. 'And today I went to the big house and met the old man in the garden. He cried out and wept when I tell him who I am, and he shouts at me my father is dead. So I run away.'

Feemie felt little electric shocks of excitement go down her spine. She had someone really special here. 'Er – what old man would that be now, dear?' she enquired delicately.

'He is – I suppose – my grandfather, William Alexander.' Fredrika frowned. 'I go to the Alexander shop often. I stare in the windows, but I do not dare go in. My clothes, you see.' She bit her lip and turned her face to the wall. 'So I go to the house, and it is worse for me there,' she muttered sadly.

Feemie patted her hand. 'Never you mind. You be brave, girl. First, we'll get you back on your feet.'

Rising, she stood looking down at the sick lass with a troubled frown. Half-starved and ill-nourished was putting it mildly. She'd seen more flesh on a whippet. 'Beef tea to start wi', an' plenty of porridge an' cream,' Feemie decided. 'Then Scotch broth an' boilin' beef, maybe a wee drappie port wine whiles, to put colour in your cheeks, and I'm a great believer in Father Kruschen's Salts. Enough to cover a sixpence every morning will keep you right as rain.'

Fredrika's eyes filled with grateful tears. 'You are so kind, but I have little money left.'

Feemie beamed and patted her skinny, little shoulder tenderly. 'Och, you can settle up later, hen, once you've put the bite on the Alexanders. I'll chalk it up on the slate meantime, and add a wee bit extra forbye for a' my trouble,' she said happily.

Ishbel had one of her children home at last. Brian's ship had come into Leith docks with a cargo of Algerian esparto grass for the Colinton paper mills, and he'd been granted a few days' home leave while engine repairs were carried out.

'Oh, my, don't you look braw? Are you the captain yet?' enthused Catriona, clasping her hands as she admired her tanned, handsome grandson.

Brian laughed. 'Gran, I doubt if the captain even knows I exist, except when I make the cocoa. I'm the lowest form of animal life allowed on the bridge, and my duties are mostly in the cargo hold. But don't worry, I'm working for my ticket, and hoping for a job on one of the big oil tankers.'

That warm evening in early-June, Ishbel sat in the garden with her son. It was peaceful, the city noises muted in the background, shadows on the lawn lengthening as the sun sank. Brian stretched out his legs, relaxing in a deckchair. 'What news from Adrian?' he asked idly.

A faint furrow appeared in Ishbel's brow. 'Don't you keep in touch?'

'No, we don't.'

Ishbel angled her chair so she could look at him. 'Why not?'

He closed his eyes, excluding her. 'Och, woman trouble,' he grunted.

'Which woman?'

He was reluctant to speak, yet in a way it was a relief. 'A very young woman. A lassie called Joanna Wotherspoon.'

'Wotherspoon!' Ishbel exclaimed. Hannah's bairn! What a turnaround that would be if . . .

'Yes. The worthy farmer's lass. Unfortunately, Adrian and I – well, we nearly came to blows over Joanna. It's safer to stay apart.'

'But sad,' Ishbel sighed.

'May the best man win,' shrugged Brian. 'Unfortunately that usually m-means Adrian.'

Impulsively, she laid a hand over his strong, tanned fingers. 'Don't be beaten, my darling.'

He smiled. 'Mam, it's up to the lassie. I don't envy her. How d-do you choose between identical twins?'

Brian had resolved not to visit Joanna, but of course, he weakened. Finding himself at a loose end on Saturday morning, he borrowed the car and drove into the country-side. It was no surprise when, after driving aimlessly, he found himself turning down the road leading into the estate. The gates to the Big House gleamed with fresh paint, and he smiled to himself as he left the car and followed the high stone wall where the twins had once found Joanna perched. He recalled there was more ornamental ironwork round the back.

The manoeuvre paid off. Brian's heart leaped as he saw a slender figure clad in dungarees standing beside the south entrance, engrossed with paintbrush and black paint. She was taller, more womanly. Ah, she was beautiful! He approached quietly, savouring the moment, just wanting to look at her with delight.

'Need a hand?' he said casually.

Joanna jumped. She'd been painting with such absorption she hadn't heard him arrive. She smiled. 'Oh, it's you, whoever you are! Yes, I could do with a hand. This gate's bigger than the other, and it's taking ages. You'll find a brush over there. Mind and not get paint on you.'

It was good working side by side. It gave Brian a novel insight into her determined character. She had patiently chipped all the old paint off the rusting bars of the massive gates. She had smoothed the bars lovingly with sandpaper and painted them with iron oxide to counteract rust. He could see her fingers were roughened and reddened and taped here and there with sticking plaster. His heart felt so full it hurt his chest.

'Did you know my grandmother died?' she said.

'Oh, Joanna, I didn't know. I'm s-sorry!' He knew how much she'd loved the starchy old lady.

Joanna dipped the brush slowly in the paint pot. 'She left everything she had in the world to me. The house, all the little bits of jewellery she couldn't bear to part with. She'd been selling things in order to maintain the house and keep it weathertight for me. She never told us the struggle she'd had to keep it going, because she was too proud. It makes me so sad to think . . .' She stopped abruptly, and he caught the glint of tears.

Gently, he laid down the brush and took her in his arms. She nestled there, her head pressed against his chest. It was the most wonderful moment of his life. He rested his cheek on her shining, dark hair. 'I love you, Joanna,' he told her simply.

She looked up at that, wide-eyed. 'Which one are you?'

'Which one d'you th-think?'

She pondered, frowning. 'Adrian, I suppose.'

'Brian hasn't enough s-spunk in him to kiss a girl?' he teased.

Her eyes were troubled and bewildered. 'I don't know. You change identities and muddle me. I don't know where I am with either of you, I don't know who you are, half the time.'

There was a sudden angry shout as Wotherspoon strode up the drive, a sheepdog trotting to heel. 'Here, what's going on? You leave her alone!'

Brian released Joanna, who whirled round and frowned at her father. 'Dad, he's doing me no harm!'

'Oh, isn't he?' grunted Wotherspoon. 'Joanna, every time these lads come visiting you're upset for weeks after. Just look at ye! You've been greetin'.'

She hastily scrubbed her cheeks. 'Maybe I have, but it wasn't his fault.'

Wotherspoon scowled at Brian. 'I'm takin' no chances. On your way, my lad!'

'Dad!'

Brian caught her arm. 'It's OK, Joanna. I'm g-going. I don't want trouble.' He grinned down at her. 'I'll come back sometime and help finish the gate.'

She watched him go, then turned indignantly to her father. 'Dad, you spoilsport! He was just going to kiss me.'

'Och, you're a mite young for kissing,' said Wotherspoon. The dog rolled over on its back and the farmer gently rubbed its tummy with his boot. 'You don't want to bother wi' those city lads, Joanna. Why don't you look out for a nice farmer's boy?'

She took his arm fondly. 'Just like you?'

'Maybe a wee bit younger an' bonnier,' grinned Hugh Wotherspoon, who had mellowed remarkably under his daughter's influence.

Joanna stared abstractedly after Brian. 'I never know which is which anyway, so what's the use? Unless . . .' An elusive memory bothered her, something that had been said once, something she'd noticed just today. Her brow cleared and she dropped her father's arm. 'Dad, I just remembered!' She was off, running fast, chasing after the young man.

Joanna rounded the corner of the long wall in time to see the car drive off. She leaned panting against the warm stone. Too late! Och, well, Joanna thought, maybe Dad's right. Maybe I am a mite young yet for kissing.

In between consoling the widowed Eleanor, Catriona helped out more frequently in the fitting room, for Doris's eyesight was deteriorating. 'It's those wee windows in the workroom looking on to that dark alley, Ishbel,' Catriona complained. 'The light's bad enough for sighted folk, let alone poor Doris wi' her cataracts.'

Ishbel took the complaint seriously. Studying the work-room, she could see the solution would be a larger window slapped in the opposite wall, facing west. There was a snag, however. A job like that meant one must employ the best, so there was nothing else for it. It meant calling in Allsop's.

To Ishbel's astonishment, it was not Sandy MacArthur who was shown into her office some days later, but Lady Sarah Allsop.

Sarah seated herself in a convenient chair and smiled at Ishbel's startled expression. 'Sandy is engineering, dear. I am building works.'

'I'm sorry. I mean, I didn't know—'

'That I am a working woman? My dear, anything you can do, I can do better. I had to prove it to Sandy.'

'Did you really?' Ishbel said gently. Somehow she felt sorry for Lady Sarah. She leaned her elbows on the desk. 'Forgive me for asking a cheeky question, but why haven't you and Sandy married?'

The other woman stared down at her hands, an expensive ring winking on the engagement finger. 'Complex reasons. You for one. And fear for another.'

'Fear? Of what?'

'Sandy's a ruthless man, by his own admission. A climber. I love him dearly but I'm afraid to marry him.' She looked up sharply, meeting Ishbel's eyes. 'You can tell me. Is he a hard-hearted man?'

'I never found him so,' she answered truthfully.

Maybe it was the wrong answer. It annoyed Sarah. She stood up angrily. 'Oh, you! You're the ghost at my wedding feast. Why did you send that wretched American away? Why must you still be free and available?'

Ishbel was hurt and infuriated. 'And you have a nasty, suspicious mind! If you can't bring yourself to trust Sandy, then don't marry the poor man, Lady Sarah, don't ever marry him!'

Sarah gathered up the notebook and measuring tape she'd been carrying when she arrived. 'I'd be obliged if you'd show me the building work you want done, Mrs Alexander,' she said icily.

Towards the middle of July, Sandy had a tip-off from one of the lorry drivers that MacPhee the tinker had turned up in Blairgowrie for the berry-picking. He went at once to Sarah.

'I'm taking two or three days off, love. Can you hold the fort?'

Sarah's eyes narrowed. 'No, I can't. Why can't Grierson do it? He's our manager. Anyway, Sandy, where are you going?'

He wouldn't look at her. 'I've to go to Blair to see a man.'

Sarah recalled a conversation they'd had some time ago. 'I know!' she said triumphantly. 'You're off to confront that wretched man MacPhee. I don't know what's behind all this intrigue, Sandy, but if you intend to harm that person, I'm coming with you. I don't want any trouble.'

'There'll be no trouble, my lass, so long as MacPhee doesn't mak' any,' Sandy said grimly.

'Exactly! I've no intention of letting you go off on your own.'

His fiancée was formidable when she'd made up her mind, and Sandy had no option but to give in. All the same, he wanted no onlookers when he caught up with the tinker and found out whether he still owned Big Bob. If he found the man had ill-treated the horse, Sandy knew he wouldn't be responsible for his actions.

On longer journeys Sandy tended to drive Freddie Alexander's Silver Ghost, though it was almost an antique now and folk stared. Somehow he couldn't bring himself to get rid of the man's car, although he had never sat easy in it.

Sarah enjoyed the comfort of the big car, though she couldn't resist a dig. 'This was Freddie's car once, wasn't it? Did Ishbel ride in it, I wonder? Maybe that's why you won't sell it.'

'Maybe,' he replied cheerfully, teasing her. He drove to South Queensferry, only to come down the hill to join the long queue of vehicles waiting to board the busy little ferry-boats plying to and fro across the Forth. Freddie sighed and leaned on the steering wheel. 'When'll they get around to building a road bridge?' he wondered.

Still, when they eventually boarded the boat it was a pleasant crossing, and warm and sunny driving through the bonnie countryside of Fife and Perthshire when they reached the opposite shore. Sarah was happy until she glanced at Sandy's abstracted expression, then she grew nervous. 'Sandy, what has he done, this man MacPhee?'

'I don't know, yet,' he answered, in a tone which did not encourage further questions. Sarah pressed her back more firmly into the comfortable seat and tried to overcome her fears. She loved him so much. If only he weren't such a hard, dangerous man!

The air round the Blairgowrie raspberry fields smelled rich and sweet as wine, so extensive were the fields, so heavy the crop, and so many the folk who swarmed through orderly rows of raspberry canes. Freddie rolled the car to a halt and he and Sarah stared in silence at the scene of activity. Every old charabanc and bus that had wheels and a reasonable engine had been pressed into service to bring berry-pickers in hordes from Dundee and Perth and the surrounding district. The transport remained parked in a varied, rusting fleet round the edges of the fields, awaiting the homeward journey.

The fields themselves were bright with assorted sun-bonnets and head scarves and active with hands that flew from red fruit to baskets and various receptacles tied around waists. Wee, busy bairns pecked away at lower levels to fill their cans, mouths red with berry juice. Marks of the berry-pickers' industrious passage showed in white stalks of gathered fruit which peppered the bushes. A foreman was perched upon a weighing platform, the scales surrounded by noisy men, women and bairns beside a stack of wooden barrels ripe with the reek of raspberry juice. Sandy called out to the man, 'Have you seen MacPhee the tinker?'

The foreman stopped his hot work with the scales and scratched his head. 'I've seen a wheen o' MacPhees, maister. There's a whole tinkie's camp o' MacPhees here this season.'

'Where?'

The man waved a hand. 'Down by the woods. Yonder where the smoke blaws.'

Sandy left the car parked in a lane. He looked at Sarah. 'You'd better bide here.'

'No,' she insisted. 'I'm coming with you.'

They almost missed the tinkers' camp in the clearing, it blended so cunningly with the bushes. Only drifts of woodsmoke gave away the location. There were several small homesteads, made with curved withies covered in weathered tarpaulins. Some small children played around the clearing under the watchful eye of an older woman, busy making clothes pegs from wood and wire. Sandy removed his hat. He was very conscious of intruding as the bairns gathered round the old woman, suddenly quiet.

'Excuse me, ma'am, but I'm looking for Mr MacPhee.'

She expertly completed a clothes peg and dropped it into a waiting basket before replying, 'Is it *The* MacPhee you're wanting?'

'Aye, I suppose.'

She gave a fluting whistle, and presently a thin, grey-haired man stepped into the clearing. He wore a bonnet of large proportions, braces over a spotless white sark, and a debonair red and white spotted kerchief knotted round his neck. His eyes were small, keen and bright as a sparrow's. He looked Sandy and Sarah up and down and formed his own conclusions. 'Aye?' he said warily.

'A good while back you bought a horse, a Clydesdale, from a farmer in the Mearns,' Sandy said. Sarah gave him a startled glance.

'So I did.'

'Where is it?'

'Who's askin'?'

'An auld horseman.'

MacPhee narrowed his eyes and measured Sandy up for several long seconds. 'The beast's hobbled yonder,' he grunted, angling his head.

Sandy's heart was beating fast. He hardly dared look towards the horse, his dear old friend, for fear of what he might do to this man. 'If you've—' he began wildly, but Sarah clutched his arm, silencing him. MacPhee watched with a wee amused smile. Silently, he turned and led the way through the trees, the quick bairns darting after, the old woman coming up curiously behind.

The horse was grazing peacefully at the edge of the wood, well accustomed to the rope hobble. His coat had grown long with outdoor life, the long tail matted with burrs, the mane lying all anyhow. But it wasn't the shaggy condition that brought salt tears to Sandy's eyes, it was the lack of pride in the drooping neck, the dull resignation of the once proud beast, all the spirit gone out of the old horse. Sandy swallowed. 'Ah, Bob! Bobbie!' he cried.

The horse's head jerked up at the remembered sound of his master's voice. His white face swung round to Sandy, ears pricked. Hobbled and limping, he came over fast, nuzzling Sandy eagerly, breathing on him with his sweet, grassy, horse's breath. Sandy leaned his head thankfully against the horse's broad white blaze while tears ran down his cheeks. He whispered The Word that only horsemen know, watched a trembling shiver go through the big animal, a new light appear in the patient brown eyes. 'Bobbie. Ah, Bob!' he said again huskily, for he could say little else.

MacPhee had been watching the reunion impassively, hands in pockets. 'He's a willing beast, maister, but he's too big for my cart. I've been on the look-out for a wee cuddy that'd suit me better, if I could just get a fair price for the big yin,' he remarked idly.

'Name your price, man,' said Sandy tersely.

'He's worth thirty bob.'

Something snapped inside Sandy. 'No, he's no'!' he shouted. He hauled out his wallet. Feverishly, he counted out ten-shilling notes, pound notes, then fivers, the

367

contents of the well-filled wallet spilled recklessly at MacPhee's feet, the notes rustling on the grass like leaves in the wind. 'That's what he's worth, and more!' he yelled at the man.

MacPhee's mouth fell open and he gulped two or three times before he could speak. 'Then tak' him, maister!'

Sandy released the hobble and took hold of Big Bob's bridle. 'Hup, lad!' he said, clicking his tongue.

The old Clydesdale arched his neck and stepped proudly forward, well enough cared for, a little lame, shaggier than he ought to be, but those faults could easily be put right, Sandy thought. It was the prideful lift of the dainty big feathery hooves that mattered. He spoke gently to the horse, as was his habit when he held the lonely plough stilts, the sliced furrows gleaming fresh behind his bonnie, honest Clydes. 'There's a farmer nearby, Bobbie, a guid friend o' mine. If I ask, he'll keep ye in comfort 'til I come for ye. It'll no' be long, my lad, and we'll be together for aye, I promise!'

Sarah trotted beside them. She looked up at Sandy with amazement. 'Sandy, you're crying!'

'Aye, I'm a big softie at heart, Sarah,' he admitted sheepishly. 'I'm sorry.'

Sarah reached up and kissed his wet cheek thankfully, her eyes shining with joy and relief. 'Oh, my darling, bonnie lad, I'm not!'

Feemie Geddes had restored her prize lodger to something resembling health, thanks to good plain Scots fare and Father Kruschen's salts. The young woman was still too skinny for Feemie's ample taste, but she was of the whippet breed, Feemie decided, and you'd never get good honest fat on her. It was time for the lass to strive for her birthright as an Alexander. On the wrong side o' the blanket, but never mind. Feemie took Fredrika one Saturday morning to Beany's barrow in the Grassmarket.

Beany had a reputation for quality cast-offs, and Feemie had a picture in her mind's eye of how a lady should look, based on visits to the sixpenny matinee at the Playhouse and a glimpse of the bonnie new Queen and her two pretty wee lassies at Holyrood Palace.

They passed a happy forenoon haggling and arguing, for Fredrika and Feemie's tastes differed widely and Beany's was something else again. In the end all three settled on a wide-brimmed navy hat with a big white bow in front; a long pale blue dress and jacket the dead spit o' the one the Queen wore, Feemie swore; nice enough white gloves and high-heels, and a long white feather boa, the nearest Beany could find to fox fur. Recklessly, Feemie splashed out on a pair of artificial silk stockings for 1/11d. They returned to the close flushed with success, having spent nearly five bob, which Feemie solemnly entered on the growing list on the slate.

Dressed in all her finery, Fredrika surveyed herself doubtfully in Feemie's looking glass. 'You are sure this is how a Scottish lady looks?'

'You could've stepped right oot o' a Holyrood gairden pairty this very minute,' Feemie assured her.

'Then I will go now to my father's shop,' Fredrika decided.

'You ask for Mrs Alexander. She's your pa's widow, and the heid bummer in the shop. She's no' oot o' the top drawer hersel', so she's your best bet, and a nice enough woman by all accounts,' Feemie instructed, following

Fredrika anxiously to the door. A full slateful of tick
depended upon this encounter. Besides, strange as it might
seem, she'd grown fond of the lass.

Head high, one hand anchoring the hat against a west
wind, Fredrika swept along Princes Street. Folk stopped
and stared, but she did not pause until she reached the
shop. Flicking the end of the long boa over one shoulder,
she marched in regally and looked around. Her entrance
made a small, breathless hush within the shop. Sensing an
unusual presence, Clara appeared and hurried forward.
'Good afternoon, what can we do for you?'

'I wish to speak with Mrs Alexander, if you please, on
very important private business,' Fredrika said.

Ishbel was seated at her desk studying a list of recent
products and marking those she thought might sell, when
her secretary popped her head round the door. 'Mrs
Alexander, there is – er – someone to see you.' A lift of the
secretary's eyebrows prepared Ishbel to receive someone
out of the ordinary.

The young woman the secretary ushered in was dressed
outlandishly in someone's cast-offs. She stared dumbly at
Ishbel, as if suddenly afraid to speak. Even her eyes looked
scared, huge and dark and frightened. Ishbel smiled
encouragingly. 'You wanted to see me?'

'Yes, but it is – very difficult. You see, I am Frederick
Alexander's daughter.'

'What?' Ishbel's smile vanished. She stood up. 'What are
you saying?' she demanded sharply.

The angry change in tone helped Fredrika's fighting
spirit to assert itself. She lifted her chin and met Ishbel's
eyes squarely. 'Frederick Alexander seduced my mother
during the war in France. When I was born she wrote a

letter asking him to help us. He did not answer, neither did his family. I know he is dead, but now I have come to make claims, for my mother's sake.' She choked back tears, for she had no way of knowing now if her mother was dead or alive.

Ishbel was disturbed and angered by this outrageous claim. Her lip curled. 'And I suppose if we refuse to give you money, you'll spread this ridiculous story the length and breadth of Edinburgh!'

Fredrika's eyes flashed furiously. 'It is not ridiculous story. It is truth!'

Ishbel stood up. 'My dear girl, I assure you there was no letter, and I doubt if you have the slightest proof to back up your claim. If this had been true, my husband would have told me. We had no secrets from one another. My husband was a gentleman, and he would not have shirked his responsibility. He was an honourable man.'

'He was not! He shamed my mother and deserted her, and you dare deny it!' Fredrika's voice rose dangerously.

Ishbel was furious. She moved swiftly round the desk and faced the young woman. 'Listen, you are trying to blacken my husband's memory, and I'll no' stand for it. You have thought up this cruel lie to extort money from his family. Well, I warn you, you won't get a penny out o' me. If I hear any more of this, I shall go straight to the police.'

Police! Fredrika stepped back in terror. Ah, she'd had more than enough trouble with police in Germany! Dumbly, she stared at this angry, pretty woman. For the first time she appreciated how tastefully Mrs Alexander was dressed, the fine quality of the simply cut costume and creamy blouse. Fredrika looked down in dismay at her own garish outfit and her self-confidence crumbled. This was

not how a Scottish lady dressed, this was only dear
Feemie's idea of finery.

'Leave now and I promise no more will be said about
this,' Ishbel said coldly.

Fredrika backed away, then turned and fled. She vowed
tearfully she would never return to beg help from her
father's harsh family. I am proud, she thought. That is all I
have left. Pride.

Chapter 17

Fredrika hurried home to Feemie's close, glaring fiercely at passers-by who dared look askance at the garish outfit. There was a muddy group of little urchins playing tig round the door.

From the huddle choosing who would be 'it', the master of ceremonies caught sight of Fredrika and broke off proceedings with a yell. 'Hey, wifie, have you been to a fancy dress pairty?' There was much giggling, and Fredrika slammed the door angrily upon their ridicule.

Feemie came hurrying from the kitchen quarters. 'Did ye put the bite on Mrs Alexander? How did it go?'

Fredrika's lip quivered. Now the ordeal was over she felt weak. Her eyes filled with tears. 'She would not believe. She must have proof, and I have none.'

Feemie planted her big red fists indignantly on her hips. 'Did you no' say your name, lassie? Fredrika, after your pa. What mair proof would the woman want than a daft foreign name like that?'

'She wants documents, letters, Feemie,' sighed Fredrika tiredly. 'My mother wrote, but Mrs Alexander says she never see that letter, and I believe her. She is a very pretty, angry woman. She says if I don't go away, she will call the police, so I go away quick.' Fredrika started shivering with fear, and Feemie looked serious. She didn't want police coming in about the place. She'd always kept respectable.

But the poor, downcast lassie was her first concern. This afternoon's fiasco had undone all Feemie's good work, and Fredrika looked ill and sick at heart, as well she might after getting the kick from the Alexanders. Feemie put an arm round her. 'Come awa' ben into the warm, hen, it's chilly out here.'

There was a pot of tea stewing on the stove and Feemie poured out a cup, dosed it with plenty of sugar and milk and handed it silently to her lodger. Fredrika closed her cold fingers round the cup and drank. A little colour crept back into her cheeks. 'I will never go back to the Alexanders to be insulted. Never!' she declared fiercely.

Feemie was alarmed. 'Och, here! There's no call to go into the huff,' she cautioned anxiously.

Fredrika's expression softened. 'Feemie, I will find work. I will work very hard, and every bob you have put on the slate I will repay and more. I swear this to you.' She drained the cup and stood up with fresh purpose. Going to the landlady, she put her arms round Feemie's capable bulk and hugged her. 'Oh, Feemie, I do love you so! You are the only one who has been kind.'

Feemie went beetroot red with embarrassment. 'Och, awa' you go!' she mumbled faintly.

Fredrika smiled. 'Yes, I go to take off the beautiful clothes you have bought me.' Her brown eyes twinkled merrily at Feemie for a moment, then she was gone. Feemie stood motionless in the middle of the floor. Love? She couldn't think of anyone who'd loved her. Her heart felt all soft and wrung out like chamois leather. Slowly, she reached for the damp dishcloth and wiped the slate clean.

Ishbel sighed and shook her head when the young woman fled at mention of the police. It was sad to see poverty driving young people to crime these days. There had been an increase in shoplifting and other offences, but at least she expected no more trouble from that scared young woman. What an odd way to extort money! Clever, though. She must have believed the family would do anything to avoid a scandal of that nature.

Ishbel returned to the list of products she'd been studying, but found she couldn't concentrate. Her thoughts kept turning to the woman's outrageous claim. Ishbel wished she'd questioned her more closely. Perhaps she'd been put up to this by someone who'd worked in the shop and knew the family history; someone with a grudge, she thought. That must be it, but it was an uneasy thought. She stood up and crossed to the window, staring out across the gardens and upwards to the castle. Freddie had been very much in her thoughts recently. It was very strange that girl turning up out of the blue.

'May I come in?'

Ishbel looked over her shoulder to find Lady Sarah Allsop already in the office. This was a very different Lady Sarah from the cool, professional individual who had supervised installation of the large window which had revolutionised work in the workroom. Sarah positively glowed with happiness.

'What can I do for you?' Ishbel asked.

Sarah laughed. 'You can come to my wedding.'

Ishbel sank on to a chair. 'You're going to marry Sandy after all?'

'Yes. We're taking the plunge quite soon. Very quietly, mind you, just family and a few friends, but you must come.'

'Why? You were filled wi' doubts and suspicions when we crossed swords a wee while ago. You accused me of being a ghost at your wedding feast. What's changed?' Ishbel asked suspiciously.

Sarah laughed merrily. 'My dear, not a ghost, a guest! We both want you there. Sandy wants it for old times' sake. I want it to prove to my canny heart it's really me he loves.' Her mood changed and she leaned forward, speaking softly. 'Ishbel, you were right. Sandy *is* a big softie at heart, and to think it took an old Clydesdale to convince me!'

Ishbel was thoroughly bewildered. 'What are you blethering about?'

And so, joyfully, Sarah told her the whole touching story of Sandy's search for Big Bob.

Eleanor Alexander had put off going through her husband's personal papers, but as the summer of 1937 drew to a close with a nip in the air, and the smoky, mellow scents of autumn invaded the garden, Eleanor turned resolutely to the task. Catriona took time off from work in the shop to be at her old friend's elbow. She knew better than most the anguish of stirring the dust of old, sweet memories. In her usual practical way, Catriona kept a good fire going for the disposal of papers unwanted in the clearout, and the two elderly friends started at the desk in the study and gradually worked their way round to the bureau in the smoking room. Dear old Foxy's daughter and grandson, Foxglove and Foxtrot, stood by to offer sympathetic support, silky ears and wet noses available as usual.

When Eleanor and Catriona had mopped their tears over William's faded love letters which Eleanor would not part with for a ransom, and the fire was thick with the powdery ash of other papers, Catriona blew her nose. 'That's it then, lovie. How about a nice cup o' tea? I'll go down an' give Florrie a shout.'

Eleanor did not remember William's wall safe until her friend had gone. Moving across to Grandmother Alexander's portrait and swinging it aside on hidden hinges, she selected a key from William's keyring and opened the safe.

Tears started anew as she gently lifted out William's most precious and intimate keepsakes. He had treasured every shy, little note she'd sent him before their marriage, and carefully preserved the red rose he'd plucked from her wedding bouquet before she threw it gaily to her laughing bridesmaids. Photographs of herself as a young woman, and their two dead sons as babies, boys, and grown young men, were carefully preserved along with schoolboy letters and postcards from Scout camps. All the rich wealth of a full, long life. Aye, and all the tragedy too!

At the bottom of the pile she came across a much-travelled envelope with a foreign stamp and postmark, and picked it up curiously. It was addressed to:

> *M. Alexander,*
> *le Magasin Alexander,*
> *EDINBURGH*

William had written 'Freddie' on it, underlining the name twice darkly. Just looking at it gave Eleanor an odd, anxious flutter of the heart. She opened the flap, took out the letter it contained and scanned the pages slowly. She soon realised it was intended for Freddie's eyes only, but William must have opened it by mistake. Though it was written in a strange mixture of French and English, the meaning was plain enough, and the writer's anguish and desperation came through clearly. Her knees felt weak as she read, and she sank on to a chair.

'Oh, Freddie!' she groaned softly.

He had got this poor French lass into trouble. Eleanor glanced hastily at the postmark: 1917, just after Freddie and Ishbel were married. She could understand why William had kept quiet about this unfortunate woman. Had he shown Freddie the letter? Knowing her son, she did not think so. Freddie had been good-hearted and honourable. If he'd known about this letter and the woman's plight, Eleanor had no doubt he would have moved heaven and earth to locate her and help the mother and his baby.

Eleanor put a hand to her heart in distress. But what about Ishbel? She obviously knew nothing of this tragic state of affairs. The old lady levered herself shakily to her feet, the letter clenched in her fist. Dear William had decided to keep this sorry episode in Freddie's past from Ishbel, and Eleanor must respect her dead husband's wishes. Twenty years was a long time. Far better if Ishbel never found out about Freddie's lovechild.

Impulsively, Eleanor bent down to the fire. With a quick, jerky movement, she flung first the letter, then the envelope into its red heart. The thin sheets of paper curled and blackened, then flames flared up, consuming them. The old lady straightened slowly. There. It was done.

With a rattle of teacups, Catriona came in. 'The cup that

cheers!' she beamed, placing the tray on the table. She glanced across at Eleanor. 'My dearie, you could do with one. You look as if you've seen a ghost.'

'Maybe I have, Catriona,' said Eleanor quietly, staring down at fragile black ash drifting in the grate.

Brian's ship came into Granton with general cargo, and the skipper was not so liberal with shore leave. Brian was kept busy helping with the unloading of the holds. The September evening was peaceful though, with the ship at rest in her berth and those members of crew lucky enough to be off duty away to the pub and the fish and chipper. Brian leaned on the ship's rail and looked out across the wide mouth of the river towards the Fife coast. Auntie Nellie and Uncle Jock still lived there, very elderly now but hale and hearty. He thought with great affection of the quiet old fisherman and his canny ways. The water was golden-red, lit with phosphorescence, surely a night for the 'burning fishing'. Brian wished he had the skill to chap the gunwale and watch the silver darlings answer in the dark water, but the old skills were fading fast. If he transferred to oil tankers, as he hoped to do one day, he would have little time to study the surface of the sea for the clean, quiet jump o' the herring.

Brian frowned as a noisy car horn intruded into the peacefulness, and crossed the deck to the starboard side to see what all the din was about. He had an odd sixth sense which was proved correct when he recognised his mother's car, with Adrian at the wheel. However, it was Adrian's passenger who caused Brian's heart to miss a beat. He gripped the rail tightly. 'Joanna!' he breathed.

He went apprehensively down the gangplank and

frowned at his twin. 'What are you d-doing here?' His heart ached to see the girl he loved sitting beside his handsome, dashing brother. May the best man win, he'd said once, but which was the best man?

Adrian's eyes were wary, watchful. 'The little lady wanted to see you, wee brother. I persuaded the Gru – uh – Mr Wotherspoon to let me take Joanna for a spin.'

Brian looked at her. 'Why d-did you want to see me?'

She climbed out of the car and stood in front of him. 'I wanted to tell you that you can't fool me any more. I know you are Brian.'

He smiled faintly. 'Of course you know. I have the whole weight of the Merchant Navy behind me at the moment to prove it.'

She moved a little closer. 'Brian, I don't need that sort of proof. I'll always know you were the one who helped me paint the gate, the one who held me close and told me you loved me, and wanted to kiss me.'

'Hey!' Adrian had been jealously following every word. He leaped from the car and slammed the door. 'I helped you with that wretched gate, Joanna, I hugged you, and I love you best of all the girls I know. What's he got that I haven't?'

Joanna reached for Brian's hand and held it in both of hers. 'He is caurry-fisted, left-handed. You told me once, Adrian, and I do not forget details. When I saw Brian take the paintbrush in his left hand, then I remembered.' She smiled her beautiful smile. 'Brian, I will always know you, by your caurry-fist.'

Unexpectedly, Adrian began to chuckle, then gave a great bellow of laughter. He slapped Brian good-humouredly between the shoulderblades. 'Well, I'm blowed, wee brother. Seems you have the edge on me!'

'Seems I have, old man,' he said dazedly.

Joanna linked arms with the two young men. It felt good to be friendly again. Better than good – wonderful. Arm in arm, the three of them walked along the quay until they reached the end. They stood silently looking over the Forth to the Fife coast, where friendly lights were already beginning to shine through the gloaming. Pity I'm a little young for loving and kissing and settling down, thought Joanna regretfully. But one day I will be old enough, and then, maybe – who knows?

Lady Sarah Allsop and Sandy MacArthur had chosen to be married in the ancient, stone-roofed kirk of Corstorphine. It was a glorious, breezy autumn day when Ishbel joined a small, select gathering inside the kirk. A drying wind from the north stirred the red and gold leaves of the old sycamore nearby. It was a wind of the sort they called 'droothy' on the farm and welcomed heartily for the drying of sheaves at hairst. Ishbel took her place diffidently beside Edinburgh's heid bummers and their wives, the folk Sandy associated with nowadays. Who would have dreamed the young horseman who'd once been her shy sweetheart would one day be a name to conjure with in the city? Ishbel brushed away a tear. Dear Sandy. She would always cherish the memory of that innocent love affair, and always regret the heartache she'd inflicted upon a vulnerable young lad.

There was a stir in the kirk as Sandy and his best man emerged from the vestry and took their places before the altar. Ishbel hid a smile as she recognised the foreman who'd worked with Sandy for many long months in the shop. Trust Sandy to make his own choice of best man, and make no concession to airs and graces! The foreman, hair slicked carefully over a bald patch, looked ready to burst with pride.

Then they were all on their feet, for Sarah was coming serenely down the aisle, her hand resting lightly on her father's arm. Ah, but she looked everything a bride should be, quiet wedding or no'! thought Ishbel. Sarah reached Ishbel's pew, and their eyes met for an instant. Both smiled. They would be good friends. They were two of a kind.

Ishbel listened intently to the old familiar words of the marriage ceremony. They seemed even more solemn and binding to her in maturity. Until death us do part, she thought with tears in her eyes. Ah, darling Freddie, always loved, always mourned! But Matthew, the man who filled all her thoughts today, remained unattainable, married to another woman, gone from her life forever.

She roused herself to find the register had been signed, and the new husband and wife were walking out of the kirk, their guests following after. Unobtrusively, she mingled with a crowd of well-wishers gathered in the kirkyard, but Sarah sought her out, dragging Sandy with her. 'Ishbel, we did it! We finally tied the knot!'

Ishbel kissed her cheek. 'Och, my dear, I never doubted you would. Sandy's a determined chiel.'

Sarah was accosted by more guests, and Sandy and Ishbel were left alone together briefly. 'I'm so happy for you, Sandy,' she said softly. 'You have a lovely wife, and in the end you found Big Bob, your bonnie Clyde.'

He grinned. 'Aye. The two seem connected somehow, in a way I can't quite fathom. Bob's safe in the paddock beside my house, smartened up daily wi' the dandy brush and eating his head off. I'm to use him to keep my hand in turning a good straight furrow at the ploughing championships, Ishbel. It does a man no harm to mind his roots once in a while, and Bobbie needs to work.'

She gave him a straight look. 'No regrets, Sandy?'

'Not a one.' He hesitated then went on quietly, 'When you turned me down for Freddie, I vowed one day I'd stand before ye and taunt ye wi' wealth far greater than his, then I'd laugh in your face and walk away. It was a bairn's boast, Ishbel, but it's come full circle today, and I want to tell you it's a hollow victory.'

She reached up and gently kissed his cheek. 'Aye, but without that vow, you wouldn't have been driven to climb the ladder right to the top. You wouldn't have met the woman you love, and you wouldn't have been half the man you have become. It's gey strange, my dear, the way life twists and turns.'

'So it is, Ishbel,' Sandy agreed with a hint of awe, as his laughing little bride returned to claim him.

There was no grand reception, only a dram for those who wanted it at Sir Stewart Allsop's mansion, accompanied by tea, sandwiches and a slice of wedding cake. The wedding was none the worse for that, in Ishbel's opinion. The happiness of the newly-wed pair lit the occasion with a glow that warmed the heart. Sandy and Sarah departed on honeymoon in a new, sporty Jaguar, a car that Freddie would have relished. Sandy caught Ishbel studying it and smiled. 'I sold Freddie's Silver Ghost to a man who appreciates fine things, Ishbel. It never really belonged to me.'

'Too many memories?'

'Aye, maybe so.' He revved the powerful engine, and Sarah opened the window and threw out the posy of flowers she'd been carrying. Ishbel instinctively reached out and caught it. She stared down at the little bridal bouquet, and everyone laughed at her dumbfounded expression.

'You're next!' shouted Sarah.

Sandy drove off to rousing cheers. There was no traditional pour-out of pennies for the bairns for there were no bairns to enliven the occasion. No rattling tin cans and old boots trailed behind the car. No notice proclaimed the pair were 'JUST MARRIED'. No confetti marred the well-kept flowerbeds and gravel. A very restrained do, Ishbel thought, aware of disappointment.

She remembered her own country wedding years ago; Mam's clootie dumpling, the dancing in the barn, and the fun it had been. Matthew had accused her of being a country girl at heart, and perhaps she was. Depression settled upon her now the newly-weds had gone. Once she would have been eager to hurry back to work, but the daily discipline of the shop had palled since Matthew left. Perhaps if Elspeth had shown an interest in the business, or the twins had been cast in the mould of other clever Alexander sons, things might have been different, but there was nobody to take over when Ishbel grew old. When that time came, the shop would pass out of the family's hands forever and go to strangers. Ishbel sighed. She must go back to work. It was only mid-afternoon, what else was there to do?

'I've found work for ye,' Feemie announced to Fredrika.

'Oh, Feemie, good!' Her lodger's brown eyes sparkled and she clasped her hands rapturously. Work had proved more difficult to find than Fredrika had expected. 'Is it in a shop?' she asked eagerly.

'Aye, weel, a kind of a shop,' said the landlady doubtfully. 'Rizzio's fish an' chipper round the corner. Being foreigners theirsels, they don't mind taking on a woman wi' no experience an' a funny name.'

'Fredrika sounds funny to you?'

'Not funny ha-ha, lovie, just funny peculiar. Pity you didn't say it to Mrs Alexander. That would've floored the wumman.'

The Alexander question was still a source of friction between landlady and lodger. Feemie nursed hopes, though she'd come to recognise there was steely determination hidden within her lodger's skinny frame. No' so skinny these days, mind you, thought Feemie proudly. The lass was real bonnie now she'd filled out. Suppressing a sigh, Feemie watched Fredrika's chin lift stubbornly. She knew what that meant.

'If the Alexanders want me, they must seek me. I will not go again to them, begging.'

'Hoity toity,' sniffed Feemie glumly.

Fredrika abstractedly chased a crumb across the kitchen table with a fingertip. 'But it was a lovely shop, Feemie. Never have I seen such beautiful things. I think to work in a shop like that would be Heaven,' she said wistfully.

Feemie trapped the crumb with a duster. 'Aye weel, missie, I'm afraid it'll feel more like the Other Place, when they start frying tonight in Rizzio's fish an' chipper.'

There was a notice in the window that said 'Frying Tonight, Peas, Pies, and Black/White Puddings', and a small queue already at the door when Fredrika turned up at Rizzio's.

She had dressed carefully in a neat, dark dress and jacket selected from Beany's barrow, and added a snowy white collar she'd made in fine crochetwork. Some boys in the queue whistled.

Every corner of the shop, every nook and cranny of wall and ceiling, wore a thick shiny coating of grease. The Rizzios themselves, Mama, Papa, Pia and Maria, shone and glistened as they dealt expertly with great vats of boiling fat, trays of battered fillets, and a heap of chipped potatoes that Papa was tipping merrily into the fat, which greeted them with a terrifying, bubbling hiss. The heat made Fredrika's neat dress stick to her back the moment she set foot in the doorway. Feemie was right. It was like the Other Place.

Mama wrapped her in an apron and set her to work in the back premises, peeling potatoes and then chipping them with a heavy latticework device operated by a handle. Fredrika set to work grimly. The task was monotonous and surprisingly arduous, and she found her thoughts turning longingly to the Alexanders' shop, which was so different. As she worked, she dreamed she walked on thick carpets, admired shining woodwork, entered lifts that moved smoothly up and down. In her imagination she touched fine silks and sniffed lovely perfumes and lovingly arranged fine gold necklaces where they caught the best light. She hugged the memory of her father's shop to her heart, and longed wistfully to be part of it.

But Mama had returned, pleased with Fredrika's efforts. 'You are doing well, *cara mia*, very quick. Soon you will be in the front shop frying with us, when Maria leaves to be married,' she promised.

Fredrika came down to earth and found herself once

more in the cheerless back shop, with bare stone walls, the cold tap and sink and big wooden table white with potato starch, with promotion to the blistering heat of the front shop to look forward to. She blinked away tears. She wanted to run far from cold Edinburgh, from her father's unfriendly family, from endless potatoes and the heavy smell of hot fat that already clung to hair and clothes. But she could not run. Kind Feemie had found this work for her, and she must do it well, until all the bobs on Feemie's slate had been repaid.

The film starring Polly and Elspeth arrived in Edinburgh early in 1938, and Ishbel took an afternoon off to see it. She sat in the concealing darkness with tears dripping slowly down her cheeks, although it was a funny film, a masterly performance, and the cinema echoed to laughter. The loving bond which gradually formed between the American mother and the adopted Scottish daughter was beautifully portrayed and utterly convincing, probably because it was a real-life situation, Ishbel thought. There were tears as well as laughter in the audience, and Ishbel's heart ached with wistful emotion when the film ended with Elspeth secure in Polly's arms.

She came out of the picture house and made her way slowly to the shop, head bowed in thought. It was nearly closing time, but the various departments were still busy, with customers taking advantage of sale offers. Matthew's elevators were packed, but she just managed to squeeze into one. The doors closed and they began the smooth journey to the upper floors.

'I guess we should think about escalators next. Harrod's in London have had escalators for decades,' remarked a well-remembered, well-loved voice in her ear.

She spun round, 'Matthew!' It was no dream, no illusion, he was there, smiling down at her with the beloved, quirky grin she remembered so well. She felt weak, filled with relief and joy and a strange anguish. Regardless of the interested spectators, she eased her arms free of the crush and flung them round his neck, pressing her cheek against his, savouring his solid, comforting warmth. 'Oh, Matthew, how I've missed you!'

'Second floor, gowns, nightwear an' ladies' unmentionables,' sang out the little liftboy, a recent product of Archie's colourful training. The elevator emptied tactfully, the wee boy grinned widely and continued the upward journey with eyes strictly to the front.

Matthew held Ishbel in his arms and kissed her gently. 'Brings back memories, doesn't it?' he whispered.

Indeed it did. The lift reached its destination and they went hand in hand into the office, scene of their confrontations, their anguish, and their love. In the privacy of that quiet place, Ishbel rested her head thankfully on Matthew's broad chest while he embraced her. 'I can't believe you're here, holding me. I'll wake up and find you gone. Oh, Matthew, that's happened so often since you left me without hope. I can't believe you're real and not a dream.'

'I'm real,' he said. Urgent and warm, his lips sought hers and convinced her.

Some time later, they sat together in the flat that had once been Matthew's and Polly's. The air smelled stale and musty, but Ishbel had opened the windows a crack to let in a sharp, cleansing east breeze from the sea and turned on the gas fire for warmth. She imagined there was still a faint trace of Polly's scent.

'Matthew, what about Polly?' she asked, steeling herself. That was a problem that must be faced. There was no escape from it.

He sighed. 'It didn't work out. Polly and I went our separate ways, and I guess we ended up just friends with memories of good times shared when we were young. The marriage was dead, Ishbel, it was over.' He smoothed a soft, dark tendril lovingly from her brow. 'Polly and I were divorced. It was the only honourable course to take for both of us. I met you and loved you like I never loved Polly. Our marriage had become a sham, and I guess we were both too honest to put up with that. The divorce was amicable – a few tears, sad regrets, but no recriminations.' He took her hand. 'One other thing, love. Elspeth and I had a long talk. She longs to come home, but reckons Polly still needs her. Elspeth's a good kid, Ishbel. She loves you, and one day, when the time is right, she'll come back. Can you live with that, honey?'

Ishbel's heart was heavy but she smiled. 'Yes, I can live with it. I can be generous because you've come back. I can live with your divorce, Matthew. It seemed shocking to me once, but now I'm older, wiser and more tolerant, and this country has been shaken to the roots by a king who gave up his throne to marry a divorced woman. Attitudes are changing, even here in douce Edinburgh.'

'Oh, my darling, then will you—?'

Quickly, she laid a finger on his lips. 'No, don't ask me yet, Matthew. It's too soon. We have all the time in the world, my darling.'

He stood up abruptly and moved to the window, staring out. Sensing how troubled he was, she went to him. 'Dear, what is it?'

389

He looked down at her. 'Have you read what Winston Churchill said in the Commons recently, about appeasement?'

Ishbel wrinkled her nose. 'Och, the man's a scaremonger! Mr Chamberlain says that Germany won't dare—'

'President Roosevelt doesn't think he's a scaremonger,' Matthew broke in. 'The President told me he believes there could be war in Europe. He can't see a situation where America would be drawn into it, but I guess he's taking no chances. My job is to work hand in glove with the RAF, pinpoint possible sites for airfields throughout the UK, and assess strategic positions for US air bases.'

She felt dark shadows gathering, threatening their new-found happiness. She put her arms round her loved one and held him tightly. 'You're warning me you'll go away and leave me, my dearest, and I thought you'd come back to me for good? I thought . . .' Her voice broke.

He tilted her chin. 'Yes, I'll leave you, but only for a short time. When this assignment's over I'll come home to Edinburgh and the shop. I got to work out where to site those escalators, remember?'

She smiled bravely. 'Ah, yes. The escalators. Now that's pricey! Do you still intend to bankrupt me, my darling?'

He grinned, and kissed her lightly on the nose. 'No, honey, only to marry you soon as possible, and argue happily ever after.'

Working in the fish and chip shop had its compensations; most mornings and afternoons Fredrika was free to think and plan. Every spare bob she earned went into the pouch she had made and hidden beneath the mattress, to repay the debt to Feemie. She never mentioned it now but

Fredrika was determined the debt would be repaid. Rizzio's was grimy, greasy and hot as the Other Place, but it was a shop, and it fired Fredrika's imagination. She remembered restaurants she had visited with her parents in happier days in Berlin, and looked thoughtfully around the fish and chipper, seeing in her imagination a very different scene.

Papa Rizzio's mouth hung open when he came upon his new employee with a pail filled to the brim with hot soapsuds, assaulting the layers of grease on the walls. 'What you do, Rika?'

'I clean. See, this is blue!' She showed him the pale, clean colour appearing through the grime. She dipped the cloth once more into hot soapy water and vigorously attacked another patch. 'An ice cream parlour with coffee and teas would be nice next-door,' she remarked.

Papa roared with laughter. 'Ice cream and fish and chip? You want to talk with my young cousin Enrico. He has very good Italian recipe handed down from his Papa in Napoli, but no shop.'

Papa Rizzio bustled away, but Fredrika went on doggedly with her self-appointed task. She determined to have a word with young cousin Enrico in the not too distant future.

Although living frugally and saving bobs, Fredrika occasionally allowed herself a visit to the interesting small cinema in Princes Street which showed a succession of cartoons, travel films and news items. On rainy afternoons she sat enthralled by Mickey Mouse and Donald Duck or dazed by the *Flying Scotsman*'s long journey south telescoped into several racing minutes. News items invariably filled her with dread. She watched Germany's leaders posturing on the screen, and vast German armies marching, and wept silently for her dear mother and beloved Vati.

Fredrika longed to stand up and shout a warning to the unheeding audience. 'Take care! Terrible deeds are done in Germany today to innocent folk just like yourselves. Can't you see these men are dangerous?' But of course she did not dare make a scene and have the dreaded police in tall helmets remove her.

On one such afternoon, Fredrika left the cinema with tears on her lashes. She came out blinking into sunshine, to find the early-afternoon rain had cleared. She had just crossed Princes Street and was heading for the Grassmarket when a heady scent of flowers was borne to her nostrils on an unexpected breath of air, tempting her.

Fredrika paused irresolutely. She had never dared walk in Princes Street Gardens because of their proximity to the Alexanders' shop, but how beautiful they looked today, the trees so fresh and green with new leaves! She could not resist the pull of their sunlit attraction, and went hesitantly down the steps. A riot of yellow and red wallflowers scented the air and scarlet tulips nodded approvingly at her in the sunshine.

Fredrika lifted her face to the sun in pure delight. Its warmth touched her brow like a kiss. Ah, she had not known it was so pleasant to walk here, with lovers strolling hand in hand beneath the trees! Well, she had no lover, but somehow, strangely, she did not feel alone as she wandered on beside the glowing flowers.

The sun in her eyes, Fredrika did not pay much attention to the lady and the tall man walking arm-in-arm towards her. Then suddenly she recognised the lady and her heart gave a flutter of sheer panic. There was no mistaking those striking features. It was Mrs Alexander! Fredrika looked around wildly, but there was nowhere to run and people all around her. If Mrs Alexander summoned the police, Fredrika would be grabbed.

And then she recovered her good sense. Why should I run? she thought defiantly. I have done nothing wrong. It is the Alexanders who have wronged my mother and rejected me. Straight-backed, she marched on. Eyes front, she walked mechanically towards the couple. They were laughing, happily absorbed in one another and in their love. As she passed them, Fredrika could not resist a quick, curious glance. Mrs Alexander glanced up at the same moment, and for a second their eyes met. A brief, fleeting moment, then it was over. Fredrika marched on, quickening her pace, hurrying down the slope towards the safety of the concealing bushes.

I do not need the Alexanders now, she thought proudly. I will work, and I will prosper. I am Fredrika!

Ishbel paused suddenly, looking back over her shoulder with a frown. Wasn't that the girl who—? No, it couldn't be! The young woman walking briskly away was well dressed in a neat blue costume with a touch of white lace at the throat. She was quite a different person. It was only the eyes, those beautiful, dark eyes—

'What's wrong, honey?' Matthew asked in concern.

'It's just – I imagined I recognised somebody. But I was mistaken.'

He smiled gently. 'Ghosts from the past?'

'Something like that, my dear.'

Smiling at one another, they walked on, out of the shadow of the trees, into the sunshine.

Chapter 18

Ishbel knew Matthew must leave soon. Even walking with him in the spring sunshine she knew it. She glanced back nervously once or twice as they climbed the steps to return to the shop, expecting to see stormclouds gathering on the horizon, but dark rainclouds had dispersed, and there was nothing menacing to be seen.

'Something bothering you, honey?' Matthew asked.

'Yes, Matthew. Must you go?'

He nodded. 'I must.'

She was frustrated and angry, for there was nothing tangible to fight, only rumours of a war that might never happen. 'It's daft, sending you on a wild goose chase,' she complained. 'As if we need American air bases in our own country!'

'I hope you're right, but in the meantime the Air Ministry has plans for new strategic airfields if war comes, and I'm one of the guys selected to do a discreet survey. I guess I had valuable experience in that sector during the last war.'

'Oh, all this talk of war makes me sick! And there's nothing I can do!'

'Yes there is. You can marry me right away.'

Her step faltered, and her breath came fast. 'It's too

soon, darling. I don't want to rush into this.'

His expression was sorrowful as he looked down at her. 'Ishbel, don't you want to marry me?'

She pressed close to him. 'Of course I do. I love you so much, but I can't forget Freddie married me in haste because he was going back to France. I don't want that for us, Matthew. We have all the time in the world.'

'Do we?'

'Of course we do!' she protested sharply, his grim tone alarming her.

He paused and faced her. 'Listen, Ishbel, I appreciate what you're saying, but I think we should get married soon. I was figuring we could fix up a trip to the registrar's before I leave for London.'

'The registrar's?' Ishbel repeated in blank dismay. Her wedding to Freddie may have been hasty, but it had taken place in the beautiful chapel on the Hawkertons' estate, and that had given the simple ceremony special meaning. Ishbel was aware of a crushing sense of disappointment. It was difficult to hide one's feelings from Matthew Clark, however. He tilted her chin with finger and thumb, the better to examine her crestfallen appearance. In his intuitive way he guessed at once what was bothering her.

'You'd be marrying a divorcee, Ishbel, whether you liked it or not, and I guess that means making sacrifices and facing censure. Are you sure you love me enough?'

He looked so sad, Ishbel kissed him. 'Sure, I'm sure, my darling,' she said.

'I never thought I'd see the day my daughter would walk out wi' a divorced man,' complained Catriona, stabbing her needle more forcefully than usual into the small garment she was sewing for one of Dorothy's Bootless Bairns.

Eleanor laid down the crossword puzzle she had been frowning over and studied her friend. 'You've little need to worry on that score, dear. Matthew's a fine, stubborn man, and well able to handle a spirited woman like our Ishbel. Besides, he's American, and they think nothing about divorcing one another over there. Film stars do it all the time.'

'More fool them. I don't know how they can be bothered,' sniffed Catriona.

Ishbel chose that moment to enter the parlour. It was a spring holiday, and the shop was closed that Monday for the welcome break. Matthew had headed for Montrose further up the coast, on one of the mysterious missions about which he remained tight-lipped. Ishbel held Brian's latest letter, and wasn't sure whether to be delighted or dismayed by the news it contained.

'Brian's very full o' himself this time!' she said. 'He's transferred to an oil tanker, a huge ship. He just managed to scribble a note before they left Grangemouth bound for Rotterdam.'

Both grandmothers looked proud. 'Brian's done very well,' Eleanor nodded complacently.

Ishbel seated herself beside the elderly ladies and stooped to pat the two sleepy terriers snoozing on the rug. The dangers of Brian's transfer had mercifully escaped the older women, and she was glad they were not worried. Her own imagination had been running riot since she'd received his letter. Ishbel deliberately concentrated upon the more light-hearted aspects of the move. 'Brian says he's the lowest form of animal life allowed to crawl on to the bridge,' she said.

'Och, he was aye modest. It takes the other yin to blaw his ain trumpet enough to deafen ye, now he's sitting his finals at the university,' remarked Catriona.

'Yes. The Alexander family has always been blessed with clever sons,' said Eleanor proudly.

The words caused Ishbel an unexpected pang. She recalled Freddie's rueful expression when he'd told her about generations of clever Alexander sons who had built up the business. She could sympathise with his predicament, for she was the last of the line now. The younger generation of clever Alexander sons had no interest whatsoever in their heritage. Elspeth had made her preference for acting quite clear and showed no signs of returning to Scotland. The mother and daughter act with Polly was proving very popular in the States.

'Where's your American man gone today?' enquired Catriona, breaking into her thoughts.

Ishbel glanced up, resentful of her mother's tone. 'If you mean Matthew, he had to go north on business.'

'Business? Huh!'

Ishbel felt herself bristling. 'What's that supposed to mean?'

'I wonder you can trust a divorced man, that's all.'

'I'll trust Matthew wi' my future, Mama, when the time comes.'

Catriona dropped the sewing and stared aghast. 'You're never going to marry him!'

'Catriona, love – please don't—' Eleanor ventured apprehensively. As she grew older, she had a dread of scenes. Arguments upset her, but she could see the pair of them were too intent upon the quarrel to pay the slightest attention to her. The little dogs stirred and wakened, sensing their mistress's mood.

'Of course I'm going to marry him!'

'Nonsense! He's divorced. The kirk won't agree to it.'

'If they won't, then there's always the registrar.'

'The registrar!' Catriona gave an outraged howl. 'Ishbel, you couldna!'

'Why not? It's legal.'

'Will you listen to the woman!' Catriona turned to Eleanor, who cringed. 'Legal, she says! Well, I'm telling you, Ishbel Alexander, I'll no' allow a daughter o' mine to marry in a heathen office. That's no' for decent Kirk folk like us. I absolutely forbid it!'

'Oh dearie me!' moaned Eleanor weakly. Tempers were rising, and it was the angriest confrontation she'd witnessed in years. The dogs sat up, growling.

Ishbel was furious. 'You can't stop me. I'm no' a biddable young lassie now, I'm near forty years old! You can't boss me around like a bairn any more, Mam.'

'Och, I never could! You were aye a self-willed, stubborn wee—'

Eleanor wrung her hands. Foxtrot began a series of short, ear-piercing barks which added to her distress. She plucked at Catriona's sleeve. 'Catriona, I don't feel—'

Catriona impatiently shook off her friend's restraining hand. 'Ishbel, if you marry Matthew Clark in the registrar's, don't expect me to be there giving you a blessing.'

'Don't worry, I won't!'

Both paused for breath, dismayed by the ferocity of the quarrel. Ishbel felt like weeping. She hadn't wanted this row and wasn't sure how it had happened. She'd favoured a leisurely courtship to allow her mother to mellow a little and accept Matthew as a future son-in-law. Trust Mam to pull the rug from under my feet, Ishbel thought.

Catriona was just as dismayed by the upset. She couldn't see a peaceful solution, for she swore she wouldn't set foot in a registrar's office even if Ishbel went down on bended knees and begged her. Catriona was determined not to budge an inch.

'Oh dear, I'm afraid I don't feel at all well,' faltered Eleanor weakly. So saying, the old lady slid gently off the chair and landed in a dead faint at their feet. The dogs began howling and barking miserably, in unison.

'Nothing to worry about,' decided Michael Burton, after examining Eleanor thoroughly and prescribing a few days' rest and an iron tonic.

Ishbel and Catriona sighed with relief, united again in their concern for the old lady. 'Just a wee turn! And here's me thinking the worst,' Catriona declared indignantly.

The doctor smiled. 'In my opinion she'll be in fine shape for a good few years yet. Only,' he paused and frowned thoughtfully before continuing, 'I can't help feeling there's something preying on her mind, judging by her behaviour when she was coming round from the faint. She mentioned a letter. Has she had any disturbing news recently?'

Ishbel looked anxious. 'We had a letter from Brian today with the news he'd taken a job as deck officer aboard an oil tanker, but that didn't seem to worry her.'

'I know!' broke in Catriona. 'She was having a clear-out of William's papers the other day, and reading his letters upset her at the time.'

'Ah, that solves the mystery!' nodded the doctor sympathetically. He rose, preparing to go on his rounds. 'Keep her quiet and make sure she follows the diet sheet I left for her. She's a little anaemic but we'll soon put that right. Dorothy will be round to see her this evening once our Bootless Bairns are safely tucked up in bed,' he promised.

Although Fredrika was very shaken after the close encounter with Mrs Alexander, she was encouraged by the fact she had not been recognised. Fredrika decided she had changed out of all recognition from the terrified refugee in odd clothing who'd tried unsuccessfully to be accepted into her father's family. This change for the better was thanks to Feemie's hearty good cooking, not to mention Fredrika's own tasteful selections from Beany's second-hand barrow.

A few weeks after seeing Mrs Alexander, the Rizzios promoted Fredrika to the front shop, Maria having married a local potato merchant and secured Papa Rizzio's potato supplies for life. 'Frying Tonight' was a step up, and although Fredrika found the front shop blistering hot, the work was much more interesting. Fredrika, with her good-humoured repartee and sparkling brown eyes, was soon a firm favourite with the clientele. Papa had acted upon Fredrika's suggestion and persuaded his wiry little cousin Enrico to join the firm, bringing with him the secret recipe for Neapolitan ice cream.

All summer Fredrika worked long hours. She worked happily and with a goal in sight. Her ambition to succeed in spite of the Alexanders' rejection spurred her on, and besides, she could visualise the big storeroom in Papa Rizzio's shop as it would look when scrubbed clean and painted in pale colours. Over the summer months her vision of a coffee and ice cream parlour became reality.

Mama, Pia and Fredrika sewed gingham table cloths to cover second-hand tables and painted chairs to match. A big industrial refrigerator, bought on the never-never, hummed in the background while Enrico, sparkling in spotless white overalls, manufactured quantities of wonderful ice cream.

The weather turned cold in October, and ice cream sales dropped, but Mama provided coffee from an old Italian recipe, topped with whipped cream and grated chocolate. Little Pia produced thoroughly wicked iced cakes and pastries oozing with fruit and cream. New customers continued to appear, some even forsaking cafes in the New Town as fame of the ice cream parlour spread. The Grassmarket had never seen the like in its long, turbulent history. The pouch filled with shillings, beneath Fredrika's mattress, grew fatter and heavier week by week.

Fredrika trailed tiredly home to Feemie's lodgings one cold October night, threading her way through Saturday night revelry as pubs disgorged merry customers on to pavements. She absent-mindedly fended off amorous imbibers begging kisses, and politely turned down offers to partner cheery individuals doing 'The Lambeth Walk, Oi!' down the steep, cobbled wynd.

Fredrika's mind dwelt on higher things. Ice cream trade had been so successful that, God willing, Papa and Enrico had agreed 'Stop Me and Buy One' barrows throughout the city were an idea worth considering for summer 1939. She gave an eager smile, for the future looked good. The smile soon faded, for behind Fredrika's happiness lurked sadness. There was no way of knowing what had happened to her mother and foster father, in Germany.

Feemie was waiting up for her. The landlady kept an eye on the clock, and had been known to appear on the streets, ready to do battle, if Fredrika was late. Feemie looked ruffled, drawing her lodger hastily into the kitchen and shutting the door with elaborate care, having first cast an eye up and down the corridor, to make sure there were no working men daring to eavesdrop.

'The police have been,' she whispered.

Fredrika turned pale. 'Oh, Feemie, no!'

Feemie nodded. 'Aye. They're on to you. I near died when I found a great big bobby standing on the doorstep, seeking a list o' my lodgers. Beany tipped me the wink a wee while ago that they were checking up on foreigners, after that Jordan woman in Dundee turned oot to be a German spy and no' a hairdresser at all. Since she was put in the nick the police have been on the lookout for spies. I never thought to see them here though. I've aye kept respectable.'

'But Mr Chamberlain came from Munich with an agreement!' wailed Fredrika. 'I saw for myself in the News Theatre. He stepped from an aeroplane waving a piece of paper signed by the German Chancellor, and then he told everyone there would be peace. I was so thankful I cried. My papers were stamped by immigration, so what does the bobby want with me?'

'God knows!' said Feemie despondently, pouring two brimming cups of tea.

Fredrika drank with a shaking hand. It was the nightmare that haunted her dreams, come to life. Now the bobby knew where she was, they would come, and this time there was no Vati to make a clever hiding place for her beneath the coal. She furtively dabbed her eyes.

'The police will take me away and lock me up!'

'Over my deid body!' Feemie swelled her formidable bosom and stuck out her chin. 'Anyroads, your papers are in order 'cause I'd a good look at them when you came. The bobby said they want a'body in the country registered for identity cards, especially casual workers, so I had to give him a list to keep my ain nose clean. I told him your father was a guid honest, deid Scotsman and you were born on the wrong side o' the blanket.'

Fredrika's eyes widened with horror. 'Feemie, you didn't say—?'

She sighed regretfully. 'I never let bug it was Freddie Alexander if that's what you're thinking. I'm no' one to break a promise.'

Fredrika looked wildly round the warm kitchen seeking a safe hiding place, but there was none. 'What will I do if the bobby comes? Where can I run to?' she groaned. Already she imagined she heard heavy fists beating on the door and the thunder of jackboots pounding up the close.

Her landlady put an arm around her shaking shoulders. 'You sit tight, love. Feemie will look after ye.'

So Fredrika laid her head thankfully against Feemie's stoutly corseted bulk, and felt safely harboured. Let the bobby come! she thought bravely. When he returns I will not be here to bring trouble for Feemie. Soon there will be one hundred shillings in the pouch to repay the ticks on Feemie's slate, and then I will leave Edinburgh, she decided.

No amount of money could ever repay Feemie's kindness, Fredrika thought, but one hundred shillings would help. She would be lost indeed without Feemie, but she loved her friend too much to stay.

* * *

1938 had been a bad year for farming. The wages farm workers could expect were lower, and men were not keen to work upon the land. Income tax stood at 7/6d in the pound for struggling farmers. Even with increased mechanisation, Wotherspoon had difficulty making ends meet, although the estate now belonged jointly to himself and Joanna, on the death of Lady Hawkerton.

'There's more profit to be had out o' leisure activities these days,' he complained woefully to his daughter. 'Thon Billy Butlin's holiday camp at Skegness is packed out wi' folk. Maybe we should turn this place into a holiday camp, Joanna.'

'No fear!' she replied stoutly.

He hid a pleased grin. It was the reaction he'd hoped for.

Joanna toyed thoughtfully with a plate of Bunty's excellent broth. 'Maybe we shouldn't turn up our noses at leisure activities though, Dad. There's salmon fishing and shooting. Leasing stretches of the river and moorland would bring in some income, and there are empty cottages we could let as holiday homes for city folk.'

He broke a slice of bread and dipped it in the broth. 'It's turning the clock back. That goes against the grain.'

'Well, the grain hasn't brought much profit, has it, Dad? Grain prices are depressing,' she pointed out quickly.

Wotherspoon fell silent. He had a high regard for his daughter's opinion. She had a keen mind, but like all young folk the heart often ruled the head. What he had in mind would hurt her, he knew, but it must be said. 'Aye, well, keeping the Big Hoose watertight is pouring good grain money doon the drain, Joanna. Better to tak' the roof off, then we wouldn't pay rates on the auld ruin.'

She looked stricken, ready to weep. 'Oh, Dad, must it come to that?'

Relenting a little, he patted her hand. 'We'll struggle on yet awhile before taking that drastic step. Meantime, I'll think about letting reaches o' the river for fishing and a beat o' the moorland for shooting, and we'll rent out cottages to city folk as you suggest.' He gave her a keen glance. 'By the by, Joanna, have you given thought to what you'll do now you've left the school?'

Joanna hesitated. Her ambition was to learn about paintings, furniture and restoration work so that she could return the mansion to its former glory, but that was not an option at present. How could she attend Edinburgh Art College, and desert her father when he needed her most? She couldn't fail to notice Wotherspoon had grown appreciably older and more stooped with worry recently. He had always worked hard for long gruelling hours, and now he should be taking things easy, he must work harder than ever. Life wasn't very fair, Joanna thought.

'I've decided I'll work on the farm, if you'll have me, Dad,' she told him, and was rewarded by the joy that lit her father's tired eyes. Being Wotherspoon, he made no comment on the decision. He stood up and stretched.

'Aye, weel, Joanna, put on your wellies. We'll away to the potato fields and get the tattie-howkers started on the tattie-lifting.'

It was an unexpected meeting with Sandy MacArthur that opened Ishbel's eyes to dangers ahead. At the beginning of September, Matthew had left for London, and because she was so lost and alone without him, Ishbel threw herself energetically into hard work required to stock the shop adequately for Christmas. It was only the end of October, but she was determined Christmas 1938 would be one to remember.

When Sandy was announced and shown into her office one blowy October day, Ishbel enquired kindly after his wife.

'Sarah's fine. I'm to be a father, soon,' Sandy said.

Ishbel was delighted. 'Sandy, that's wonderful news!'

He grinned. 'Aye, the next generation's on its way.' The grin quickly faded, and he looked so serious Ishbel felt an uneasy qualm. Something warned her this was not a social call.

'What is it, Sandy? Why have you come?' she asked sharply.

'Air raid precautions, Ishbel. Princes Street is in my ward,' he answered.

She stared at him. 'Air raids? You mean bombs? Surely it'll no' come to that!'

'Aye, it will. If war breaks out they'll bomb the cities. We must be prepared. For instance, those huge shop windows of yours. Have you given a thought to what would happen if a bomb fell and shattered the windows when the shop's crowded wi' folk?'

A horrifying picture formed in her imagination, and she half rose in protest. 'Sandy—'

He went on relentlessly. 'Have you thought about the possibility of poison gas seeping through the store? Have you planned where staff and customers could shelter in an air raid? Have you considered how you'll fight fires if incendiaries fall, and how to black out your shop? Ishbel, have you given a single thought to what could happen in the city of Edinburgh if there's war?'

She sank back in the chair. 'I don't dare think about it. Will it come to that, Sandy.?'

He sighed. 'I wish I could be optimistic, but I'm not. I'll no' be called on to fight, so I volunteered to be an air raid warden at the Local Defence meeting. My task is to help shop-keepers like yoursel' to be prepared, Ishbel. Women and bairns will find themselves in the front line, this time,' he warned.

Sandy's visit gave Ishbel cause for concern. After he had gone she walked through the shop, studying the premises with new eyes. What she saw filled her with dread. She had always loved the beautiful glass cupola, which flooded the central shopping arcade with light and sunshine, but now she stood, gripping the gallery railing, and looked upwards in horror. If all that glass came crashing down the consequences didn't bear thinking about. From the gallery, she descended into the basement and was reassured by the depth and strength of the stone walls. Staff and customers would be safe enough down here.

In the economical light of a few bare bulbs, Ishbel looked around the gloomy basement and shivered, imagining the area filled with frightened women and children. She felt a sudden panicky sense of urgency. Up until that moment she had believed there was plenty of time to plan a peaceful future with the man she loved. Now she wasn't so sure. She couldn't rid herself of a superstitious dread that she was fated to lose those she loved dearly.

Matthew returned in November, just as Ishbel took delivery of half a dozen stirrup pumps, each complete with thirty feet of hose. As a precaution, she'd previously ordered ten dozen jute sandbags, to be filled with sand if the need arose. After years of depression jute mills in Dundee were working overtime to supply a huge demand for sandbags throughout the land. It was an ill wind that didn't blow somebody some good, right enough!

With a glad cry, Ishbel ran into Matthew's arms. 'My dear, how I've missed you!'

Kissing her, Matthew immediately sensed her anxiety. He studied the cartons containing the stirrup pumps, which were stacked high in the office. 'What's all this, love?'

'Air raid precautions. It's cost us well over twelve pounds, Matthew, and that's just a start. I feel safer now, more prepared.'

'I guess you're wise, honey. The news from Europe's not so good. The policy of appeasement will sacrifice Czechoslovakia, I guess. Hitler must be laughing up his sleeve.'

She put her arms round him, suddenly frightened. 'Matthew, I don't want to wait. I want us to get married.'

His arms tightened round her. 'You're sure?'

'I'm sure, even if we marry in the registrar's and my mother blows her top.'

When Ishbel and Matthew announced they planned to marry as soon as possible, it was Florrie who came up with a compromise that saved the day. Florrie attended one of the kirks at Holy Corner, so called because a cluster of four churches congregated in that hallowed spot. Florrie's minister was young and go-ahead, and had no objection to marrying Matthew and Ishbel in the vestry.

Catriona received the decision with relief. 'Aye well, the vestry's near enough the kirk,' she said, and graciously agreed to attend and sanctify the union with her blessing.

Brian was far away, heading for Port Harcourt in

Nigeria, but Adrian had gained his honours degree in mathematics and was doing a spot of tutoring in the city while pondering his future. He was quite overwhelmed with delight when Matthew asked him to be best man.

On Matthew's modest stag night, the two men shared a beer together, and Adrian seized the opportunity to seek Matthew's advice on a decision which had been worrying him. It was a novel experience to have a father-figure to consult.

'I want to join the RAF, Matthew,' he admitted.

'Following in your father's footsteps?'

'That's right. I want to learn to fly, and I'm also interested in this new tracking device they call radar. Have you heard about it?'

Matthew nodded. 'Sure, I've heard. Enough to know sometimes it works, sometimes it don't.'

Adrian took a thoughtful swig from his glass. 'If it could be made foolproof, it would be mighty useful if war breaks out.'

Matthew gave the handsome young man a keen glance. 'I hope you realise you'll be in the thick of it, if it does.'

He met Matthew's eyes with a tight grin. 'Why d'you think I've kept quiet about this? No sense worrying my mother, until I have to.'

Ishbel's only worry on the sunny December day chosen for the wedding was whether her hat, a pillbox affair swathed in veiling, would withstand a northerly breeze tugging playfully at the airy concoction as she stepped from the taxi. Breaking with tradition, Catriona had decided it was in order for her to give her daughter away. There was a lump in Catriona's throat as she thought about Donald, and wondered what he would have made of it all. Strangely enough, she suspected Donald and Matthew would have liked one another. She had a sneaking affection for the big American. He was patently honest, and so obviously in love with Ishbel that Catriona's misgivings had been laid to rest.

'Hurry up, Ishbel. Hang on to your hat, mind, lest it ends up on top o' the steeple,' Catriona warned, hanging on to her own bonnet. She linked arms happily with her lass, and they walked companionably towards the rear of the kirk.

It had been a very different occasion from her first wedding, but none the worse for that, Ishbel thought. Adrian passed the wedding ring to Matthew, who slipped it on to her finger.

They were man and wife at last, with no hymn singing, no pews packed with guests. The frills didn't matter, Ishbel thought happily, as Matthew kissed her. Dear old Florrie sniffed emotionally in the background and Eleanor Alexander and Catriona furtively wiped away tears as the simple ceremony ended.

Dorothy's Bootless Bairns had been judged too many and too boisterous for inclusion in the vestry, but the bairns waited outside, armed with packets of multi-coloured confetti which deluged the happy couple and scattered like apple blossom across the churchyard, hastened by the mischievous wind.

'North Berwick for a honeymoon at this time o' year! I never heard anything so daft. You'll freeze to death!' declared Catriona, when informed of Matthew and Ishbel's immediate plans after the wedding breakfast.

'Oh, no, we won't.' Matthew grinned and kissed his new

mother-in-law before assisting his bride into the car. Ishbel was in a daze, but she was determined to observe tradition. She handed Matthew the bag of pennies and halfpennies she'd been hugging.

'Here, Matthew. It's an old Scottish custom, a pour-oot of money for the bairns. It's meant to bring luck.' Her husband honked the horn loudly and drove off, scattering the money recklessly along the driveway. The Bootless Bairns descended upon the unexpected bounty with delighted whoops and squeals.

Again remembering that other joyful occasion years ago, Ishbel sighed. 'No old boots and tin cans this time around, Matthew.'

'I drew the line at old boots, honey, but I left Adrian's notice an' the balloons. We've got 'Just Married' tied to the back bumper!'

Even without the notice and the balloons on the back of the car, which Matthew had removed before their arrival, the proprietor of the small North Berwick hotel guessed shrewdly they were a honeymoon couple. 'There's no' many hardy souls visit North Berwick this time o' year,' he remarked as his guests signed the register.

'So we've been told,' said Matthew. 'I guess we just enjoy peace and quiet.'

'Man, you'll no' get peace and quiet wi' a nor'easterly gale blowing on this shore!' predicted their host with feeling.

He was right. They went walking before early darkness settled on the seashore, and were forced to hang on to one another, leaning into an icy wind that sent spray and blown sand to sting their laughing faces. Wild seas raced from the seething base of the Bass Rock to crash against the harbour wall, where fishing boats jostled uneasily in the sheltered lee. To a country woman and a city man, it was a timely reminder of the might of the ocean, a scene they would remember for the rest of their days. Ishbel worried about Brian, and found the turmoil of the sea difficult to contemplate without a shiver of foreboding.

But they found a bright fire burning in the bedroom grate that night, a warm, flickering glow that lit the white walls as they lay in one another's arms. Ishbel had never felt so happy, so fulfilled. 'To think I resented you when you joined the firm, Matthew. I didn't trust you an inch; remember how we fought and argued for months?'

He smiled. 'Yeah, it was fun. I guess we'll always argue, honey. You're no pushover, and there's still the question of the escalators.'

She kissed him. 'You may be sure I'll always speak my mind. I promise I'll keep no secrets from you, my love.'

Matthew lay still and silent. There was a secret he had never told her, one she ought to know. Now they were man and wife he could help her come to terms with a tragedy from the past. 'Ishbel, I have a confession to make,' he said quietly.

She turned her head to look at him, and he could see the amused gleam of her eyes in the firelight. 'A confession? That sounds ominous. What have you been up to, my lad?'

'It concerns Freddie.'

Her eyes grew dark and the smile vanished. 'Freddie?'

'Yes. Before he met you he had an affair with a French girl. There was a child, Ishbel.'

'Oh, Matthew!' she whispered.

Holding her, he could feel the shock tremble through her. Concerned, he held her closer and quietly told her

413

about Freddie Alexander's ill-fated affair with Marietta. She heard him out in such a frozen silence it unnerved him.

'Honey, try to understand,' he begged. 'It was wartime, the Germans were poised to attack, and an airman's life could be mighty short. You mustn't blame Freddie too much for what happened. Rightly or wrongly, I advised him to do nothing about the child. Freddie had just married you, so I guess he took my advice. There was no way he could trace Marietta and her baby. They were far behind enemy lines.'

She suddenly pulled out of his arms and struggled into a sitting position, hugging her knees. 'There was, Matthew! There was a letter,' she cried.

He was startled. 'Ishbel, what are you saying?'

She began sobbing, tears pouring down her cheeks. 'A young woman came to see me months ago. She claimed to be Freddie's daughter. She swore her mother had written to Freddie when she was born, but there was no reply. I told her I didn't believe a word of the story. I even threatened to call the police, and she was frightened then, and ran off. Oh, Matthew, what have I done? Did I really send Freddie's daughter away, when she badly needed our help?'

Chapter 19

Matthew kissed his bride to comfort her. 'Don't blame yourself, darling. I accept all the blame for this. I guess I should have told you long ago about Marietta and Freddie's baby. It was on the tip of my tongue several times, but I thought it would distress you.' He lay there looking wretched. 'Gee, Ishbel, I never expected Freddie's child to turn up in Edinburgh. I feel bad about it, kind of responsible for a tragedy if this poor kid really was his daughter.'

'I'm sure she was. Oh, Matthew, she looked half starved.' The gale rattled the window frames and whistled with renewed fury in the chimney of the firelit bedroom. Ishbel shivered and nestled closer to her husband. She badly needed Matthew's comfort. Her imagination was running riot. Closing her eyes, she recalled details of the girl's pale, thin features and remembered anew the pathetically hopeful light in the dark eyes. There had been a proud tilt to the chin that had lent a certain dignity to the ludicrous, jumble-sale outfit. The poor girl's abject terror when threatened with the police had been perfectly genuine. Ishbel groaned. 'She was terrified, Matthew. I should have guessed she wasn't a criminal!'

Matthew hugged her. 'Honey, don't you fret. We'll find her somehow.'

'How can we? We don't even know her name, of if she's still in Edinburgh. She may have moved on somewhere else.'

'Sure, she may have,' he agreed. 'But if she's still around, Ishbel, I promise you that somehow, some day, we'll find her.'

Travelling the high seas in the oil tanker *San Merino*, Brian was better placed than most to assess what was happening in the rest of the world, and the prospect of war in Europe appalled him. He loved the life at sea, the spice of danger when the long deck of the tanker dipped deep into the troughs and rose again, awash to the bow. He had confidence in the ship, ungainly as she might seem. The long-bodied deck was spanned by a catwalk, the high superstructure of the bridge and the crew's living accommodation placed well aft. He felt safe even in the fiercest storm, because he had faith in his ship, his own ability, and the skill of her crew.

But what if a hidden enemy lurked out there, waiting underwater with the grim intention of turning the ship into a fireball? Brian turned away abruptly from his contemplation of the sea. If that ever came to pass he'd be so damned mad at the outrage, he'd do anything in his power to outwit the predator. He wouldn't see his mates burn and choke in thick, black oil.

Thoughts of war were far from Brian's mind in May 1939, however, although plans had already been put forward by Edinburgh Corporation to evacuate children from the capital. Brian had three or four months' leave in which to work for the next stage of his ticket. It was a pleasant change from shipboard life to live at home for a spell and attend classes in navigation and seamanship at technical college. It was also a novel experience to find he had a stepfather.

Matthew and Ishbel had decided to make their home in Knoxhall House, although Ishbel secretly hankered after their own establishment. It was virtually impossible to enjoy the peace and privacy they craved after busy days spent working, since Catriona and Eleanor were always in attendance in the evenings. But the two ladies were getting on in years, and Eleanor, in particular, was in need of care. Dear old Florrie, who had served the family faithfully for many, many years, was becoming so lame and slow she could hardly manage the stairs. Ishbel hadn't the heart to suggest that the old soul should retire, so the household struggled on valiantly with the doubtful help of a succession of disinterested young lasses, who came and went with depressing regularity.

Although Brian's thoughts had turned as usual to Joanna Wotherspoon, he was reluctant to take the plunge and visit her. He had broadened his outlook and been mildly attracted to many pretty women on his travels, but a vision of the young Joanna continued to haunt his dreams. He had a course of action in mind, but was reluctant to put it to the test. He wanted to hold on to his dreams. If they were shattered, he wasn't sure how to reshape his future. If he had a future, that is. As the beautiful, tranquil summer of 1939 passed into uneasy history, the future seemed bleak.

Shortly before he was due to sit his final exams, Brian took courage in both hands, borrowed his stepfather's sporty MG and, with hood lowered and wind ruffling his hair, drove through fields of ripening wheat to Dalkeith.

He was forced to slow down upon reaching the driveway of the Big House, running the gauntlet of a procession of giggling schoolgirls on bikes, headed by a severe school-mistress who eyed the car and its handsome young driver with stern suspicion. Brian's heart lurched when he had parked the car and finally tracked down his young love. She had grown tall in the months he'd been away. The breeches, stockings and stout shoes topped by a plain white blouse merely accentuated a delectable figure. He discovered he wanted her more than ever.

She was attending to his grandfather's beehives, her face darkly shadowed beneath a bee-keeper's hat and veil. The scene gave him a momentary twinge of sadness, remembering old Donald lying so still and peaceful on the fresh green grass. He walked up softly behind Joanna. 'Telling your troubles to the bees?' he asked.

She turned in surprise, her eyes dark and mysterious behind the veil. He saw her shadowy features light up. 'Hullo, there! I say, hang on to this for me, will you?' She handed over the small smoke bellows she used to pacify the bees, then giggled. 'Ah, caurry-fist! You're Brian!'

He laughed. 'Joanna, we must work out a more reliable method of identification in future!'

'What do you suggest?'

He wanted to say, a kiss? But instead he asked curiously, 'Aren't you afraid of bees?'

'No,' she answered. 'Your grandfather wasn't, so why should I be? I love the busy wee creatures. I haven't been stung yet.'

He watched the bees buzzing around her. 'You're rather

wonderful, Joanna. Unique and special,' he told her softly. He felt such overwhelming love for her, he was sure it must show.

The ridiculous veiled hat guarded her expression. He guessed she was embarrassed, for she hastily changed the subject. 'Did you know we leased the mansion house to a girls' boarding school? Now that was a brilliant idea of my father's. It's saved the roof coming off.'

'Judging by the lively lassies I met in the drive, I'd say the roof was in danger of being raised somewhat,' he remarked with a smile.

He took her hand and led her out of range of the hives, then gently removed her hat and veil. He studied intently the young face that had drifted through his dreams on many restless nights. Her skin was smooth and clear, tinted gold by the sun, the eyes looking into his were grave and fearless. He folded her in his arms and held her close to his breast. That was enough for several long moments, and then it was not nearly enough. 'I love you, Joanna. Do you remember when I tried to kiss you?' he said unevenly.

Her eyes were bright, amused. 'You were caught in the act. My father came.'

Brian glanced around warily. 'Where is he now?'

'Mucking out the byre.'

'That's OK then.' He kissed her. He put more into the kiss than he'd intended. All his longing for her went into the passionate embrace, his loneliness in the long watches of the night and his fear for the future. To his incredulous joy, he felt her respond, shy and hesitant at first, then as eager and wholehearted as he would have wished.

'Joanna, will you m-marry me?'

The kiss had left Joanna confused and disorientated. She

had not told him Adrian had come wooing her. Adrian, in RAF uniform, dashing enough to steal any girl's heart. Adrian, with wings on his breast and daredevil ways. Adrian, who buzzed her father's fields mercilessly, flying so low in the slow biplane he had driven Wotherspoon to fist-shaking fury and sent black stirks and dairy herd romping madly through new-sown turnip fields. Adrian, who kissed her casually and made her laugh. Oh, why must she fall in love with twins?

'No, Brian,' Joanna said in a small voice. 'I'm sorry, I can't marry you.'

He released her abruptly. His expression had gone so blank and dead it frightened her. 'Is there someone else?'

'Yes – no – ohh, I don't know!' she cried tearfully.

His eyes narrowed thoughtfully. 'It's Adrian, isn't it?'

She could only nod mutely.

'Damn him to hell!' said Brian quietly. He turned his back on all his dreams, and walked away.

When Brian had left for Liverpool to rejoin his ship, Ishbel felt unsettled and desperately anxious. Both her sons were in danger if war broke out. Edinburgh Corporation was already prepared. Gas masks in square brown boxes had been distributed to everyone, and Sandy visited the shop to fit these symbols of terror and explain how to use them when yellow contamination boards indicated the presence of poisonous gas. Ishbel pitied Sandy's wife Sarah, who must put her very young son into the cage-like contraption evolved for babies, which Sandy also demonstrated. It looked likely to frighten the life out of a baby. Fitting on the claustrophobic mask with its strong rubbery smell made Ishbel feel sick, and she had great difficulty breathing, the rubber flapping uncomfortably against her cheeks as she struggled with nausea and attempted to breathe.

She was often unwell these days, a fact she put down to worry and an early approach of what her mother called the 'difficult age'. As if every age didn't have its difficulties! Ishbel thought, but at least Matthew was at home just now to lend his support. The Air Ministry and Fighter Command were considering his recommendations for strengthening air defences around the Forth.

Matthew had suggested painting the cupola with a black tarry substance which served both as blackout material and a safeguard to prevent flying glass. The resultant gloom inside the store took some getting used to, but nobody complained. There was disruption elsewhere in the capital, anyway. Part of Princes Street Gardens had been dug up to make underground shelters and deep trenches appeared in Inverleith Park and elsewhere. Anderson shelters cropped up in private gardens, and nobody objected to black paint and black drapes over the doors, and shop windows criss-crossed with brown sticky tape. In fact, it was a reassuring sight for most folk. Edinburgh was ready.

A particularly severe stomach upset sent Ishbel reluctantly to the doctor, and after a thorough examination she came out of the surgery in a daze and headed unsteadily towards the shop. Matthew was in the office, and looked up in concern when his wife walked in and slumped wanly in a chair.

'Honey, what did he say? Did you get a tonic?'

'Oh, I got a tonic all right!' she answered. 'Matthew, we're going to have a baby.'

Matthew's jaw dropped. Somehow, because of Ishbel's age and his lack of success with Polly, it had never crossed his mind they might be blessed with a child. His baby! He felt so awed and excited he nearly wept. Recovering from the initial shock, his emotions were in chaos. He wanted to sing and dance and turn cartwheels, and at the same time he was so darned scared he felt sick. Would Ishbel be OK? At that point, he wished it hadn't happened. 'Honey, are you sure about this?' he demanded anxiously.

'Sure, I'm sure. At least, the doctor is. He thinks I'm nearly five months gone. And I thought it was middle-aged spread!' She smiled weakly. She couldn't remember feeling quite the same with other pregnancies, but she'd been a younger woman then. Matthew was on his feet. He came across and kneeled beside her, taking her hand. It felt cold and limp, and his anxiety mounted.

He chided himself bitterly for this state of affairs. He loved her so much, he should have noticed long ago the dark shadows like bruises beneath her tired eyes. He lifted her hand to his lips and kissed it humbly. The skin was fine, with a faint scent of flowers. Matthew had no words to express his emotion, his immense gratitude for the child she was giving him.

'Honey, from now on you take things easy, you understand?' he said gruffly. He wished he could do the suffering for her. That was impossible, of course, and Matthew thought that his suffering would be all the greater, because of his helplessness.

Ishbel smiled and patted his cheek. 'How can I take it easy when there's so much to do?'

'I know a way,' he said firmly. 'You send right now for Elspeth. You need your daughter. Polly can survive without her. My darling, I guess the time's come to insist that she comes home.'

* * *

Elspeth was usually up before Polly in their Los Angeles abode. It was a lovely place, as befitted the successful partnership. There was an orchard of peach trees right behind the house. In springtime, the scent of blossom invaded every room, and the ground was strewn with petals like a pink snowfall. And yet, now that her mother's letter had arrived with its disturbing news, Elspeth was aware of deep, far-reaching relief. She had an excuse to leave.

She could tactfully end the partnership with Polly and launch out on her own, if she went home to Scotland. Elspeth sat down on the shallow steps bordering the swimming pool and looked across the artificially blue water, her mother's letter clutched in her hand. Acting in Hollywood had been exciting at first, but now she longed for an end to the role she was forced to play. She wasn't a child actress any more, and she was sick of frilly dresses and cute curls, simpering dimples and smart dialogue. Yet that's what their contract demanded. I want to act properly, Elspeth thought. I want to be Ophelia and Juliet while I'm young, and Lady Macbeth when I'm older. I want to work hard and learn to be an actress, not a cute little turkey. If I stay here tied to Polly and light comedy, I'll never have the chance.

Elspeth hugged her knees unhappily. But I love Polly so! I wouldn't hurt Polly for the world, and yet I must. I really think I must.

'Hi, honey!'

Polly was up. Dressed in a flouncy blue housecoat, she carried a glass of orange juice, her usual breakfast. Her pretty, kindly face was scrubbed clean of makeup, and the clear skin shone as innocently as a little girl's in the morning

sunlight. She sat down at the table beneath the shady
umbrella and took a sip of juice. 'What you got there, my
love?' Polly asked idly.

'It – it's a letter from Mam.'

Polly was instantly alert. She studied the girl closely and
could tell she was upset. She felt an icy chill of premonition.
'I hope it's not bad news?' she asked carefully.

Elspeth frowned. 'Depends how you look at it, Polly.
Mam's expecting a baby.'

Ishbel was expecting Matthew's baby! How that hurt!
The possibility of a baby had occurred to Polly when she'd
heard Ishbel and Matthew had married, but she'd persuaded herself it would never happen. I was a fool, I
should've been prepared, Polly mourned. I should've built
defences.

Well, it was too late now, and she must accept the raw
deal Fate had dealt her. Polly took a sip of icy, tart juice. It
burned like fire all the way down her aching throat, but
steadied her nerves. 'I guess Matt will be over the moon.
He always wanted babies,' she remarked lightly, blessing
her acting skill.

'Yes,' Elspeth replied absently. She continued to crouch
miserably on the white marble steps beside the blue water.

Polly frowned. Oh heck! Was there more? 'Something
botherin' you, my darlin'?' she ventured. They'd never
kept secrets. They'd argued like a real mother and
daughter, hollering at one another, but they'd never held
grudges nor kept secrets.

Elspeth turned resolutely to face the woman who was her
dearest friend. 'Polly, I've got to go home. Mam's sick with
this baby and she needs me. She says they're preparing for
war back home. I got to go, Polly, I'm sorry.'

'Honey, if war breaks out you'll be in danger in Britain. You're safe here, Elspeth. Your mam wouldn't want you running into danger, would she? Besides, your career—'

Elspeth stood up in one lithe, graceful movement. 'Polly, if I carry on with little-girlie roles, my career is finished. I have to move on. I've got to leave you and strike out on my own.' In tears, she ran to Polly, hugging her. 'Oh, Poll, I'm sorry! They'll terminate your contract if I go.'

Polly was stunned by this cruel blow. She knew she acted as the motherly stooge in their sparkling partnership, and without Elspeth she was finished. She was a professional, though, and she could see the only way forward for so talented a young actress was to break the mould and go solo. Time to let go, Polly old girl, she told herself wryly. Time to give the acting performance of your life.

Indignantly, she shoved Elspeth away. 'Say, are you tellin' me I got no talent? You think I need your cute looks an' smart ways to make me a star?' Polly tapped her chest proudly. 'Well, you jus' think again, honey-baby. I got "it". I got "oomph". I got glamour! So you go on home, Elspeth love. I'll be OK.'

Rizzio's 'Stop Me and Buy One' barrows had become a familiar sight in Leith, Portobello and most places where Edinburgh folk gathered to enjoy the brilliant sunshine. The summer of 1939 was the best anyone could remember, ice cream was in great demand, and Fredrika was highly delighted with the prosperity she'd brought to the kind Italian family. She had very nearly collected one hundred shillings, and was preparing for a stealthy departure from the city within the next few days. Feemie had heard no more from the dreaded police, and gradually Fredrika's fear had faded. Why should she be afraid anyway? she thought. Her papers were all in order, stamped by immigration.

One warm day in August, Feemie left Fredrika in charge of the lodging house and headed for the marketplace to haggle for weekly provisions, a task Feemie grimly relished. It was Fredrika's morning off, and she sat by the open kitchen window idly enjoying a mid-morning cup of tea. She could hear happy shrieks and laughter coming from children in the nearby school playground. Glancing out, she watched little girls skipping to a rhyme which echoed merrily in Fredrika's ears.

> *Jeelly on a plate, Jeelly on a plate,*
> *Wiggle-waggle! Wiggle waggle!*
> *Jeelly on a plate!*

Fredrika laughed merrily as they wiggle-waggled their small bottoms and swung their neat, pleated skirts. Oh, it was good, that!

She was still smiling as she rose to answer a gentle tapping on the front door. Fredrika found a young man standing on the doorstep, and was delighted to see a new customer for Feemie. Two or three of Feemie's regulars were on the Army Reserve and had gone off recently to join their regiments. Fredrika subjected the man to keen scrutiny, and was satisfied. He seemed clean and respectable, dressed neatly in jacket and flannels with blue shirt and navy tie.

'You want lodgings?' she asked pleasantly.

He seemed taken aback at finding Fredrika instead of Feemie. 'Er – well, I—'

'Lodging is sixpence per night, but it will be a shilling if you want a good breakfast with porridge and sausage,' said Fredrika cunningly. These were inflated prices, but times were hard and he looked as if he could afford it.

He didn't answer for a moment, giving her a long, considering look. 'Excuse me, but are you Fredrika Klein?'

She stared. 'Yes, that is my name.' She had Vati's name, and was proud of it.

'I wonder if you will answer a few questions for me, Miss Klein?'

'Questions?' Fredrika repeated uneasily. 'You don't like these high prices?'

'It's nothing to do with that, miss. I'm a police officer,' he announced calmly.

Fredrika collapsed against the doorpost, otherwise her legs might have given way. 'You're a bobby!' she gasped in horror.

He raised his eyebrows. 'Well, yes. I just have to ask you—'

'Where is your uniform? This is not fair play, coming without uniform!' cried Fredrika angrily, recovering her spirit.

'I am Detective-Sergeant Murray Gibson, of the plain-clothes branch, Edinburgh City Police,' he explained coldly. 'If you will just answer one question for me I'll not take up more of your time, Miss Klein. We understand you are illegitimate, and of course we will be discreet, but we need to know your father's name for our records.'

'That is none of your business!'

'Oh, but it is.' He frowned. 'You'll appreciate we must check everyone's story very carefully these days.'

Fredrika folded her arms. 'I will not tell!'

Murray Gibson was annoyed. This was a job he detested, and this young woman was one of the many awkward customers he had to deal with. 'If you refuse to reveal your father's name, Miss Klein, then you must report to the police as an alien until the present emergency ends,' he warned.

Fredrika swallowed nervously. 'If I go to the police I will never be seen again!'

'Oh, nonsense! Nothing will happen to you as long as you make no attempt to leave the city,' he explained patiently.

'You mean I may not leave Edinburgh?' She went quite white with dismay.

Well, well! So she was planning to scarper, Murray thought grimly. Shock tactics would not go amiss with this young woman. He leaned down to her, face to face. 'Miss Klein, if you sneak out of Edinburgh without telling us what we need to know, I shall come after you personally and haul you back. Understand?'

She nodded, dark eyes so terrified they struck a sympathetic chord, and he was sorry he'd scared her. He was on the point of adding a soothing word when she suddenly turned defiant and started shouting at him. 'I thought you were nice working man. If I had known you were a bobby, I would never have opened Feemie's door to you!'

Coldly, Murray drew himself up to his full height: an impressive six feet. 'I shall expect to see you at police headquarters, Miss Klein, two o'clock sharp, Friday afternoons, from now on,' he ordered officiously.

The door slammed in the policeman's face with a bang that rivalled the garrison's one o'clock gun. 'Ouch!' he winced, and walked away, smothering a grin.

* * *

Ishbel could hardly believe she had her daughter home at last. Elspeth had arrived by sea just in time. Even as the delighted family gathered round to celebrate Elspeth's arrival, Poland was being bombed into submission and Britain had issued a hurried ultimatum to Germany. Trainloads of bewildered evacuees had left Edinburgh already that Friday morning, bound for reception centres in the surrounding countryside. At the first hint of trouble, the Scottish Crown Jewels were hastily removed from the Crown Room in Edinburgh Castle, packed carefully in a stout chest and stowed in a vault carved deep in the rock, protected by sandbags and locked safely behind fireproof doors.

But thoughts of war were mercifully far from Ishbel's mind at that moment. She lay on a sofa propped up with cushions, Elspeth kneeling beside her. She'd had a fainting spell in the shop, and had been warned there was a danger she might lose this precious baby if she didn't rest. Ishbel held her daughter's hand tightly. 'Och, I feel useless lying here! I was strong as a horse when I had you and the twins.'

Elspeth leaned over and kissed her cheek. 'Well, you deserve a little pampering, Mam. Don't you worry, Matthew and I will take care of everything.'

'You mean you intend to work in the shop, darling?' asked Ishbel, incredulously. Had her daughter got the acting bug out of her system at last? she wondered.

'I guess it won't hurt me to try,' said Elspeth. One look at her mother had shocked her so much she'd immediately abandoned all thought of theatre work at present. Ishbel looked ill and drawn. Long years of worry and hard work had taken their toll on her natural good health, and pregnancy had been the last straw. She must have rest, the doctor had insisted. There was nothing else for it, Elspeth must help in the shop.

'I can't believe they'll be so daft as to start another war,' grumbled Catriona, airing a favourite topic. 'They've handed out gas masks, and as if that's no' enough to scare the living daylights out o' folk, there's ration books coming and threats o' shortages o' decent food and clothing. You can just imagine what that'll do for our trade!'

'Everyone will be in the same boat, Catriona,' said Eleanor, patting the sleepy little dog on her lap. She couldn't stop admiring her granddaughter's looks. Such a strikingly bonnie lass, with such a strong resemblance to dear Freddie it brought tears to her eyes.

Ishbel's heart had lurched at Eleanor's innocent remark about boats. Brian was at sea, but where exactly the oil tanker was, Ishbel didn't know. She only knew the country was on the brink of war and her son was in terrible danger. Matthew sat down beside her and gave her his warm, loving smile. Strange, she thought, Matthew always knew when she needed the comfort of his love, to see her through the bad times.

Saturday afternoon in Edinburgh seemed perfectly normal on that last day of peace. The sun shone upon crowds watching Hearts beat Motherwell 4–2, Princes Street was crowded with shoppers and there were queues at the cinemas.

Adrian knew it was a deceptive normality. Working in the ops room at RAF Turnhouse, Adrian knew that all personnel at airfields round about had been placed on alert and high-explosive shells of gun batteries round the Forth were fused and ready. Only by a stroke of luck, and by working several boring night shifts, had he managed to wangle twelve hours' leave that Saturday. He'd phoned Joanna right away, and she'd jumped at the chance of a few hours' respite in the city, away from the farm. Farming with old Grumpy – as he termed Wotherspoon – couldn't be much fun, thought Adrian as he waited for Joanna's train to arrive. She was much too beautiful to be buried in the country.

He caught his breath as she alighted from the carriage and came towards him. Her skin was tanned, her dark curls upswept to a ridiculous little hat perched on top, a scrap of veiling over the eyes. Her costume was very plain, very smart. 'You look good enough to eat,' he remarked, as they kissed lightly.

Taking his arm, she laughed. 'Funny you should say that, because I'm jolly hungry.'

'OK, we'll walk along and inspect the air-raid shelters in Princes Street. I'm something of an expert on shelters, 'cause I've helped dig a few around the air base. Then I suggest we have a good old Scottish high tea before joining the queue to see John Wayne in *Stagecoach*.'

Her eyes danced. 'That sounds perfect!'

Joanna was proud to be seen on the arm of such a dashing and handsome airman. Other girls stared enviously. Best of all, the outing was nothing more than harmless fun to lighten her hard working life, and she could afford to relax and flirt a little and enjoy herself. Joanna hung on tighter to her escort's arm, feeling carefree and happy. She knew where she was with Adrian. He had dozens of girlfriends, none of whom he took seriously. To him, she was just one of many.

With Brian it was different. He was vulnerable and easily hurt, and she must be sure of her feelings before committing herself. It had upset her dreadfully when Brian proposed, because she was unsure of her own emotions, and would not give him false hope. She smiled a little sadly to herself. One thing was sure: there was no risk of breaking Adrian's fickle heart.

Having satisfied their healthy young appetites with bacon and eggs, scones, jam, and cakes, washed down with cups of tea, they joined the long queue outside the cinema. Once seated inside with the lights turned out, Adrian found it hard to concentrate on the programme. Even disturbing scenes of German conquest in the Gaumont newsreel couldn't distract his attention from the girl by his side. In fact, war sharpened emotions, he thought. He was not an experienced pilot, but if the need arose he would be called upon to fly the new Spitfires rumoured to be arriving any day now. He might die, and he wanted to live. Oh, how he wanted to live when he stole a glance at the beautiful young woman by his side! Cautiously, he slid an arm along the back of her seat and eased it gently around her shoulders. Joanna turned her head and glanced at him, smiling, then nestled closer. Her hair was delicately scented. He touched it with his lips. 'You smell like roses,' he whispered.

She giggled. 'Friday night is Amami night.'

He nibbled her ear. 'Joanna, I love you.'

'Ha-ha! Me and a dozen other girls.'

'I'm serious, sweetheart. I really am. Will you marry me?'

'Don't be daft!'

'Joanna, have pity! There's going to be war. I could get killed.'

'Not you. You're a born survivor.'

'Listen, I want to marry you. I mean it. Why won't you?' he pleaded.

'Because!' she replied absently, engrossed in the film.

His expression hardened. 'Is it Brian? I know he's been mooning around you lately like a lovesick calf.'

That spoiled everything. The whole pleasant, light-hearted outing went suddenly wrong. 'Yes, Adrian,' Joanna admitted crossly. 'It *is* Brian.'

'Damn him, I knew it!' exploded Adrian.

A long-suffering cinema-goer in the row behind tapped the young airman's shoulder. 'Some of us are wantin' to watch this film, son.'

'Oh, blast!' muttered Adrian angrily, settling down moodily to watch John Wayne win his girl.

Next day, Sunday, 3rd September 1939, just as the tatties were coming to the boil at lunchtime, an agitated mother flung open a window in Tollcross and shouted to her bairns playing below. 'Come awa' in and get your gas masks. The war's on!'

The news flashed through the city as folk spilled out of the kirks. The sky seemed the same quiet blue, the clouds an innocent fluffy white, but men looked upwards doubtfully. You couldn't trust the sky any more. There were air-raid shelters everywhere to prove it. Word went round that the one o'clock gun, fired daily from Edinburgh Castle, would cease firing for the duration of the war. Folk stared at one another, more frightened by this break with tradition than they cared to admit. Strange indeed that the sound of gunfire should live in their memory as a symbol of peace!

433

At Knoxhall House, Ishbel discovered her mother busy in the bathroom, filling the bath to the brim with cold water. 'Mam, what on earth are you doing?'

'I'm getting ready for the incendiaries falling, Ishbel. I'm filling this bath and keeping it filled till the war's over. There's buckets of sand and a stirrup pump in the hallway, too,' replied Catriona grimly. 'I dinna trust thon Auxiliary Fire Service. The postie's one o' them and they sound an amateurish bunch to me.'

Although Ishbel laughed at the time, she was soon forced to admit her mother had a point. After a few uneasy weeks, war came with a vengeance to Edinburgh. On a beautiful day in early October, a black bomber came screaming out of the sky to attack two cruisers in the Forth, close by the railway bridge. All that afternoon determined air attacks persisted round the naval base at Rosyth, while Spitfires scrambled from Drem and Turnhouse RAF bases, giving chase to waves of the German bombers. In the gun battles that followed, shrapnel and spent shell caps rained down over the city, falling on Haymarket and Rutland Square and over a wide area uncomfortably close to Alexander's. The Scottish capital had the unwelcome distinction of being singled out for the first air attack on British soil.

Ishbel had regained some of her strength and energy as her pregnancy advanced, and had ventured into the shop on that memorable afternoon to see how Elspeth was faring. She worried about her daughter, sensing that Elspeth had difficulty adjusting to the work.

Unfortunately, Ishbel arrived just as her daughter had received a mild telling-off from Clara. Elspeth made a face at the manageress's back. 'Old cat! Honestly, Mam, am I expected to grin and bear it if a customer is downright rude? I was mightily restrained, anyway. I only told the grumpy guy to quit complaining, there's a war on.'

Ishbel hid a smile. 'You know what they say, my love. The customer's always right.'

'Huh! That'll change while I'm around!' declared Elspeth ominously.

Ishbel said no more, but she could anticipate trouble. She left Elspeth behind the counter and made her way slowly up the wide stairway to the gallery. She felt cumbersome and heavy, and arrived breathless from the climb, pressing her hand against a painful stitch in her side. She stared upwards at the darkened dome of glass above her head. Its gloom on this pleasant October day seemed doubly menacing. All of a sudden there was a mighty crash, a splintering of wood, and a long, jagged crack appeared in one of the darkened panes. Ishbel screamed. She gripped the railing and shouted at the pitch of her voice. 'Evacuate the store, get everyone outside!'

Archie appeared at her elbow. 'Wait a moment, ma'am, it's just as bad outside, there's shrapnel falling everywhere. I've just had word there's a raid on, and bombs are falling in the Forth. You can hear the guns firing, if you listen.'

She clutched his arm, 'Get everyone down to the basement, Archie. They'll be safe down there.'

Matthew appeared at a run, as Archie hurried off to clear the store. 'Ishbel, what's happening? They say there's an air raid, but I'm darned if I heard any sirens,' he cried.

'There was no warning,' she gasped. 'Matthew, look at the roof!'

He glanced upwards and blanched. 'My God! If that falls . . .' Matthew put an arm round his wife and urged her towards the stairway. 'I guess there's little we can do about

435

it till the raid's over. Ishbel, I want you to go down to the basement with the rest.'

She leaned against him, swaying a little. The stitch in her side had increased in intensity. It faded, then cramped her breathing once more. She paused, then the truth hit her. 'Matthew, the baby's coming!'

He stopped in his tracks. 'What, now?'

'Yes,' gasped Ishbel urgently. 'Right now.'

Chapter 20

The baby wasn't due for three weeks, but Matthew had been warned by Catriona that babies were notoriously unpunctual. In fact, they seemed to take a positive delight in choosing awkward moments, Matthew thought as he supported his wife. This sure was a mighty awkward moment! He could hear aircraft overhead, and it sounded like a full scale battle was going on up there. With all that danger in the streets outside, he couldn't risk taking Ishbel to hospital, so what was to be done?

While Matthew swithered, a sherd of glass loosened from the dome above and fell past them like a spear, to shatter on the shop floor below. Ishbel clung to Matthew, terrified. 'Darling, the rest of that glass could come down any minute!'

He made up his mind. 'We'll go to the basement, honey. At least you'll be safe down there.'

A strange scene met them when they reached the basement. The large, gloomy space was packed with customers and staff, most of them clutching square brown boxes containing gas masks. They were seated on benches that Ishbel had provided on Sandy's advice, and there was a loud buzz of excited conversation, which ceased abruptly as Matthew shouted, 'Say, is there a doctor in the house?'

They stared anxiously at Ishbel, then hopefully at one another, but nobody stirred. 'A nurse?' he tried desperately. Ishbel sagged beside him, eyes closed as she endured another spasm of pain.

'I have a first aid certificate, Mr Clark,' volunteered Cathy, the plump, little lady whose job in Alexander's covered everything from tea lady to dispenser of aspirins.

'That'll have to do, Cathy,' Matthew decided. 'My wife needs a woman to care for her while I go fetch a doctor.'

Cathy swiftly took in the situation and patted his arm. 'Dinna fash yoursel', dear, I've had four o' my ain.' She put an arm round Ishbel and led her to the small room which served as first-aid post. Elspeth followed, thoroughly alarmed. 'Mam, what's wrong?'

'Your mammy's havin' a bairn, that's all, lovie,' Cathy said cheerfully, making Ishbel comfortable on the trestle bed while Matthew stood watching worriedly.

'I'm leavin' now, honey. I'll be back soon with the first doctor I can find,' he said.

Ishbel reached for his hand. 'Darling, take care! It's dangerous out there. I heard gunfire just now.'

He kissed her. 'Don't worry. I had plenty of practice dodging bullets during the last show. I'll be back in a jiffy.'

When Matthew had departed on his mission, Cathy gave Elspeth an understanding glance. 'You don't have to bide, lass. I'll manage fine on my own.'

Elspeth hesitated. The very thought of the birth scared her, and she didn't want to witness it. She studied her mother anxiously. Ishbel's eyes were pain-filled and beads of sweat stood on her brow, but she made no complaint.

Mam's so brave! Elspeth thought admiringly, and was suddenly ashamed of her own cowardice. She knelt beside the bed and slipped an arm round her mother's shoulders. 'I'll stay,' she said staunchly.

Looking back afterwards on that frantic hour, Elspeth wondered where she'd found the courage to remain calm. At times her mother cried out and clutched her arms so tightly it hurt, but Elspeth spoke soothingly and hugged her until the pains eased and she relaxed.

'My, this wee bairn's in an awful hurry, but its mother's fair exhausted, poor soul. What's keeping the doctor?' remarked Cathy with an anxious glance towards the door. She had her sleeves rolled up, frizzy grey hair standing on end. Elspeth began praying fervently as time dragged by with no end to the struggle. Oh, please, let the doctor come!

When Elspeth was beginning to think mother and baby would die, there was a flurry of activity outside and Matthew ushered in a professional-looking gentleman, who took in the situation at a glance, flung off his jacket and took command. Several minutes later came the sound Elspeth had been praying for, the newborn baby's cry, sounding loud and lusty in the confined space.

'It's a boy!' the doctor announced triumphantly.

Cathy wiped the baby's face and wrapped him warmly in a towel before handing the crying baby to Elspeth. 'Here, Elspeth, tak' your wee brother an' gi'e the mite a cuddle while we see to your mammy.'

Elspeth took the little bundle gingerly. He seemed very tiny to be making such a protest. His eyes were tight shut like a little blind puppy, and he was making a great show of indignation, tiny hands emerging from the folds of the towel to beat the air. Elspeth laughed delightedly. This is my brother! she thought with a joyful leap of the heart. I saw him born, I was with him from the very first moment of his life. This is my own, my special little brother!

She had never known such a tender feeling. Oh, she loved the twins dearly, but they had one another, and didn't really need a sister. As she stood with her small half-brother in her arms, Elspeth could see how lonely her childhood had been. Never knowing a father's love, excluded from her brothers' close companionship, and with Mam forced to work hard to keep the three of them in comfort, she had been a very lonely little girl indeed. Poor Mam! Elspeth thought compassionately. She'd abandoned her hardworking mother in favour of childless Polly, who'd had plenty of time on her hands. Well, that was in the past now. A new chapter was beginning with the birth of this little boy.

She examined the baby with wonder. He had stopped whimpering and opened his eyes. She knew he was far too young to focus on anything, but he seemed to study her features with curiosity. She smiled. 'Howdy, wee half-brother. You're beautiful!' she told him.

'Oh, Elspeth, let me see him!' Ishbel cried eagerly. Smiling, Elspeth placed the baby in his mother's arms and stood aside.

Matthew peered round the door at that moment, and Elspeth cried out joyfully. 'It's a boy, Matthew!''

His face broke into a beaming smile and he came bounding in. He kissed his wife, then gingerly stroked his son's cheek with a finger. 'Well, what d'you know?' he whispered in awe. 'Ain't he the handsomest baby you ever saw in your life?'

Ishbel laughed and kissed their son. 'How does the name Ryan Donald Clark appeal to you, Matthew?' she asked thoughtfully.

'You mean, call this little guy after my father and yours? Ishbel, that's a swell idea!' Matthew agreed, bursting with pride.

While little Ryan Clark was making a dramatic appearance, brand new Spitfires scrambled from the air bases at Drem, Turnhouse and Leuchars were proving their worth against the first enemy aircraft to attack Edinburgh since Zeppelins ventured across the coastline years ago. RAF pilots learned new battle tactics fast, and the skies over Fife and the Lothians thrummed with action as the small fighters dived on the larger, slower bombers. Meanwhile, anti-aircraft batteries pounded away at the target whenever the Germans came within range.

It was a hotter reception than they had bargained for, and soon one of the Junkers spun helplessly out of control and plummeted into the Forth. The crew of a small trawler working nearby cautiously picked up the survivors, and found them to be remarkably ordinary, half-drowned, young men, grateful to be alive.

It was not easy for the Spitfires to be everywhere at once, however, and a convoy moving up-river towards the boom defence came under heavy attack later that afternoon, one of its destroyer escort being badly damaged and several crewmen killed. Nobody in Edinburgh was in any doubt the war had started, and the rest of the country watched in trepidation, and waited.

It was not long before sirens sounded frequent alerts and although Morningside and Alexander's had escaped more serious damage, Ishbel, safely home with her new baby, heard tales of bombing and fierce aerial battles taking place in the surrounding district. Everyone was tight-lipped, mindful that 'careless talk costs lives'. Posters everywhere warned the public of that very real danger, and it was difficult to have a clear picture of events. Ishbel was seriously worried lest Adrian had been involved in the dog-fights. She knew her adventurous son would be in the thick of it. Adrian had boasted recently of his skill when flying solo in an old Gladiator; he had hoped to transfer to Spitfires in due course, and the very thought of him speeding recklessly through the sky petrified his mother.

Nobody knew where Brian was, and that was a source of added anguish. Attacks on convoys mustering in Methil Bay brought home to Ishbel the danger Brian faced every day at sea. His letters were guarded and few and far between. She could only guess he was running the gauntlet of U-boat attacks, bringing home the petrol and oil that was so essential to the war effort. Both her sons were in such grave danger that Ishbel shed many despairing tears as she lay helplessly in bed, cuddling her miraculous, new baby. Her thoughts often strayed to Freddie's lost daughter, but secretly she despaired of ever finding her. It was just another worry, another sorrow to bear.

Adrian phoned later that week, much to everyone's relief. He had heard rumours of casualties in the city and he, too, was concerned. Matthew was able to reassure his step-son and proudly announce the arrival of Ryan, the twins' half-brother.

Adrian was delighted. 'Matthew, many congratulations! I bet Mam is over the moon.'

'Still a bit dazed by the speed of events, I'd say, Adrian. We both are. I guess she'll be mighty relieved to know you came through the air battle in one piece.'

There was an awkward pause, then Adrian said sheepishly, 'Well, actually, Matthew, I wasn't flying.'

'You weren't?' Matthew was surprised.

'No. I was – er – needed elsewhere. I can't talk about it, Matthew. It's – um – frightfully hush-hush.'

'An important mission?'

'Oh, definitely! Extremely important. Daren't say more, you understand.'

'Yeah. Careless talk costs lives,' Matthew remarked mildly.

'You bet! Matthew, I have to go now,' Adrian said hastily. 'Give my baby brother a kiss from me, and tell Mam jolly good show.' With evident relief, he rang off.

Matthew replaced the receiver and stood gazing thoughtfully at the silent instrument. He would bet his last dollar Adrian was hiding something. Even the hush-hush bit sounded to Matthew like a lot of baloney. What was the word that had sprung to mind during that odd conversation? Matthew pondered for a moment. Sure, that was it: Bravado!

Adrian heaved a huge sigh of relief once he'd phoned home. He'd dreaded telling his nearest and dearest he'd failed the flying course and would not now be entrusted with a Spitfire. Failure was acutely painful. Adrian couldn't remember failing anything he'd set his heart on, and the humiliation had shaken his self-esteem. He'd been dux in maths and physics at school, and at university had joined an elite and pampered band of research students. Beautiful girls came running when he smiled, falling over themselves for his attention.

Except Joanna Wotherspoon. She had turned down the first serious proposal of marriage he'd ever made to anyone, another blow to his confidence. The deadly rival was dear old Brian, of course. Adrian could sympathise with Joanna's quandary. It must be confusing for the girl to be courted by two identical, brilliant, handsome chaps, he thought.

Back at his desk, Adrian frowned absently at the complex figures and radar diagrams spread before him. His thoughts kept straying agonisingly to his recent interview with the Station Commander. He could recall every single word of the roasting, which was branded deep into his memory. He'd stood rigidly to attention and his back and calf-muscles still ached. Eyes fixed on a point one inch to the right of the SC's left ear, he'd felt cold sweat gather in beads on his brow.

The Station Commander had slapped a sheaf of letters on the desk. 'You know what this is, Alexander?' he'd snapped. 'It's a mass of furious complaints from the general public which tell a tale of reckless disregard for safety and wilful misuse of a valuable biplane that is almost beyond belief. These people write of women miscarrying, horses bolting, cattle rampaging in terror through crops, sheep falling down gullies, cows withholding milk and hens off the lay. The reputation of the RAF lies in shreds and tatters in the Dalkeith area, because one damn fool decides to show off. Fortunately, because of your dangerous and unlawful low flying, you were clearly identified.'

Identified? Adrian was startled. He'd thought recognition was an outside chance, or he would never have risked the exhilarating show of aerobatics intended to impress Joanna. He had a sudden vision of a furious, fist-shaking figure down below in a neep field. Adrian groaned inwardly. The Grumpy. I might have guessed!

Then the sentence had been pronounced, the death-knell to all Adrian's hopes. 'You've failed the course, Alexander. God knows we need pilots, but not reckless idiots. I have no hesitation in grounding you for good. As from today, you'll be transferred, and assigned to desk duties. Dis-miss . . .

Adrian returned abruptly to the present, still smarting. So here I am, he thought drearily, working in the Chain Home Radar Station at Drone Hill. The station was part of a radar network stretching from Devon to Caithness, and as if to humiliate Adrian thoroughly, the installation had developed gremlins and broken down twice at crucial moments during recent air raids. The trusty old Observer Corps had been of more assistance to fighter squadrons and ack-ack batteries, and there had been rude remarks and scorn poured upon the installation.

Still, it was interesting work. Adrian pored over figures and diagrams and studied the radar screen before him. Rightaway he could spot a weakness in the system he hadn't noticed before. He settled down diligently to eliminate the flaw.

Catriona had become even more safety conscious, with a baby in the house. Apart from the Anderson shelter in the kitchen garden and the bath, brimful with water, shovels and buckets of sand in dark corners to deal with incendiaries posed a threat to the unwary. Curtains were heavily lined with blackout material and the gas-proof refuge room in the wine cellar was provided with every item Catriona could tick off a long list issued by the Local Defence. These included a first-aid kit equipped with bleach ointment for blister gas, sal volatile for faints and tannic acid jelly for burns. A pencil served both for notes and for a tourniquet. Finer details included ear plugs to protect ear-drums from bomb blast, tranquillisers for distressed dogs and chewing gum to soothe Florrie's frayed nerves when sirens sounded. Florrie could puff her way through a whole packet of twenty Gold Flake in moments of stress, and Catriona strictly banned smoking in the refuge room. Florrie was forced morosely to chew gum.

Ishbel had regained strength quickly after the birth, and was back at work by the end of the year. This time she was determined not to be parted from her child. Little Ryan Clark accompanied his mother and father to the shop every day, and for the most part slept peacefully in a Moses basket in the office.

Catriona was incensed by this plan. Secretly she'd hoped to have full charge of the infant, Florric being past coping with a young baby, and Dorothy and her doctor husband fully occupied running a large house in the country filled to overflowing with evacuees and Bootless Bairns.

'I wonder at you, exposing a poor wee bairn to such dangers, Ishbel!' Catriona sniffed.

Ishbel laughed and hugged her mother. 'Nonsense, Mam! He's safe as houses with us. Whenever the siren goes, he's whisked down to the basement. I get the impression the wee rascal loves all the attention. Anyway, you have your hands full running the house and queueing for rations, not to mention doing your bit with the WVS.'

Catriona was silent. It was true. She had joined the

Women's Voluntary Service and helped in a forces' canteen, though it left her very little spare time. Florrie wasn't fit and servants no longer available, so the work of keeping house fell upon Catriona. Eleanor was too elderly to be of much assistance apart from a little dusting. The old lady was in a great state of nerves since Local Defence Volunteers had commandeered the lodge, which had a fine view of the crossroads. Eleanor was convinced they stored guns and high explosive shells in there and Knoxhall House and its occupants were in danger of being blown sky high. She had challenged the commanding officer on the subject and received a rueful reply. 'Och, wifie, I only wish we had explosives, instead o' one Boer War rifle an' a couple o' pikes!'

Although Catriona continued to grumble about the danger to the baby during the first freezing winter of the war, Ishbel stood firmly by her decision, much to the secret delight of Matthew and Elspeth; they could spend time with Ryan at odd moments during the working day.

Elspeth found the baby's presence a solace, for she could not settle to work in the shop. Nearly every aspect of the retail business irked her. She was impatient with long, wearisome hours spent standing behind counters, smiling, always smiling, even when your feet ached. Then there were shortages and empty shelves, as the German blockade and attacks on convoys took effect. Customers grumbled in consequence, good-natured complaints for the most part, but quite enough to try Elspeth's small store of patience. She was responsible for the large notice which appeared one day in the tearoom, causing a considerable stir of indignation. Ishbel hid a smile at her daughter's down-to-earth approach to a wartime problem.

'Tearoom customers who wish to use the Shelter in the event of an alarm, kindly inform their waitress, who will present the bill immediately.'

'Well, why should they sneak out without paying, just because there's a raid on?' argued Elspeth.

She endured life in the shop throughout that long, hard winter, but often, as she lifted Ryan from the Moses basket and sat rocking him on her knee, Elspeth made plans to get away. Her acting career must wait until after the war, but she longed to do something worthwhile to bring that moment closer.

Ryan was nearly six months old when the first hint of spring warmed the air at last. He had graduated to a large wooden cot which was kept in a corner of Ishbel's office. He could sleep there or play with his toys and watch all that was going on. A pram was stored downstairs, and there were always volunteers to take him out for a breath of fresh air. He was a good baby, blessed with Ishbel's dark curly hair and Matthew's roguish grin. Sometimes, as Ryan lay playing with his toys Ishbel was surprised by his strong resemblance to her father. It was a likeness that delighted her. 'Ryan, you'll no' go far wrong if you take after your grandpa,' she told him.

He gave a gappy grin, then began chuckling and kicking his feet in the air: a sure sign Elspeth had come into the office. 'Are you busy, Mam? Could I have a word?' she asked.

Ishbel laid down her pen. 'What is it, love?'

Elspeth crossed over to the baby, leaning over the bars of the cot. She put a hand down to him, and he grabbed it, trying to pull himself up. 'I've decided to join up,' Elspeth said.

'Elspeth, you don't have to!' Ishbel protested in dismay. 'You're needed here. If they start conscripting women you could apply for exemption.'

Her daughter lifted the baby out of the cot, kissing and cuddling him as if gathering strength from his innocent wee face. 'Mam, you don't understand. I've thought long and hard about this. You have Matthew to help you now, and I'm not really needed here. Besides, to be honest, I'll never make a shop-keeper. I went along to the ATS recruiting centre yesterday and offered to do my bit for the war effort. They were delighted to have me, and said I could begin basic training as soon as I liked.'

'Oh, Elspeth!' Ishbel said brokenly. All her young ones in the forces now!

Elspeth kissed Ryan's round, pink cheek. 'I'll miss you, my wee one!' she told him tearfully. Sensing troubled times ahead for his big sister, Ryan opened his mouth and yelled.

Elspeth left a few weeks later to join her unit some-where in England, and that signalled more changes in Alexander's. The most heart-warming was Doris's return to the workroom after a successful cataract operation. Matthew and Ishbel had paid for it to be done by a specialist in the field, and Doris was back at work with her sight restored, adapting austerity fashions with her usual flair. That success helped cheer Ishbel after the departure of her daughter.

All the younger men on the staff who had passed fit were conscripted to the army. The greatest blow came one fine spring morning, when the elevator manager appeared in Ishbel's office, looking resolute. 'I got my call-up papers, ma'am,' Archie told her. 'I've to report to Fort George in two weeks' time. I'm to be in the Cameron Highlanders.'

She was shaken by this news, for Archie had blossomed remarkably well since promotion, and become one of the pillars of the firm. His patient wife Katie had done much to overcome Archie's disability, and he now had enough skill in reading, writing and arithmetic to get by. He had confided to Ishbel he was looking forward to learning more when his little son reached school age, so that he could keep one jump ahead of the lad.

'Oh, Archie, I thought they wouldn't take you. You're quite indispensable!' Ishbel cried.

'Och, nobody's that!' he laughed, then paused for a moment. 'Would you and Mr Clark keep an eye on Katie and the bairn for me, ma'am? She has nobody of her ain to see to her, and she wants to volunteer for factory work while I'm awa'. My granny has offered to look after the bairn when Katie's working. I wasnae keen at first, but maybe it's a good enough idea. The work'll keep Kate frae fretting.'

'Don't you worry, Archie, we'll see to them,' Ishbel promised.

'One thing,' he said thoughtfully, 'I'm no' bandy-legged, thank God. I'll look no' too bad in the kilt!'

Wotherspoon was surprised to find his popularity had risen dramatically, now U-boats were preying upon convoys and shelves in food shops were emptying fast. City dwellers came hopefully to the farm seeking eggs, butter and cream. Some of them would almost go down on their knees to him, begging tearfully for half a dozen fresh eggs and a wee pat of farm butter.

It was one of the finest springs Wotherspoon could remember, though in the war zone the year had begun with disasters, and seemed set to go on in that vein. Hitler's armies had invaded Norway and Denmark, walked into Holland and Belgium with comparative ease, defeated France and swept the British Expeditionary Force in disarray on to the Dunkirk beaches. It was thanks to a flotilla of brave wee boats that most of the weary, defeated army escaped across the Channel to fight another day.

'Aye weel, we ken where we stand noo, Mr Wotherspoon, no allies to bother aboot, just us,' remarked Wotherspoon's trusty old bailie, cheerfully forking muck in the byre. 'Mind you, we've to mind oot for invasion. They're sayin' in the pub there'll be Jerry parachutists floating down from the sky dressed as nuns.'

'Och, nuns'll stand oot like sair thumbs in this parish,' grunted Wotherspoon. He didn't give much credence to the invasion scare sweeping the country just now. The gentlemanly Neville Chamberlain had made way for that renowned battler, Winston Churchill, and the farmer could sense a change of heart and toughening of sinew.

The popular theme abroad in the beleaguered land was 'Dig For Victory', and Wotherspoon was allotted half a dozen Land Army girls to make up a work force sadly depleted by conscription. Joanna had already volunteered for the Women's Land Army, and was delighted to be joined on the farm by six companions. These were girls from all backgrounds, but Joanna took an instant liking to one, a Glasgow townie called Ruby Reid.

Ruby was big and cheery, her eyes sparkled with fun and her red cheeks glowed as brightly as her name. Nothing could dampen Ruby's spirits, not even knocking muck along the furrows in the chilly early morning light, a longstanding, wearisome task which was loathed by the other girls. 'Doesn't this get you down, Ruby?' groaned Joanna, leaning wearily on the fork as they followed the lurching muck-cart.

'No fear! I intend to stay firmly up, with this stuff lying around,' declared Ruby, knocking an unpleasant heap neatly into the furrow. She gave Joanna a shrewd glance. 'When is your RAF lover-boy due for leave, Jo? He seemed very keen last time. I was tempted to throw a bucket o' cold water over him!'

Joanna sighed, bending her back to the task. 'I'm keen on Adrian, but the trouble is he has an identical twin brother, Ruby, and I'm keen on him, too. I hardly know which to choose.'

Ruby paused, startled. 'You don't mean to tell me there's two like Sergeant Big-head?'

Joanna laughed. 'Only in looks, dear. Brian is quite different in temperament.'

'Well, thank heaven for small mercies!' breathed Ruby, getting on with the job.

As the two young women worked their way down the drill, Joanna's thoughts turned to Brian. She had not seen him for months, and though he wrote friendly, non-committal letters to her, she knew his voyages were long and dangerous. She prayed that he would be kept safe, and would come home soon. If only I could see Brian again, she thought, perhaps I could decide which twin it is I really love.

Fredrika considered herself fortunate to obtain a nearly new outfit from Beany's barrow that beautiful summer.

Beany's clientele had been swelled by many well-to-do customers who sneaked furtively across the bridges, but Fredrika, as a regular, had her pick of the good stuff. The outfit cost two precious shillings, but was well worth it. It was warm pink with a neat white collar.

'Pink makes the boys wink,' remarked Feemie.

'It will not make the bobby wink. The man's heart is marble,' declared Fredrika grimly.

'Och away! The bobby must have a soft spot for ye, or he'd have had you put behind barbed wire along wi' a' the other foreigners.'

'That would be better than reporting every Friday,' grumbled Fredrika. 'Papa Rizzio tells me there is a big ship called the *Arandora Star* leaving soon for Canada with interned Germans and Italians on board. If the bobby had a soft spot, I would be on it, sailing far away from the Alexanders.'

This was a sore point with Feemie, and she looked sour. 'Well, if you won't tell the police who your pa was, what can you expect?' she said, her face scarlet as she doggedly ironed sheets that hot June day.

'Why should I tell? Mrs Alexander has another husband and another baby. I will never be welcome there, Feemie.'

Feemie folded the dazzling white sheet in silence. The lassie was quite right. She'd missed her chance.

Feemie heaved a sigh. Everything was changing now that the war was on. There were fewer working men to fill Feemie's lodgings because they were all away to the Forces. Those that were left behind were too fussy by far. For instance, there had been a mild rebellion that morning over scrambled eggs made with dried egg. Feemie picked up the offending packet and put it on the shelf. 'Egg, whole egg, an' nothin' but egg. Some folk dinna ken when they're weel aff,' she muttered. She glanced at the clock. 'You'd better away to the cafe, lovie. You're late.'

Dressed in the new pink outfit, Fredrika stepped out. It was a beautiful day, a day to forget war and the random raids which frightened everyone. The cold stone pavement felt warm for once beneath Fredrika's white peep-toe sandals, and she felt young, pretty and light-hearted that lovely summer morning.

She heard the strange noise for the first time as she turned the corner. It was an oddly menacing sound which she'd heard before somewhere. She frowned as she tried to remember.

The noise varied, sometimes loud, then sinking to barely a murmur. It sent a shiver down Fredrika's back. She looked around anxiously, but the street was quiet, quite deserted. Somehow the absence of people made her afraid. It was not right; usually she was greeted right and left by friendly faces, women leaning on the window sills, looking out. There was nobody to be seen, today.

The noise began again, closer, a growling sound rising to a roar. Fredrika stopped, the lovely summer day had suddenly grown evil and threatening. She had gone icy cold with terror, for she recognised the sounds now. She had heard them the night her mother and Vati were taken, and they were the sounds of hatred and of violence. Fredrika began running towards the scene. She ran desperately, hoping she was wrong, knowing instinctively she was not.

Racing round the corner, she found herself on the edge of an angry crowd surrounding the Rizzios' shop.

'Shut their shop! We dinna want enemies in our midst,' somebody shouted, and there was a roar of approval.

'No!' gasped Fredrika. She couldn't believe it. She knew Papa and Mama Rizzio had lived happily in Edinburgh for many years and were British citizens. They were kind people, and little Pia would not harm a fly. It made no sense. She turned fiercely on a woman standing near. 'Why do they do this terrible thing?'

The woman studied Fredrika apprehensively. 'Did you no' hear on the news a wee while back that Mussolini has joined up wi' Hitler? The Italians are his allies, and some of these folk have lost sons and husbands in the war. You canna blame them for wanting the Italian shops closed doon. Best stay out o' this, lassie. They'll have the Rizzios oot o' there, and there's little you can do about it.'

'No, you are wrong. There is much I can do!' cried Fredrika furiously. She pushed her way through the crowd, shoving and using her elbows to good effect where necessary. When she reached the shop window, she turned and faced the angry mob. 'You will stop this nonsense at once!' she ordered them.

Her sudden appearance startled the unruly mob into silence. Somebody whispered, 'Hey, that's the lassie who works in their shop.'

'She's an alien, too! A Jerry,' a woman cried, and such a menacing uproar broke out that Fredrika could not make herself heard. At last, a more urgent cry came filtering from the rear. 'Watch oot! Here comes the polis!'

For once in her life, Fredrika welcomed the arrival of police. Her heart lurched then raced faster as she recognised one of the policemen. She smiled radiantly and waved. 'Bobby! I prayed you would come!'

The crowd had begun melting away as the squad of police officers approached, but one grief-stricken woman picked up a stone and sent it flying erratically through the air, aimed at the shop window. Murray Gibson saw the danger, and shouted. 'Fredrika, look out!'

Fredrika was so relieved the nasty incident was over she had started to run towards her rescuers, and the shouted warning came too late. She ran straight into the path of the flying missile, which caught her squarely on the temple and sent her crashing to the ground.

For a horrified second, Murray couldn't move, then he raced forward and knelt beside the motionless young woman. He took her limp hand in his. 'Fredrika?' She was unconscious, a trickle of blood running down her cheek. He hardly dared touch her in case he made the head injury worse. Quickly, he stripped off his jacket and laid it tenderly over her for the pavement was cold beneath his knees, and her pink dress was of fine silk which clung softly to her slim figure. He remained there beside her, until an ambulance arrived, and Fredrika was lifted gently aboard.

Chapter 21

While Elspeth was engaged in basic training with the ATS, Ishbel and Matthew struggled to maintain high standards under wartime conditions. It was not easy, with the character of Alexander's so drastically changed by enemy action. The glass dome, which had been a feature of the shop, had been repaired, but Matthew had decided it must be boarded up for safety's sake. Ishbel found the resulting gloom depressing, the main shopping area lit only by a few meagre light bulbs for economy's sake. She and Clara did what they could to cheer the scene with draperies and hangings in rich colours. Customers appreciated their efforts and there were no complaints, though there were plenty of grumbles on the home front, Ishbel found.

At breakfast that morning, Catriona curled up her nose. 'I canna stand this National wholemeal bread. Will you just look at the colour of it! Dirty grey. I'd be ashamed to bake bread like that. As for the wee scrape of margarine, that's whale oil, and tastes like it.'

'There's a terrible shortage of wheat, Mam. It'll maybe improve after harvest,' Ishbel said, spooning porridge into Ryan's eager little mouth.

Catriona sighed. 'There's a terrible shortage of everything. Four ounces o' bacon, butter an' sugar a week, doled out on points from your ration book and not much more than two shillings worth o' beef. That's not enough to feed a wee mouse.'

Matthew was opening the mail, but he glanced up. 'Atlantic convoys are doing their best to bring in supplies, Catriona, but I guess it's mighty hazardous with U-boats around.'

Ishbel shuddered. 'Especially on an oil tanker.'

Eleanor slipped a sly piece of bacon to the dogs beneath the table. It was difficult feeding hungry pets these days. 'I'm down on my poor old rheumatic knees every night praying for Elspeth and those laddies,' she said. 'Thank God, Brian's been lucky so far, and Adrian's safe, working away at something secret.'

Ishbel's attention turned to her husband. His expression had changed, and he frowned as he slowly re-read the letter in his hand. She wiped the baby's milky chin. 'Matthew, what is it, my dear?'

He looked up. 'Fighter Command's impressed by the performance of Spitfires in defence of Rosyth and the Forth, Ishbel. They say German pilots have named this area "Suicide Corner", and I'm wanted down south to have a word on the siting of squadrons and ack-ack batteries in the light of what we learned up here. I figure they're expecting an attack on London any day, and they aim to be ready.'

Her heart quickened with fright. 'Darling, if they bomb London you could be in danger. How long will you stay?'

'I don't know,' replied Matthew soberly. 'It could be a month, or it could be longer, it all depends. American coastal shipping's been attacked by U-boats, and the feeling is America will be forced into the war sooner or later. That means more bases in Britain for US planes, and more work for me.'

'Oh, Matthew! When will this madness end?'

Ishbel struggled not to cry, because the baby sensed emotional upsets, but Ryan's lower lip was already quivering ominously, and Ishbel hugged him reassuringly. The pattern of life had not changed. One by one her loved ones were being taken from her. *Perhaps it's a judgement on me for sending Freddie's daughter away so harshly,* Ishbel thought sadly. She had never ceased to rue the day she'd refused to help the poor, scared refugee.

Matthew lifted his son out of the highchair. 'You look after your mammy while your dad's away, Junior. I'm countin' on you, mind.'

Ryan gurgled with delight and solemnly tweaked Matthew's nose.

Fredrika's mind drifted in a confused state as she lay semi-conscious in hospital. Faces floated before her, dear Mama and Vati, arms round one another, smiling at her lovingly. She knew she would never see them again, and the bright faces faded into dimness. She called out to them, sobbing pitifully. A voice said, 'Steady, girl!' and a hand held hers. A strong hand, a man's hand. Fredrika hung on for grim death.

'The police shall not take me away!'

Somebody laughed close by. 'No chance, Fredrika. You know what they say about the Leith police?'

'No. What?' The conversation was baffling, but she was curious.

'The Leith police dismisseth us. Go on. Say it,' urged the voice.

Fredrika mustered her wandering thoughts. 'The Leith poleeth . . . dithmisses uth—'

Another voice spoke in a lower tone, a woman's voice. 'That's encouraging. She's coming round nicely. No brain damage, I think.'

Brain damage? Her head felt odd, tightly bound and restricted. The feeling frightened her. What had happened? She couldn't remember. Fredrika struggled to raise a hand to her brow, but her arm seemed weighted with lead. Her fingers encountered bandages, and then it all came back in a rush. The Rizzios! Her eyes shot open and she struggled up in panic. 'Stop them! The Rizzios are good. They are kind,' she shouted.

The light in the small, white room was too bright. It pierced her eyes like needles. Her head throbbed and the room spun, whirling her round, driving her into a man's comforting arms. She hung on, spinning wildly out of control, but the arms steadied her. The room gradually righted and darkened, and a nurse came into view bending over her.

Fredrika smiled weakly, though it was painful. 'Leith police dismisseth us,' she repeated carefully.

The nurse patted her hand. 'Very good, love. Now, no more gymnastics while I go and report to the doctor. Promise?'

Fredrika nodded. That hurt too. She nestled into the warmth of the supporting arms. She felt safe and protected from harm there. It was the same feeling she'd had when crouched in the hidey-hole Vati had made for her in the coal bunker, that good man's last gift of freedom to the girl who had been like a beloved daughter to him.

She felt pleasant warmth against her cheek. Opening her eyes cautiously, she saw for the first time the man who held her so close, his unshaven cheeks resting against hers.

'It is the bobby!' she groaned. So, she had not escaped. He was still watching and questioning. 'What happened?' she asked dully.

'You walked into a stone intended for the Rizzios' shop window. You've had severe concussion and a hairline skull fracture, and have been out cold for nearly forty-eight hours,' Murray Gibson told her. He couldn't disguise his relief. Every minute he could spare had been spent at her bedside. He hadn't realised how much she meant to him until the awful moment when he saw her struck down. At times he'd been filled with a terrible fear she would never recover. He had never known fear like it, and now her dark eyes were wide open, he had never experienced such relief. He wanted to hug and kiss her for joy. He wanted . . .

'What happened to the Rizzios?' she demanded, breaking into his thoughts.

'They closed the shop. The family left Edinburgh and went to relatives in Alyth. It's a small, country town, and they'll be happier there.'

She sighed. 'I'm glad for them, but now I have no work.'

'Listen, if you will tell me who your father was, I can help you. I promise I'll be very discreet, Fredrika.'

She lay looking at him speculatively, eyes very dark beneath a white cap of bandages. 'Shall we make bargains?' she said. 'I will tell you the name if you will agree not to speak to my relatives, and promise to arrange passage for me on board the ship that leaves soon for Canada.'

461

He hesitated. Canada! If she went to Canada, he might never see her again. It was a desolate thought, but for her sake he struggled to remain detached. The *Arandora Star* was due to sail for Canada, and a passage could easily be arranged for Fredrika. She could make a fresh start, and perhaps that was best for her. He made up his mind. 'Very well, Fredrika. It will be done, I promise you.'

Fredrika lay back with a contented smile. After weeks of reporting to the bobby, she had learned to trust his word.

'Frederick Alexander was my father.' It was a relief to say it, the end of a long battle with the past, a new beginning.

He stared at her, amazed. 'You mean, from Alexander's, the big store?'

'Yes, but my father's family do not want to know me, Bobby. You must promise never to tell them where I am.' She was growing drowsy, her voice dropping to a sleepy murmur. 'It is beautiful, my father's shop, with lovely dresses and nice things, Bobby, but my pink dress from Beany's barrow is lovely too, and cost two shillings. Pink makes boys wink, you know.' Fredrika yawned and curled up like a child, drifting into a deep, natural sleep.

Murray Gibson stood for a long time staring down at her, then leaned over and gently kissed her cheek in farewell.

Alone again! Ishbel thought in despair. She and Ryan had watched Matthew leave that morning on the London Express, then they had returned to the shop. Carrying the little one in her arms, Ishbel stood in the doorway of the office and wondered where she would find the strength to carry on. 'You did it before, my lass!' she told herself sternly.

But I was younger then, and welcomed hard work, she thought. Now I'm in my forties, sick of war and difficulties and shortages. I want to take life easy and watch Matthew's son grow.

With a sigh, she entered her office and put Ryan in his playpen. He immediately howled in protest, hauled himself up and stood shakily, hanging on to the bars and screaming. Ishbel sighed again, in defeat. She'd get little work done with that din going on, and she knew perfectly well what the little rascal wanted. He wanted to rove around freely.

'OK, have it your own way,' she said resignedly, lifting him out.

Ryan stopped yelling and beamed, then he was off exploring, crawling at high speed. Ishbel checked the office for hazards, then settled down at her desk. The baby played happily, emptying the wastepaper basket of all its interesting rubbish while Ishbel became absorbed in her own paperwork. There was much more of it now everything was rationed and scarce, and she forgot about the baby as she wrestled with allowances of tea, sugar and milk doled out to restaurants under Lord Woolton's decree.

After a while, an unnatural silence alerted her and she looked up. 'Ryan?'

No sound. Ishbel rose hastily and glanced round the room. A tiny gap in the partition between the two offices told its own story. It was just wide enough for a determined baby to creep through. 'Ryan!' she shouted in panic.

He wasn't in the other office, but the door was ajar, and she ran to it in terror, remembering the steep stairs leading down to the landing. Reaching the corridor, Ishbel froze. The baby had crawled to the top of the flight of stairs, and was poised there, pondering how best to tackle this new challenge. Ishbel screamed. 'Ryan, no!'

Her warning shout startled him. He tried to turn, lost his balance, and before Ishbel could move, the baby had gone rolling and bumping out of sight. She raced to the top and looked down, then clung to the bannisters, feeling sick and faint. Ryan had rolled a few feet, but was quite unhurt, scooped up in Adrian's arms.

Immediate reaction set in, and Ishbel burst into tears. Adrian bounded upstairs, his small half-brother in his arms. 'Hey, steady on, Mam!'

'Oh, Adrian, I took my eyes off the bairn for five minutes and he could have died!'

'But he didn't,' said Adrian gently.

He put his free arm across his mother's shoulders and led her into the office. Ishbel collapsed gratefully into a chair. Adrian placed Ryan firmly in the playpen. 'Sit, boy!' he ordered, wagging a finger. 'Now, stay!' Ryan gaped in awe, stuck a thumb in his mouth and did not utter another squeak.

Adrian smiled airily. 'That's a trick I learned from Joanna when she was training her collie pup. It seems to work.'

Ishbel was recovering from her fright, mopping her eyes. She hadn't been aware he was seeing so much of Joanna Wotherspoon. 'You're friendly with Joanna?' she asked.

'More than friendly. I'm crazy about her,' he admitted. 'I love outdoor girls in breeches and big muddy boots. There's something awfully appealing about them.'

Ishbel's heart was aching for Brian's sake. She knew he had loved Joanna faithfully for years. If she chose Adrian, Brian would be devastated. 'So you're courting

Wotherspoon's daughter. What does Wotherspoon have to say about that?'

He looked uncomfortable. 'Oh, he's coming round to the idea. Slowly.'

Adrian had already crossed swords with Grumpy. By misfortune, they had met at the edge of a turnip field ruined when the dairy herd stampeded, having been alarmed by Adrian's aerial stunts.

'Good afternoon, sir. Nice day,' Adrian had greeted him politely.

Wotherspoon scowled. 'I'm glad you think so. Look at my neeps.'

Adrian surveyed the sorry sight morosely. 'You'll be pleased to learn you had your revenge, Mr Wotherspoon. I'm grounded for good.'

'Aye, I'm pleased to hear it,' the farmer growled. Wotherspoon narrowed his eyes and stared into the far distance. 'By the by, you seem awfy keen on my lass.'

'I've asked Joanna to marry me. She's considering it,' replied Adrian boldly.

Wotherspoon glanced at him. 'Oh aye? And what about the other lad?'

'Brian? He's far away at sea.'

'Then I'd advise Joanna to hold her horses till he's back.'

The farmer prepared to go on his way, then paused. 'Mind you, my daughter will go her own way, no matter what. Joanna will make up her own mind, and when she does, nothing on this earth will change it. I'm just warnin' ye, my lad.' For an instant Wotherspoon's keen eyes had twinkled humorously, and Adrian had almost liked the man.

Ryan remained quiet and well-behaved, obviously none

the worse for his escapade, and Ishbel wondered what had brought Adrian to the store at that opportune moment. 'Do you have a spot of leave, dear?' she asked hopefully.

''Fraid not.' He perched on the edge of the desk. 'I just popped in to tell you I've been posted to Arbroath, on loan to the Marines. The old kitbag is downstairs with Cathy, and I'm actually on my way to the station. That's all I can tell you, Mam.'

'Hush-hush?'

'You bet. German U-boats would be shivering wrecks if they knew.'

Ishbel laid a hand anxiously on her son's arm. 'But you won't be in danger, will you, love?'

His expression became suddenly bleak. 'It's a desk job, and there's absolutely no risks attached, Mam,' he assured her.

Completely recovered from the head injury, Fredrika was preparing to leave Britain any day now. The hardest part had been telling Feemie she was going, but Feemie, surprisingly, had made no comment apart from a few expressive sniffs. Wait until she saw the pouch overflowing with shillings, though! Fredrika thought, hugging herself in delight. Then Feemie's slate would be wiped clean of debt, with interest added.

For the formal presentation, Fredrika chose the cosy hour she spent every evening in the kitchen with Feemie. Feemie was stewing tealeaves she'd saved from breakfast, but looked up with interest when her lodger came in with her hands held behind her back. 'What you got there?'

'It is very big surprise for you, Feemie.'

'It's half a dozen eggs!' exclaimed Feemie, her eyes

gleaming. The ration was one egg per person per fortnight, and was hard to bear.

'No, it is better.' Fredrika produced the pouch with a flourish and poured all the shillings on to the kitchen table in front of Feemie in a jingling, silver heap. 'There!' she cried proudly. 'It is payment for all your kindness. Now the slate will be clean.' It was strange; Fredrika had expected to feel wonderfully happy, but this was like the sad ending of a good chapter in her life, and brought only grief.

Feemie hadn't moved. She sat frozen, staring at the shining heap. Then came the most dreadful sound Fredrika had ever heard, a dry, creaking noise as Feemie's leathery heart finally softened and broke, the pain of the heartbreak bursting from her in an agonised howl. She took her large fist and swept it furiously right and left, sending the money flying off the table to fall clattering in a rain of silver coins, on to the floor. 'You think I want your siller?'

Fredrika turned pale. 'B-but, Feemie, the ticks. The slate—'

Feemie lumbered unsteadily to her feet and pulled open the drawer. She dragged out the slate and flung it on to the table with a crash. 'Look at it. Go on!' she shouted.

Terrified, Fredrika looked. She couldn't understand what she saw. She stared and stared, then looked up slowly at Feemie. 'It is clean,' she said in a small, bewildered voice.

'Aye, it's clean,' Feemie sank down on the chair and stared at Fredrika. 'My God, lassie, when will you understand? You're the only person on God's earth that's ever loved me. You gave me wealth I never knew. I wiped the slate clean months ago. Oh, Fredrika, I dinna want your money, I only want you to bide!' With a forlorn wail,

Feemie buried her face on her arms. Her heartrending sobs were all the more painful, because she was so sadly out of practice.

With a cry, Fredrika ran to her friend. She stretched her arms round Feemie and rested her cheek against her grey hair. Holding Feemie in her arms, Fredrika felt as if her own heart had broken. She was young, she would work hard in Canada, and she would survive and maybe even prosper, but what of Feemie's future as she grew old and sad in the Grassmarket with all the working men gone and nobody to love her? She gently kissed the sternly regimented grey curls on Feemie's temple. 'Feemie, don't cry any more. I will tell Bobby I will not go on the ship. I will bide with you, and take my chances.'

Feemie looked up with sudden hope. 'You'll bide?'

'I promise. Only – don't cry.'

The landlady fumbled for a hanky and blew her nose. 'Och away, I wasna greetin' at all, it's just this damn cold in the heid.'

'And you will take the money?' persisted Fredrika.

Feemie looked sheepish. 'Och, it seems a pity to refuse the good siller right enough, lovie, when it's so kindly meant.' She took Fredrika's hand in her work-worn fists, and the radiant smile she bestowed upon her beloved lodger transformed Feemie's stern, homely features to something approaching beauty.

Heavy air attacks on London began in earnest in September, and listening to accounts of the Blitz, on the wireless, Ishbel knew no peace from that moment on. Matthew was in the thick of it, and so was Elspeth, who was stationed somewhere on the outskirts of London. For days on end

Ishbel would hear no word from Matthew as relentless destruction cut normal lines of communication, then there would be a hurried phonecall from her husband.

'I'm OK, honey,' Matthew assured her. 'When I need to recharge my batteries after helping with rescue work, I sleep safely in an underground bunker, courtesy of the Air Ministry. When I'm not working out how we can hit back, I'm down in the Underground trying to organise some comfort for Londoners crowded in there.'

Ishbel was not reassured. She read between the lines and knew Matthew was taking risks. Eleanor, always an avid radio fan, listened in to the gloating tones of William Joyce, nicknamed Lord Haw-haw, and it was hard to discount his extravagant claims of victory in Europe and destruction all over Britain.

Eleanor was not impressed, however. 'Did you ever hear such blethers?' the old lady would snort, switching over indignantly to Tommy Handley's *ITMA* to enjoy a good laugh.

Meanwhile, Edinburgh did not escape attack. On a peaceful early Sunday morning in late September, a bomb fell squarely upon the Caledonian Distillery, starting a blaze in the whisky store. Crowds, evacuated hastily from their nearby homes, were forced to watch the mournful sight of many gallons of the national spirit going up in spectacular fashion as flames leaped hundreds of feet into the Edinburgh sky.

Sneak raids continued less frequently throughout another harsh winter, but Catriona was in her element during the severe weather, cheerfully dishing out warmth and comfort in the shape of tea and sandwiches to soldiers and civilians alike, in the WVS canteen. She did what she could to help her daughter in the shop and care for her small grandson, but mostly Ishbel struggled on alone.

Ryan was a lively handful now, toddling around. He had graduated from the cumbersome apparatus required for small babies into a Mickey Mouse gas mask, which he thought great fun. Ryan's boundless curiosity took him into anything in the store that could be opened or manipulated by dextrous little fingers, and Ishbel was forced to watch him every moment of the day. Even so, her determination to keep the child by her side was as fierce as ever.

Matthew came home after an anxious spell in April and May 1941; attacks on London had reached new ferocity, then began tapering off as the Battle of Britain was won in the air. Ishbel rushed into her husband's arms with relief. 'Oh, darling, they've just announced they're to introduce clothes rationing. That's the last straw. If you hadn't come home I think I would have given up.'

He kissed her tenderly. 'Not you. You'd have coped.'

She tugged eagerly at his arm. 'Wait until you see your bairn. He's wonderful, thriving on cod liver oil and rose hip syrup and National dried milk.'

'Of course he's wonderful! See what handsome parents he's got,' declared Matthew proudly.

Next day, after Ryan had greeted with interest the tall stranger who was his father, then settled obediently for a nap, Ishbel linked an arm through Matthew's as they walked in the garden of Knoxhall House. The scene on that pleasant Sunday afternoon was very different from pre-war days; Eleanor had generously decided to hand over the extensive grounds to those who wished to dig for victory, and the lawns, rose gardens and kitchen garden had been divided eagerly into small allotments tended by folk who had no land of their own. Neat rows of vegetables and drills of potatoes stretched away on either side of the path.

'Will you have to go back again, darling?' Ishbel asked anxiously. Matthew looked thin and tired after all he'd been through.

'I guess not. Unless America is dragged into the war, of course.'

'Is that likely?'

He shrugged. 'It's possible.' Matthew didn't want to talk about war. He'd seen the horror of it at first hand in the London Blitz, and the memory of destruction and carnage would stay with him for the rest of his life. He longed for peace, but then, didn't everyone?

'I met Elspeth,' he said. 'We had lunch together in a little hotel in Richmond. She's working with an ack-ack unit, doing a good job tracking enemy aeroplanes.'

'Oh, Matt, how was she?' Ishbel asked eagerly.

He laughed. 'Hungry. I gave the waiter a wink, and somehow the good guy produced second helpings for her!' He paused, wondering how his wife would take his next piece of news. 'She's been acting again, honey. They gave her a part in the Easter army revue, and she was a wow. One of the big theatrical agents has offered to find her all the work she can handle, after the war.'

Ishbel watched keen gardeners tending their tiny plots. Her attitude to life had changed since war disrupted everything. If Elspeth had talent, then she must exploit it, even if that meant there was no future for the family firm. 'I'm glad she has a promising career lined up,' Ishbel said quietly. 'But you know, Matthew, I often think about Freddie's other daughter. I wonder where she is, and what she's doing. I wonder if she's happy. It would be good to find her, but I don't know where to start.'

Fredrika was highly delighted. She hummed to herself as she hurried along to report at Police Headquarters on Friday afternoon. Now the police knew her background the need for Fredrika to report as an alien had been relaxed, but she still continued to visit Police Headquarters. It had become a habit, and she would miss talking to Murray. They met often, and not always in his office. They had walked in Edinburgh and talked and laughed together, and she had allowed him to hold her hand. Once he had almost kissed her, but she would not permit that, although she had wanted his kiss very badly. There was no future in kissing her, for him. He was a bobby, ambitious to rise high in the police force, and she was nobody at all, and would hold him back socially.

She had good news today, though. Tapping discreetly on the door of his office, she went in. He was alone, and his expression was so grim and tight-lipped she felt tender and loving towards him. She crossed the room and planted a kiss on the pursed mouth. 'Bobby, I have news. I have a job!'

He smiled and reached for her. 'Good for you! What is it?'

She jouked neatly out of range. 'It is in engineering works. I am to be a welder.'

'A welder!' He couldn't help laughing, though it was no laughing matter. That was hard, hot, dangerous work for a woman.

'I don't know what is funny,' she said severely. 'Working men have gone to be soldiers, so I learn to weld. What is funny in that?'

He straightened his face. 'Nothing, Fredrika. It's a very worthwhile job, I just wish you'd found something easier, that's all.'

'Life is never easy. It would have been just as hard for me in Canada.'

Murray was silent for a moment. 'Fredrika, I have something to tell you,' he said gravely. 'I just heard that the *Arandora Star* was torpedoed some time ago. There was heavy loss of life amongst the internees aboard.'

She stared at him in horror as the full implication of the sinking dawned on her. 'Oh, Murray! If Feemie had not begged me to bide, then perhaps, maybe—'

'I could have lost you forever, my dear little love,' he said quietly.

The nine o'clock news on 7th December 1941 dealt another shattering blow to Ishbel's peace of mind, for it carried the announcement of an unprovoked attack by Japanese planes on the American Fleet in Pearl Harbor. She turned to Matthew. 'This will bring America into the war, won't it?'

'I guess so,' he nodded.

Catriona was knitting khaki socks for the Forces, her busy needles clicking. 'That'll mean an end to Polly's food parcels, I suppose. They've been a perfect godsend,' she sighed. Catriona's thoughts circled around food these days. Rationing and Lord Woolton's price controls made everything scarce, and sometimes she was at her wits' end to feed the family. Polly Clark's parcels had arrived from America at intervals, containing such luxuries as tinned ham, dried fruit, the inevitable Spam, and on one occasion a mysterious drink called Instant Postum, to which Eleanor had taken a strong fancy. The old lady had grown thin and spare. Catriona suspected her friend of starving herself to feed her dogs. Although the loss of the elderly Foxglove had caused Eleanor much grief recently, it had been a relief to Catriona when the little dog was laid to rest in the orchard. Foxglove's son Foxtrot was still lively and provided consolation, while wallowing happily in his mistress's undivided attention.

'The Christmas pudding's safe, anyway,' Catriona said aloud. 'I got a grand recipe from the Gas Council. It's breadcrumbs, flour and dried egg, then Polly's dried fruit, prunes, marmalade, carrots and grated potato, then you add treacle, or a wee tickie golden syrup and gravy browning, and mix it all up wi' lemon squash.'

'Sounds an absolutely revolting mixture, dear. I'm sure it'll be delicious,' said Eleanor comfortably.

While America prepared for outright war that festive season, Polly was facing up to her own future. Without Elspeth, the Hollywood studios didn't want to know her. That wasn't unexpected. She sold the sumptuous house she'd bought in the days of stardom and moved into a more modest apartment while she considered her next move.

Being Polly, and honest to the core, she took a mirror into the most cruel light she could find, and examined her assets. Fair, plump, and undeniably forty. 'Well, old girl, so much for "it" and "oomph",' she told her reflection cheerfully, 'I guess you got to concentrate on mature glamour, if you want a job.'

Polly had a facial and hairdo, and splashed out on fancy clothes before paying a visit to her agent. He was pleased to

THE ALEXANDER INHERITANCE

see her, shaking hands warmly and seating her with some ceremony, before relaxing behind his desk and giving Polly a long, hard appraisal. 'You know, honey, your outfit's all wrong, if you don' mind my saying so,' he said pleasantly.

Polly was indignant. 'How d'you mean, it's all wrong? I spent nearly a hundred dollars on this stuff, not to mention on the hair an' the face.'

'Forget the glamour. That's not your style, love.' He leaned forward eagerly. 'Listen, Polly. We're at war, right? You can bet your last dollar that when our boys are sent overseas they'll be homesick, missing their wives and girlfriends, missing their moms. That's where you could come in, honey. I guess you don' know it, Polly, but you're everyone's idea of their favourite momsy. One look at you, the toughest GI in the unit will be dreaming of homemade apple pie, an' blubbering.'

'But I can't cook!' wailed Polly.

He slapped his knee and roared with laughter. 'Heck, you don't need to cook, you just look as if you can!' He sobered up. 'Polly, you can sing an' dance real nice, an' you look pretty as a picture even though you're kinda long in the tooth. I've been on the lookout for somebody your age to entertain the troops. There won't be a fortune in it, but you'd be doing your bit for the war effort. What d'you say?' He leaned forward, flatteringly breathless with hopeful anticipation.

Momsy! thought Polly caustically. Well, maybe the guy was right. She'd got nowhere until she'd played a motherly role with Elspeth, whose departure had left a big void in Polly's life. Momsy! Well, there was an irony, she thought. A woman who couldn't have kids of her own, acting mother figure to thousands of homesick GIs. Well, at least she'd be helping those poor young guys. 'OK. When do I start?' Polly said.

The agent relaxed and slid a form across. 'Just sign here, Polly. Oh, by the by, I forgot to mention you might find yourself in the war zone one day, darling,' he warned smoothly.

Sandy's very elderly Clydesdale, Big Bob, had returned to Wotherspoon's pastures some months ago. Bob's paddock in Corstorphine had become too dangerous. Even nearby Edinburgh Zoo had not escaped damage, although fortunately all the animals were safe. The chimpanzees and orang-utans were particularly disturbed, and had kept up an angry screaming and scolding for hours after an air attack damaged their cage. Sandy had decided enough was enough, and evacuated his old friend to the comparative peace and safety of the countryside.

The old horse was a particular favourite of Joanna's. She enjoyed grooming Bob with a dandy brush until he shone. It was a restful occupation, during which the mind could wander. Her friend Ruby usually accompanied her to the stable, though the city lass was no lover of horses. Perched on the ladder leading to the hayloft, Ruby chewed on a straw and watched. 'Penny for your thoughts, Joanna, love. You were miles away,' she remarked.

'So I was,' Joanna laughed. 'I was actually at sea, thinking about Brian.'

'Ah, yes. The wandering sailor I've yet to meet,' Ruby said. 'I'm surprised he even crossed your mind, seeing as how you and Sergeant Big-head are thick as thieves these days.'

She sounded aggrieved, but Joanna didn't notice,

absently brushing the horse's mane. 'Brian hasn't been home for ages, but he writes lovely letters that make me laugh, although I think that where he is, there's very little to laugh about.'

'Love letters?' asked Ruby with interest.

Joanna sighed. 'No, not love letters. You know, Ruby, I've often wondered, why not?'

Brian could have told her why he deliberately kept his letters light and noncommittal. He had been damned lucky, but by the law of averages his luck couldn't last. He'd seen too much destruction and too many shattered lives to have much hope for the future. Ruthlessly, he'd driven all thoughts of love and marriage out of his mind, and lived for the day, no further. He couldn't forget Joanna, but she dwelt as a wistfully beautiful memory of what might have been, a tender spot in his hardened heart which ached painfully when touched.

He'd been on the tanker *San Merino*, based in Canada, until this present trip, their job being to re-fuel escort ships in the mid-Atlantic, but the old vessel had developed engine trouble, and they'd put into port in Halifax. Repairs would take weeks, and Brian found himself transferred with some of his shipmates to another convoy. Brian had been sent as deck officer to the escort vessel *Jessica*, an armed merchantman. It was the largest convoy he had seen so far, fifty slow, lumbering vessels in all, escorted by a destroyer, frigate and four corvettes of the 'grey-funnel line', as the merchantmen nicknamed the Royal Navy. Not to mention the *Jessica* herself, loaded with vital spare parts for Liberator bombers and armed with depth charges and useful guns fore and aft.

In Brian's estimation, the one bright spot upon a

dangerous horizon filled with lurking U-boats, was the fact the ships were heading for Liverpool, and he hadn't set foot on British shores for over three years. He was impressed with improved technology aboard *Jessica* and said so to the skipper. 'You can thank the boffins ashore who've improved radar and asdic,' the skipper said. 'It's not hit and miss now, but a real threat to the subs, and they know it. With luck, we might bring this lot safely into port. God knows, they need the supplies at home.'

Up on the bridge, Brian lifted his binoculars and studied their companions doubtfully. The convoy consisted of the usual flock made up of nine columns about four miles long, vulnerable tankers in the middle rank, the others plodding along at six knots, a safe distance apart, while the escorts swooped anxiously around the perimeter. He shifted the binoculars to the horizon and pursed his lips. The sky didn't look too good. It bore out the weather forecast of nasty weather ahead.

The convoy ran into a storm out at sea forty-eight hours later. Storms were a mixed blessing, Brian had discovered. High seas kept U-boats submerged, and a submerged submarine was a slow and sluggish enemy, easily tracked on the Asdic screen. On the other hand, Canadian Air Force Catalinas operating from Newfoundland could not provide air cover in bad weather to make sure the submarines stayed well under. The sailors nerved themselves to endure conditions which were hard, but preferable to that other deadly menace.

When the wind and the seas moderated, the scattered convoy re-formed, but everyone remained on edge. The skipper took a quick sweep around with the binoculars to discover how the convoy had fared, and he frowned. 'I don't like the look of old *Gertrude*. She's dropped behind more than she ought.' Radio silence was observed for safety's sake, so he glanced at the Signals Officer. 'Give her a flash, will you, Jake?'

The Morse query flashed out, then followed the quick wink of the oil tanker's reply. 'Engine trouble, Skipper. They're trying to fix it,' the Signals Officer reported.

The captain groaned. 'We can't leave her. She's a sitting duck. We'll have to ride shotgun.'

Brian felt his nerves tighten unbearably. The rest of the convoy and the Navy escort would go on, while the two stragglers must do their best to catch up once the tanker's problem was fixed. Safety lay in numbers, and the situation was extremely dangerous for a lone escort and a lame duck.

The grey silhouette of the frigate loomed up to starboard, her signal lamp winking furiously. 'What does she say?' Brian asked.

The skipper laughed. 'She says, "*Jessica*, dear, your ship is slowing."' He turned to the Signals Officer once more. 'Explain the situation, Jake, and ask permission to escort *Gertrude*, will you?'

Once more, swift Morse signals flashed out in response from the frigate's grey mass, before she turned away to resume her watch.

'What now?' asked Brian.

'"God speed and good luck, girls," she says, and by heaven, Brian, we'll need it!' answered the captain grimly.

Chapter 22

The sea seemed empty once the convoy had gone on its slow way, but the crews on the two stragglers knew they lay tossing in a deceptive calm. The escort captain gave Brian a meaningful glance. 'Go see what's on the wireless, Brian. And I only hope it's Tommy Handley.'

Brian left the bridge and went below. The Asdic operator was fine-tuning the transmitter on the hull, ears keenly attuned to changes in the monotonous, pinging sound of underwater echoes. 'The skipper wants to know if you've picked up *ITMA* yet,' Brian remarked.

The operator grinned. 'No such luck. Nothing whatsoever to report, thank God. Tell him he'll be first to know.'

Returned to the bridge once more, Brian relayed the message. There was nothing to do but wait helplessly, engines ticking over as the escort moved in slow patrol around the wallowing tanker. Sounds of hearty hammering drifted across the water, and the captain shuddered. 'What are they doing over there? Don't they realise they could bring the whole wolf pack down on us?'

But as a gloomy pitch darkness fell, it became clear to watchers on the bridge that the U-boat pack had other targets in mind, and somehow, incredibly, *Jessica* and *Gertrude* had slipped through to escape the onslaught. A red glow lighting the sky beyond the far horizon told its own grim story of a fierce attack on the convoy. It was lit intermittently by the clear white light of snowflake flares as the beleaguered escorts attempted to target their enemies, who were lithe and speedy adversaries when upon the surface. Brian watched and listened to the distant echo of explosions with horror. Many of his shipmates were there. The Morse lamp on the *Gertrude* winked briefly. 'OK. Ready to move. Where to, sister?'

The captain glanced at Brian. 'You're a young lad who's been trained to deal with tricky situations, so what do the textbooks say?'

'Blast the textbooks!' answered Brian grimly. 'The wolf pack's attention is centred on the main convoy, which indicates they've been tipped off by the decoders and are lying in wait ahead. My guess is they don't know about us, or they would have picked stragglers off long ago. To save our precious cargoes, my instinct is to steal quietly away from this diversion, head well to the north where we can call up air protection from long-range bombers and the wolves won't gather in numbers because of bad weather. I suggest we change course for Iceland.'

'Live to fight another day, hmm? My sentiments exactly,' said the escort captain, thoughtfully studying the dangerous glow lighting the night sky. He frowned. 'Fuel could be critical, though.'

'Then our navigation better be spot on,' smiled Brian. He felt eager to go, ready to pit his wits against the enemy and the ferocity of the Northern Atlantic. The engines speeded up, thudding more powerfully beneath his feet, echoing a quickened heartbeat. If they made it this time and reached port safely, Brian vowed that nothing on this earth would stop him marrying Joanna Wotherspoon.

Except, possibly, Joanna herself.

Adrian had been lying comfortably in the lee of a haystack, with Joanna resting sleepily beside him. The strange feeling came upon him gradually, ending in a terrible fear that made his heart beat fast and jerked him into a sitting position. Joanna opened her eyes. 'What's the matter?'

'It's Brian! Something awful's happened to Brian. I know it.' Sweat broke out on Adrian's brow. His brother's danger oppressed him. A dark, formless menace bore down on him. Adrian couldn't put a name to it, he only sensed it was there, threatening.

Joanna sat bolt upright in alarm. 'How do you know?'

'I've always known when Brian was in bad trouble. I've always helped. But I can't help him now, Joanna. There's nothing I can do.'

His words terrified Joanna. She thought about Brian, her gentle, funny, caurry-fisted lover. She closed her eyes, and he was there, every detail clear and alive in her mind, the warm lovelight shining for her in his eyes. Grief overwhelmed her.

You never told me in your letters you loved me! You never mentioned it, and so I thought that maybe Adrian was the one I loved. Oh, Brian, why didn't you tell me you loved me? Joanna cried silently to the fading vision. She opened her eyes, and there was Adrian, his head bowed with sorrow. 'Adrian, is Brian dead?' she faltered. She never doubted that somehow his twin would know.

'I don't know. He might be. The feeling's bad, Joanna. Very bad,' Adrian groaned wretchedly.

A pitchfork landed dangerously close. 'Oh, I beg your pardon!' said Ruby Reid caustically. 'It's hens' eggs I'm after. I didn't expect to find lovebirds.'

Joanna had to get away, to come to terms alone with her fear and sorrow. She scrambled to her feet. 'Ohh – Ruby! I've had such terrible news!' she announced brokenly. There were no words to express how bad she felt so, without another word, she fled.

Ruby stared after her. 'What's up with Joanna?'

'I had a premonition my brother's in danger. It was so strong it scared us both to death,' Adrian told her.

'Ah!' Ruby nodded wisely. She sat down beside him. 'The mysterious bond between identical twins. I've heard about that.'

He clenched his fists angrily. 'Something has happened to Brian, Ruby, I know it has. You can scoff if you like!'

She looked at him seriously. 'Adrian, I'm not scoffing. I could weep for dear Joanna's sake. I believe she's found out too late which twin is her soulmate.'

He scowled sulkily. 'Are you suggesting Brian is?'

'I'm not suggesting anything, 'cause I don't know your brother. I know you, though, and you would make Joanna miserable.'

'Listen here—' he protested furiously.

'No. You listen.' Ruby jerked a thumb towards the mansion house. 'Do you care what happens to the Big House when the war's over?'

'That mouldering old heap? No, frankly, I don't give a damn.'

'Joanna cares. She cares passionately, and from what

484

she's let slip to me, so does Brian. They're a pair of stubborn, sentimental idealists, the sort who tackle the impossible and accomplish it. Maybe you wish you were more like your brother, but you never will be, because you have other strengths, which incidentally I admire. You've kidded yourself you love Joanna, but you don't.'

He lay back, staring at her. 'You seem to know a heck of a lot about me.'

Ruby chewed pensively upon a straw and refused to look at him. 'Aye. Maybe I do.'

There was a long, thoughtful silence, filled only with the peaceful sounds of the countryside, and the rustle of hay as Adrian edged closer. 'I wish you'd put that blasted pitchfork away, Ruby, it makes me nervous,' he said. 'You know, I may not be in love with Joanna, but I do admire girls in breeches and muddy boots. I find them most appealing.'

'I know you do, love.' Ruby tossed the pitchfork aside and smiled invitingly, a dimple in each cheek.

Nothing had prepared Fredrika for the dirt and ugliness of the engineering works. Working in the Rizzios' shop had been hot, but Fredrika had cleaned and freshened the shop, and with hard work had made it a pleasant, attractive place. No amount of cleaning and scrubbing would beautify these surroundings, though. For hours on end, Fredrika toiled. Black, oily machinery with pistons and flywheels roared and thundered in her ears, shooting out sooty sparks which died in the cold air before reaching the blackened roof. The machinery was of such vast strength it crushed and mangled steel plates into odd shapes as if they were made of cardboard. Fredrika's job behind the protective mask was to make strong welds in three precise locations with the blow torch. This she did grimly to the very best of her ability, all day long, every day of every week, on and on through the months, except for blessed Sundays.

The knowledge she was doing vital war work might have been enough for another person, but Fredrika had discovered something shocking and surprising about herself, as she worked in the dark, ugly place. She needed beauty in her surroundings, just as she needed air and water, and she threatened to fade away without it.

The tide had turned in the war at last. Allied troops had landed in Europe that summer. Optimism had been high in Edinburgh for a speedy end to the war by the autumn of 1944, but such hopes were unfounded: troops were faced with a long, hard slog through France and Belgium and on into Holland, fighting all the way. A fierce, cruel winter came early to Europe, and as the armies became bogged down in sleet and snow, it seemed the war would never end.

Fredrika worked harder than ever to help the fighting men, carefully making her three crucial welds on the essential equipment. She suffered, but it seemed only right to suffer, when soldiers were suffering more. She caught cold, and developed a hard, painful cough which wouldn't go away.

'I'd give ye honey, if I had any honey,' said Feemie worriedly.

Fredrika curled her thin fingers gratefully round a mug of tea. Her hands and fingernails, once so white and clean, were scarred and stained with oily dirt which no amount of scrubbing would remove. She shed silent tears over ruined hands and broken fingernails, but she summoned up a smile for Feemie. 'I am very fine,' she said. 'Dear Bobby gave me good cough lozenges today, and I am much better.' So saying, she was gripped by a fit of coughing that left her weak and gasping.

Feemie said nothing, but her worried thoughts went racing on. Fredrika was fading away before her very eyes. The lass was thinner than ever, hollow-cheeked, eyes dark-circled with fatigue. Enough was enough, decided Feemie grimly. She knew exactly what must be done. 'Away to your bed, lassie. I put a stone piggie in, to warm it,' Feemie told her young lodger kindly.

They had told Ishbel that Brian was missing, presumed drowned. There had been tragedy before in Ishbel's life, but this loss had taken the heart out of her. Naturally enough, it was Adrian who'd first sensed something was far wrong. He'd made discreet inquiries, and discovered that the survivors of Brian's battered convoy had limped into Liverpool some time ago. Brian's ship wasn't with it, and the Convoy Commander could only conclude the stragglers had been picked off by a stray U-boat. Brian's fate was vague and inconclusive, and his mother did not know whether to mourn or hope. It was so cruel, Ishbel thought, as she struggled miserably to concentrate upon rationing and clothing coupons in the quiet of her office.

Ryan tugged at her sleeve. 'Another wee piece of paper, please, Mam? he begged hopefully.

Ishbel put an arm around the little boy, gaining comfort from hugging the bairn. 'What did you do with the other bit I gave you, lovie?'

'I writed all over it,' he said proudly, holding up for her inspection a sheet of paper covered back and front with busy scribbles. Ryan was always scribbling, pretending to do grown-up writing, calculating long lists of endless squiggles he swore solemnly were sums. A wee business tycoon in the making, Matthew declared fondly.

Ishbel ruffled her small son's dark hair. 'Paper's mighty scarce, you know, honey-bun.' She reached into the desk drawer and took out a notebook, which she handed to the delighted child. 'That's an old order book, Ryan. We don't need it now. There's precious little to order anyway, and what's left is so skimpy it's scarcely worth considering. No double-breasted jackets, not more than three pockets or three buttons on a garment. Trouser legs not more than nineteen inches wide, no permanent turnups, no elastic, no zip fasteners. Och, Ryan, restrictions are endless!' Ishbel sighed. Ryan nodded wisely, though the list made little sense to him. Ishbel had been lonely so often with Matthew called away frequently to London, she was in the habit of speaking her thoughts aloud to the child. Today, with much anxiety clouding her mind, Ryan's company gave his mother special comfort. The small boy had lost interest in the conversation, and was examining his latest acquisition eagerly. 'What's this, Mam?'

'It's carbon paper, lamb. Here, I'll show you.' Ishbel was introducing Ryan to the entrancing properties of carbon paper when her secretary hurried in. The girl looked troubled. 'Someone to see you, Mrs Clark. The lady had no appointment, but I thought you'd want to see her right away.'

It took Ishbel a moment or two to place the young woman who was ushered into the office, and then recognition dawned. It was Katie, the young wife of Archie the lift manager. Ishbel smiled at Ryan. 'Darling, take your book downstairs and show it to Cathy. Ask her to look after you for half an hour, will you, my love?'

He trotted away obediently, and Ishbel closed the door and seated her visitor on a chair.

'You have a fine wee laddie,' Katie remarked.

'Aye, I'm lucky.' Ishbel smiled. She sat down behind the desk. 'Katie, how's Archie?'

The young woman didn't answer right away. She stared down at her hands. The wedding ring caught a glint of sunlight, and shone bright gold. 'Archie won't be coming home, Mrs Clark,' she answered evenly. 'I just heard yesterday he was killed in a place called Goch.'

'Oh, no!' Ishbel cried. She could hardly believe the tragic news. She'd missed Archie very much since his call-up. Alexander's would never be the same without him. 'Oh, Katie dear, I'm so very sad,' she said sorrowfully.

'Aye. I thought you would be,' said Katie dully. The young woman seemed very calm. Too calm, Ishbel thought uneasily. It was as if shock had frozen all Katie's emotions. 'I thought he'd come through it, Mrs Clark,' Katie went on. 'It never entered my heid he wouldn't come home to me and the bairn. He's been in the thick of it wi' the Highland Division since the D-Day landings, and never had a scratch. But – but his luck ran oot.'

The room fell silent. Sadness bore down on Ishbel, another burden for her heavy heart. 'He was a fine man, Katie, one of the best,' she said.

'So he was, Mrs Clark. He looked braw in the Cameron kilt.'

'I'm sure he did, my dear.'

'He was pleased because he wasna bandy legged, like some o' them,' Katie said with a tight little smile. With that, the ice that froze her poor, grieving heart cracked and melted, and with a distraught wail she covered her face with her hands and burst into a storm of weeping.

Ishbel hastened to the young woman and gathered her in her arms. She was secretly relieved to see the wild storm of grief released, and when it had abated she hugged Archie's young widow compassionately. 'Katie dear, there will be a trust fund set up for you and Archie's bairn. I gave Archie my promise Alexander's would care for you both, and so we will,' Ishbel told her.

'That's another one done for!' said Elspeth with satisfaction as the guns boomed out. She was becoming an expert at tracking doodlebugs. The wretched, pilotless, winged horrors came droning over ack-ack positions on the southeast coast with unfailing regularity, and Elspeth had plenty of opportunity to perfect her skill. Still, some got through, and she counted these a personal failure, knowing they meant possible death and destruction in poor, battered old London. The only hope was that the flying bombs they missed would become entangled in a forest of barrage balloons positioned between the coast and the capital.

Elspeth eased the pressure of the heavy tin hat, which was making its usual aching furrow on her brow. Oh, how weary she was of the war! Hopes had been high it would end very soon, but it dragged on and on. She scanned the sky. Doodlebugs came winging across the Channel at all times of day and night, and recently there had been a more sinister development about which the War Ministry remained tight lipped. Gun batteries were ineffective against rockets which came whistling straight out of the stratosphere, bent upon indiscriminate destruction. Horrible!

Elspeth shuddered and turned her attention to dreams of the future, while the gun crew waited for the next emergency. She clung to future hopes like a lucky charm. When the war ended and she was demobbed, she planned to go home for a month or two to enjoy the company of her family and adorable little half-brother. Ryan had been just a toddler when she last saw him, but the bond between them had proved as strong as ever.

After that spell of rest and recuperation at home, Elspeth was confident that with hard work, her success as an actress was assured. She knew she still had much to learn in her chosen profession, but she was young, and dear Polly had coached her well in the basics. Elspeth rubbed her tired eyes. She often thought about her dear friend and wondered guiltily what had happened to Polly's career after their partnership ended.

'Watch out, here's another!' somebody shouted.

Instantly, Elspeth was alert. She trained her sights upon the droning menace and gritted her teeth. This one wouldn't get away.

Well, I guess I was warned about the danger of entertaining the troops, Polly thought wryly. There was gunfire starting up all round the Belgian town they were in. The stage of the hall packed with GIs started shaking beneath her tap-dancing feet. She tapped all the louder, drowning the sounds.

Namur had seemed a peaceful enough spot when she and her accompanist Jimmy and the rest of the troupe arrived from Brussels that misty, wintry morning. The river Meuse had flowed quietly beneath the bridge, and there had been a large, comforting presence of American soldiers going about their business. The front line was way to the west, so where did gunfire come from all of a sudden? Polly wondered.

She danced across to the piano and did a few high kicks. Her soldier audience laughed and cheered. Their own moms were not usually that supple. 'What's goin' on out there, Jimmy?' she whispered.

'Search me!' he shrugged. He launched into 'Ma, I miss your apple pie,' which had become Polly's signature tune. The audience joined in lustily, stamping their feet. The stage manager appeared in the wings, his eyes popping, waving his arms in agitation. 'Get off! Get off, Polly, for God's sake! We got to get out, 'cause the Germans have launched a surprise attack on the Ardennes. The others have gone to the truck already, and we don't aim to wait around for stragglers. You got five minutes, honey. After that, too bad!' With that ultimatum, he turned and fled.

Polly and Jimmy looked at one another. 'If we run, we leave these poor young GIs to panic their way out of this place. That don't seem right,' murmured Jimmy, his agile fingers flying lightly over the keys. 'I reckon I'll stay until they get out safe and orderly. You buzz off, Polly.'

'Oh yeah?' hissed Polly indignantly. 'You stay, so do I! I'm Momsy to these poor kids.'

She turned and ran to the footlights, holding up her hands for silence. Jimmy's piano playing died away, and there was a sudden hush in the over-crowded church hall. Everyone could hear the gunfire now. It sounded dangerously close, and the men looked at one another nervously. Polly smiled around pityingly. 'You poor guys. They promised you Dorothy Lamour, an' what did you get? You got me!'

There was a roar of laughter, and someone shouted. 'Momsy, we don' mind. Dorothy's in Hollywood, you're here. You're OK!'

Polly spread her arms to embrace them. Her heart felt full to bursting. She loved them all dearly, every last one of these threatened young men. They were her sons, her darlings. Momsy. What a wonderful name!

'Now you listen here, boys,' she told them. 'I guess the war is coming to this place, and you have to clear the hall an' prepare to fight it. But don't you panic and don't you fret, I'll be right here with you, singing while you march out. Just like your own Mom back home, you can depend on me. I won't leave you, I won't ever run out on you, my dear boys.'

Jimmy struck a chord and launched into a defiant medley. Polly's sweet, powerful contralto rang out, challenging the sound of gunfire as the men filed from the hall in orderly ranks. There was no panic. They marched out into the freezing darkness, singing and whistling as they went.

In the empty hall, Jimmy rose from the piano and flung his arms round Polly. 'Polly, you were great!'

'You weren't too bad yourself,' she said shakily.

The din of shelling was coming closer. He looked around anxiously. 'Polly, we've got to get out of here somehow. The truck will have gone long ago.'

A lone soldier appeared in the doorway. 'Hey, I been detailed to drive you back to Brussels safe and sound,' he called to them. He gave Polly a wide, happy grin. 'You take care of your boys, so I guess your boys will take care of you, Momsy, dear.'

* * *

Joanna's life had changed drastically since Brian went missing. She had never felt so unhappy, The harsh weather did not help. She lifted a heavy stone and brought it crashing down on ice that had formed overnight on the cattle trough. Water spilled through, dark and icy, and she thought about Brian, and shivered. The other land girls, muffled to the nose in scarves, jerseys and jackets, hacked freezing turnips and distributed them to hungry sheep, ekeing out a meagre ration of sheep mix. In her sadness and despair, Joanna had withdrawn into herself. The others were sympathetic, and treated her gently. At that moment, Ruby was grimly slicing the pile of swede turnips allocated by rights to Joanna.

Adrian visited often, but his visits failed to cheer Joanna. The time for light flirtation was over. She knew where her heart lay drifting aimlessly for ever more with Brian, in the cold relentless sea. Her eyes stung, tears frozen by the keen wind.

'Hey, Jo!' called Ruby kindly. 'How about biting Bunty's lug for a flask of hot tea? Much more of this, and my feet'll be frozen to the ground!' Ruby was endlessly tactful and observant. She seemed to know when Joanna needed solitude. Obediently, Joanna plodded across a skim of frozen snow towards the farmhouse.

Reaching the track, Joanna saw from a distance that her father was greeting visitors at the farmhouse door, and she paused uncertainly, for she felt in no mood to chat. Walking on reluctantly she recognised Adrian, out of uniform for once, but the other man was a tall, bearded stranger. She would have slipped unnoticed round to the back, but she had been spotted. Adrian waved, and the others turned, watching her approach. With trepidation, she forced herself to go on, wondering what more bad news this stranger brought.

Seeing her strained expression, Wotherspoon put an arm round his lass and drew her close. Nobody spoke for a long moment, then the stranger held out a hand.

'Joanna dear, don't you remember me?'

She stared at him then gazed stupidly at the hand held out to her. 'Caurry fist,' she whispered. She moved closer, her heart leaping. 'Brian! Oh, my darling, Brian!' Her relief at finding him alive was so tremendous, she could hardly move, only reach out and grip his strong left hand as if she'd never let it go.

Adrian laughed delightedly and punched his brother lightly on the arm. 'I told you the face fungus would fool her!'

Brian laughed. 'In the North Atlantic, boy, a beard's excellent insulation. The thicker the better.' He felt wonderful. The love shining in Joanna's eyes, the fierce warmth of her grip, gave him hope. More than hope: certainty! He took Joanna in his arms, and she snuggled against his chest with a contented sigh.

Adrian watched a trifle dismally. 'So, the best man wins. I guess it was inevitable she would choose you, wee brother. You came limping into port a hero, with cargo and lame duck intact, while I spend my days safe at home, sitting on my bottom, staring at charts and screens and screeds of figures.'

Brian smiled fondly at his twin. 'Och, there are no heroes in this cat-and-mouse game, big brother, we're all dependent upon one another. You helped me more than you know. I wouldn't be here now if long-range bombers hadn't been equipped with an improved radar system. The planes

495

circled round us for many hours, keeping at bay a stray U-boat intent upon sinking us. Their depth charges drove him deep under the surface and kept him there, until we reached Reykjavik safely.'

Wotherspoon gave a deep rumble of delighted laughter and clapped Adrian on the back. 'So I was right! You were a menace in the air, but a useful lad, when grounded!'

Adrian grinned sheepishly. You know, he thought to himself, I'm beginning to like the old Grumpy!

Life in the engineering works was no better as winter wore on. Worse, in fact, Fredrika thought. Stubbornly, she refused to give up her job despite Feemie's pleading. There were sound reasons why she couldn't give up. With overtime, the pay was good, and she knew Feemie was dependent upon the rent. Nearly all the working men had gone, as the army dug deep into the barrel, and Feemie would be in dire straits but for Fredrika's money.

Leaving the works, Fredrika pulled her threadbare coat closer round her neck. It was a horrible night. Sleet stung her cheeks viciously, and a cruel east wind gleefully sought out weaknesses in her inadequate clothing. She shivered as she left the yard with the other dark, shrouded figures who had shared her misery on the late shift.

When two people stepped out of a nearby doorway and one of them grabbed her arm in the darkness, Fredrika was terrified. Memories from the past rose up, and she acted instinctively, tearing the arm free and dodging away. The man was too quick for her. He side-stepped, blocking her path; she struggled, then collapsed against the wall, coughing.

It was the most severe fit she'd ever had, the harsh pain of it wrenching her chest so that she could hardly breathe. When the pain eased, there was somebody holding her arms and she was a prisoner. She groaned. 'Oh, why won't you leave me alone?'

'You've been alone too long, Fredrika,' a woman's voice said. It was a kind voice, tearful with compassion, and it was vaguely familiar.

Fredrika peered cautiously at her captor. She couldn't see her very well in the blackout, but she suddenly remembered the subtle perfume she wore. 'It is Mrs Alexander!' Fredrika gasped.

'Mrs Clark now,' Ishbel said. Matthew, her companion, was supporting the sick young woman on the other side. Ishbel's heart went out to Freddie's daughter. 'Oh, my dear, I've been heartbroken because I sent you away,' she cried. 'I didn't believe your story at first, but Matthew, my husband, had met your mother in 1917, and he confirmed all you'd told me. We couldn't think how to find you again. We didn't even know your name, but at last today we were told everything about you and where you could be found, so we came at once.'

Fredrika's thoughts were desolate. Her trust had been betrayed, and by the man she loved! Yes, she admitted it, she loved Bobby dearly, but he had broken his word, and above all she had loved and admired his integrity. 'Bobby told you!' she cried.

Matthew frowned. 'Who the heck's Bobby?'

'He is policeman, and I trusted him, but now I can never trust him again,' Fredrika answered tearfully.

Ishbel laughed. 'My love, it wasn't your bobby who came to us and told us where to find you. It was someone else.'

Fredrika was bewildered. 'But only the police know who

I am and where I work. There is nobody else!'

'My dear Fredrika, you forget, there is someone. There is Feemie,' said Ishbel gently.

Feemie was in the nerves after the bold step she'd taken that day. Since returning home from the Alexanders' shop she'd been shaking like a leaf. Not because of that nice woman, Ishbel Clark, and her American man, mind you! Feemie had been greatly relieved to discover they were grateful to be told where Freddie Alexander's daughter could be found. It was facing Fredrika herself that Feemie dreaded.

She'd broken her solemn promise to the lass. No matter if it was kindly meant and done in desperation because Fredrika was slowly killing herself, it was still a broken promise. In a frenzy of worry, Feemie had scrubbed the close and polished and cleaned the lodging house frantically. Exhausted by her efforts, she was now brewing up the last of a week's ration of tea, to give herself strength as she awaited Fredrika's arrival.

As it happened, Fredrika came in so quietly she caught her landlady by surprise. Feemie's jaw dropped, and she spluttered over a mouthful which had gone down the wrong way, for Fredrika was not alone, Mr and Mrs Clark accompanied her. They were parlour folk, and here they were, standing large as life in Feemie's kitchen. Fredrika crossed the room and stood sternly in front of her landlady. 'Feemie, why did you tell? You promised not to. I am proud, and I was managing to live.'

'Managing to live?' Feemie exploded indignantly. 'More like managing to kill yoursel'! You think I'd stand by and watch you fade away in that place? No' likely!'

Ishbel broke in. 'Feemie, we've told Fredrika there's no

need for her to go back to the engineering works. She admits the work is ruining her health. I want her to come and live with us, and help us in the shop. It's up to Fredrika, of course. I've assured her we'll abide by her decision.'

Feemie stared at the lass she loved like her very own. So this was the parting of the ways, she thought. Nobody with an ounce o' common sense would turn down such a braw offer. 'Aye weel, Fredrika, you'll no' likely be wanting the sausages I queued up for, but maybe you an' your folk will tak' a cup o' tea afore you go?' she said wistfully.

'I am not going,' Fredrika said.

'In the name of a' the Wee Folk! Why not?' howled Feemie angrily.

Fredrika flung her arms around her. 'Because I will not leave you, Feemie. I would rather fade away in horrid works than leave you.'

Feemie turned apologetically to Ishbel and Matthew, her eyes brimming. 'The poor lassie's a wee bit soft in the heid, ye ken, only being half Scottish. She's blethering a lot o' nonsense.'

Ishbel smiled. 'Oh, I don't think so, Feemie. She's saying she won't abandon her best and dearest friend, and I don't blame her.' She gazed thoughtfully at the two for a moment. 'Look, I've been thinking. Our dear old cook is hoping to retire and live with her widowed sister, but my mother and mother-in-law are getting on in years, and can't cope with the big house without help. Would you consider moving to Knoxhall House as our housekeeper, Feemie? The family would be delighted to have you!'

'And so would Fredrika, I guess,' added Matthew with a smile.

Housekeeper! Feemie's bosom swelled. It was the best

offer she'd ever had in her life, a huge step up the ladder to live with toffs in Morningside. Feemie looked at Fredrika and her expression softened. The improved status didn't matter tuppence to her. She'd be on hand to keep an eye upon her lass and make sure she settled happily with her new family. Feemie took a dainty sip of tea, because it didn't do to seem too keen. 'Aye weel, it mightn't be a bad plan, Mrs Clark, so I'll accept the offer,' she agreed grandly, then added hastily, 'for Fredrika's sake, of course.'

The long winter ended at last, and with the thaw and the green shoots of spring came renewed hope. Almost a year after the D-Day landings had optimistically promised a speedy ending, the conflict ceased. Matthew kept the shop open that wonderful day, broadcasting Winston Churchill's speech at three o'clock that afternoon throughout the store.

Now the war was officially over, Ishbel and Fredrika ransacked the shop for red, white and blue bunting and ribbons to make a patriotic show in the bare windows, and that evening when the shop had closed and dusk fell, the depleted family gathered in the drawing room of Knoxhall House. With pleasure that knew no bounds, Ishbel pulled aside the blackouts and let the light from the chandelier shine out for the first time in nearly five years. She wished the twins and Elspeth could have seen the sight, but they were still on active service, celebrating elsewhere.

Ryan ran to the window and stared out in amazement. There were twinkling lights shining like stars all over the city. Searchlights played across the night sky, fingers of light pointing towards the old castle perched upon its spine of rock. Orange bonfires glowed on hillside cairns all over the Lothians and Fife that night. It was a sight for a small boy to remember all his life.

Eleanor Alexander, with a burned letter lying heavily on her conscience, studied Fredrika who sat holding hands with the nice policeman who was so obviously smitten. Dear Freddie's lovely daughter, Eleanor thought emotionally. What an unexpected joy to find her at last.

Eleanor was tempted to confess her secret, but decided to let the matter rest. Matthew had verified the claim, and Fredrika was restored to her rightful family, fully recovered from bronchitis and working happily with Ishbel and Matthew in the shop. Fredrika showed signs of exceptional talent in that direction, and the old lady was comforted to know the future of Alexander's rested in capable young hands. Dear William would have been pleased about that, she thought. One day I will tell Fredrika the whole story and ask her forgiveness, Eleanor decided. But not today. 'I have a bottle of fine old champagne hidden away for this very special occasion,' she announced smugly.

Catriona stared. 'I've never seen it. Where is it, dear?'

'In the refuge room, hidden in one of your buckets of sand. You said yourself that was the safest place in this house,' answered Eleanor blandly.

When Matthew had unearthed the bottle and persuaded Feemie to leave the kitchen and join them, he charged their glasses and held his up to the brilliant glow from the chandelier.

'Here's to Alexander's, and to dear old Edinburgh. God bless us all!'

The toast drunk, he sat down beside his wife and put an arm round her waist and kissed her. 'Penny for your thoughts at this wonderful moment, my love,' he said softly.

'I was thinking about Polly,' Ishbel said. 'I'm glad she found fame and fortune, Matthew. I bet she deserved the medal they gave her.'

'Yeah. Polly's a real trouper,' Matthew agreed.

She looked down at the sparkling drink in her glass, and many memories stirred. She remembered dear Freddie's merry smile, and those other young men, the victims of another dreadful war, who'd clapped and cheered when she sang Harry Lauder's songs for them. She remembered a dark-haired young country lass in a reach-me-down dress, and her first, wary sip of champagne. Perhaps that's where it all began, the start of the long road leading to the shop, to Matthew and this fulfilling moment.

I must tell Ryan the whole story, one day, thought Ishbel, as she took another sip of champagne.

More Enthralling Fiction from Headline:

HARRY BOWLING

The new Cockney saga from the bestselling author of GASLIGHT IN PAGE STREET

The Girl from Cotton Lane

Cotton Lane in dockland Bermondsey is one of the many small cobbled streets which serve the wharves. And on the corner is Bradley's Dining Rooms, the favourite eating place of the rivermen, trade union officials and horse and motor drivers. Since her marriage to Fred Bradley, Carrie has been building up the business, and trade has picked up considerably since the end of the Great War. Yet everything is not well between Carrie and Fred. And though they have a little daughter they both adore, neither of them is truly happy.

Carrie's parents, Nellie and William Tanner, live in Bacon Buildings, the tenement they were forced to move into when George Galloway sacked William after thirty-seven years. But their hearts lie in Page Street, their old home, and with their friends there: redoubtable Florrie 'Hairpin' Axford and her gossiping companions; scruffy old Broomhead Smith; the fighting Sullivans, and young Billy, who, unable to box after a wound sustained in the trenches, is determined to set up a gymnasium to help the local youngsters keep off the streets; and new arrivals, Joe Maitland, who's doing well with his warehouse in Dockhead, though his dealings are not always strictly above board, and Red Ellie, the stalwart Communist who brings the street together to fight their slum landlord, George Galloway.

Don't miss Harry Bowling's previous Cockney sagas, GASLIGHT IN PAGE STREET, PARAGON PLACE, IRONMONGER'S DAUGHTER, TUPPENCE TO TOOLEY STREET and CONNER STREET'S WAR, also available from Headline.

FICTION/GENERAL   0 7472 3869 3

More Enthralling Fiction from Headline:

JOY CHAMBERS
who plays the popular Rosemary Daniels in 'Neighbours'

An epic saga of nineteenth-century Australia

Eve Herman and her sister Clare find themselves orphans in Sydney town, 7000 miles from the land of their birth. Clare – beautiful, impressionable, addicted to pleasure – soon takes the easy way to earn a living, and Eve – strong and reliable – is left alone.

Naval sea captain Alan Fletcher intends to take up his rightful position as Squire of Long Moss. But his ruthless cousin's plotting means he is instead transported on a convict ship bound for New South Wales.

Revered and respected throughout the colony, John Stuart Wakeman is the owner of Mayfield, the largest, richest and most renowned property in New South Wales. The first moment he sees Eve he is captivated.

On their wedding day, Eve's life is forever altered by a fateful meeting in the bush, and the realisation that there is a secret she must keep from her husband. When she is brutally attacked, her secret comes back to haunt her and cause bitter estrangement between her and her husband. Heartbroken, Eve is all too vulnerable to the magnetism of Alan Fletcher – the man her husband has sworn to destroy...

MAYFIELD is a story of the overwhelming and consuming love of two men for the same indomitable woman, and of the valour, losses and sacrifices that each must make in the fight for her love.

FICTION/SAGA   0 7472 3863 4

More Compelling Fiction from Headline:

—— HARRIET SMART ——

The magnificent Scottish saga from the author of *A Garland of Vows*

GREEN GROW THE RUSHES

In the long hot summer of 1900, a group of people is brought together in the decaying splendour of the Quarro, a Scottish country house owned by the down-at-heel Lennox family.

Jessie Macpherson, newly appointed cook, dazzles the Lennoxes and their guests with her skill – but even in her triumph, she realises there has to be more to life. Sholto Hamilton, a poor, ambitious lawyer, offers her a glimpse of other delights, and Jessie is quickly trapped in the sensual web he has woven. But what future can there be for a gentleman and a servant?

For Celia Lennox, daughter of the house, there can be no more eligible a suitor than Ralph Erskine, heir to an Edinburgh steel magnate. He certainly admires her, but it is another man who catches her eye – and perhaps her heart.

Ralph's sister Alix overcomes parental opposition and society's disapproval to win herself an education and against all expectations finds a man who shares her view of life – until a shocking stroke of fate robs her of happiness.

As their lives touch, new alliances are formed – some doomed to failure and bitter despair, others that will endure against the odds to bring lasting happiness.

A sweeping, panoramic saga that moves from country house to industrial slums, from bohemian free-thinking to High Tory politics, *Green Grow the Rushes* is an outstanding successor to Harriet Smart's first novel, *A Garland of Vows* ('precisely and lovingly observed... excellent' *The Sunday Times*), which is also available from Headline.

FICTION/SAGA   0 7472 4050 7

A selection of bestsellers
from Headline

THE LADYKILLER	Martina Cole	£5.99 ☐
JESSICA'S GIRL	Josephine Cox	£5.99 ☐
NICE GIRLS	Claudia Crawford	£4.99 ☐
HER HUNGRY HEART	Roberta Latow	£5.99 ☐
FLOOD WATER	Peter Ling	£4.99 ☐
THE OTHER MOTHER	Seth Margolis	£4.99 ☐
ACT OF PASSION	Rosalind Miles	£4.99 ☐
A NEST OF SINGING BIRDS	Elizabeth Murphy	£5.99 ☐
THE COCKNEY GIRL	Gilda O'Neill	£4.99 ☐
FORBIDDEN FEELINGS	Una-Mary Parker	£5.99 ☐
OUR STREET	Victor Pemberton	£5.99 ☐
GREEN GROW THE RUSHES	Harriet Smart	£5.99 ☐
BLUE DRESS GIRL	E V Thompson	£5.99 ☐
DAYDREAMS	Elizabeth Walker	£5.99 ☐

All Headline books are available at your local bookshop or newsagent, or can be ordered direct from the publisher. Just tick the titles you want and fill in the form below. Prices and availability subject to change without notice.

Headline Book Publishing PLC, Cash Sales Department, Bookpoint, 39 Milton Park, Abingdon, OXON, OX14 4TD, UK. If you have a credit card you may order by telephone – 0235 831700.

Please enclose a cheque or postal order made payable to Bookpoint Ltd to the value of the cover price and allow the following for postage and packing:
UK & BFPO: £1.00 for the first book, 50p for the second book and 30p for each additional book ordered up to a maximum charge of £3.00.
OVERSEAS & EIRE: £2.00 for the first book, £1.00 for the second book and 50p for each additional book.

Name ....

Address ....

....

....

If you would prefer to pay by credit card, please complete:
Please debit my Visa/Access/Diner's Card/American Express (delete as applicable) card no:

Signature .... Expiry Date ....